# WHEN THE STORM PASSES

# OTHER TITLES BY MANEL LOUREIRO

## Apocalypse Z Series

*The Beginning of the End*

*Dark Days*

*The Wrath of the Just*

## Other Novels

*The Last Passenger*

*Only She Sees*

TRANSLATED BY THOMAS BUNSTEAD

# WHEN THE STORM PASSES

A THRILLER

MANEL LOUREIRO

Previously published as *Cuando la tormenta pase* by Editorial Planeta in 2024. Translated from Spanish by Thomas Bunstead. First published in English by Amazon Crossing in 2026.

Published by Amazon Crossing, Seattle

www.apub.com



EU product safety contact:
Amazon Media EU S. à r.l.
38, avenue John F. Kennedy, L-1855 Luxembourg
amazonpublishing-gpsr@amazon.com

ISBN-13: 9781662532085 (paperback)
ISBN-13: 9781662532078 (digital)

Cover design by Brian Lemus
Cover image: © ANTIVAR, © Oskari Porkka / Shutterstock

Printed in the United States of America

*This book is dedicated to Antonia Kerrigan, of course.*
*There are no words to describe the huge*
*void left by her absence.*

# 1

## The Island

***Isle of Ons. January, present day.***

The dock emerged gradually into view.

It was a long, pitifully narrow concrete breakwater, battered by the waves, some of which would wash over the top and sweep across its entire surface.

Struggling toward the dock was a potbellied fishing vessel, rocking from side to side each time the waves lifted it up like a child's toy, the paint flaking from its hull. The *Punta Suido*, its name painted in red letters on a bronze plaque attached to the front of the cabin, had clearly seen better days.

Hunched in the bow, the sole passenger contemplated the rugged silhouette of the island, dominated by a hill with a towering white lighthouse perched on top. Just to the south of the main island lay the smaller, inaccessible islet of Onza, inhabited only by seabirds and surrounded by a tumult of roaring foam that broke against its cliffs.

Whenever a wave shook the boat, the man's knuckles turned white as he gripped the gunwale.

Although Roberto Lobeira was hardly the type to flee danger, he loathed the sea with every fiber of his being. And yet here he was. Because he had to reach the island.

Roberto registered the intense concentration of the skipper—a sinewy man with a thin beard and a hard expression, wearing a yellow oilskin—as he maneuvered the boat, applying careful bursts of the throttle and pulling hard on the wheel. Upon leaving Bueu, Roberto had been told that in these conditions, there was no question of docking and that the best they could do was to bring the boat in close to the breakwater and for him to jump.

When they were just a few yards from the dock, he broke into a sweat. The tension was palpable as the crew slung tires over the edge of the boat. The conditions had grown markedly worse during the crossing, and the vessel reared and plunged like a wildly bucking horse.

"Everyone, get ready!" shouted the skipper, leaning out of the side of the cabin. "We only have one shot at this!"

The engine roared as a particularly strong wave buffeted the boat, and the *Punta Suido* came within inches of striking the cracked concrete of the breakwater. One of the tires hanging over the side screeched as it scraped against the concrete, leaving a long scar of black rubber, which the water immediately swept clean.

"Now!" cried the skipper. "Jump onto the dock! Jump!"

Roberto eyed the gap. Those few feet might as well have been a million miles. A narrow strip of black water foamed furiously between the side of the fishing boat and the concrete, gaping like a hungry mouth. It shrank and expanded as each wave hit. If he fell in, he'd be crushed like a grape in a winepress.

"I'm not sure about this!" he shouted, turning his head. "I think we're going to—"

"Stop messing around!" the skipper yelled, spittle flying. "Just fucking jump!"

Roberto didn't wait to be told again. He tossed his baggage off the boat and leaped after it just as the tires along the hull jammed against the dock with a long, ominous creak. His feet hit the concrete as a wave crashed against the dock and transformed into a cascade of icy water.

Before he could wipe the salt water from his eyes, the fishing boat had pulled away with a powerful burst of its engines and was spinning around so that its bow was pointed toward the horizon.

"See you in a month's time. Take care!" shouted the skipper from the stern, before adding something that puzzled Roberto. "And stay out of trouble!"

Another surge of seawater brought him back to the task at hand. A wave-battered dock was hardly the most sensible place to hang around. He dragged his bags to the end of the breakwater and paused to consider his next step.

He looked around. Behind him, the visitor reception booth—where in the summer there would have been a line of hundreds of tourists—was boarded up until next season.

*Welcome to paradise,* he thought to himself.

The Isle of Ons was part of a national park, and visits were strictly regulated. Even so, during the summer months, it was busy with day-trippers and vacationers who rented houses or flocked to a campsite on one of the few flat areas of land that the island had to offer. Ferries arrived every few hours, unloading hordes of travelers and then returning to gather them up at the end of the day, sunburned and revitalized by this rugged getaway just an hour from the mainland.

In the fall and winter, things were very different.

When October arrived, the flow of travelers came to a halt, and the island was left deserted and silent. The tourist ferries were laid up in port, waiting for the following summer, and the rocky, windblown den of Ons went into hibernation.

Hence having to hire a fishing boat to get here. Ons would be completely cut off until the good weather returned.

And completely cut off was precisely what Roberto needed to be.

Disconcerted, he looked around for some indication of where to go. To his right, a path led uphill to a cluster of houses, the nearest thing to a village to be found on the island.

With freezing hands, he took his permit from his pocket. Somebody should have been there to meet him, to check that everything was in order, and to give him the keys to his rental cottage. But there wasn't a soul to be seen, and the only sounds were those of the breaking waves, the whistling wind, and the cry of seagulls overhead.

He was gripped by the disturbing thought that he would have to spend the next month alone, like some modern-day Robinson Crusoe, but checked himself. There had to be somebody around.

Just then, he heard voices coming from up the hill.

He made as if to shoulder his heavy backpack but put it down again. The one thing he could be sure of was that nobody was going to steal his baggage in this desolate place. Halfway up the hill, he realized he had made the right choice. Roberto kept himself fit, but by the time he reached the top, he was completely out of breath.

Now he discovered the source of the voices.

Two figures stood in the middle of the road, oblivious to his presence.

One of them was a tall, well-built man in his forties. Wearing a black raincoat, waterproof pants, and thick rubber boots, he had a round face and a bushy, white-flecked beard. The other was a boy of about fourteen, with pale skin, tousled blond hair, and green eyes that sparkled with anger.

The man was holding a cardboard box above his head, out of reach of the boy, who was jumping up and trying to grab the box. Every time he did so, the man just took a step back.

"Give them to me!" The boy was clearly upset. "They're mine!"

"You want them?" said the man. "Here you are!"

He reached inside the box and threw something at the boy's feet. When the boy bent down to pick it up, the man gave him a shove, sending him sprawling to the ground. The boy got up, covered in mud, his face red, and started jumping up again in a vain attempt to grab the box from the man's hands.

"Go on, then, you little prick," he mocked. "Pick them up; pick them up."

Without stopping to think, Roberto strode over to them.

He'd never been able to stand bullies. Perhaps in other circumstances, he would just have remonstrated with the man or threatened to call the police, but the nearest police officer was on the mainland, more than an hour away. Roberto's whole body ached; he was tired, wet, and in a rotten mood—a bad combination that set him off like flames beneath a bubbling cauldron.

Some people can keep their calm in any situation, whatever happens. Others have outbursts of temper that rage like a fire, short but intense. And then there are people like Roberto who generally belong to the first group but who, on occasion, lose their cool. He didn't like it when that happened because then things got out of control.

But he couldn't help himself.

A couple of years earlier, he'd gotten into trouble when sharing a trench with a unit of soldiers in a desolate corner of the Balkans while writing a series of articles on the sufferings of war. On another occasion, he'd almost ended up dead in a ditch while researching Mexico's Gulf Cartel.

Nobody could say that Roberto Lobeira was a coward.

Before he'd had time to think, he charged up to the man and shoved him in the back. Caught unawares, the bully staggered, eyes wide in surprise. The box was jolted through the air and hit the ground, its contents spilling. Thor and Iron Man looked up at him from where they lay in the mud.

*It's a bunch of toys,* Roberto noted in some part of his brain that seemed to be dispassionately observing events. *It's a load of superhero figures.*

"What the fuck?" the other man shouted. "Who are you?"

"Leave the kid alone." Roberto's voice sounded as if it belonged to somebody else.

"This freak?" The man glanced at the boy, who was scrabbling about, picking up the figures scattered on the ground, oblivious to the altercation. "Who's going to make me? You?"

"If I have to."

The man glared at him, smiling derisively. Roberto could imagine what the man saw—a skinny stranger, five feet ten, his black hair plastered to his head, a tired expression on his angular face. The man was at least four inches taller than Roberto and must have outweighed him by a good thirty pounds. Beneath the man's raincoat, Roberto could make out the bulging muscles that were the product of a lifetime of working on boats. From the man's expression, it was clear he had made the same calculation and reached a similar conclusion. But it was already too late.

The man's smile widened as he peeled off his raincoat and dropped it to the ground, leaving him freer to move. Roberto tilted his head to one side and took a step forward, the blood roaring in his ears. Maybe it was then that the man became aware of the look in his adversary's face, the emptiness in his eyes, the abnormal determination behind the grimace.

"Fine," grunted the man, suddenly hesitant. "There's no need to—"

"Luis! Stop it right now!"

A woman of about forty was standing a little way off. She wore an old navy-blue sweatshirt, faded jeans, and muddy black rubber boots. Her body was wiry, and she had uneven features, her high, classic cheekbones bisected by a nose that was a little too long. She was attractive without being beautiful. She leaned casually on the shaft of a hoe, the iron blade at the end of it clearly sharp. In the right hands, that farming tool could just as easily make furrows in a person's head. And Roberto had no doubt that her hands were exactly the right ones.

"Fuck's sake," groaned the man. "Stay out of this, Antía."

"You started it," she replied. The boy was cowering behind her legs like a beaten puppy. "Or am I wrong?"

"This is none of your business."

"Of course it is." Her eyes flashed.

"I don't have to listen to you."

"Maybe not." She shrugged and jutted her chin at one of the nearby houses. "But possibly to him you do."

Up on a balcony, a white-bearded man was calmly smoking a cigarette while contemplating the scene. He gave a slow shake of his head, before turning and going back inside the house.

Big, burly Luis scowled, but all his grit seemed gone, and there was a look of relief in his eyes. He stooped to pick up his raincoat, shook the mud off it, and barged past Roberto.

"We'll be seeing each other," he muttered. "This is a small island."

When he was gone, Roberto heaved a sigh. The overpowering fury had passed, and only the adrenaline remained. His heart was still racing, and he plunged his hands into his pockets in an attempt to calm himself.

He went over to the woman. She had dropped the hoe and was hugging the boy, who was sobbing loudly.

"Thanks," said Roberto. "If you hadn't shown up, things could have gotten pretty ugly."

"It's me who should be thanking you. For defending Diego. Poor kid has no idea what to do in situations like that."

Roberto took a closer look at the boy, who was gazing gratefully up at him, his big green eyes full of tears. Roberto had thought, given the youngster's small, lean frame, that he was just a kid, but realized now he must be at least sixteen or seventeen.

"Hi, I'm Roberto." He held out his hand to Diego, who just stared at it, seemingly unsure what to do, before throwing his arms around Roberto, almost knocking him over with the embrace.

"I'm Diego," said the boy, unleashing a dazzling smile. "And now we're friends. Friends forever, right? Friends, friends, friends!"

"Forever's a long time." Roberto smiled back. "But we can start with today."

"Are you a secret agent?" trilled Diego.

"What?"

"You've come to the island in the middle of winter because you're a secret agent, on a special mission, right?"

"He isn't a secret agent, Diego," said the woman. "He's the writer Roberto Lobeira, and he's going to be spending a few weeks at the Escudero place."

"News travels fast." Roberto frowned.

"More than fast, in a place as small as this." She shrugged. "Especially if a famous author comes to visit."

Roberto thought he detected a hint of sarcasm.

"And you are?"

"Antía Freire," she said curtly. She had a firm handshake. "I'm Diego's sister, and I've got the keys to your rental property."

"And who was the idiot I almost just had a fistfight with?"

"Luis Docampo." She winced, as if the words tasted bitter. "Son of Ramón Docampo, the gentleman on the balcony."

"Let me guess: You guys aren't best friends."

"That doesn't quite cover it," she said. "Let's just say that the Freires and the Docampos have a few long-standing differences."

"That's why he was like that with Diego?"

She shook her head. "No," she sighed. "That's just because Luis is an asshole. When did you get in?"

"Just now," said Roberto, struck by how alike the siblings were with their bright blond hair and their green, storm-tossed eyes. "My bags are down by the dock."

"Then you should go get them straightaway." Antía started in that direction. "There's a big storm coming in. Don't suppose you want your stuff getting washed out to sea."

"No," he said, startled. "No, I really don't."

"Hurry, then!" she said, clearly incredulous at such a rookie error.

Roberto turned and dashed back toward the dock. On finding his bags just where he'd left them, still a good way clear of the rising swell by the visitor booth, he heaved a sigh of relief. He grabbed his backpack and slung it over his shoulder.

Antía eyed his luggage critically.

"I hope you've brought enough stuff for your stay. If the sea gets worse, we won't be seeing a supply boat anytime soon."

"I've brought enough food for a month, don't worry," he said, still smiling. "I knew this place didn't cater to visitors in the winter."

Antía muttered something but was obviously relieved. She and Diego helped Roberto gather the rest of his luggage, and they started up the hill. As they climbed back toward the houses, he saw that the woman was right—the sea was turning rougher. He was no expert, but even he could tell that the docking maneuver would have been far harder in the current conditions.

"How far to the house?"

"About a twenty-minute walk," Antía said. "There are only a couple of tricky slopes. Steep, and a bit of a scramble."

"Can't we drive there?"

Her look spoke volumes.

"Considering you know so much about the island, Roberto Lobeira, I'm surprised you don't know that Ons has barely any paved road. This isn't the mainland. There are a few drivable sections, but the rest is all dirt tracks, most in pretty bad shape. That's why there aren't any vehicles. They're forbidden."

"Forbidden?" He could hardly believe it.

"We're in a national park, remember. People go pretty much everywhere on foot."

"No cars." Roberto looked gloomy. "Great."

"I *say* pretty much everywhere—actually, there is some transportation. The lighthouse keepers have a pickup truck; there's a truck at the campsite, though that's closed in the winter; and the park rangers have an SUV."

"And will anyone give us a ride?"

"The lighthouse guys keep to themselves. There won't be anyone at the campsite until summer, and none of the rangers are working today. Ons isn't exactly busy at this time of year."

"No problem, I'll manage," snorted Roberto, picturing the walk up to the house. He was already exhausted and didn't want to think about traversing "tricky" slopes for another twenty minutes.

"Don't worry," said Antía eventually with a half smile. "The rangers' SUV is near here, by the generator behind the church, and I happen to have a set of keys."

"I appreciate it." Roberto shook his head. "I'm not sure I can face carrying all this stuff."

"No problem," said Antía. "Give me a minute, and I'll go get the SUV."

Antía went off, leaving Roberto alone with Diego. Roberto observed him as the teen concentrated on wiping down his mud-spattered superhero figures. At a glance, there was nothing out of the ordinary about Diego, but little details of body language and facial tics showed he wasn't completely normal. He was subtly but noticeably different—some mild form of autism, possibly. Roberto didn't know enough about such conditions to be any more precise, but there was no doubt that Diego had already forgotten the incident with Luis Docampo and was extremely content, lost in a fantasy world that only he could access—he and his superheroes.

"Do you live on the island?" Roberto said to break the ice.

"Mm-hmm . . ." was all the answer he got.

"All year round?"

"Sometimes I go to the mainland with Antía, when I have to see the doctor. I don't like the doctor," he added, gaze still pinned on his figures.

"And you don't get bored?"

"There're lots of people in the summertime." He shook his head. "It's winter now, which is worse."

"Of course, there can't be much to do."

The boy blinked slowly a couple of times, which in any other person would have seemed affected and ridiculous but in his case seemed entirely natural.

"No, not because of that . . . In the summer, with all the people, *he* hides. But in the winter, he always comes out and does things. Nasty things."

Roberto felt an icy shiver down his back. Diego's tone was fearful in a way that made it clear he didn't mean the bully Luis.

"Who are you talking about?"

But they were interrupted by a vehicle's headlights. Roberto looked up to find a hulking white SUV with the Spanish national park emblem on the doors, and Antía motioning to them from behind the wheel. They loaded up the luggage, Roberto and Diego got in, and Antía pulled onto the track.

As they were driving away, Roberto glanced out the window and saw the white-bearded Ramón Docampo once again. He had returned to the balcony and was watching them steadily, cigarette in hand. The sky was so dark with clouds now that it was almost as if night had fallen. In the gloom, Roberto couldn't make out the man's expression, but a thought came to him that further darkened his mood.

*Stay out of trouble,* the skipper of the *Punta Suido* had said.

And he, within ten minutes of being on the island, had probably made enemies of half its inhabitants.

# 2

## A Gift

The paved road ended after a hundred yards, and the SUV began hurtling along a narrow dirt track with deep drainage ditches at either side. Every now and then, they passed an unlit, empty house.

"In the summer, almost all the houses are occupied, either by their owners or by vacationers," Antía explained, without taking her eyes off the road. "But at this time of year, you can go a whole day without meeting a soul, if that's what you want."

The SUV shook as it tackled a steep slope.

"Did you bring enough food?" she asked again.

"Yes. I was told to bring everything I needed."

"Good. There's a store and a few restaurants, but they only open in the summer. The Docampo bar, the one next to the dock, sometimes opens during the winter but only when there's a fishing boat in port. I doubt they'll serve you, but you can always try."

"I seem to have gotten off to a pretty bad start with the Docampos."

"Maybe," she sighed. "But these are our problems really, not yours. My mother wouldn't agree with me, but you ought to go to the bar at some point and try to smooth things over."

"You're telling me to make peace with the guy who I nearly got into a fight with, two seconds after arriving?" Roberto gave her a quizzical look.

"I'm telling you not to get drawn into our quarrels," she replied. "It's . . . complicated. Anyway, this is the place."

The SUV lurched to a halt next to what appeared to be an overgrown mound, barely visible in the darkness. Only when they got out did he realize that it was a small cottage with irregular stone walls and a moss-covered roof. By the door stood an old fig tree, gnarled and twisted by the wind, which was no doubt a welcome source of shade during the summer but right now looked more like something out of a horror movie.

Antía handed Roberto the key, and he turned it in the lock. Once inside, he felt around for a light switch, but nothing happened when he flicked it on.

"You should be so lucky . . ."

With a click, Antía illuminated the interior of the house with a powerful flashlight.

"Electricity on the island is rationed," she explained. "There's a generator in the village that supplies the whole place, but it only runs for a few hours a day."

"And the rest of the time?"

"We get by without electricity." She shrugged. "It's not so hard once you get used to it. But don't worry, there's usually some power early in the evening. It should come on soon. Diego, honey, go look for a lamp."

The boy went to the kitchen and quickly came back with a propane lamp and a triumphant expression on his face. Antía opened the valve and pressed the igniter; with a quiet hiss, gentle gaslight illuminated the room.

"This place has a hot water tank, like almost all the houses on the island, but it's quite small, and it takes a while to refill. So no chance of long showers, I'm afraid. And the flame on the boiler has a tendency to go out."

"How do you know so much about the place?"

"It's my work during the summer season." Antía smiled. "I rent out houses to tourists, fix any problems, deal with the owners. Most of them haven't set foot on the island in years. That isn't unusual—having visitors out of season is."

"I'll try not to be any trouble," he replied.

Roberto looked around the cottage. It consisted of a spacious living room with a couch and a table with four chairs, and a tiny kitchen in which stood an old fridge, its door ajar. At the far end were a small bathroom and a bedroom containing a double bed that looked antique.

"It's not very big, but it's south-facing and it's warm," she said. "And as soon as the weather clears, you'll see that it's got spectacular sea views."

"It's more than enough for me."

"The fridge only works some of the time, but if you keep it closed, it should more or less conserve whatever you put inside it. There's a map of the island on the back of the door if you want to go for a walk. See you around, no doubt."

Roberto observed her silhouette in the doorway. Once again, he was struck by the graceful fluidity of her movements, while at the same time she seemed slightly tense, on alert. She was keen to get going; he could tell.

Roberto took his cell phone from his pocket.

"There's no electricity, but there is coverage," he murmured. "That's weird."

"It's because of the tourists," Antía explained. "In the summer, people complained about not being able to post on Instagram, so a cell tower ended up getting installed, up by the lighthouse. The cell tower and the lighthouse are the only two places with their own generators and electricity around the clock."

"That's good to know."

"You shouldn't have any trouble." She gave him another one of her curious half smiles. "We have to go now. Diego, say goodbye to your new friend."

To Roberto's surprise, the boy came over and threw his arms around him, hugging him tightly. Antía's goodbye came in the form of another robust handshake.

"One last thing," she said as she turned to leave. "The island can be a dangerous place at night, particularly in the winter. Take care if you go for a walk."

"Dangerous?" replied Roberto in surprise. "What do you mean?"

"Oh, nothing sinister, don't worry," she said. "Just that the paths aren't lit, and the ground is very rough. You could fall and break a leg. It's no joke."

"I wasn't planning to go trekking in the middle of the night," he assured her.

"Aren't you going to say anything about the Tangaraño?" Diego fidgeted behind his sister.

"What does he mean?"

"Nothing," Antía said sharply. "Just his usual nonsense. Fantasies. Don't pay any attention, or you'll go crazy with his stories, like everyone else. Okay, see you around, Roberto Lobeira. It's been a pleasure to meet you."

Out they went, and as the SUV roared away into the gloom, Roberto felt the crushing weight of loneliness bearing down on him.

By the light of the propane lamp, he looked around again. The place that, just a moment before, had seemed cozy and welcoming, like a hobbit's hole, now seemed cold and bare, his prison for four weeks that stretched interminably ahead—a whole month stuck on this island, with no possibility of going home; no way to call a taxi or an Uber or to jump on a train. And he couldn't walk back the way he'd come, of course . . .

He'd locked himself in a prison of his own making.

He had always believed in being open to new experiences, but this wasn't turning out to be easy. He hoped the monastic seclusion would enable him to make good progress with his novel. That was what had brought him here, after all.

He spent the rest of the evening arranging his belongings, having dinner, and preparing a suitable corner in which to work. As he was finishing, the ceiling lamp buzzed quietly a couple of times, and suddenly the house was filled with light, just like Antía Freire had promised.

He turned on the electric heaters. The house warmed up almost immediately, and he felt his mood lift. The place seemed welcoming again, and the ugly imitation Persian rug even managed to lend the ensemble a touch of elegance. The pictures on the walls were cheap prints bought in some home-decor store, but at least they fitted with the rest of the room. The couch sagged slightly in the middle but had not yet reached that point when it would become a torture instrument.

Things were looking up. Even the rain had desisted, and the darkness outside no longer seemed so threatening.

He felt the urge to inspect his new domain, if only by taking a short stroll. He didn't intend to go far. He'd have plenty of time to explore the island properly in the coming days.

He put on his parka and grabbed the lamp. He turned up the flame and caught his reflection in a mirror that hung next to the door, its painted frame flaking. With his hood up and holding the lamp, he looked like some character that had stepped out of the nineteenth century.

The yard was overgrown and would clearly benefit from the expert hand of a gardener. Ivy and brambles had smothered the low stone wall that ran around the house, and spread like a brown-green stain across the lawn with its dormant grass. By the faint light of the lamp, he did a circuit of the cottage, but apart from a ramshackle woodpile, the water tank, and an abandoned chicken coop, there wasn't much to be seen.

He wandered a short way until he reached the main track. It was made of beaten earth, but the winter rains had washed away much of the surface, and here and there, large potholes had been filled in with rubble and gravel. Taking care not to twist an ankle, he followed it uphill. He meant to go only as far as the next curve before returning to the cozy warmth of the cottage.

Suddenly, something moved among the vegetation to his right.

Roberto started, but even with the lamp, he could see nothing more than a few stunted trees. A second later, there was a flash of light behind him, and he saw something moving again.

He laughed with relief. It was just his own shadow.

And once again, a huge flash illuminated everything. He looked around, searching for the source of the light. Then, almost immediately, there was another shaft of light. He suddenly realized that it was the lighthouse, its powerful beam sweeping across the path.

He counted slowly between one flash and the next. When he had counted to twenty-four, the pattern was repeated—three flashes, followed by a pause. He wondered if the light would also reach the cottage.

He shivered. That was enough for one night. He retraced his steps, but as he entered the yard, he stopped short.

Somebody had been there.

There was no doubt about it. He had definitely closed the door behind him, but it now stood ajar, and a yellow strip of light from inside stretched across the sodden lawn.

But that wasn't the strangest thing.

There was something lying on the stone threshold.

He approached slowly and, as the light from the lamp slowly illuminated the object, he felt a ball of ice forming in his stomach.

It was the decapitated head of a rabbit, resting on some twigs.

He looked around warily.

"Who's there?" he shouted. "Hello! Is there anyone there?"

The only reply was the sighing of the wind and the pitter-patter of the rain. It was as if the island were holding its breath.

He crouched down to inspect the macabre gift. The poor beast stared up at him through watery, lifeless eyes, its teeth bared and a startled expression on its face. The head had been severed cleanly, and there was hardly a trace of blood. He laid the back of his hand against it. It was still warm—the animal had been dead for only a few minutes. He entered the cottage, holding the lamp out in front of him like a weapon.

He went through all the rooms, but there was nobody to be seen, and it would be impossible for anyone to hide in the cottage. He checked his belongings: Everything was just as he had left it. Disconcerted, he took a pack of cigarettes from his pocket and lit one.

He tried to remember. He'd closed the door, he was sure of that, but he hadn't locked it, so anyone could simply have turned the handle and let themselves in. But there was no trace of a visitor.

Nothing to indicate that anyone had been there.

Apart from the decapitated rabbit's head at the entrance. That could hardly have gotten there on its own.

He took a deep drag on his cigarette and stared out into the darkness, wondering what else this island had in store for him.

Whatever it was, something told him it wasn't going to be pleasant.

# 3

## The Poacher

The night was long, and he barely slept.

The ghosts of the past had accompanied him. It was always the same—memories of a dark night with cries and screams all around, a constant bombardment of them, until eventually he woke, drenched in sweat. It had become a familiar routine over the past four years. Every time he thought the ghosts had finally been buried, they showed up again, like gate-crashers ruining a party.

He checked the windows, jammed a chair up against the door, and went back to bed, hoping to sleep, only to wake every few minutes, alert to the slightest noise. Each time, it turned out to be nothing more than the wind or the rain. It was nothing, and it was everything.

He knew it was all inside his head. But it was one thing to know something and quite another to really believe it. Anxiety and fear are slippery beasts, hard to tame once they've escaped from their cages.

When the sun finally showed itself above the horizon, he had slept no more than a couple of hours.

After spending a while struggling with the controls of a gas stove that looked as old as the island itself, Roberto brewed a pot of strong coffee. While the aroma pervaded the room, he took a quick shower to wash away the last traces of sleep. He shivered in the tepid trickle of water, but once he was dressed and had a mug of coffee in his hand, he began to feel better.

Until he opened the fridge door. There, on the top shelf, inside a plastic bag, was the rabbit's head, tangible proof of the previous night's events.

He closed the fridge and went outside. The sun occasionally peeked through the clouds, which were racing across the sky toward the mainland, driven by a wind that set the tops of the trees swaying. Sipping his coffee at a moss-covered stone table in the middle of the yard, he replayed what had happened.

Applying the same analytical reasoning he used when constructing the plots of his novels, he took out a leather-bound notebook and began to write.

He knew there couldn't be many more than thirty people on the entire island, and none of them lived very near the cottage. On top of that, nobody had driven there, because he would have heard the engine. At the same time, if someone had come on foot, surely he would have seen the glow of their flashlight.

It was true that he didn't know the terrain like the locals, but he doubted that anyone could find their way along those rutted tracks without some help. And he had done a circuit of the property before setting off on his walk, so the possibility that somebody had been lying in wait until he left could also be ruled out.

He crossed out one after another of the lines he had written. He glanced over at the plastic bag containing the rabbit's head—he had brought it out with him, and it lay on the table next to his packet of cigarettes.

He ran his fingers through his hair. His quiet getaway wasn't turning out precisely as he'd hoped.

*You're imagining things. The most likely explanation is that some predator caught the poor creature and just dropped the head on your doorstep.*

That made more sense. His pen scratched furiously on the paper as he developed the idea. No doubt a fox or a weasel had killed the rabbit and dragged it there while he was out. Startled by his return, it had fled, abandoning the head. As for the door, perhaps he hadn't closed it properly, and the wind had blown it open. It definitely made more sense than all the crazy ideas that were bouncing around inside his head and were no more than feverish imaginings.

*None of that explains the absence of blood,* insisted a small voice. *If some predator had been devouring a rabbit on your doorstep, there would have been a real mess. But there wasn't a single drop of blood.*

"No," he said determinedly as he circled what he had just written. "That's the only thing that makes sense."

The rabbit had been caught and eaten, like dozens of other creatures that had no doubt encountered the same fate that night, in the never-ending game of hunter and prey. The predator carried the head in its jaws to finish off the feast in a quieter location and had ended up at his doorway. End of story.

The idea felt liberating. Suddenly, all the fears and concerns that had haunted him throughout the night evaporated like morning dew.

Everything was going to be okay. He'd write a great manuscript, his agent would be happy, and the world would give him a break for a while. Nothing could go wrong.

How easy it all seemed by the light of day.

He went inside and tidied up, and it was only then that he realized that the previous night, with everything that had happened, he'd forgotten to charge his laptop. The battery icon flashed red, mocking his expectations. And, of course, now there was no power.

Roberto wasn't going to let that ruin his good mood. He would leave the computer plugged in, and as soon as the electricity came back on, it would start to charge. Anyway, he was a night owl when it came to writing, so it wasn't such a big deal. He could use the time to go for a walk and acquaint himself with the setting of his novel.

With that in mind, he left the cottage, making sure to lock the door behind him. As an additional measure, he plucked a hair from his head and delicately fixed it across the corner of the doorframe. It was virtually invisible, but if someone were to open the door, the hair would be dislodged, giving him a sure sign. It was a trick he'd learned years before, from a member of the Gulf Cartel in Tamaulipas. It was a precaution against being ambushed and caught in a hail of bullets when you walked through your front door. He wasn't envisaging anything like that here on this little Atlantic island, but better to be safe than sorry.

Setting off, when he reached the track, he turned in the direction of the main cluster of houses on the island. He wanted to explore at his leisure and, if possible, take a walk along the island's beaches—he was planning to set the start of the novel on one of them.

Under the pale winter light, the narrow track he had ascended the previous day in the SUV seemed positively bucolic. He was beginning to see why vacationers might choose to return year after year.

The sea shimmered in the distance, and flocks of seabirds wheeled overhead. He turned off the track onto a white gravel path that snaked its way through dense thickets of juniper. Occasionally it skirted a copse of trees that looked like tormented sculptures in a land thrashed by salt-laden sea winds. Almost the whole island was a vast, uninterrupted expanse of low scrub, although even that was relative because, in some places, the untended vegetation grew to the height of his head.

The island had been densely populated in the past, but over time, with widespread emigration, nature had reclaimed almost every inch of it. Roberto half glimpsed the occasional weed-choked stone ruins of an old fisherman's hut. He imagined what it must have been like in centuries past when the land was cultivated. But nothing remained of that now other than memories and tumbledown walls.

Gravel crunched beneath his feet, and he realized he was actually walking on a layer of cockle and clam shells, crushed and spread across the path. No doubt there would be dozens of similar paths all over the island. He was wondering to himself just how many decades it would have taken to create them when, up ahead, he saw somebody approaching.

In one hand the stranger carried a bulky sack, while the other gripped a short pole with a blunt, rust-spotted blade at the end. The man seemed to be just as taken aback to find Roberto there, but it was too late to pretend they hadn't seen each other.

The man was about fifty, tall, and well built, with brown, twinkling, watchful eyes. His beard was badly in need of some attention, and although the same went for his hair, that was at least meticulously combed back, with just a few curls tumbling over his ears. His clothes, worn but practical, looked as if they belonged to someone accustomed to hard work.

They eyed each other with a mixture of distrust and surprise. Finally, the other man broke the silence.

"Morning," he said in a gruff monotone.

"Good morning," replied Roberto.

"I don't know you. Are you a park ranger?" There was a hint of hostility in his voice. "You guys are meant to be in uniform. You can't fine me if you're not on duty, right?"

Roberto scrutinized the man again and noticed that he was making a futile attempt to hide the heavy sack behind his back.

"Don't worry, I don't have anything to do with the park." He raised both hands in a reassuring gesture. "And whatever you've got in your sack is none of my business."

The other man muttered something to himself but seemed to relax a little.

"Just a few crabs," he admitted eventually, in a thick accent that was difficult to understand. "I've got a permit. Honestly. And, anyway, they're legal size!"

"I'm sure they are," Roberto said, though he didn't believe a word.

The man was clearly a poacher, presumably of some sort of seafood. The path he had appeared along led directly to the rocky shoreline.

"I'm Roberto Lobeira." He held out his hand to the man, who showed absolutely no interest in returning the greeting. "I'm staying on the island for a little while."

"It's not the summer season yet," replied the poacher, who did not seem inclined to reveal his own name.

Roberto lowered his hand.

"Yes, it takes a bit of explaining . . ." he said. Then, faced with his companion's silence, he gave up. "Anyway, have a good day."

The man nodded. Seeming to think for a moment, he then put his hand in the sack and produced a spider crab.

"Here, have one," he said, "but don't tell anyone you saw me around here."

"There's no need." Roberto shook his head without taking his eyes off the creature, which clicked its claws insistently. "As far as I'm concerned, we've never met."

The poacher grunted and returned the crab to the sack, allowing Roberto to catch a brief glimpse of a writhing mass of legs, pincers, and seaweed-covered shells.

"I'm Víctor Pampín," the man said as he jutted his chin in the direction of the other side of the island. "I live close to Punta Xubenco. If you want any fish or seafood, come and find me. You won't eat better."

"Do you live here all year round?"

The man gave an ambiguous shrug.

"You're the first person I've met here who isn't either a Freire or a Docampo," Roberto went on, ignoring the poacher's reticence. "I heard that everyone who stays on the island over the winter is from one of those two families."

"Most, yes," replied Pampín. "But there are a few of us who don't have anything to do with them. And there're the lighthouse keepers, of course."

"Isn't it tough here?"

"Tough?"

"I just mean, it's pretty cut off in the winter, harsh even, given the lack of electricity and the poor connections with the mainland."

"This is my home," the poacher said, as if no further explanation were required. "I've always lived on the island, and I hope to die here. Some stay because they don't have anywhere to go on the mainland,

and others because this is their place, and they want to make sure everything's in good order."

"Really? What do you mean?"

"Haven't you seen all the vacation homes on the island?" replied Pampín, who was gradually becoming more talkative. "And then there're a couple of restaurants and a grocery store. This place turns into a theme park in the summer. And it's all controlled by the same people."

"The Freires and the Docampos," hazarded Roberto.

"Exactly, the fucking Freires and the fucking Docampos." Pampín's face was suddenly contorted by rage. "They're the bosses of the island, and they behave as if everything belongs to them by divine right, even the things that don't."

"You're not so keen on them, I'm guessing."

"They're a bunch of thieving bastards, the lot of them. They have contracts with the park; they own the boats that bring the tourists; I'm pretty sure they're in with the authorities too." Pampín spat on the ground in disgust. "God knows what shady dealings they've got going on."

"How did they get their hands on everything?" Roberto looked around. "I thought this place wasn't much more than an isolated fishing village until the 1970s. Where did they get the money from?"

"That's a question you'd have to ask them." Pampín's expression became much more opaque. "Anyway, I don't want any problems, and I've probably said too much already."

"Don't worry, I won't say a word," Roberto assured him.

It was clear that the island, like all remote, rural places, had its own collection of stories, rivalries, and jealousies. But the reporter inside him couldn't help being intrigued. How had two fishing families managed to amass a fortune and basically take possession of the whole island while the rest had had no choice but to emigrate?

He added the enigma to the long list of things he couldn't quite believe.

"And what's that for?" Roberto pointed at the pole with the blunt metal blade.

"This?" He shook it in front of him. "It's a scraper. For pulling goose barnacles off the rocks. Best goose barnacles in the world. You should try them."

"Isn't it dangerous?" Roberto asked, vaguely remembering a documentary he had once seen about the men and women who risked their lives to gather this prized seafood from the treacherous rocks below the tideline.

Pampín muttered something unintelligible and looked down at the ground. Roberto would have bet anything that the man had never seen a fishing license in his life.

"How do you manage to make a living on the island?" he asked.

"From the sea, of course," the poacher replied. "In the summer, I sell my catch on the mainland; in the winter, I just feed myself. Octopus, mussels, fish . . . Between that and the vegetable patch, I get by."

"You don't get bored?"

"No," the man laughed. "There's always something to do. I don't stick my nose into other people's business, and I try to make sure they don't stick their noses into mine."

"The rangers in particular," Roberto joked.

"Yes," grunted Pampín, clearly irritated, before abruptly falling silent.

"What's up?" asked Roberto, inwardly cursing his inability to lay off the irony.

But the poacher didn't answer. Instead, he turned and walked off to one side of the path. The slope grew gradually steeper until it reached an old, half-ruined wall. The man pointed to something on the slope.

"That wasn't there two days ago," he said.

Roberto looked in the direction Pampín indicated, trying to make out what he was referring to. Eventually, he spotted something of a beaten track through the bracken and brambles. He would never have noticed it without the poacher pointing it out.

"Someone's come this way recently," Pampín said nervously.

"Some animal, I bet," Roberto ventured. "Maybe a rabbit or a badger."

"There's nothing big enough here to make a path like that." He shook his head. "It has to be something else."

They cautiously approached the beginning of the path. Pampín put his sack down, grasped the scraper with both hands, and held it out in front of him. He seemed nervous. Using the scraper, he pushed the vegetation aside, clearly on edge.

Underneath, there were just earth and the droppings of some small rodent. The man sighed in relief and straightened up, but Roberto quickly shattered his tranquility.

"What's that?"

Pampín looked where Roberto was pointing.

It was a drop of dried blood; there was no doubt about it. A bit farther on, following the track through the undergrowth, was another—and another.

Once he'd seen it, the trail of blood was clear as day. Whatever it was had left a series of drops, running up to the crest of the hill and out of sight.

"Let's see where it leads," said Roberto.

"You're joking," replied Pampín, his eyes wide open. "I wouldn't go up there if you paid me."

Roberto didn't answer. The trail of blood on a lonely path pulled at his reporter's instincts with the insistent force of a tugboat.

Accompanied by a reluctant Pampín, he followed the trail. Every few yards, there was another drop of blood, leading them on like the breadcrumbs in a fairy tale. Finally, they came to the top of the hill and stopped at a drystone wall.

"Holy Mother of God!" muttered the poacher, crossing himself. "This is the work of the devil!"

Next to the wall, somebody had built a small structure of branches, anchored firmly to the ground. Tied to the branches with twine was the dismembered body of a rabbit, like some macabre imitation of the crucifixion. Whoever was responsible for this scene had carefully opened the animal up and taken out its intestines, arranging them around the corpse like colored streamers in a complicated, indecipherable pattern.

"It's got no head," Pampín murmured anxiously. "Where's the head?"

*In my fridge, inside a plastic bag.*

"That doesn't matter." Roberto crouched next to the dismembered animal in search of clues. "Do you have any idea who might have done this?"

"I don't know, and I don't care." Pampín again crossed himself and took a step back. "The devil's work, I tell you. The sooner we get out of here, the better."

Roberto gave him an inquisitive look. Pampín seemed genuinely terrified. Here was a hard man, someone who risked life and limb daily on wave-battered rocks, now trembling like a child at the sight of this small, headless animal.

"Have you ever seen anything like this before?"

But Pampín didn't deign to answer, and instead turned around and set off back down the path. Roberto got out his phone and took a couple of photos of the rabbit before following the poacher. A thousand different ideas occurred to him, but one in particular stood out.

Whatever had happened the previous night, it had not been the work of an animal or some coincidence. Someone, whoever that might be, had left a message for him on his very doorstep. And, while he didn't know what the person was trying to say, they clearly weren't friendly.

Pampín was already on his way, pack over his shoulder.

"Hang on a moment!" shouted Roberto. "Are you sure you haven't seen anything like this before?"

By way of a response, Pampín merely crossed himself again and kept going, almost at a run. At the last moment, he turned his head.

"Talk to Elvira!" he said. "She'll explain it better than me."

"Elvira? Who's Elvira? Where can I find her?"

"Elvira Couto, the old woman who lives by Melide Beach, at the far end of the island," the poacher shouted over his shoulder. "She knows about these things! Tell her Pampín sent you!"

And without another word, he set off, almost at a run, leaving Roberto Lobeira with a head full of unanswered questions.

# 4

## Elvira

Roberto hesitated, but eventually, with a shake of the head, he took the neatly folded map of Ons from his pocket. Melide Beach was at the northeast tip of the island, away from the main cluster of houses. There was no proper road there, but he reckoned it wouldn't take him long.

He set off to find Elvira Couto, hoping to solve the mystery.

He'd thought it might take him fifteen minutes to get there, but soon realized he'd misjudged both the distance and the terrain. The narrow track, barely wide enough for a couple of people, zigzagged erratically as it clung to the coast, rising and dipping with the contours of the landscape.

From time to time, as he rounded a corner, he would startle a rabbit that would instantly scamper away, but apart from those and the eternal seagulls and cormorants, there was no other sign of life.

He might as well have been the last man on the face of the earth.

After more than half an hour, his ankles aching, he followed the track around a hairpin bend that gave way to a gentle downhill slope. The track ended at a short flight of cracked cement steps, and here a hand-painted sign with faded lettering identified a nudist beach.

He looked around. He thought it would be an incredible place to swim naked in the summer, but right now—with a chilly wind, and the damp air trying to penetrate the defenses of his expensive parka—stripping off was the last thing he could imagine wanting to do.

The beach was a solitary expanse of fine white sand stretching away into the distance. The waves breaking on the shoreline sent foamy ripples across the wet sand, with the cloudy sky reflected in the sheet of water left in the foam's wake. It was one of the most beautiful scenes he had ever set eyes on.

But of Elvira Couto there was no sign.

"If she's anything like Pampín described, I doubt she's sunbathing on the beach," he said to a seagull that was eyeing him from a few feet away. "Let's see if we can find where she lives."

He headed along the beach, trying to stick to the hard sand without getting his feet wet. The tide was coming in, progressively diminishing that strip. At the far end of the beach, he came upon a narrow path that sloped back inland. After weeks of winter weather, the path was a sure invitation to sprain an ankle, but he didn't see an alternative.

Certain sections had to be clambered with great care, and soon he was panting from the effort. He couldn't believe there wasn't an easier way to get there, but not knowing the island paths had forced his hand. After five minutes, the path widened out. His hopes rising, he walked for some distance, casting around for anything that could be Elvira Couto's house.

It was so hidden that he nearly missed it. The gorse and brambles were so high that they almost completely concealed the tiny dwelling nestled in a hollow to his right. Only the terra-cotta tiles made it stand out. He retraced his steps a little way until he hit the path to the house. There was no other sign of any human presence, so this had to be the place.

A few yards down the path, he came to a wooden sign on which somebody had written, in shaky letters, **PRIVIT PROPARTY, KEPE OFF**. The author, apparently no fan of spelling conventions, was clearly none too fond of visitors either. He pushed on regardless.

It was a low, stone dwelling, with a couple of windows that were little more than arrow slits, a roof that was crying out for repairs, and a dilapidated water tank at the rear. The front yard was in relatively good order, however, with neat rows of carefully tended plants.

From the eaves hung small figures that swung in the wind. Roberto moved closer, and a shiver ran down his spine. Many of them were little stick people, from which hung shells and pieces of glass tinkling in the breeze. Others were pieces of wood upon which strange symbols had been traced in a brown liquid of uncertain origin. The place would have looked like a witch's hovel were it not for the almost infinite quantity of junk piled up around the outside of the building: a jumble of timber, old plastic sacks, moldy pallets, and masses of uncovered scrap metal, slowly being devoured by rust.

An irrational burst of fear urged him to turn around and flee. The solitude had such a powerful effect on him that he nearly did just that, but his curiosity ultimately won out.

Something strange was happening on this island, something that involved him—or which, at least, had touched on him. And the woman who lived here might have the answers.

He approached the peeling door and knocked twice. Nothing happened. Wondering if it was empty, he felt a momentary sense of relief, but then there came the sound of a key turning, and the door creaked open.

A little old woman looked at him unblinkingly. Roberto, unable to calculate her age, thought he had never seen such a dirty, wrinkled face. She couldn't have been more than four feet nine and was hunched over. She was dressed from head to toe in black, with the only concession to color a blue headscarf that almost completely covered her hair, a few white strands poking out from underneath it. Her hands—knotted and twisted by arthritis—held a dishcloth, and the intense, ferocious gleam in her eyes was the only sign of vitality.

"What do you want?" she asked in a voice like broken glass.

"Hello, I was looking for . . ." Roberto trailed off, unsure of how to introduce himself. "Are you Elvira Couto?"

"And what if I am?" she replied.

"I'd like to talk to you. Ask you some questions . . ."

"I don't have time." She went to close the door. "I'm extremely busy. Go away."

"Wait!" Roberto pleaded. "Víctor Pampín sent me! He told me you'd have answers!"

"Pampín talks too much. You've no business being here. Off you go!" she grunted, before slamming the door in his face.

The key scraped mockingly in the lock. Roberto stood staring at the closed door. He'd anticipated all sorts of reactions but nothing as overtly hostile as this. Frustrated, he was about to turn and leave when he decided to have one last try.

"It's about the dead animals!" he shouted at the door. "A rabbit's head appeared on my front step! I found the rest of the body! Please, I need answers!"

For what seemed like an age, nothing happened, and he thought the woman was simply going to ignore him, but just then, the lock turned again, and the door swung open. Elvira, on the threshold, observed him inscrutably.

"You don't need answers," she said dryly. "You need protection."

"Protection? What are you talking about?"

"Are you just going to stand there asking stupid questions, or are you going to come in?" the woman replied. "I don't have all day . . . and you're running out of time."

That, more than anything else, made Roberto's mind up, and he stepped over the threshold.

# 5

## The Dead Man's Kiss

The interior was dark, and it took a while for his eyes to become accustomed to the gloom. The first thing that hit him was the acrid smell, a mixture of stale sweat, cooking, and stuffiness, and under it all a faint hint of decay. The house was little more than a hovel, consisting of a single room, crammed with the most varied collection of objects imaginable. Glancing at a corner, separated from the rest of the room by a moth-eaten curtain, Roberto made out the filthy bed where the woman no doubt slept. Nearly every square inch of the walls was covered by shelves on which stood tins, dried-out plants, stones, pieces of wood, and items Roberto didn't even want to know about.

The woman cleared a pile of old newspapers from a wooden stool and gestured to him to take a seat. Roberto obeyed.

"Okay, tell me what's happened," she grunted, drying her hands on the grubby cloth. "The whole story, please."

*I might as well,* he thought to himself. *I don't see what harm can come of it.*

Roberto told her everything that had happened since the moment he had been confronted with the rabbit's head on the doorstep. The woman interrupted from time to time to ask him to expand on some detail, in a manner that struck him as surprisingly methodical and professional. When he had finished, he squared his shoulders and looked expectantly at the woman.

"So?" he said. "Do you have any explanation for all this?"

"I most certainly do," she replied with a bitter laugh that sounded like a truck unloading gravel. "But you aren't going to like it. They've cast a *meigallo* on you."

"A what?"

"A *meigallo*. A curse," she said, as if talking to a child. "The dead man's kiss."

Roberto raised his eyebrows. "You can't be serious."

"Do I look like I'm joking?"

"The dead man's kiss." He swallowed, incredulous. "What's that?"

"A powerful spell," the woman muttered. "It will dry your life out, bit by bit. You'll gradually become weaker and weaker. First, you'll stop eating; then you won't be able to sleep; and finally . . . you'll die."

"That doesn't sound like much fun."

Roberto was a rational person. During his lifetime, he had seen evil incarnate more than once, but on each and every occasion, there had been a common denominator: the darkness of the human soul—fratricidal hatred, a thirst for vengeance, mindless pillage. He'd seen suckling infants murdered, women raped by guerrilla fighters, ditches piled with corpses. The horror always arose from the blackness of somebody's heart, but it took forms you could recognize. What the old woman had told him sounded more like a tale to scare children. It couldn't be true, even if Elvira Couto's expression was utterly somber.

"I don't believe in all that stuff. A rabbit's head is just that . . . a head. It can't harm me."

"Ah, but whether you believe or not makes no difference," she replied. "Evil doesn't need your consent to exist."

"Well, that's one thing we agree on," he said. "And I don't suppose you have any idea who could be responsible for this . . . dead man's kiss?"

"There are dark forces at work on this island," she muttered, rubbing her hands. "Something arrived on Ons many years ago, and it stayed among us."

He had hoped the woman might give him a clear answer: *This is a trick we play on tourists.* Or *It's a gory local custom. We're on an island in the middle of nowhere, and we do strange things to pass the time.* He certainly hadn't expected to be dealing with some kind of voodoo.

"Okay. So what do I have to do to get rid of the curse?" he asked impatiently. "Dance in the rain? Throw salt over my shoulder? Walk under a ladder?"

"You shouldn't joke about these things."

Roberto raised his hands placatingly. This was a waste of time.

"Okay, I didn't mean to upset you. What do I have to do?"

But Elvira had turned away and was rummaging through a pile of junk in the corner. Finally, she let out a victorious yelp and held up a bundle of dried twigs, held together with some elaborately knotted red thread.

"What's that?" Roberto asked. "What are you—" The woman had struck him across the face with the bundle of twigs as she muttered something unintelligible. "Ouch! What the hell are you doing?" Before Roberto could stop her, she whipped him three more times in quick succession, mumbling as she did so.

"The graves of the dead, from near and far, from sea and land, from streams and mountains . . ."

The rest was incomprehensible gibberish that Roberto couldn't decipher. He patiently allowed the woman to hit him nine more times, hoping that the ridiculous ritual would eventually come to an end.

"And now you have to jump over the fire." The woman pointed at the hearth. The flames had almost consumed the log that was burning in it, leaving just a few embers. "Three times."

"How am I meant to jump there?" Roberto answered, losing his patience. "Do you want me to get into the fireplace?"

Her only response was to walk over to the hearth and kick the embers, scattering them across the stone floor of the hovel. One of the embers rolled into a corner and almost set light to the cloth hanging down from an old side table, but Elvira stamped it out.

"Jump," she ordered in a voice that brooked no dissent. "Jump if you want to save yourself. Three times, neither one more nor one less."

Roberto was tempted to make a run for it, but eventually he groaned and stood up. Feeling ridiculous, he jumped three times across the embers while Elvira observed him with a clinical gaze, watchful for anything the ritual might be missing. When he was done, she seemed satisfied.

"Nearly done." She leaned toward Roberto, who wrinkled his nose at the acrid odor. "Keep this in your pocket for protection," she said, pressing something into his hand.

It was a short length of fishing line tied around some dried leaves with a fragrant smell. Not wanting to argue, he did as he was told.

"So?" he said. "Is that it?"

"That depends on the strength of the *meigallo*," she answered as she gathered up the embers in her hands and tossed them back into the hearth as if they were already cold. "But in principle, yes. You're clean."

"You don't have any idea who might have done it, do you?" insisted Roberto.

"This is the Tangaraño's doing," Elvira muttered, making a sign to ward off the evil eye. "It's always him."

"Who's the Tangaraño? It's not the first time someone has mentioned him."

"I'm not going to say anything else." The woman shook her head.

"Is he a local?" Roberto asked. "I only arrived on the island yesterday, and I haven't had time to make enemies."

"Who have you met?"

"Let's see," he replied, counting on his fingers. "Antía and Diego Freire. One of the Docampos. Víctor Pampín, who told me to come and find you . . . and yourself. It isn't a very long list."

"Don't trust the Docampos or the Freires," she muttered. "Both families have dark secrets. And don't forget that, however friendly they may seem, they'll always want something from you, even if you don't realize it."

*The same warning as the poacher gave me,* he thought to himself. *They might be powerful on the island, but they aren't exactly popular.*

"Dark secrets? What do you mean?"

"That's not for me to say." She held out her hand. "And now, my payment."

Roberto looked at the open palm for a moment, until he realized that the woman was demanding compensation for the ritual. Feeling like a tourist trapped by a sideshow huckster, he wondered as he took out his wallet how many innocents the old woman fleeced each summer.

"I don't want money," she hissed. "Don't insult me."

"So what do you want?"

"Something personal," she replied bluntly. "It doesn't have to be valuable. It just has to be something of yours. Something you really care about."

He hadn't expected that. It clearly wasn't some ruse for tricking unwary tourists.

He patted his pockets, looking for something that might satisfy the strange woman's demands. Finally, he found an old fountain pen. It wasn't expensive, but it had accompanied him on his many journeys, starting with his very first trip as a reporter, in Aleppo. He hoped it would suffice as payment.

He offered it to the woman, who snatched it from his hands and inspected it, her eyes glinting. After a moment, she gave a satisfied grunt and tossed it nonchalantly into a nearby chest.

"We're done." She pointed at the door. "You can go now. And remember what I said: Don't trust anybody on this island. Appearances can be deceptive."

Roberto left the hovel, mystified. When the door slammed behind him and he heard the key turning in the lock once again, he stretched and let out a loud sigh. The salty air provided a refreshing contrast with the strange atmosphere inside the house.

He took one final look around and shook his head.

*What a waste of time.*

He walked away, his head already back in his book. Perhaps he could even make use of this episode.

Before long, he was on the beach again, sitting on a rock, watching the waves break on the shore. A hungry seagull, perhaps the same one as before, approached hesitantly, on the lookout for a free morsel.

"This place is full of lunatics," he muttered to the seagull as he took out a cigarette. "And I seem to have met all of them."

The seagull spread its wings and let out a squawk. He tossed a handful of sand at it, and the bird took flight indignantly.

He lit the cigarette, no mean feat in the wind, took out his notebook, and started to search for his pen when he remembered that he no longer had it. He looked at the notebook again.

In his head, he was re-creating the whole experience, and the more he thought about it, the more absurd it seemed. All Elvira Couto needed was a wart on her nose, a black cat, and a bubbling cauldron to turn her into a character out of the Brothers Grimm. At the same time, the woman's smell, the grime, the poverty, the collection of old junk and garbage told another story that was far sadder and also, undoubtedly, far more real—the story of someone suffering from some kind of mental illness.

He didn't believe a word about the dead man's kiss, of course, but he had no doubt that, whoever had performed the ritual—the mysterious Tangaraño perhaps—the aim was to frighten him. The question was why? However much he worried away at it, he couldn't think of a reason, other than the possibility that his presence on the island might have been an unforeseen inconvenience for somebody. And that opened up such a wide range of possibilities that just thinking about it made his head hurt.

He stubbed out the cigarette in the sand, put the butt in his pocket, and took out the pack to light another one. It was a bad habit he had given up a while ago but which he had slipped back into. He didn't feel proud of himself, but right now he urgently needed to smoke. He gave up after a couple of tries. The rain had become heavier, and the little cylinder of soggy paper was falling to pieces in his hands.

The change in the weather appeared to have frightened away even the seagulls, which were no longer gliding overhead with their raucous cries. Only the monotonous sound of the rain and the roar of the waves crashing against the barnacle-and-mussel-encrusted rocks accompanied him, lulling him into a stupor.

He was startled out of it by a sudden ringing sound. It took him a moment to realize that the noise was coming from his jacket. He struggled with his zipper until he managed to take out his phonc. His agent's name flashed up on the screen.

Carmen Gavín had been his literary agent ever since, with very little preamble, he had submitted his first manuscript. Back then, Roberto had already decided to abandon the hazardous and reckless life he had led until that moment, and he had seen her as somebody he could trust. Carmen was nearing retirement, although she had every intention of dying in the saddle or at least at the desk of her agency in Barcelona. She was pragmatic, as caring as a grandmother when required, and as tough as a sergeant major when the circumstances called for it.

*The Fleeting Glance* should have been one of those novels that languished on the shelves at the back of bookstores, far from the tables groaning with titles put out by major publishers that always occupied the space near the front. It was the literary debut of a war reporter who had seen enough death, misery, and destruction to fill three lifetimes, a simple novel of curious detectives who resolve crimes thanks to their mental acuity and ingenuity. The truth was that he had no great hopes for that manuscript when he signed the contract with a small publishing house.

But things had turned out quite differently.

Everything had gone crazy.

Two weeks after its launch, *The Fleeting Glance* had topped the bestseller list, to his surprise and to that of his publishers. Word of mouth did the rest, and the book's popularity spread like the ripples on the surface of a pond. Things got completely out of hand when a well-known presenter recommended it on primetime TV. Sales went through the roof, and with the speed of a hurricane, the book became "the publishing phenomenon of the year," as the media put it.

But then the source of ideas inside his head, the one that had enabled him to write *The Fleeting Glance*, dried up. And that was how things had stood until a solution had presented itself a few weeks ago.

As he was pouring a second gin and tonic in front of the TV, images of a green island surrounded by cliffs battered by a raging sea had appeared on the screen: a few scattered houses, beaches of white sand, low vegetation whipped by the wind, and standing guard over it all, a huge, lonely lighthouse on the highest point of the island. A wild paradise in the mouth of the Pontevedra estuary, the Isle of Ons was a patch of land barely two square miles in total, which could be reached only by boat.

In his head, the ideas had started to flow. He had spent the rest of the night in an almost fevered state, scribbling down notes: a tale of shipwrecks, sailors washed up by the waves, a torrid and moving love story. All the pieces fitted together perfectly.

There was only one problem.

He didn't know anything about the place.

He needed to visit it, to allow his reporter's instinct to fill the missing gaps in the story.

And that was why he was here, in the middle of winter . . . although things weren't going quite as he had imagined.

Roberto took a couple of deep breaths before accepting the call.

"Hi, Carmen."

"Hi, Roberto!" Carmen's energetic, singsong voice was clearly audible at the other end of the line. "How's your island retreat going? Productive?"

"Well, it's certainly been an interesting experience so far," he replied, without answering her question.

"Are you all settled in? Is everything okay?"

"Yes, it's all good. I'm hoping to make some decent progress with the novel over the next few days."

"That's great news!" enthused Carmen at the other end of the line.

In the background were the noise of Barcelona's downtown traffic and the buzz of the human beehive of a large city. She must be calling from the street, on her way to a meeting—just like Carmen.

He had a sudden pang of nostalgia. Even though he was here, trapped in the time bubble that was the Isle of Ons, the world continued turning at full speed. Suddenly, in the middle of a lonely beach, he felt an irrational need to be in Barcelona, London, Paris, or any other great metropolis, strolling down a busy sidewalk, on his way to a restaurant or a bar. The desire to be surrounded by people caught up in their own affairs, at once solitary and accompanied, was intense. He wanted to return to a modern world, one in which ritually sacrificed bunny rabbits, electricity rationing, witchcraft, and illicit fishing were nothing more than picturesque details in a movie you watched from the couch at the end of a long, hard day.

But Carmen was nearly a thousand miles away, and, as far as Roberto was concerned, she might as well be in another galaxy because he had no way of leaving this accursed island for another four weeks, when the *Punta Suido* was due to return for him.

"Are you sure you're okay, Roberto? You seem a little . . . distant."

*I almost got into a fight with a total stranger, someone's put a spell on me with a rabbit's head, but thankfully an old crone who would really benefit from an urgent visit from social services removed the evil eye from me. And all in just twenty-four hours.*

"I'm fine," he lied. "I've never felt better. I'm looking forward to sharing my draft with you. I'm sure it's going to be good."

"If anything happens to you . . ." Carmen suddenly sounded worried. "If you run into any problems . . . you'll call me, right? If you need help, I'll make sure someone comes to get you."

The sudden show of concern moved him more than he wanted to admit.

"Everything's fine, Carmen, I promise," he said. "Thanks for looking out for me. I've got to go now—I'm in the middle of a tricky paragraph, and I want to finish it before lunch."

"Don't forget to call me," she insisted. "Take care, Roberto."

"You too," he replied before ending the call.

He put the phone back in his pocket and breathed out very slowly. *One Mississippi, two Mississippi, three Mississippi* . . . He inspected his hands: His fingers were stained with blood, no doubt from when he had touched the crucified rabbit.

He wiped them on his pants and checked the time. It was almost midday. He decided he'd had enough for one morning. He'd go back to the cottage and write for a few hours, to clear his head of everything that was buzzing around inside it. And, while he was at it, he'd take the rabbit's head that was sitting on the top shelf of his fridge and bury it a long way away. Just in case.

God, he could use a drink.

# 6

## Secrets and Quarrels

His second morning on the island wasn't much different from his first, except that he had managed to sleep more than five hours straight, something of a record for him, after spending most of the evening working on a draft that he was quite pleased with. However, his sleep was not exactly restful because recurring nightmares featuring Elvira Couto woke him up more than once. After his shower and his morning coffee (and after checking the front step in case any new nocturnal gifts had appeared), he decided to explore the village.

Although it was downhill all the way, the state of the track left a lot to be desired. When, half an hour later, he finally reached the smooth cement surface of the road, his ankles were aching.

As he rounded the final corner, he came across an unexpected scene. Two women were sitting on a low wall in front of the church, a large rubber bucket between them. They were lost in conversation and didn't notice his arrival. One of them was in her late fifties, with curly gray hair; she was short and stocky, and despite the temperature, her broad, muscular arms were bare. The other was younger; she couldn't have been more than eighteen or nineteen years old. Thin and delicate, her head a mass of blond hair, she was the opposite of her companion. The girl's eyes were the same stormy green as Antía's and Diego's. Roberto wasn't one for gambling, but he'd happily bet that she was a member of the Freire clan.

The older woman held a thin, sharp knife in her right hand. Roberto observed with a certain fascination as she thrust her hand into the bucket and brought out a huge purple octopus. In one fluid movement, she turned it upside down, and, the octopus still waving its tentacles, she inserted her knife where the animal's mouth was, twisted the blade, and, with practiced deftness, removed the entrails in one go, accompanied by a viscous sound. Before he had time to fully absorb what he had just seen, the woman was already taking her next victim from the bucket.

Just then, the girl noticed the new arrival, leaned toward her older companion, and whispered something in her ear. The woman dropped the octopus into the bucket with a splash and turned to look at Roberto.

Her eyes were the same color as the girl's, but her expression was harder, and the lines on her face spoke of a life exposed to the elements. She cleaned her hands on her apron and put away the knife before taking a step toward him.

"You must be the writer," she said in the steely voice of someone unaccustomed to being contradicted. "Antía told me about what you did yesterday to protect Diego."

"It was no big deal, really."

"When somebody helps one of my family, it's always a big deal for me," she replied sternly, holding out her hand. "I'm Rosalía Freire, Antía's mother. This is my daughter Helena, Diego's other sister."

Roberto shook her hand. It was hard and calloused.

"Apart from a few odd ones out," said Helena, "everyone here's either a Freire or a Docampo." In contrast with her mother's, the daughter's voice was smooth, with a deep and slightly disconcerting vibrato.

"Yes," said Roberto warily, "I thought so."

He decided not to mention the previous day's encounters with the poacher and the witch at the far end of the island. Something told him that the less information he gave the two ruling clans about his movements, the better.

"Do you live on the island all year round?" Roberto asked, changing the subject.

"I go to the mainland a few times a year, but I like it here," the girl replied quietly. "We all like it."

"We're in your debt," Rosalía pitched in. "The Docampos are a bad lot, every last one of them. If you want some advice, steer clear of them. And if there's anything you need, just come and ask me."

*However friendly they may seem, they'll always want something from you.* Elvira Couto's warning echoed in his head.

What had begun as a casual encounter had turned into something very different, although he wasn't sure what. There was a strange tension in the air, as if what he said next would be very important in some complex game whose rules he didn't understand.

"That won't be necessary." He shook his head, choosing the most prudent solution. "It was nothing."

Rosalía Freire scrutinized him for a few seconds with her stony expression before she finally relaxed and something akin to a smile appeared on her face.

"As you wish," she said in her powerful voice. "But if you need anything, come and find us at El Cucorno."

"El Cucorno? What's that?"

"Our family home." She pointed toward a substantial stone house that seemed to cling to the slope. "If you need help, our door is always open. Come and visit us one of these days."

"Thank you."

An awkward silence followed. Rosalía gripped her knife and waved it at the height of Roberto's chest, a few inches too close for comfort, but he forced himself not to move a muscle.

"You seem like a good man," the woman said with a half smile that could mean anything. "And I don't usually say that of visitors. Be careful when you're out and about. The island can be a dangerous place for people who don't know it well."

"Because of the cliffs?" he asked cautiously.

"Every summer someone ends up splitting their skull or breaking a leg because they've gone somewhere they shouldn't. The whole west side of Ons, facing out to the open sea, is a series of steep rock faces that tumble directly down to the shore," she replied. "If you fall down one of those, your body will never be found. Ever. Above all, take care with the Devil's Hole."

"The what?"

"The Devil's Hole," the woman replied. "A chasm that's more than forty yards deep. The bottom connects to the sea through a system of caves. But if you fall in, you're dead. If you want to see it, don't go alone. One of my boys will accompany you."

"I'll bear it in mind."

"Goodbye, Mr. Lobeira." Saying this, Rosalía plunged her hand into the bucket and pulled out another octopus, which she gutted with a flick of her wrist. Part of the animal's insides fell at Roberto's feet, but he didn't even flinch, fascinated as he was by the woman's skill. "See you around."

"Goodbye," Helena added timidly, without looking up.

Roberto walked away, thinking to himself that Rosalía Freire was one of those people whom it's best not to fall out with.

He continued along the road that ended at the dock. The two restaurants that served the summer visitors were closed, their windows boarded up to protect them against the inclement weather.

Their empty terraces were bare and soulless, and an old, sun-bleached ice cream sign advertised products that would not be available for several months.

However, he noticed that the door of one of the establishments was ajar. Roberto approached and rapped on the door with his knuckles.

"Coming!" shouted a woman's voice from inside. "Wait a moment!"

Not daring to enter, Roberto ran his eye over the terrace. There were a few tables under an awning and a stack of dusty chairs.

He dragged one of the tables to an empty part of the terrace and selected the least dusty of the chairs. Then he sat down and waited.

After a while, a middle-aged woman with the thinnest lips Roberto had ever seen appeared; her black hair was gathered into a tight bun from which a few white strands had escaped. The woman stopped and looked him up and down, apparently surprised.

"Who are you?" She furrowed her brow. "I thought it was my son knocking."

"My name's Roberto Lobeira." He stood up to offer the woman his hand, and she looked back suspiciously. "I'm staying on the island for a while."

"Ah, the writer."

*All I need is a sign on my back.*

"I was wondering if I could have a coffee," he said. "I know you're closed but . . ."

"You're staying at the old Escudero place." It wasn't a question but a statement. "You've rented it from the Freires, right?"

"I have," he answered cautiously.

"If you want a piece of advice, don't trust those people." The words came out of her mouth like bullets from a gun. "They might seem charming, but they're snakes. Believe me."

Once again, the intricate tangles of the island's ancient quarrels had ensnared him, turning even a mundane activity like having a coffee into a tedious exchange of words, reproaches, and explanations.

"Let me guess," he said in a tired voice. "You're a Docampo."

"I am."

"And about that coffee . . ."

"The machine's off." She shook her head. "And the fridge has been empty since the end of the summer. If you want, you can have a beer. We've got plenty of that."

Roberto checked his watch, hesitating. It was still only eleven o'clock in the morning. *What the hell?* he thought. It might be early, but he couldn't think of anywhere better to be than sitting on that terrace, enjoying the weak rays of sunlight that filtered through the clouds scudding across the sky. And doing something normal, like having a beer while he looked out at the sea and enjoyed the sunshine, seemed like a well-deserved prize and the perfect contrast to the events of yesterday.

"A beer would be great, thanks."

The woman nodded and disappeared into the restaurant. She returned shortly with a bottle of tepid Estrella Galicia and a bowl of tired-looking peanuts. Even so, Roberto was delighted as he sat enjoying a view that was more than a match for anything to be had from the most elegant terrace one could imagine.

The tranquility lasted no more than ten minutes. As he sat there, his eyes closed, he sensed the presence of somebody casting their shadow over him. He opened his eyes, already wary.

"Good morning," came the deep, nasal voice of Luis Docampo, the bearded man he had nearly come to blows with upon arriving on the island. "Mind if I sit down?"

Roberto hesitated. The man didn't appear to be looking for trouble, despite their previous encounter, and there was nothing to gain from being unpleasant, so Roberto nodded politely. Luis fetched a chair and dragged it across the floor, its legs squeaking on the tiles. He groaned as he eased his large body into the seat.

"I think you've already met my wife, Amaia," he said, pointing to the half-open door.

"Yes, she was very . . ." Roberto was about to say "friendly" but thought better of it. "Hospitable. And she brought me a beer."

"Do you mind if I join you?"

Roberto shrugged, and Luis Docampo took the gesture as a yes. He turned toward the door and gave a loud whistle. Amaia popped her head round the door, and a minute later she returned with another beer for her husband.

"She told me you were here," the man said, "so I came to see you. We didn't get off to a very good start the other day."

"You were tormenting a kid," replied Roberto dryly. "A kid, what's more, who has some kind of learning disability. If you want me to apologize for stopping you, I'm afraid you're barking up the wrong tree."

The man shook his head. "I wasn't hurting him. I was just winding him up. I was going to give his stupid superhero toys back."

"Even so, it isn't right."

"You don't know what you're talking about." Luis leaned on the table, which creaked under his weight. "You're like everyone else from the mainland, turning up here, thinking they know it all and we're just a bunch of hicks. That boy isn't what he seems."

"Really? What do you mean?"

"The kid's always going about spying," said the man, before taking a sip of his beer. "He's always hanging around our places, peering through the windows, trampling the fields."

"That's just a kid messing around!"

"Messing around? If only! A few weeks ago, a bunch of chickens disappeared from my coop, and later I found them with their heads chopped off." Luis Docampo stared at him before adding ominously, "I'm sure it was him."

# 7

## A Walk on the Beach

"Their heads? What do you mean?"

"Like I said! Right off!" Luis brought his fist down on the table, making the bottles clink. "He pulled their fucking heads off and chucked them on the path. I'm telling you, that boy is bad news. I was just trying to teach him a lesson, that's all. Until you turned up."

Roberto sipped his beer, which suddenly tasted bitter. He couldn't help wondering if the Freire kid had been responsible for the grisly scene with the rabbit on his own doorstep. If what the man said was true, it wouldn't be the first time he'd done something of the kind. Diego didn't seem to have the capacity to know what a curse was, much less perform a ritual of this sort. Even so, a seed of doubt had been sown.

"Are you sure it was him? The stuff with the chickens, I mean."

"Who else could it have been?" Luis glanced around. "Listen. Life here is tough, particularly in the winter. The tourists come in the summer, they get off the boat to sunbathe, take photos, eat seafood . . . and they go home. For them, this place is paradise, but for me, for us . . . it's our home. And if I have to defend it against one of those damn Freires, then I will."

*Here we go,* thought Roberto. That's why Luis Docampo had been so keen to talk to him. Once again, he was in danger of getting tangled up in the old tensions that were everywhere on this island.

For both sides, his presence meant a new piece on their infernal chessboard. Everyone wanted to enlist him.

"I don't know what problems you have with the Freires, but I'd like to stay out of them," Roberto protested. "I'm only going to be here for a few weeks, and then I'll leave."

"Nobody can stay out of things," replied Luis. "Not in the winter."

"Why not?"

"You'll find out soon enough," said Luis, swigging his beer. "You'll see, even if you don't understand right now. Your world and ours are very different."

"In what way?"

"In every way," he grunted. "Children's rights, animal rights, the environment, all that crap that people in the cities go on about . . . Here, it's just about survival. Simple as that."

"It's like you're talking about another country."

"Have you noticed where we are?" Luis pointed toward the distant coastline. "There aren't any doctors here, no police, none of the things you take for granted on the mainland. We have to be self-sufficient even if that means doing things that some people might disapprove of. Even if it means being a bit rough to teach a kid a lesson."

Roberto kept silent, trying to see the man's point of view. He didn't agree with him, but he understood his motives or, at least, what it was that led him to think the way he did. And he was keen to make the most of the opportunity. If Luis Docampo wanted to talk, there was another subject Roberto was interested in.

"By the way," he said cautiously, "I've heard people mentioning the name Tangaraño . . ."

"Bah, that's nothing but an old wives' tale," Luis snorted, although Roberto couldn't help noticing him extend his index finger and pinkie under the table to ward off the evil eye. "Did someone say the chickens were the Tangaraño's doing? No way. It was the kid; I'm sure of it."

Roberto didn't answer and instead sipped his beer.

"Ah, there's my son, Tristán." Luis pointed to a young man approaching along the road.

Tristán Docampo was about twenty years old, tall and ungainly, with unruly brown curls escaping from beneath a yellow-and-purple Lakers cap. He had dark eyes, like the rest of his family.

"Good morning," he said politely. "Dad, we've got work to do."

"I know, I know," Luis growled, grabbing his beer. Roberto observed the man's Adam's apple go up and down as he emptied the bottle in one go before slamming it on the table with a satisfied air. "Hell of a taskmaster, your mom! Anyway, Roberto, I hope I've cleared up a couple of things. And if you want a piece of advice, stay away from the Freires, the weird kid and his witch of a sister, above all. They'll only bring you trouble. This is on the house, by the way."

With those words, he stood up and, accompanied by Tristán, disappeared back down the road, leaving Roberto on his own at the table, even more confused than before.

It was madness. If he listened to what everyone was telling him to do, he should just shut himself away in his cottage like a hermit and stay there until the boat came to fetch him.

But it also felt like a lot of lies. Something told him the decapitated chickens were linked in some way to the rabbit he'd found on his first night. And what about the so-called curse that he couldn't stop thinking about? Was everything Diego Freire's doing? Did this mysterious Tangaraño—whom the inhabitants of Ons seemed to be so afraid of—really exist? Or could it be the work of Elvira Couto, the strange witch? Perhaps somebody else was really responsible? Or maybe he was just the victim of a tiresome joke, cooked up between the islanders?

He pushed away his beer, which had suddenly lost its appeal.

"To hell with the lot of them," he grunted. "I'm going for a walk on the beach."

When he stood up, he noticed a boat tied to one of the bollards, rising and falling in the swell. It was a fiberglass vessel, about fifteen feet long, with two powerful Yamaha outboard motors at the back. Just visible on the bow was a national park emblem, faded by the sun and the seawater. Every time the waves lifted the boat up, its sausage-like fenders gave a rasping squeal as they scraped against the dock.

He guessed one of the park rangers must have come to the island that morning to conduct some routine business. After all, even if it was partially inhabited, the island was also a natural reserve. But judging by the white-capped waves, it seemed obvious that the vessel wouldn't be hanging around for long.

He retraced his steps and headed north. The track was fairly level compared to the other routes he had taken, and it was flanked by numerous, tastefully restored fishermen's cottages that stood patiently awaiting the arrival of tourists in the spring. Once again, he had the unnerving sensation that some unknown entity was spying on him, but the spectacular views to his left quickly displaced that thought: This side of the island, facing toward the mainland, was stunningly beautiful, with a succession of white beaches and green meadows, dotted here and there with old houses built from irregular blocks of granite.

A crooked wooden sign pointed toward a beach called Area dos Cans. Roberto followed the path until he came to a strip of fine white sand that, combined with the turquoise water, looked positively Caribbean, although he knew the water temperature would barely exceed fifty degrees.

Just before stepping onto the sand, out of the corner of his eye, he caught sight of movement among the bushes. Roberto turned.

"Show yourself. I know you're there."

"No, I'm not," answered a familiar voice.

"I can see you, Diego," he replied patiently.

The boy peered out from behind a mass of brambles and gorse. He was wearing a faded light blue Celta de Vigo soccer shirt that was two sizes too large for him, its hems coming loose, and the name of a Bosnian player who had retired at least twenty years earlier emblazoned across the back. Roberto wondered where he had dredged that relic up from.

"It's surprisingly difficult to find some solitude on an almost deserted island," grumbled Roberto. "Can I ask what you're doing here?"

"I was following you," the boy explained, looking flustered. "I wanted to know where you were going."

"I was going for a walk." He resisted the temptation to add *on my own*. Although Diego was almost an adult, he still had the mind of a child. Roberto couldn't help being intrigued by him.

"Can I go with you?" Diego's eyes sparkled. "Can I? Can I?"

It was clear that if Roberto was looking for solitude, he'd have to go quite a bit farther from the village.

"Okay, if there's no alternative, you can join me." He nodded. "You can be my guide."

Once they were on the sand, Diego bounced along at his side like a puppy. Completely immersed in his role as guide, he pointed in every direction, gabbling confused explanations as he went. Roberto struggled to follow what the boy was saying, and the fact that he seemed to be randomly pointing at trees, piles of washed-up seaweed, and things that were visible only to him didn't exactly help.

Roberto observed him carefully. There was no question that Diego was not "normal," whatever the word meant, but he had a powerful aura of curiosity and innocence. Roberto was quite sure he spent most of his time snooping around, including on the Docampo land, but try as he might, he couldn't picture the boy coldheartedly decapitating chickens.

Then again, just three days ago the idea of someone leaving a dead animal at his door had also seemed unbelievable. As Luis Docampo had said, the place was different. Perhaps, in that remote, rural location, killing an animal was no big deal, even for a kid like Diego.

The beach was better than he'd dared hope. He could understand why, in the summer, it would be packed with sunshades, towels, and dozens of bodies glistening with sunscreen as they roasted in the sun.

If it weren't for the icy wind that blew in off the sea—not to mention the overexcited boy skipping around—he would have been tempted to lie down for a while.

"Tell me something, Diego." Roberto tried to interrupt the boy's games. "What did you want to talk to me about the other day, at the cottage?"

The boy looked at him as if he didn't understand. Roberto had another try.

"You said something about 'the Tangaraño.' What were you talking about?"

Diego's expression immediately darkened, as if a cloud had covered the sun. Instead of answering, he lowered his head and concentrated on making a hole in the sand with his feet.

"I don't want to talk about it."

"I'd like you to tell me."

"I'm scared," he said in a low voice. "I don't like it."

"Is it the Docampos?" He remembered his arrival, with Luis Docampo bullying the kid. "Is it one of them? Is it them you're afraid of?"

The boy shook his head.

"So . . . What are you scared of, Diego? Tell me."

"The Tangaraño," he whispered. "And the witches."

Roberto smiled to himself. *Don't pay any attention, or you'll go crazy with his stories, like everyone else,* Antía had said. So that was what it was about.

"Are you scared of Elvira Couto?"

Diego opened his eyes wide in surprise. "No, no. Not Elvira! She's good; she isn't a witch."

"Witches don't exist, Diego. And the Tangaraño doesn't either. You don't need to be afraid of them. They can't hurt you."

The boy's reaction surprised him. He raised his head, his face contorted with anger.

"He does exist!" he yelled. "In the summer, Tangaraño hides, but in the winter, when we're alone, he comes out again. He always comes out again."

"That's your imagination," Roberto said, trying to reassure him. "I promise you."

Then Diego spoke more quietly, but his words hit Roberto as if he were shouting at the top of his lungs.

"That's not true." He shook his head. "I've never seen him, but I've seen what he does to the animals. He hurts them. He kills them."

The rabbit's head appeared in Roberto's mind.

"Why does he kill them, Diego?" The day suddenly seemed colder and more hostile. "Who is this Tangaraño? Where does he live? Tell me."

But it was impossible to get another word out of the boy, who retreated into a mute silence. Roberto understood that there was nothing to be gained from pressing him, so he gave up. He still didn't believe a word of the boy's fantasy of witches and monsters, but he couldn't deny that the coincidence was, to say the very least, disturbing.

They continued along the beach in silence. The sand felt almost silky underfoot, it was so fine. The waves were crashing onto the shore, leaving a flotsam of seaweed, driftwood, and discarded junk.

And then, his life changed forever.

# 8

## The Bundle

It was just a fraction of a second. Later, he would ask himself what would have happened if he hadn't turned his head at that precise moment. How different everything would have been. But when fate rolls the dice, there's nothing you can do.

He spotted it out of the corner of his eye, just when the cold was close to sending him back inland in search of refuge. About twenty yards out, bobbing in the water, was an orange buoy.

"What's that?" he asked.

Diego narrowed his eyes, trying to make out what Roberto was pointing at, but the buoy had disappeared.

"I can't see anything." The boy hesitated. "Oh, wait . . . I can see it now! It'll be a pot that's been washed up by the tide."

"A pot?"

Diego launched into a convoluted explanation of lobster pots and how they were designed so that lobsters could get in but not out, but Roberto soon stopped listening. About five yards from the buoy was a bright yellow object. The same yellow as the oilskins he'd seen many of the sailors wearing in the port at Bueu.

"There's someone there!" he shouted. "We have to help them!"

"The sea's very rough." Diego looked out dubiously. "And I can't swim."

The kid was right about the sea. It was growing wilder by the minute, and each time the waves broke against the shore, they clawed away at the beach, dragging sand with them as they retreated.

Roberto was caught in a dilemma. All the ghosts of the past had suddenly come back to haunt him, trapping him on the shoreline, unable to move a single muscle. He felt dizzy. He could hardly breathe. And yet, he had to do something, even if it was almost certainly too late to save anyone. He looked around, hoping to see somebody else, but the only sign of life was the seagulls scrabbling in the sand.

"I bet he's drowned," Diego announced, as if to confirm Roberto's fears. "He isn't moving."

*But you can't be sure of that,* said the voice in Roberto's head. *Whoever it is, they need your help. You can't just stand here doing nothing.*

And anyway, it wasn't the same as the other time. Whatever was out there was floating close to the shore. A child could do this.

"It's only twenty yards," he muttered, trying to convince himself as he sat down on the sand and removed his shoes, his coat, and his woolen sweater.

He wasn't a great swimmer, but the yellow oilskin was so close that he felt as if he could almost reach out and touch it. The cold January wind whipped his skin, and something inside him—something with which he was all too familiar—yelled, *Don't do it!* so loud that it almost immobilized him. But he pressed on, because if he let the thing take control in a moment like this, then the rest of the time he spent on the island would become a nightmare in which he would be consumed by his inner demons. He had to do it. He had to.

In his underwear, he walked gingerly forward and put his feet in the water. He gasped as the icy water bit his ankles. It couldn't be more than forty-five degrees.

He took slow steps forward, struggling against the waves. Pulled by the undertow, the sand slipped away beneath his feet, as if it had a life of its own. As the water reached his waist, he found it increasingly difficult to keep his balance.

When a particularly high wave came crashing in, he held his breath.

The wave broke over his head, covering him with a whirl of water, seaweed, bubbles, and sand. For a moment, he didn't know which way was up, but then he kicked downward, thrust his head out of the water, and gulped a lungful of air.

The wave had dragged him three or four yards out to sea, and now he was floating, keeping his head above water, his body rising and falling with the motion of the sea.

He started swimming toward the oilskin, trying to keep his head above water. Every now and then, a wave crashed into his face, forcing him to shut his eyes tight. Even so, his eyes stung from the salt water, and his throat was itching.

That was when he realized his first mistake.

Either he had miscalculated the distance, or his target was moving away from the shore, because he had the sense that he was no closer than he had been at the start. The icy embrace of the water numbed his limbs, and his arms and legs felt heavier and heavier.

His second mistake, he realized, was to assume that swimming in open water, in the middle of an Atlantic gale, was the same as doing so in the placid setting of a swimming pool. The waves pounded him pitilessly, and his strength was waning fast. He knew his energy would soon run out, and he sensed the fear, even icier than the seawater, rising inside him.

But just then, almost by accident, he discovered that if he swam diagonally, he could make much better progress than if he swam in a straight line. A current pulled him along and, instead of fighting it, he could use its power to reach his objective.

The distance narrowed. Suddenly, the yellow bundle was less than twenty feet away, and it would soon be within reach. The problem was that he could see it only briefly before the waves obscured it again, and he was forced to tread water as he got his bearings, using up valuable energy.

When he finally reached his goal, he didn't exactly do so with style; rather, the bundle was washed against him by yet another wave. It struck him on the side, and for a moment he panicked and couldn't breathe. When he turned, he saw a streak of yellow right next to him, and he threw out his right arm, expecting to feel a body under the plastic.

Two things happened at once. The first was that he discovered that the thing he was holding was hard—too hard to be a human body. The second, almost at the same time, was that something slimy had wrapped itself around his legs, and he yelled with fright. He kicked with all his strength to get rid of it but, whatever the thing was, it had bound itself tightly around his ankle.

The voice in his head spoke up again. *You can't do it. You're going to die; you're finished. You should've listened to me while you had the chance.*

Roberto let out an angry, fearful roar. He reached down to his ankle, inadvertently swallowing more water in the process, and his fingers closed around the rough texture of a plastic rope. He pulled hard and managed to free himself. Drawing on his last reserves of strength, he grabbed hold of the yellow bundle, which had now become his salvation.

"Shit!" His voice was hoarse, his throat sore. "Come on, come on. For Christ's sake!"

In the interval, the current had dragged him closer to the shore, to where the waves were breaking. When the water washed back, he could see rocks poking out like stony, barnacle-encrusted knives.

From some unknown place, he summoned his last ounce of strength and kicked hard, using the bundle as an improvised flotation device. If the waves dashed him against the rocks, he was surely done for. He was fighting a losing battle. The combined forces of the current, the waves, and the undertow pushed him relentlessly, and all effort was futile. The words **THE END** lit up like a neon sign in his mind's eye. He was overwhelmed by a mixture of primal terror and incredulity, and yet too tired to resist. An avalanche of water covered his head, and he gasped.

Just then, something jolted him sideways. When he managed to push his head above the waves, he couldn't believe his eyes.

On a rock, some ten yards away, Diego was holding the rope that was attached to the orange buoy. The waves must have washed it ashore, and the kid, overcoming his fear, had somehow made his way across the slippery rocks and grabbed it.

"Hold on!" came Diego's muffled cry. "Hold on tight!"

It was easier said than done. The bundle—covered with plastic and offering no easy handholds—slipped from Roberto's grasp. Suddenly, his fingers felt the links of a chain, and he gripped on to them with all his might. The sense of relief was almost dizzying. At least he wasn't going to drown.

But there was still the problem of the rocks. Diego pulled with all his strength, but the combined weight of Roberto and the bundle was too much for his skinny arms. Roberto could see the boy tensing his neck muscles and clenching his jaw, oblivious to his surroundings. His feet were planted on bare rock, but just a few inches away was a carpet of dark, slimy seaweed. If Diego wasn't careful, he'd step on it, lose his footing, and end up in the same situation as Roberto. Worse, Roberto corrected himself. The boy couldn't swim.

"Watch out!" He coughed and spat out water as he shouted, so his words were barely intelligible.

Luckily, the waves had washed him to a more sheltered spot, where the current no longer tugged at him with such manic force. The boy drew the rope in, pulling Roberto to quieter waters.

When he finally felt seaweed beneath his feet, he heaved a huge sigh of relief. He could stand now but felt so weak that he could barely drag himself ashore. Eventually, he collapsed onto the comforting safety of a rock.

A lump of granite had never seemed so appealing. He felt rather than saw as Diego grabbed him beneath the arms and pulled him farther out of the water, and then he lay back on the rock, snorting like an ox. He was shivering violently with the combination of the cold and the adrenaline that was coursing through his system. Next to him, the boy—also at the very edge of his limits—had collapsed in a heap.

A couple of minutes passed before Roberto opened his eyes. The overcast sky moved above his head, and a few cormorants eyed the pair quizzically, wondering no doubt what these strange creatures were up to in such stormy seas. Finally, he sat up.

He had come close to dying. Very close indeed.

But now, as he looked around him, he realized that his problems were far from over.

# 9

## "Dope or Snow?"

"We have to get back to the beach," Roberto panted as he stood up. "This is dangerous."

Diego's chest was rising and falling like a bellows. "Yes. The beach, the beach."

Although no longer in the water, they were far from safe. They were clinging to a rock, and the tide was coming in. If they stayed there much longer, the waves would cover it, and they would be in an even worse situation than the one they had just overcome.

Clinging to each other like a pair of war-wounded comrades, they made their way across the seaweed-covered rocks, helping each other at the most difficult points. Roberto was amazed at Diego having made it out to the edge of the rocks. He might not be the sharpest tool in the box, to use an unkind expression, and he wasn't particularly strong, but he was as brave as a lion.

When they reached the spot where Roberto's clothes lay in a pile on the sand, Diego collapsed in exhaustion. Only then did Roberto realize that Diego had had the good sense to wrap the rope from the buoy around his waist so that the bundle came ashore with them. Roberto's respect for the boy grew.

Still shivering, Roberto got dressed. With each layer of clothing, he felt the life returning to his body.

"I told you it was dangerous!" The boy stabbed his bony finger into Roberto's chest. "Dangerous, dangerous, dangerous! You didn't listen to Diego!"

"You're absolutely right." Roberto's teeth were chattering violently, and he struggled to pronounce each syllable. "I was a fool. I'm really sorry."

The boy glared at him, still put out. The right sleeve of his soccer shirt had ripped and was flapping like a flag.

"You saved my life, Diego." Roberto shook his head as he spoke, still shocked by how close he had come to drowning. "You're a hero."

"Like Iron Man and Thor?"

"Much better than Iron Man and Thor, believe me." He ruffled the boy's hair. "They're not fit to lick your boots."

"I'm a superhero!" Diego jumped up and down. "A superhero!"

Watching as the boy proceeded to make a series of explosive noises to go with the imaginary lasers he was firing, Roberto was overwhelmed by a sense of affection and gratitude.

While Diego fought with hordes of invaders in another dimension, Roberto turned back and looked at the raging sea. He'd had a near miss. The waves had dragged the yellow bundle to the shoreline and left it half submerged in the sand. Grabbing the rope, he pulled it out of the reach of the sea.

It was very heavy and, seeing it up close for the first time, he wondered what the hell it was.

It was a rectangular package, measuring about five feet along the sides, and one foot high. It had thick yellow plastic around it, enclosed with a pair of stout chains for good measure. At the point where the chains crossed was a huge padlock, and tied to this junction was the rope with the orange buoy at the other end. Fixed to the sides was a pair of sturdy plastic fenders, like scaled-down versions of the ones he'd seen on the national park boat earlier that morning. The fenders were no doubt there to ensure that the whole arrangement stayed afloat.

Roberto gave the bundle a shove and guessed it must weigh at least one hundred pounds. Underneath, attached to the chains, was another rope, the one that had wrapped itself around his ankle, but this was only six feet long and hung loose. It must originally have been attached to a weight, which would have kept the bundle underwater, far from the coast. The buoy would float on the surface while the bundle moved along a few feet below, supported by its fenders, safe from becoming snagged on the seabed but also hidden from prying eyes.

It was a simple but ingenious system. And given where they were, he thought with a shudder, the puzzle was not difficult to solve. The bundle must have been dropped by drug smugglers or narcos to be picked up by their partners in crime, but the sea had torn it free from its weight, and the waves had then washed it ashore, where he had spotted it by pure chance. If it hadn't been for that coincidence, the bundle would have been smashed against the rocks until the air-filled fenders had been torn to pieces, and then it would have sunk to the bottom of the sea, with only the fish to witness its demise.

Instead, there it was, at his feet.

He smelled trouble, and the temptation to throw the thing back into the sea was almost irresistible, but his curiosity got the better of him—that and the fact that he'd almost died retrieving it from the waves.

"What's inside?" asked Diego, who had been watching him inspect the bundle.

"I don't have a clue, but that's not our problem." Roberto could feel another, harder layer below the plastic. "We have to take it to the village. Then we can call the Guardia Civil to take care of it."

"Will they come in a hillycopter?" Diego's eyes opened wide in excitement. "Last summer one came for a sick tourist. It was cool!"

"It's called a 'helicopter'—and I don't have a clue how they'll come." He patted the boy on the shoulder and stared out toward the horizon.

"But looking at the state of the sea, I wouldn't be surprised. We're going to need help, Diego."

"I'll go!" The boy jumped up, scattering sand as he did so, and before Roberto could say another word, he ran off, leaving a trail of indignant seagulls in his wake.

Roberto lay back down on the sand. The heat was gradually returning to his extremities as he overcame the shock. His hands trembling, he took out a cigarette and eventually managed to light it.

He exhaled, lost in thought. No doubt he'd be able to use the experience for a good scene in his novel. Or at least for a good anecdote. *Did I ever tell you about the time I almost drowned rescuing a hundred-pound bundle of cocaine?*

But right now, he didn't feel like laughing. He'd just realized he would be buried by an avalanche of tiresome bureaucracy as soon as the authorities arrived. Statements, hearings, and the rest of it.

But that wasn't the worst thing. The bundle no doubt had an owner. An angry owner who would be looking for it.

Who possibly already was.

*Stay out of trouble,* the skipper of the *Punta Suido* had told him.

*For Christ's sake, Lobeira! It didn't take you long.*

A while later, a shout roused him from his thoughts. Fifty yards away, walking along the beach, was Diego, jumping with excitement, accompanied by two people pushing a wheelbarrow.

He was surprised to see that one of them was Diego's sister Helena, the girl who had been at Rosalía Freire's side, and that the other was Tristán Docampo, the son of Luis. Perhaps the two clans set aside their differences when there was an emergency. Or maybe they distrusted each other so much that if something unexpected happened, they sent a joint delegation. Whatever the explanation, he was delighted to see them. Even in peak condition, he would barely be able to move the bundle on his own, and after his near-death experience, it was out of the question.

When they reached him, they stared at him open mouthed. Their gaze flitted from the yellow bundle to Roberto and back to the bundle, as if they were faced with an impossible mathematical problem.

"Hi, guys." He raised a hand. "Diego and I found this. Can you help us?"

"Where was it?" Tristán asked when he finally recovered the power of speech.

"Floating close to the shore. We dragged it in."

He omitted the part where they had almost drowned. The last thing he needed was to be told off for putting the boy's life at risk. There would be time to explain properly later.

"This could be a problem," Helena mumbled.

"These things are always a problem," Tristán agreed, in a way that suggested this wasn't a first. "A massive pain in the ass."

"What do you think it is?" the girl asked. "Dope or snow?"

"That doesn't matter," Roberto interrupted, keen to get off the beach as quickly as possible. "It's obviously a bad business. Let's take it to the village and call the Guardia Civil to come get it."

The two youngsters looked at each other but said nothing.

"We have to hand it in," Roberto repeated. "There's no alternative. Help me get it into the barrow."

Between the four of them, they lifted it up. With its heavy load, the wheelbarrow sank into the soft sand, and it took them more than ten minutes of pushing, shoving, and cursing to get to the foot of the ramp.

When they reached the village, a small crowd was already waiting for them in front of the church. Both the Freires and Docampos waited expectantly, the two clans forming distinct groups. The tension was palpable when, sweating, they finally unloaded the barrow. Helena and Tristán gravitated automatically toward their family groups, but Diego stayed by Roberto's side, oblivious to everything.

"Where was it?" Rosalía Freire asked. "Who took it out of the water?"

Roberto considered his answer carefully. There was something in the atmosphere that he couldn't put his finger on but worried him.

"I found it." He placed his hand on the yellow plastic. "On the beach at Area dos Cans."

"What's inside?" Ramón Docampo spoke. The old man looked from the bundle to his grandson Tristán with an impenetrable expression on his face, as if the boy had something to do with the bundle's unexpected appearance.

"I don't have a clue, but it doesn't matter," replied Roberto, exasperated. "We have to notify the authorities. Let them deal with it."

A heavy silence greeted his words, more eloquent than any reply.

"On the island, we like to resolve our problems in our own way." Ramón Docampo clicked his tongue. "Let's take a look inside."

"Come on!" Roberto protested. "We can't open it. It could be evidence of a crime. We can't handle it without permission. Don't you see?"

"There might be nothing illegal about it," said another Docampo, a short, stocky man. "It could just be a float or some equipment."

"That's true," Rosalía Freire chipped in, to his surprise. "What if it's just some floating garbage? We'd have made the Guardia Civil come all the way out here for nothing, and with this weather, that would probably mean a helicopter trip. That doesn't come cheap."

"They wouldn't be at all happy about that." A strange smile had spread across Ramón Docampo's face. "They'd be furious."

"Absolutely raging."

Roberto looked around for someone to back him up, but they all seemed to be in agreement. He had to admit that they weren't completely wrong. He didn't want to think about what would happen if they called the authorities to open up a bundle of old clothes. The recrimination, the jokes. What people would say about the islanders panicking for no reason.

Only Antía, standing beside her mother, seemed to share his doubts, but she remained silent, a worried look on her face. Roberto exchanged a glance with her. *My hands are tied,* she seemed to say.

"Okay," he said. "Let's open the damn thing and see what's inside."

"That's the spirit!" Luis Docampo clapped him on the back, so hard that he almost choked. "We need tools."

Someone ran off and returned with a hammer, an axe, and a chisel. They presented the tools to Luis, but he shook his head and pointed to Roberto.

"The one that finds it opens it," he said with a twisted smile. "Come on, writer. Go ahead."

Roberto picked up the hammer and the chisel and squatted down beside the bundle. He rested the end of the chisel against a link of the chain and struck it with the hammer. There was a loud clang, and the chisel almost jumped out of his hand.

"Harder, man!" Luis urged him. "We don't have all day."

Roberto gritted his teeth and struck another blow. He quickly got into a rhythm and hammered away at the chain with gusto. At each blow, small shavings of iron flew off, and the dent in the link gradually grew larger. He was soon sweating from the effort. His hands were burning and his arms were heavy, but that didn't stop him.

A sharp clink brought him back to reality. The link had split in two, and the chain hung loose.

"Here." He passed the hammer to Diego without looking at him. "Hold this for me."

He pulled the chains off and, with the tip of the chisel, slashed the yellow plastic. Underneath was another layer of plastic, transparent and much thicker—someone had gone to a great deal of trouble waterproofing whatever was inside. There was layer upon layer of cellophane, which he gradually cut his way through.

Finally, when he had opened up a hole large enough for his fingers, he put down the chisel and pulled hard with both hands. The plastic ripped, exposing a gap about eight inches long.

There was just one final layer of black plastic. Holding his breath, Roberto tore it off, and his eyes almost popped out.

For all his speculation about what might be inside, he hadn't expected this.

"So?" asked Luis Docampo, impatiently. "What is it?"

By way of reply, Roberto thrust his hand inside and gingerly turned around, as if he were handling dynamite.

A faint murmur of surprise rippled through the onlookers.

In his hand was a wad of five-hundred-euro notes, held together with a rubber band. And under that was more. Much more.

The yellow bundle that had almost cost him his life was full of money.

More money than he could even imagine.

# 10

## "A Whole Lot of Money"

Rosalía Freire was the first to recover the power of speech.

"Is that . . . money?" she asked, her voice tight with tension. "Real money?"

"Looks like it," said Roberto. "I'm not sure but, yes, I think so."

"How much?"

"There's only one way we could find that out." He pointed at the bundle. "We'd have to count it."

"So what are we waiting for?" Ramón Docampo stepped forward impatiently. "Open it up."

"Hang on!" protested Roberto. "We already know what's in there. It's the Guardia Civil's business now."

"How much do you think there is?" Ignoring Roberto's words, Luis Docampo had extracted another wad of notes from the bundle.

"Don't touch it. You'll cover them with fingerprints—the police will hardly thank you."

"I'm wearing gloves, Mr. Writer," replied Luis as he stuffed the wad into his coat pocket. "And you touched them too."

Roberto stared at the wad in his own hand as if seeing it for the first time, and cursed inwardly, before dropping it on the ground.

"We'll tell the officers when they arrive," he insisted. "We have to hand it over."

It would be so simple: Just one call to the authorities and they'd arrive in less than an hour, whether by sea or by air. He didn't have the slightest doubt that it was the right decision. His hand was halfway to the pocket where he kept his phone, but he stopped when he saw that Ramón Docampo had raised his arm.

"Not so fast. There's an alternative."

"What?"

"We could keep it."

A murmur spread through the group, like fire through a barn. There was no need to look at them to know which idea was more popular. Far more popular.

"You can't be serious."

"Why not?"

"Well, to start with, because the money doesn't belong to us."

"And who does it belong to?" Ramón Docampo looked around theatrically. "I don't see anyone here but us. What the sea washes up on the shore belongs to whoever finds it."

A chorus of agreement echoed around him.

Roberto was astonished.

"Come on, be reasonable! It's clearly a stupid idea!"

His heart sank when he saw that nobody agreed with him. Everyone was staring at the wad of notes on the ground with the greedy expressions of hunting dogs eyeing a hare. Even Antía seemed undecided. "This money belongs to someone." He tried to find another angle. "They're bound to be looking for it."

"They don't need to know that it's ended up here," Luis cut in. "It could have washed up anywhere."

"Listen to me, everyone." Roberto tried to sound as authoritative as possible. "Nobody ties a bundle of cash to a buoy in the middle of the sea if they aren't doing something illegal. It's not like putting it in a piggy bank. This money must be linked to drug trafficking."

"And what's that got to do with us?"

"Because the owner will be looking for it, for Christ's sake!" Roberto exploded. "They're not the sort of people you want to get on the wrong side of, and believe me, that's exactly what will happen if you steal their money. We need to tell the Guardia Civil. Now."

"Not so fast," interjected Ramón Docampo. "My son's right. Nobody needs to know this money is here. It would be like it never existed."

Roberto stared at them impotently. They had been overcome by greed; he could see it in their eyes.

"Don't you understand that what you're proposing is a crime?" he insisted. "We could end up in jail. Think about it."

"Maybe we keep just some of it." It was the first time Antía had spoken since they'd opened the bundle, and Roberto felt his stomach tighten to see that even she was considering it. "Just a few thousand. Then we can call the Guardia Civil to come and get the rest, and everyone will be happy."

"They'd realize the money was missing." Roberto shook his head. "They'd see the gap, and they'd put two and two together. Anyway, what do you think will happen when you start flashing the cash a few weeks after a narco hoard has been washed up? Do you think nobody's going to notice?"

"That's why we can't hand it in." Rosalía Freire shook her head. "As soon as news gets out that the money's appeared, the narcos will know that we found it. And it won't matter if we keep some of it or not. Those people are suspicious by nature."

"So?"

"They'll assume that we've kept some of it, and they'll come to Ons to get their revenge," she replied. "You aren't from here; you don't know them like we do. It doesn't matter what we do; as far as they're concerned, it'll be our fault that they lost their money. They'll think we've hidden some of it. You said it yourself: They're not the sort of people you want to get on the wrong side of."

"We can't tell anyone, particularly not the authorities," Ramón Docampo said, backing her up. "We'll just divvy it up and be done."

A deathly silence ensued.

"No way." Roberto shook his head as he took out his phone. "I'm not getting caught up in anything like that."

"That's easy for you to say," interrupted Luis Docampo's wife, Amaia, with a hint of bitterness. "You don't live here. In a few weeks, you'll go home, return to your comfortable writer's life, and nobody will know you had anything to do with this. It isn't you they'll come after. We'll have to pay the price."

Roberto stopped, his fingers hovering above the screen of his phone. There was truth in what the woman said. But the very idea of taking the money revolted him. In Mexico, he had seen at close quarters how many broken lives the narco empire left in its wake.

"I have a suggestion." Ramón Docampo held his hands palm outward. "Why don't we count the money first to see how much we're talking about? There could be something else under the top layer of bills. Or maybe there's nothing at all. We need all the information before we make a decision."

Roberto had to admit that his logic was impeccable.

"Okay," he conceded. "But everyone has to wear gloves when they touch the money."

It was as if he'd fired a starting pistol. Everyone threw themselves on the bundle and began to tear the wrapping off, sending bills flying everywhere.

"Calm down, calm down! Let's take it slowly."

Order was soon reestablished. Roberto, Antía Freire, and Luis Docampo counted out the wads as if they were the tokens in some children's game. The rest of the islanders milled around, watching carefully.

It was more complicated than it had seemed at first sight. Beneath the top layer of five-hundred-euro notes was a layer of hundred-euro notes, grouped together in thick bricks. Below that, the familiar features of Benjamin Franklin greeted them from a layer made up of hundred-dollar bills, his enigmatic expression reminding Roberto of the *Mona Lisa*. When they reached the final layer, another surprise awaited them.

"What the fuck is this?" Luis Docampo held up a wad of long purple notes.

"They're Swiss francs," replied Roberto, interrupting the count for a moment. "They're worth a lot."

"Really?"

"Yes." He nodded. "Each of those notes in your hand is worth about a thousand euros, give or take."

"It looks like Monopoly money." Luis smiled as he dropped the wad into his lap.

Roberto fell silent, his suspicions growing. This wasn't going at all how he'd envisaged it.

Finally, the last wad emerged from the package. He'd been keeping a tally in his leather-bound notebook, and he went over the figures again in silence as the others watched impatiently.

"So? How much is it?"

Roberto ignored the question and checked the total again, incredulous.

"The dollar and Swiss franc exchange rates vary but—" he began.

"Stop beating around the bush!" interrupted Luis. "How much is there?"

Roberto looked up very slowly.

"Seventy-five million euros . . . give or take."

Once again, everyone fell silent as they each pondered the ridiculous sum of money piled up in front of them in the wheelbarrow, like paper bricks.

It was Diego who broke the moment of concentration.

"Is that a lot of money?" he asked.

"Yes, Diego, it's a lot of money." Roberto squeezed his arm, trying to feign a cheerfulness that he didn't feel. "A whole lot of money."

The exchange had a liberating effect. Suddenly, everyone was clapping and laughing, and hugging each other, although the division between the two families remained firmly in place. Roberto felt like one of those journalists sent to cover the story of a lottery jackpot won by a village syndicate. They just needed someone to spray the crowd with champagne. Everyone was euphoric.

Apart from him.

At the beginning, he had assumed the cash was the payment for a drug shipment that some cartel had smuggled into the estuary. But if that was the case, it would all be in either euros or dollars. Not a combination of the two, and certainly not with Swiss francs thrown into the mix like spare picture cards.

No, this was something else—the combined payment for multiple illegal operations. And that was much worse, because a cartel might be able to afford losing the payment for a single operation. That was a calculated risk, one that occurred from time to time—part of the business. But a fortune like this—in a number of currencies, in used, nonconsecutive bills? That was something else. Getting this much money together in this way would have taken time, and would be difficult to do without arousing suspicions in the banking sector. Somebody had gone to great lengths to prepare this particular consignment; it was the dream of some criminal who moved in the black market and wanted to launder their ill-gotten gains.

And if they'd gone to such lengths, Roberto very much doubted that they'd swallow the money's disappearance so easily.

He needed to make the islanders understand, whatever it took. Right now, though, drunk with euphoria, they wouldn't pay him any attention. Only Antía remained silent, lost in thought. Roberto went over to her.

"This is madness. We have to put a stop to it."

The woman remained silent for a while, so long that Roberto thought she hadn't heard him, but finally she gave him a deep, sorrowful look.

"I know," she replied, "but right now it'd be easier to drag this island to the mainland than to get them to listen to us."

"Maybe if you talked to your mother . . ."

"There's no point." She shook her head. "Look at her—when she gets something into her head, she's unstoppable. And anyway, we'd still have to convince the Docampos. They've just discovered they're sitting on a gold mine, and there's no way they're going to change their minds."

"So what should we do?"

"I don't know," she admitted. "I don't have a clue."

"Okay, that's enough!" Ramón Docampo clapped loudly to get everyone's attention, then threw his cigarette butt to the floor and ground it out with his heel before speaking. "How are we going to divvy it up?"

"Half and half, obviously," replied Rosalía Freire immediately. "Equal parts between the Freires and the Docampos."

"What about him?" Ramón jutted his chin in Roberto's direction. "How much does he get? The same as us?"

"There's only one of him," Luis protested, "and there's lots of us. It wouldn't be fair."

"But he's the one who found the money." Ramón Docampo observed him carefully. "I wonder what he has to say about it."

The celebrations gradually died down as all eyes turned on Roberto.

He looked steadily back. He was aware that the disposition of the pieces on the island's chessboard had changed completely in the blink of an eye, and that everyone else had realized too. He was no longer an eccentric visitor who had come to spend a few weeks on the island out of season. Suddenly, he was someone who could claim a considerable piece of the pie. Or pose an even greater threat by involving the authorities.

In other words, he had become a problem.

And, it occurred to him, there was nothing to stop them from eliminating that problem without further delay. They were miles from the mainland and the nearest authorities. There were no other witnesses.

He could already imagine the headlines: *Tragic death of Roberto Lobeira in island accident. Literary world mourns his loss.*

His head was buzzing. They wouldn't dare to. That would be *murder*, for Christ's sake. That line was surely one they wouldn't cross.

But something on Ramón Docampo's face told Roberto that the old man was making the very same calculation. And he didn't look like the hesitant kind.

These were island people, tough people. Merciless if they needed to be.

"Hang on." He raised his hands placatingly. His mouth felt dry. "I've already said a thousand times that I don't want a single cent of that money. But even so, I still think you ought to—"

"Someone's coming," interrupted Diego in his singsong voice. "Down the path."

# 11

## Consequences

Everyone turned their heads in unison, in a gesture that would have been comical in any other circumstances. A man was striding down the path toward them.

"It's the poacher," grunted Luis Docampo. "What's that lunatic doing here?"

"It's Víctor Pampín," whispered Antía, unaware that Roberto had already met him the previous day. "A hermit who lives at the other end of the island. He's a bit strange, but he's harmless. He doesn't interfere with anybody, and he just gets on with his life, fishing for shellfish on the rocks."

"Cover that money up quick!" hissed Luis. "Don't let him see it!"

Someone produced a faded blue tarpaulin and pulled it over the wheelbarrow. Beneath it, all that could be seen was a bulky form that could have been anything.

When Pampín reached the group, stopping and resting on his pole, he gave them a quizzical look.

"What's going on here?" he asked.

"There's nothing going on here, Víctor." Luis Docampo spread his arms wide and offered up an apparently sincere smile. "We're just shooting the breeze."

"The Freires and the Docampos having a friendly chat on a January afternoon." Pampín looked doubtful. "Sure, Luis. You're pulling my leg."

"Aren't we allowed to talk to each other?"

"I've never seen you spend more than ten minutes together without ending up at each other's throats." His eyes came to rest on Roberto, and he frowned, surprised to see him there, but he had the good sense not to reveal that they'd already met.

"Okay, Pampín," Rosalía interrupted. "And what are you doing here? You don't usually come down to the village."

Pampín's only response was to look at the flat blade at the end of his pole, as if he had just noticed he was holding it.

"I'm glad you've asked me." His tone hardened. "I guess you know why I'm carrying this scraper, right?"

"You'll have been collecting goose barnacles, I imagine," Rosalía Freire said. "How should I know?"

"Don't play the innocent with me!" The man's angry outburst took them by surprise. "You know perfectly well what's happened! This morning, I saw two of your nephews sniffing around Con da Fervenza, and when I went down a bit later, they'd scraped the place bare! There wasn't a single barnacle left! Not one!"

"I don't know what you're talking about," Rosalía replied.

Behind Pampín's back, two members of the Freire clan exchanged a guilty glance. Roberto sighed. This was just what he needed. Not only had Pampín turned up at just the wrong moment; now an argument about poaching had kicked off.

"Don't treat me like a fool!" yelled Pampín, going red in the face. "We agreed that Con da Fervenza is my territory. I'm the only one who can collect there! Your family doesn't have any right to be there!"

"I'm telling you, I don't know what you're talking about." Rosalía's voice was ice-cold. "Anyway, this isn't a good time. It would be better to talk later."

"I don't want to talk later! I want explanations now!" Pampín shouted. Just then, his glance fell on the wheelbarrow beneath the tarpaulin, and a suspicious expression came over his face. "What have you got there?"

"None of your business, Víctor," Ramón Docampo said curtly. "Listen to Rosalía and get out of here."

"Like hell I will!" the poacher snorted. "I'm not going to let you lot make a fool of me! You always act as if the whole damn island belongs to you. And I'm sick of it!"

"Back off, I'm telling you," warned Ramón, but the man, overcome by rage, ignored him.

"I bet that wheelbarrow is full of shellfish from my beach! And I want them back!"

Later, Roberto would ask himself what would have happened if Pampín hadn't made as if to remove the blue tarpaulin from the barrow. If he had instead been content to grumble and utter a couple of threats.

But he would never know, because Víctor Pampín grabbed the end of the tarp, about to reveal what lay beneath, and—with that simple gesture—set off the terrible chain of ensuing events.

It all happened so fast. Rosalía Freire grabbed Pampín's arm to stop him. He pushed her away. She stumbled, and one of her feet hit a slab that had been loosened by the winter rains. That was enough to make her lose her balance. Her arms windmilled as she tried to stay upright, but she toppled backward. Antía stepped forward, trying to stop her mother from falling, but she was too far away. Her sudden movement startled Pampín. Maybe the man was completely beside himself, or maybe he thought Antía was trying to attack him. Who knows. Whatever the reason, in a reflex gesture, he raised the scraper and landed a heavy blow to Antía's ribs, causing her to double over and groan in pain.

After that, it was as if everything were taking place in slow motion. Roberto saw it all happening in a blur. It took him a second to realize that it was Diego, and another to understand what was about to happen. But it was too late.

"Leave them alone!" yelled the boy, his eyes wide. "Don't hurt them! Bad man! Bad, bad, bad!"

Diego was holding a hammer, the same one Roberto had used to break open the chains. In one clean movement, he brought it down on Pampín's head before the man had time to defend himself.

There was a sickening crunch. Pampín staggered, dropped his pole, and took a couple of steps backward. Dark red blood trickled down his forehead. He raised his hand to his head, incredulous, and when he withdrew it, saw that it was stained red. For a moment, he stared at his sticky fingers, as if he couldn't understand what was happening. Then his eyes rolled back into his head, and he collapsed, like a puppet whose strings had suddenly been cut.

And that was all. No more than twenty seconds could have passed, but Roberto felt as if time had stopped and he was trapped in a nightmare. Nobody moved a muscle; they were too shocked to say anything.

Diego, who was standing next to the fallen man, stared at him, unable to process what he had done. His gaze shuttled between the man and the hammer in his hand, and back again, as he searched for the connection between the two things. Suddenly, it hit him like a bolt of lightning, and he began to shake uncontrollably.

"Diego!" groaned Antía, still reeling from the blow to her ribs. "Diego! Oh dear Lord! What have you done?"

The boy was shaking like a leaf, his mouth opening and closing silently, the expression on his face that of a cornered animal. A dark stain began to spread across his crotch, and Roberto realized that the boy had just pissed himself.

Rosalía Freire had dragged herself to where Pampín lay and was checking for his pulse.

"He isn't breathing," she muttered. "He's dead!"

"Fucking hell, the moron's killed Víctor Pampín!" Luis Docampo broke the silence. "Who would have thought he had the balls!"

"Shut up, Luis!" shouted Antía, hugging her brother, who was weeping inconsolably.

"I didn't mean to . . . I didn't mean to . . ." He looked at his sister with eyes brimming with tears. "He was hurting both of you . . . I didn't mean to . . . no, no, no, no . . ."

"Shh, honey, shh." Antía held him tight as he sobbed. "Don't look, darling. Don't worry, it's all over."

Roberto racked his brains, trying to make sense of what had just happened. In a flash, things had taken an unimaginable turn. Not only were seventy-five million euros of dubious origin piled up next to him, but now they were accompanied by a corpse. Things could hardly be worse. They were all up to their necks in it.

Diego had reacted impulsively, driven by his limited capacity for reason. He had sought to neutralize a threat, without understanding the scope of his actions. As a result, a dead man was lying on the ground.

"Antía, Helena, get the kid out of here." His voice conveyed a confidence that he did not feel. "Now."

"What are we going to do?"

"For now, just try to calm him down." Roberto's mind was whirring.

"I won't let them take him to prison." Antía's ferocious tone, like a lioness, startled him. "It was an accident."

"Nobody's going to take him," Roberto replied, although he knew that wasn't true. "Get him out of here. We'll take care of this."

"I'm serious. I won't let them arrest him."

"And I promise that nothing will happen. Please, get him out of here. Now."

Antía looked at him uncertainly until an expression of relief filled her eyes. She whispered a silent *thank you*, and the three women—Helena, Rosalía, and Antía—took Diego away up the path. The boy had entered a catatonic trance, and his head nodded backward and forward as he emitted terrifying, incoherent sounds.

"I can't believe it." Luis Docampo had bent down to pick up the bloodstained hammer, and inspected it, still in shock. "It was all so fast . . ."

"What will happen to him?" asked Tristán Docampo, who hadn't opened his mouth until then. "Is what Antía says true? Will he go to prison?"

"I don't have a clue." Roberto shook his head. "I doubt it. They'll take his circumstances into account."

"What are we going to do now?"

"I don't know." He pressed his fingers to the side of his head, detecting the first signs of a migraine. "We need to think."

"Not so keen to call the police now, are we?" mocked Luis Docampo. "Bit of a different picture now, isn't it?"

Roberto wasn't sure what to say. The man might be cruel, but he was right.

It had been an accident, with a whole crowd of witnesses who could testify to it. But that would be the least of their problems when the Guardia Civil's green uniforms appeared on the island. Maybe Diego wouldn't go to prison, but he would certainly end up in some kind of juvenile center or health-care institution, far from the island and his family, swallowed up by the system.

It was a cruel fate for a kid who had only wanted to help; a kid who, just a few hours earlier, had saved his life.

He couldn't let that happen to him.

And yet, there was no alternative.

Antía and her family would hate him forever, and he would be responsible for every terrible thing that happened to poor Diego, but try as he might, he could see no way out.

They were all in a terrible mess.

# 12

## The Hammer

His headache was getting worse, and now he felt a drop of water on his cheek, followed in rapid succession by two more. He looked up and saw that the clouds had darkened and it was starting to rain.

"We have to get the body out of here." Ramón Docampo pointed at Pampín with his cigarette. "It's going to get soaked."

"We can't move it until the authorities and the pathologist arrive. They'll have to take photos and record all the details . . ."

"Hold it, Lobeira." The old man rested one of his heavy, calloused hands on Roberto's shoulder in an almost intimate gesture. "You're a man of the world, and I'm sure you know all about police procedures and magistrates and the rest of it . . . but you don't have a clue about how this island works."

"What do you mean?"

"When it rains, all the water runs down from up there . . ." He pointed at the hills, dotted with empty vacation homes. "And it will find the easiest route to the sea. That route runs along this road. If we don't get the body out of here, it'll get totally soaked. It might even get washed away if it rains hard. We have to move it."

Roberto nodded. He was starting to feel completely overwhelmed.

"Okay," he agreed reluctantly. "And where will we put it?"

"Our little supermarket is just over there." Ramón pointed to an aluminum door plastered with faded, soft-drink stickers. "It's empty right now."

Ramón Docampo thrust his hand into his pocket and brought out a bunch of keys, which he gave to his son, Luis. As he handed them over, he whispered something into his son's ear, and Luis gave a discreet nod.

"While we sort this business out, I suggest we put the money away." He tipped his head in the direction of the wheelbarrow, which the previous few minutes had put out of people's thoughts. "We can't leave it out in the rain."

"Locked away in your shithole of a store?" One of the Freires spat on the ground. "Fat chance."

"Where then?" Ramón replied. "In one of the hovels you lot rent out, so that you can keep guard over it?"

You could have cut the atmosphere with a knife. Roberto saw that there was a very real chance of more violence breaking out.

"Isn't there some neutral ground, somewhere that's acceptable to both families? The church, say?"

Behind him stood a modern brick building adorned with the ugliest bell tower imaginable.

After a tense pause, everyone agreed.

"Okay, in the church," said Ramón Docampo reluctantly. "We'll take care of it. You and Luis deal with Pampín. Let's get a move on!"

That was enough to jolt everyone into action. While some opened the doors of the church wide, others hurried to raise the wheelbarrow into the air, like a bizarre parody of an Easter procession, and carry it up the steps. Roberto watched them disappear inside, from where he heard muffled voices. He couldn't tell if they were talking about the murder they had just witnessed or what to do with their share of the money. The sense of unreality, of sliding at full speed down a slippery slope, was only accentuated by his migraine.

"Come on, Mr. Smart-Ass," said Luis Docampo with his strange, twisted smile. "Quit daydreaming and help me move the corpse."

Roberto took the body by the ankles, and Luis grabbed it under the arms. Pampín was heavier than he looked, and Roberto's muscles soon began to burn as he struggled toward the supermarket.

When they reached the store, they laid him on the ground so that Luis could unlock the door. Inside, the place was dark and smelled slightly mildewed. He could just make out a long counter, behind which was a series of shelves that in the summer would be stacked with products but just now were half empty.

The freezer compartments—lying open, the electricity turned off—were like the abandoned sarcophagi of a lost civilization. With one final effort, they lifted the corpse onto the long wooden counter.

"And now what?"

"We should stick him in one of those freezers." Luis Docampo pointed at one of the chests, as if he'd read Roberto's mind. "We can't leave him on the counter, can we?"

"Aren't they disconnected?"

"So what?" Luis said. "We'll stick him in there and—"

Just then, a groan came from behind them. They both spun to face the counter, where Víctor Pampín's body was trembling slightly.

"Jesus fucking Christ!" groaned Luis. "The bastard's still alive!"

Roberto ignored him and leaned over the poacher. The man had opened his eyes, his expression blurry and disconcerted. His chest rose and fell almost imperceptibly, and he opened his mouth as if to speak. When he managed to focus on Roberto's face, he gripped one of his hands, in a mute request for help.

A huge wave of relief overcame Roberto. The blow hadn't killed Pampín; it had just knocked him out. He was disoriented and weak, but there was nothing that the right medical care couldn't fix. No doubt he'd have a fractured skull, but that was nothing compared to the nightmare they'd been facing.

The situation was still an absolute mess, but at least it wasn't murder. And Diego wasn't a killer.

Everything might turn out all right in the end.

"Give me some room." Luis Docampo appeared at his side. "Let me see."

Pampín was now breathing more evenly, and Roberto stepped to one side, without releasing the man's hand.

Then, without saying a word, Luis Docampo took the hammer from his belt and brought it crashing down on the poacher's skull.

One, two, three times.

With the final blow, blood spurted out and splashed their faces.

Roberto staggered back. The whole place was spinning, and he could hardly breathe. He had just witnessed a display of pure, primal violence, but Luis Docampo's face didn't betray the least sign of emotion.

"Now he's dead," he muttered, as if it were completely natural.

Roberto was unable to utter a single syllable. He grabbed on to a display stand full of yellowing postcards to keep himself upright, and tried to process the horrific scene.

"What have you done?" he asked in a hoarse whisper. "The man was alive. He was alive, you maniac!"

Luis's only response was to shrug and put the hammer, which had blood and hair sticking to it, back in his belt.

"You killed him!" Roberto pointed at him. "You murdered him in cold blood!"

Luis Docampo opened his eyes wide and affected a surprised expression.

"Me?" A twisted smile spread across his face. "You seem to be a bit confused, my friend. It wasn't me."

"What the hell do you mean? I saw you with my own eyes!"

"I don't know what you're talking about." Luis wiped a spot of blood from his cheek. "The only thing I know is that the Freire freak attacked the poor guy with a hammer and killed him. You saw it too."

"He was alive! He was still alive!" replied Roberto.

"No, he wasn't. He was already good and dead. And a whole load of witnesses will say the same thing."

"You won't get away with this." Roberto put his hand in his pocket and took out his phone. "I'm going to call the Guardia Civil right now and tell them what's happened."

"And what are you going to tell them?" Luis took a step toward him, and Roberto backed off, suddenly aware that they were alone and the door was a long way away. "That I killed him?"

"That's right."

"You know what I think?" He leaned on the counter, just inches away from the corpse, as if he were waiting to buy some bread. "From my point of view, you have three options. The first is to call the Guardia Civil and stick with the version that it was the Freire kid who killed this stupid busybody."

"No way."

"The second"—Luis raised two thick fingers—"is to confess that he was alive when we brought him here but that you killed him."

Roberto stared at him incredulously. "What . . . what crazy shit is this? That's nonsense."

"Not at all." Luis pursed his lips and shook his head sadly. "I saw you do it with my own eyes."

"You're out of your mind." Roberto unlocked his phone.

"Think carefully," Luis warned as he patted the hammer with his gloved hand. "This is the murder weapon, and as far as I know, the only prints on it are Diego Freire's . . . and yours."

Roberto Lobeira stared at the hammer in horror. The same hammer he had used to break the chains on the damn bundle of cash a while earlier. The same hammer that was, no doubt, covered with his fingerprints.

"Now tell me." Luis Docampo's voice had acquired a gentle, reasonable tone, the tone of someone explaining something to a child. "If you call the authorities and they turn up here . . . who do you think they're going to believe? You, with your crazy account of a senseless murder

. . . or me, backed by my relatives, who'll swear that when they heard Pampín's cries, they came running and saw you finishing him off? And that's before we get onto the subject of your fingerprints on the murder weapon . . ."

Roberto felt the jaws of the trap closing pitilessly around him.

"You had a motive, I guess. You wanted to keep the money, even though we didn't agree. Pampín threatened to call the police and . . . well, there's not much more to explain, right?"

Roberto had closed his eyes, like a child hoping for the monsters in his closet to disappear, but it was futile.

He was screwed. Completely and utterly screwed.

"Three options," he whispered.

"What?"

"You said I had three options." He struggled to articulate the words. "What's the third one?"

Luis Docampo took a step toward him and put an arm around his shoulder as if they were old friends. "The third option is the best," he said. "You keep your mouth shut, you don't say anything to the authorities, and you accept that the Docampos and the Freires divide the money equally between us. You renounce your share, because you've already told everyone that this business is immoral, indecent, and all that crap. Then, you spend the rest of your time on the island shut away in your cottage, writing, jerking off, or doing whatever the hell you feel like, and at the end of it all, you leave. That way, we can all forget about this nasty business. What do you reckon, my friend? That's a good solution, isn't it?"

"You're forgetting one thing." Roberto pointed to Víctor Pampín's lifeless body. "Him. Someone will miss him, sooner or later. People will start to ask questions."

"Don't worry about that," Luis replied calmly. "In a few days' time, we'll toss him over a cliff. Everyone will just assume that he slipped and fell, or that he was washed away by a wave while he was out scraping goose barnacles. By the time the seagulls have finished with him, he'll be so disfigured that nobody will even notice the hammer blows. *Your* hammer blows."

Roberto was gripped by a terrifying certainty. Luis Docampo, the same man he'd shared a beer with that morning, had him at his mercy. The islander had played his hand quickly, and what was worse, Roberto could see no way out.

He should have seen it coming. He'd been told that the rules were different here on the island. That they did whatever was necessary to survive.

The man had told him clearly and directly, but he hadn't understood. His brutal acts were suffused with the cruel pragmatism of someone who had to struggle each day to survive, of someone who had suddenly been presented with a golden ticket to escape from that vicious cycle.

He had underestimated the Freires and the Docampos when he had thought they were just a group of islanders caught up in trivial squabbles. The hatred they professed for each other was exceeded only by the overriding need to outdo their rivals. Something told Roberto that distributing the money fairly between the two clans wouldn't be as easy as Luis wanted him to believe.

"We're going out to join the rest of them now," Luis Docampo informed him. "So what are you going to tell them?"

"That I agree that you can all keep the money," Roberto acquiesced pathetically.

"And what else?"

"That I renounce my share."

"That's the way I like it." He patted Roberto's back. "Right, let's stick the body in one of these freezers and get the fuck out of here."

# 13

## Last Chance to Set Things Right

When they went back outside, heavy rain had set in. Just as Ramón Docampo had predicted, the concrete track was becoming a full-scale torrent, with the ditches on either side completely overflowing. However, despite the bad weather, no one had gone home.

It was as if the money were a powerful magnet and they were all mere iron filings, for everyone had remained just outside the church, waiting expectantly.

"How did it go?" asked Ramón. "Any problems?"

"It's all sorted, Dad," Luis answered, exchanging a knowing glance with him. "Nothing to worry about."

Roberto looked at them suspiciously. *Maybe the plan wasn't Luis's. Maybe it was all the old man's doing.* That made a lot more sense, although he still couldn't be sure.

"Well, Lobeira." Ramón Docampo threw his hands up theatrically. "Made up your mind? Still thinking about calling the Guardia Civil, or have you come to your senses?"

Roberto took a deep breath. The only sound was the murmur of the falling rain, and all eyes were on the two of them. The atmosphere crackled with tension.

"Perhaps I spoke too soon . . ." he started to say, but just then, the sound of an approaching engine cut him off.

"I'll be damned," Luis barked. "What's with all the people today? It's not like it's the high season!"

The roar of the engine grew louder, and a moment later, they saw the mud-spattered snout of the national park SUV coming around the corner. The vehicle kicked up spray as it rolled down the track and pulled up beside them with a screech of its brakes.

"What a filthy day!" shouted the driver as he rolled down the window. "How are we all?"

He was a bald, middle-aged man with a cheerful, olive-skinned face and a light beard, and he was wearing a park ranger's uniform. In the passenger seat was another, slightly younger, short-haired man who, after nodding to all present, had turned back to his cell phone.

"Good morning, Sobral," Ramón Docampo greeted him politely. "All fine here. And you?"

"A bit annoyed, to tell the truth." He jerked his thumb at the younger man absorbed in his phone beside him. "Martín here sprained his ankle just as we were finishing our rounds. I'm taking him to the mainland to get it checked out."

Martín's only response was an unintelligible grunt as he continued to stare at his phone.

"You should hurry." Ramón looked up at the sky and then out to sea. "Looks like a storm's coming in."

"Yes, I spotted that," Sobral said, his elbow resting on the open window. "I need to get the patrol boat off the dock as soon as possible, or we're gonna get ripped to pieces. Have you seen the forecast?"

"No, why?"

"Oh, there's a proper squall coming in." He clicked his tongue. "Hundred-mile-an-hour winds, rain, fifteen-to-twenty-foot waves. The fleet won't be going anywhere for a couple of days, I reckon."

"The Freires will have to check that their huts are all properly closed up," said Ramón. "Wouldn't want them blowing away, would we?"

"Like in that old movie we saw the other day!" laughed the ranger, nudging his companion. "What was it called, Martín? The one about the girl with the lion and the scarecrow and what all else?"

The younger man sighed and looked up from his cell phone.

*"The Wizard of Oz,"* he grumbled, "and you fell asleep halfway through it."

"That's right, *The Wizard of Oz*!" The ranger ignored the jibe and leaned over to Ramón to whisper, "He's pissed because his ankle's hurting. That's why we're a little late on our rounds—you know how persnickety he is about timekeeping."

"Sure thing." Ramón Docampo's smile hadn't budged. "Not to rush you, Sobral, but you should really get going. You're in for a bumpy ride."

"You're right." Sobral nodded. Just then, he noticed Roberto, and his eyes widened. "Well, if it isn't Roberto Lobeira, the writer! So it *was* you who asked for the winter-access permit. Gosh! I just loved *The Fleeting Glance*!"

Once again, everyone turned to look at Roberto. He swallowed hard. The two men in the vehicle were the closest thing to law enforcement on the island, and they were right there, so close he could touch them—the front wheel of their SUV had inadvertently stopped just a few inches from where the ground was stained with the poacher's blood.

He also instantly realized that if it hadn't been for Martín's sprained ankle, they would have shown up earlier, perhaps right when the money was being counted, and certainly in time to prevent Pampín's catastrophic end.

He cursed inwardly. The urge to just blurt it all out was almost overpowering.

Even now, all he had to do was point to the bloodstain and let events take their course . . .

He opened his mouth to speak, but at that moment he noticed Luis Docampo, who had rested his hand on the hammer, the head of which he'd thrust under his belt to hide the bloodstains. He gave Roberto a meaningful look while his gloved fingers drummed on the tool.

"Hey, Mr. Lobeira." Sobral was looking at him quizzically. "Are you all right?"

Roberto forced a smile. Tension seemed to be rising up from the very earth, charging the electric atmosphere still further.

"Nothing's wrong." He tried to make his voice sound steady. "Everything's fine."

And with those few words went his last way out. His peace had been destroyed in a few short hours, and he'd been powerless to prevent it. He had become an accessory to murder and robbery.

"If only I had the book here so you could sign it." Sobral clapped a frustrated hand on the SUV's door. "You staying long?"

"A few weeks." Roberto's face ached; he was sure his artificial smile must have been obvious, but the ranger seemed not to notice. "Maybe not that long—I don't know yet."

"I should be back in a few days, weather permitting." The ranger glanced warily at the boat bobbing alongside the jetty. "I hope I can get a signature then."

"It would be my pleasure." A flash of pain in his head almost made him vomit. "I'll be here."

"We'll make sure he doesn't go anywhere, don't worry." Luis Docampo winked at Roberto, as if sharing a joke. "Mr. Lobeira is settling in well. Turns out we have a lot of interests in common."

"That's great news. Tell Antía to pick up the SUV from the jetty and park it in the usual place. I don't want salt water getting on the bodywork."

"We will, don't worry."

Sobral rolled up the window and started the engine, and black smoke poured from the exhaust pipe. They watched the SUV driving the final part of the way to the jetty, where Sobral helped his companion hobble aboard the boat, even as the waves tossed it about. With practiced precision, they untied the moorings, and after less than a minute, the outboard motors roared to life and they were headed for the mainland.

The boat negotiated the growing waves, leaving white foam in its wake. Roberto, with every fiber of his being, wished he was on board. The farther the vessel went from the island, the more trapped and helpless he felt.

When the boat was no more than a speck on the horizon, someone breathed a sigh of relief. The tension, though not entirely gone, at least went down a notch. The air was still thick with menace, but a brief truce seemed to have been declared.

Roberto was surprised at the lump in his throat. The sheer enormity of the crazy situation was quite overwhelming. Ramón Docampo turned to him, no hint of a smile on his face now.

"Well, my friend," he said simply, "now that we're all in this together, there's quite a bit for us to discuss."

# 14

## An Abandoned Graveyard

The next morning, while he was still in the brief lapse between the world of dream and waking life, relief washed over Roberto. The nightmare had been far more vivid and real than the ones that assailed him most nights, but at least it had nothing to do with the burden he had been carrying for almost four years now.

But then, as the final remnants of sleep melted away, the realization hit that what had happened the previous day was no nightmare. It was like a sledgehammer.

The money was real. The murder was real. A dead man really was lying in a freezer chest, on an island full of accomplices to murder, and he was the worst of them all.

Also real was the key hanging on the thin chain around his neck. Totally, absolutely real.

The day before, once the park rangers had left in their patrol boat, taking with them any semblance of authority or, indeed, sanity, the tension between the two clans had immediately resumed. Decades of rancor and mistrust, compounded by nerves and greed. Great riches had suddenly been dangled before everyone's noses.

And he was quite sure they were all now trying to work out how to prevent their rivals from getting their hands on the wealth that had so unexpectedly appeared.

All that mistrust had led to the Solomonic decision to lock up the church and entrust the key to the only person on the island who was more or less neutral.

Not only was he an accessory to murder, but it seemed inevitable he would end up as a scapegoat if he didn't go along with the conditions that had been imposed on him. There was no way out.

When he took his cell phone out of his parka pocket, he was sorely tempted to call Carmen Gavín. To talk to her, to explain everything that had happened. No doubt she would come up with a solution. "If you run into any problems . . . I'll make sure someone comes to get you." Those had been her words. But as his finger hovered over the screen, just about to tap on her name, he stopped himself.

He couldn't drag her into this mess. It wasn't some protracted contractual dispute with a publisher, and it wasn't a case of writer's block. It was of a totally different order. Seventy-five million euros of dubious origin were stacked behind the altar of a small village church, and on them hung a huge sign painted in the most garish colors: **TROUBLE**. Above all, an innocent man had been murdered, and that would be a challenge even to someone as resolute as Carmen, especially since she was a thousand miles away.

Not to mention the fact that if he told her the whole story, she would be legally implicated. It might even make her an accessory after the fact. His mind raced with the ramifications.

He tried to apply himself to the novel for a few hours, and did manage to rough out a few pages, but he couldn't put reality out of his mind. He needed to think.

Perhaps a walk around the island would help him get his thoughts in order. Boosted by the idea, after a bite to eat, he checked that his computer was plugged in and left the house.

It was even gloomier than it had been the day before. Black clouds covered the sky, threatening a downpour at any moment.

Everything was bathed in a dim, diffuse light, and static electricity hung on the air, making for a heavy, unreal atmosphere. The wind had picked up, and the twisted trees shook with gust after gust off the Atlantic. It would be even worse, he guessed, on the side of the island that faced out to sea.

As he walked briskly toward the shore, he replayed the events of the previous day in an obsessive loop.

He suddenly stopped, paralyzed.

He had just realized something. Antía, Helena, and their mother, Rosalía, had removed Diego from the crime scene *before* he and Luis Docampo transported Pampín's body to the store. And when they'd left, everyone still thought the youngster was the murderer. Diego Freire was innocent, but none of them knew that. And he doubted very much that the Docampo family members had disabused their rival clan. It was just too valuable—an ace up their sleeve and the perfect means for blackmail.

He started walking again, his mind whirring. He was the only one who had the power to change things, by letting the Freires know the true story. In Luis Docampo's entire fiendish plan, that was the closest thing to a flaw he had come up with.

But it wasn't quite so simple. He couldn't be sure what the Freires would do if he told them the truth. They might help him out of his predicament, or, driven by their rivalry, they might see it as a chance to spare one of their own while Roberto took the blame.

The only certainty was that he had no idea what to do next. Rosalía Freire had seemed to him just as implacable as Ramón Docampo: pragmatic, hard, and inflexible. The chances of finding an ally in the matriarch seemed remote. On the other hand, there was Antía. Since his arrival, she had seemed like a reasonable woman, and something in his gut told him he could trust her.

He ought to talk to her on her own. But if he showed up at El Cucorno, the Freire ancestral home, Rosalía would most likely find a way to be a part of any conversation, since she was the one who had invited him to visit. And if he asked to speak to Antía in private, that would set alarm bells ringing. On top of that, how could he be sure the younger woman would keep the secret?

Feeling caught, he carried on walking. There was no one in sight, everyone on the island having the sense to keep themselves safe and dry in their homes ahead of the coming storm. He thought about going back to the cottage, but the prospect of being locked in there, with all these ideas going around inside his head, was too claustrophobic. He needed air.

The path curved gently around the coastline, and he only saw the signpost by chance, when he was almost on top of it. Crooked and half-buried in the undergrowth, it read **Church**, with an arrow pointing to a narrow path that zigzagged off to his right.

Roberto was perplexed. The village church, where the money had been stowed, was back in the opposite direction. His curiosity piqued, he turned onto the path, which had had so little footfall that the bracken was at waist height, and made his way uphill.

The path soon leveled off and became a little wider, and then he saw it: a stone wall, some ten feet high, of excellent workmanship and in very good shape, its expanse broken only by a rusty iron gate that led into a walled enclosure, above which, farther back, the upper part of some edifice was visible.

Roberto tried the handle. With a creak, the gate swung open, and he went through. Before him was a small graveyard, and at the far end stood a stone chapel, very ancient looking, its roof tiles almost completely covered in moss. It had no windows besides a pair of slits on the side walls that somewhat gave it the air of a little stronghold.

Doubtless this had been the island's original church, built hundreds of years before. Judging from its sturdy construction, it would indeed have served as a stronghold in times past, a place to withdraw to when pirates came raiding. Over time, the old chapel must have fallen into disuse, and eventually the new church had been built. He approached the main door, a hulking thing of wood and rivets. He tried the handle, but it refused to budge.

The place was old and disused but hadn't been abandoned entirely. There were dozens of graves, each with its own little whitewashed alcove and a cross in the ground at the head of the tombstone, and a few had fresh flowers.

He noticed that none of the burials were from later than the 1970s, so he guessed it must have been around then that the church ceased to be used. Most of the graves belonged to adults, yet the percentage of infants was chillingly high—a reminder of how hard life must have been on the island until fairly recently. He counted barely half a dozen graves whose occupants had lived beyond sixty.

It should have been oppressive and gloomy, especially with the storm that was about to hit, but the atmosphere was strangely peaceful, and as he wandered the graves, Roberto felt a measure of inner tranquility—the first in quite some time.

But he couldn't stay there forever. The sky had darkened, and the rain would start any minute. If he didn't want to get soaked, he needed to find shelter, and quickly.

Just then, there was a clap of thunder, followed by a deep rumbling. He quickened his pace as the first big, cold drops began to fall around him, leaving marks the size of coins as they hit the ground.

He had wandered too far from the cottage and doubted he would make it back before the full fury of the storm was unleashed. Cursing under his breath, he again quickened his pace, casting around urgently for somewhere to shelter. Spotting a cluster of houses on a cliff overlooking the beach, he headed in their direction.

Like most houses on the island, these were small and made of stone, with gable roofs and a lean-to in back. Formerly the dwellings of farmworkers or fishermen, they had been renovated as summer lodgings for tourists. As he drew close, Roberto saw that one had a narrow porch, only four or five feet wide, but sufficient to shelter under.

Dashing inside, Roberto shook himself like a wet dog. It was going to be a while before the downpour subsided, so he decided to make himself comfortable.

Unfortunately, that was easier said than done. The houses were in an exposed position, and gusts of rain hit him full in the face; he was almost as wet as if he'd just stayed outside.

Readying himself to see if he could find a more protected spot on the other side of the house, he pulled his hood tightly over his head and stepped out from the meager protection of the porch. He staggered in the wind and had to lean himself against the wall to make any progress while the icy rain lashed mercilessly down.

And then he heard a laugh.

It was a man's laugh, and it reverberated around the enclosed space between the tightly packed houses, as in a kind of sounding board. He would not have heard it, except that just then, the wind died down for a brief moment.

*The Tangaraño.*

He knew it was absurd, yet he still couldn't avoid the thought.

He peered about in the gloom, trying to identify where the sound might have come from. Nobody seemed to be there, and yet he was sure he'd heard laughter. As he was about to pass it off as a figment of his imagination, he heard it again. Looking up, he saw a chink of light from the window of a nearby house.

He had been wrong, it seemed, to assume the houses were all empty. It was a relief to think that he might now have somewhere to sit out the storm. Maybe even with a hot cup of coffee in his hands. He made it to the front door and knocked softly, but nobody answered. A particularly wet gust of wind smashed him from behind, and with that his patience was at an end. Without another thought, he turned the handle and went inside. Only to freeze, dumbstruck, in the doorway.

Standing in the middle of the room, Tristán Docampo looked back in horror, holding a couple of drinks and wearing only his underpants.

A few feet away, on the bed at the back of the room, hurriedly covering herself with the sheets, the young Helena Freire, completely naked, stared back wide eyed.

# 15

## Montagues and Capulets

The three of them said nothing, all too shocked to react. Eventually, Roberto closed the door behind him and stood there with water dripping off him, a puddle at his feet growing by the moment.

"Excuse the interruption." He cleared his throat awkwardly. "I knocked, but I didn't know . . . I didn't suppose . . . I mean . . ."

"What are you doing here?" said Tristán, who had gone over to the bed, positioning himself between Roberto and Helena. "Who told you we were here?"

There was something endearing about the young man's posture, a show of fierceness he absolutely did not possess. Roberto had to give it to him: It took a lot to stay cool when caught off guard in your underwear.

"Nobody told me anything," he said. "I got caught in the rain. I'm a long way from the house I'm staying at, and was just trying to find somewhere to shelter. I heard voices and knocked on the door but—"

"That's a lie!" Tristán cut in. "Who sent you? My father? Or was it Rosalía?"

"No one, I swear." He raised his hands. "It happened by chance."

"Yeah, sure."

"Please," Helena said, in barely more than a whisper. "Don't say anything to my mother or sister. I beg you."

Roberto was speechless for a moment as the realization slowly dawned on him.

Tristán Docampo, the youngest Docampo, with Helena Freire, the youngest of the rival clan, naked together in a house far away from everything. He could imagine that their families would be far from happy if they knew.

He sighed and undid his parka before collapsing into a chair.

"Come on," he said, gesturing to Tristán, "get dressed. This is awkward enough without you standing there half naked."

Tristán flushed and muttered something, bending down to pick up his pants and hurriedly hoist them on.

"Would you mind turning around?" said Helena.

"Pardon?"

"I'd like to get dressed too," she said, a little more firmly.

Roberto sighed and looked away as she got out of bed and reached for her clothes. It seemed as if the interlude of rustling clothes and zippers being done up was never going to end.

"That's it," she said at last.

Roberto turned again and saw the young lovers, fully dressed and sitting next to each other on the edge of the bed.

Tristán was holding one of Helena's hands between his and looking at Roberto suspiciously. "Are you sure no one sent you?"

"I give you my word," he said wearily. "Besides, I think we've got enough trouble on the island without creating more, don't you?"

The pair exchanged a relieved look, with that deep expression, full of unspoken understanding, that can only be shared by two people who are intensely in love. Roberto groaned in irritation.

It was all he needed. As if he didn't have enough problems already, he had just stumbled upon the island's very own Romeo and Juliet. Of course, instead of elegant Montagues and Capulets, he was dealing with a bunch of angry Freires and Docampos who would have no qualms about throwing him off a cliff if they learned he was concealing the tryst.

"Okay," he said, "want to explain what you're doing here? Apart from the obvious, I mean. That bit I can imagine."

Helena turned red to the roots of her hair and mumbled something inaudible as she looked down at her feet. It was Tristán who spoke up.

"This is our safe place. It's halfway between our two houses, and no one comes here in the winter. Antía has the keys because she rents it out in the summer. Helena managed to make copies without anyone finding out."

"I get it. Your little love nest. Fine. How long have you been coming here?"

"Almost two years," she said with a dignified look. "We're in love."

She said it with the steely determination that only a teenager in love can bestow on such a statement. Roberto looked at them sorrowfully. They certainly didn't have it easy.

The only two people their age on the island, they were both good looking, and, despite the enmity between their families, in such a small place, they would inevitably bump into each other all the time. They would have known the possible repercussions, but even so, he could see why they had ended up together.

"Does anyone in your families know?"

"No!" they both exclaimed, so completely in sync that, under any other circumstances, it would have been comical.

"I haven't been here long, but I get the feeling they wouldn't look very kindly on your relationship, am I wrong?"

"They don't understand," Tristán continued. "They've been at each other's throats for so long, I don't think they even remember why. But whatever, their problems aren't our problems."

"I doubt your father sees it like that." He turned to Helena. "Or your family, for that matter."

"Please promise you won't say anything," she said, her eyes glistening.

"And what's your intention? To just go on creeping around until you get caught? Or until you miscalculate and get pregnant one day? What's your plan?"

They both looked at each other, having another of those silent exchanges. Finally, Helena nodded, and Tristán turned to Roberto.

"We're saving some money," Tristán said, "from our jobs in the high season. We're planning to leave next summer. Go to the mainland, find some work, and live together."

"We're adults now," Helena added. "We can make our own decisions."

They both spoke with absolute confidence, as if the plan were seamless. Roberto could see plenty of obstacles to that dream, and the families' reaction was just about the least of them. But now something was occurring to him.

"It's all right." He raised his hands placatingly. "Your secret's safe with me; you have my word."

"Oh, thank you!" Helena groaned with relief.

"But . . ." added Roberto, and he saw the young lovers' joyful looks turn to stone.

"But what?" Tristán asked cautiously.

"I need you to do something for me in return. I think it's only fair."

Roberto felt bad for playing with their emotions like this but saw no real alternative. A plan was forming in his mind right then and there—one that he could see actually working.

"You want money? Is that it? We don't have very much, you ought to know."

"I don't want your money." He shook his head. "There's something I need you to do for me."

"What is it?" Helena's expression had darkened with distrust, and she had instinctively crossed her arms.

Roberto said nothing for a moment while he got his thoughts in order. With great clarity, he mapped out possible forks in the road and detours, as if he were plotting a novel with himself as protagonist and these two lovers as the supporting cast.

Presently he smiled, trying to appear more confident than he felt.

"Don't worry, it's nothing that hard." Speaking airily to Helena, he said, "I need you to talk to your sister, Antía, and give her a message."

"What message?"

"I need to meet with her, alone. And above all, without your mother knowing. It's extremely important."

"Why do you want to see her alone?"

"That's my business," he replied, putting on the sternest expression he could muster. "Tell her to come here, tomorrow at twelve o'clock. Can you do that?"

"She's very worried about Diego just now." A pained expression flashed across her face. "My brother hasn't said a single word since . . . what happened yesterday. I don't know if she'll want to leave him on his own."

"Well, you tell her that's precisely what I want to talk to her about, but it has to be alone. I can't stress enough how important that part is."

"Okay, if that's all it is, it should be fine," Helena replied after a moment's thought. "Sure, I'll do it."

"And what about me?" Tristán asked.

"I need you to look for something in your house and bring it to me. Something of your father's."

"Something?"

"A hammer, to be specific."

"A hammer?" Tristán looked confused. "There must be half a dozen hammers in our workshop. What do you want a hammer for?"

"I need one in particular. It's got a red wooden handle, with a rounded end. And it's also got bloodstains on it."

A silence fell. It lasted for three heartbeats while it dawned on Tristán what they were talking about.

"You mean the hammer Diego used to—"

"Yes," said Roberto. "Do you know where it is?"

"No idea, but I can look."

"And your father mustn't know. Okay?"

"And if I bring you the hammer, you promise you won't say anything about us?"

"You have my word." Roberto raised his right hand.

"How can we be sure you aren't lying to us?"

"You can't," Roberto snapped, more sharply than necessary, and he immediately felt bad. "You just have to trust me. Do we have a deal or not?"

Tristán swallowed and looked down at the floor, clearly worried. Eventually, he gave a nod.

"I'll get you the damn hammer," he said in a whisper, "but I'll need time."

"Three days. I'll meet you here in the afternoon, three days from now, okay?"

Tristán Docampo gave another nod.

"Great." Roberto stood up. "It looks like the weather is clearing up. Time for me to head back."

He opened the door, with a bitter feeling in his heart, but he didn't let it show. He had to see this through.

"See you guys again soon," he said from the doorway. "Oh, just one more thing . . ."

"What?" said Tristán.

"Next time, make sure to lock the door?"

He left without looking back. The rain had eased, only a few scattered drops falling now. He walked away, a heavy ball in the pit of his stomach.

It was pretty disgraceful on his part, but he had no choice. With the plan he'd just come up with, he could see a way out of this whole mess.

First, the hammer, the only physical evidence linking him to Pampín's murder: If it wasn't in Luis Docampo's possession, there was nothing to link Roberto to the murder. At a stroke, the noose around his neck would be gone.

That would put the ball back in the Freires' court, since Diego would once again be the prime suspect in Pampín's murder. More than a dozen witnesses had seen the boy hit Pampín with the hammer, and they had all presumed the poacher dead on the spot.

He still had no way of proving that Luis Docampo was responsible, but that was a bridge he would have to cross later.

As for Antía Freire, if he managed to get her alone, he could tell her the truth. From there on, he was counting on the hatred between the families, and the need to prove Diego innocent, to do the rest. As long as Antía believed him, of course.

However, none of this would help him unmask the mysterious Tangaraño. Nor would it solve the problem of the seventy-five million euros sitting inside the church in a couple of duffel bags, but again that was something to deal with later. For the moment, he was taking steps to ensure his own survival.

He felt relieved: He realized that it was the first time since the previous day that he had actually felt a smile spreading on his face. He even found it in himself to whistle a tune as he made his way back to the cottage.

Everything was going to be all right. Somehow, it would all work out.

At least that was what he was telling himself.

# 16

## Following the Light

After a rough night for Roberto, it rained almost the whole of the next day. It cascaded down out of glowering skies. An occasional, particularly violent gust rattled the windows, making the hairs on the back of his neck stand up. Sitting at his computer, Roberto was unable to write more than two coherent lines.

When he'd returned the previous evening, he realized his elementary mistake. He should just have asked Helena for Antía's phone number. He could then have called her and told her, in complete privacy, about what had happened to Pampín. But that obvious solution simply hadn't occurred to him, and after such an uncharacteristic oversight, he had no choice now but to show up at the appointed time. Presuming, of course, that she was going to be there.

Inside the cottage, he paced about like a caged lion. The dampness and cold had seeped steadily into his bones, so when the rain miraculously stopped midway through the morning, Roberto headed out, feeling relieved.

The gray skies had not cleared, the wind was still up, and the day felt far from settled, but at least he could get to the lovers' hideaway to meet Antía. He had no way of knowing whether his message had indeed made it to her and she would be there waiting, but the walk would calm his nerves in any case.

He didn't see a soul. The few inhabitants of the island, seemingly more sensible than him, weren't venturing out. Or maybe they were all too busy scheming over what to do with their share of the money. When he reached the house, he wasn't surprised to find the door locked and no sign of human activity.

He waited on the porch for forty minutes before he gave up and decided to head back. When he had almost reached the cottage, he rounded a bend, and a couple of startled hares tripped over each other in their eagerness to flee. He found it so comical that, despite his sorry situation, he couldn't help but smile. However, the smile was wiped from his face when he crossed the unkempt yard and got to the door.

Someone had been there. Again.

A clear path had been trampled in the long, uncut grass. The visitor's boots had gone straight over the flower bed to the door, instead of following the cobblestone path.

Roberto was sure it wasn't his own doing. Moreover, those footprints could not have been more than a few minutes old, half an hour at the most. The earlier downpour would have washed them away, so they had to have been made after it had stopped raining.

His whole being tensed. He wished he were armed, but he had only what was in his pockets and his bare hands. He inched warily closer to the door.

The wet imprint of a boot was clearly visible on the top step. It was at least two sizes larger than his own. The scene of Robinson Crusoe discovering a human footprint on the beach of his desert island burst forcefully and absurdly into his mind. He might have been on an island, but he was no Robinson Crusoe. Nor was he in an eighteenth-century novel, but in the real world.

He tried slowly turning the doorknob, but it was locked, just as he had left it when he went out. And the hair he had affixed to the doorframe was still there, so no one had opened it. It was then that he noticed something attached to the jamb of the doorframe, almost at eye level. He removed it as if he were handling a stick of lit dynamite.

It was a plastic ziplock bag, the kind used to store frozen goods, the same kind he had used to store the severed rabbit head a few nights before. But this one contained nothing so unpleasant. Rather, there was a sheet of paper inside, neatly folded.

Whoever had left the note there had taken precautions to prevent the rain from smudging it. He opened the bag and took out the piece of paper. It was handwritten, in elegant, somewhat old-fashioned handwriting.

> *Dear Mr. Lobeira,*
> *It would be a pleasure for us to have the opportunity to meet you and talk together a little. If you would be so kind as to accept our invitation to lunch, we will expect you today at half past two at the lighthouse. Just follow the light.*
> *Sincerely,*
> *A. Ibaibarriaga*
> *Head Lighthouse Keeper*

That was all. Roberto turned the paper over several times in his hands, thoughts rushing through his head. What a relief for the note to be a simple lunch invitation, and nothing to do with the strange curses of the elusive Tangaraño or his bind with the murderous rival clans.

But one thing bothered him. The author of the mysterious invitation knew his name, knew who he was. And that didn't make the slightest sense, unless someone had told them about him. The next question was what else that person knew. Especially concerning Pampín's death and the money.

He was tempted to ignore the invitation, but his curiosity got the better of him.

He looked at the clock: It was almost two already. The morning had sped by, and he would have to be there in half an hour. With a shrug, he turned and went back to the path, thinking about how to get to his destination.

The answer was easy, as he instantly realized. The lighthouse was at the top of the highest point on the whole island, so the only way to go was uphill.

In the general winter gloom, the lighthouse had already been switched on. He could make out the beam that swept around, following its preset pattern. It was impossible to get lost. He squared his shoulders and set off.

The road up to the lighthouse was by far the best kept on the island—a decent concrete surface with drainage ditches on either side. This, of course, made sense, given the lighthouse's doubtless frequent need of material and spare parts that could be brought only by vehicle.

Roberto walked briskly on, passing along the way a number of empty houses that gazed back darkly out of lifeless windows. The irrational feeling that he was being watched was so intense that he caught himself spinning on his heels more than once, but this part of the island was completely devoid of all human presence. The wind grew steadily stronger as he gained the exposed heights, and it began to pour again. He tightened his hood and pushed on.

After fifteen minutes, he reached the lighthouse enclosure. A rigid wire fence ran along the entire perimeter, and he passed through a low iron gate between concrete posts. A shed stood open by the entrance, and inside were a tractor and trailer, which he guessed served to transport any heavier goods from the waterside.

A movement away to the left caught his eye. A modern security camera had been installed on top of the shed, and it had swiveled around to look at him. His host doubtless knew he had arrived.

The road curved around slightly before reaching the very top. To the right was a dilapidated abandoned building that had been converted into a wood shelter and was littered with logs and big pieces of timber.

When he rounded the last bend, the lighthouse came into view, and he whistled through his teeth.

It was immense. It consisted of a central edifice flanked by two extensive wings. On top of the main block stood the tower: a tall stone-and-metal structure crowned with the gigantic glass casing for the light. He could see the light slowly rotating inside, dazzling his eyes every time it swept across him.

The whole complex was painted white, and the wide brown roofs were dotted with moss. Roberto walked over to the small stone yard in front of the main door. White tiles covered the facade, with a pair of windows and a huge twelve-foot round-arched door the only other things to interrupt that expanse.

He approached the door, grasped the heavy bronze knocker, and rapped three times. Immediately he heard footsteps on the other side, and the door swung gently open on its hinges.

"Ah, you're here! Right on time!"

Before him was a burly, somewhat overweight man in his forties. He had a shiny bald head that glistened with sweat, and inquisitive, alert, searching green eyes. He had a discreet blond beard that completed his affable appearance.

"Welcome to Ons lighthouse," he said with an unmistakable Basque accent as he stretched out a huge hand toward him. "I'm Álvaro Ibaibarriaga, the chief lighthouse keeper. I see you got our invitation in time."

"Indeed," Roberto replied, returning the man's fleshy handshake.

"Come in, come in! You'll get soaked."

Roberto crossed the threshold and looked around, instantly enchanted. The hallway was covered with the same ceramic tile as the facade, only with beautifully drawn borders. Delicately painted green tendrils ran upward, ending in ovals on which sailboats plied foamy seas. At the far end was a glass door with the legend **Ons Lighthouse** acid-etched on the glass, in a delightfully antiquated art deco typeface.

Ibaibarriaga followed his gaze and smiled at his astonishment.

"This part of the lighthouse was built in the 1920s. Everything you see is completely original; nothing's been changed at all."

Roberto looked up at the ceiling, which must have been fifteen feet high. Long teak beams stretched away to the end of the hallway, which provided a horizontal support for the two wings. There were doors at intervals along it, made of the same dark teak, all very solid and antique looking.

"Never been inside a lighthouse before, have you?"

"It's the first time, I admit. It's . . . impressive."

"This one's very special. As it's on an island, successive generations of lighthouse keepers have taken great care of it. It's not only a lighthouse; it's also our home."

"Sorry, Mr. Ibaibarriaga," Roberto interrupted him. "There is one thing that—"

"Call me Álvaro, please," the lighthouse keeper said with a smile.

"Well, Álvaro, I was just wondering how you knew my name, and that I was staying on the island," he said in the calmest voice he could muster. "I suppose someone must have told you."

"Oh no, nothing like that."

"So?"

"Probably better if I just show you . . ."

He gestured to the glass doors. "This way."

On the other side of the doors was a spiral staircase built of granite ashlars. Through a small window, he could see that they were already above the rooftops of the lateral wings, although it was still a long way to the very top. They reached a point where the stone staircase opened into a circular room, empty except for a series of modern electrical junction boxes that hummed softly. A metal staircase on one side led still higher.

"This is how you get up to the light," explained the lighthouse keeper. "Be careful where you put your feet, and hold the handrail. You wouldn't be the first to fall down these stairs."

Roberto climbed carefully, Ibaibarriaga behind him. Getting to the top, he found himself on a platform, also circular, but with its center occupied by a colossal, ring-shaped steel structure with heavy supports at the bottom.

"This is the system for turning the light," said Ibaibarriaga, mopping his brow. "That circular part you see up there is filled with hundreds of liters of mercury. The bearings for the light float on that. It's a very old system, but it never breaks down."

"Is that the way up to the light?" Roberto pointed to another flight of stairs.

"Yes, but first I wanted to show you something. Look over here."

To one side, next to the wall, was a heavy iron door, covered in rust. On a tripod beside it rested an expensive, modern-looking telescope.

"The other day, when you arrived at the island in the fishing boat, we saw you with this." The man laughed as he tapped on the device. "It's a Vanguard Endeavor ground telescope. We usually use it to check the buoys in the navigation channel, or sometimes to watch for birds, but it's also useful for checking when visitors arrive."

"So there's an observation post on the other side of that door?"

"A balcony that goes all the way around," said Ibaibarriaga. "But I wouldn't go outside *just* now!"

To make his point, Ibaibarriaga went over to a couple of huge bolts, which looked like the locking mechanisms on a ship's hatch. They gave a rasping squeak as he turned them, and he pulled on the door. A blast of air hit Roberto, and he took a couple of steps back. The roar of the wind was thunderous, and Ibaibarriaga had to shout to make himself heard.

"The wind's much stronger up here, and the storm's already going pretty hard! We'll soon be at eight or nine on the Beaufort scale!"

Roberto didn't know exactly what that was, but there was little doubt it meant "huge storm." It felt like a relief when Ibaibarriaga, pushing with all of his considerable weight, closed the door with a grunt.

"Mystery solved." Ibaibarriaga gave another smile. "Now you know how we knew about your arrival."

"Sure, but not how you know my name."

"Ah!" Ibaibarriaga let out a laugh that echoed around the room. "There's an explanation for that too."

He reached into one of his pockets and took out a battered copy of *The Fleeting Glance*, clearly much thumbed and with lots of dog-eared pages. The lighthouse keeper turned it over to the smiling photo of Roberto on the back.

"See, we already know you well," he said. "Plenty of time to read up here."

Roberto relaxed. He felt like he could breathe again. The events of the previous day had not reached Ibaibarriaga's ears. He was just someone with time on his hands—and a powerful telescope.

"If you want, I'll show you how the light works later." He pointed toward the last flight of stairs. "But I think our food's almost ready. Besides, I want to introduce you to my colleagues."

Taking particular care on the section with the metal steps, they went back down to the entrance hall. The delicious smell of cooking grew stronger as they advanced.

He followed Ibaibarriaga down a hallway on the right. There was a faint electric purring, no more than a light buzz. This reminded him that the lighthouse was the only place on the entire island that had constant power, a luxury he could now fully appreciate after the days he'd spent living by propane lamps and candlelight.

They came eventually to a large, spacious kitchen. A big wooden table stood in the middle, covered with a brightly colored oilcloth. The space was well lit and warmed by a roaring log fire. There was a glimpse of the leaden skies through rain-streaming windows, the panes of which rattled intermittently in the wind. The homey atmosphere enveloped him like an embrace the moment he stepped inside. It was, he thought, the coziest place he'd seen on the island.

A short, squat man stood with his back to them, busily chopping vegetables. His hands moved with astonishing speed as he diced an onion. Hearing them enter, he put the knife down and wiped his hands on a cloth before going over.

"This is Antonio Vázquez," said Ibaibarriaga as Roberto and the man shook hands. "My second-in-command here."

"Please, not Antonio," he said. "My friends call me Varatorta." His timid smile revealed a large gap between his front teeth. "It's a long story."

His black hair was neatly cut and combed across his balding head, and he had a goatee, but his most striking feature was his snub nose. Roberto guessed he was somewhere approaching forty.

"Varatorta is not only a lighthouse keeper but also an excellent cook." Ibaibarriaga clapped him on the back. "He spent years in the kitchens at a restaurant in Cangas before coming here."

"I'm not that good," he said, winking his dark eyes, "but better than them at least."

"It smells wonderful." Roberto's stomach rumbled as if to drive home the obvious—much to his embarrassment. "I haven't had a proper meal in days."

"Well, you'll love this." Varatorta lifted the lid off a pot, sniffed, and let out a grunt of satisfaction. "A few more minutes."

"Why don't you show our visitor around?" said Ibaibarriaga. "I'm sure he'd love to see what life is like here."

"Of course." The cook again gave that gap-toothed grin. "Come on, it's this way."

Roberto followed the lighthouse keeper down a hallway. As they advanced, he could not help but marvel at such an unusual mixture of old architecture and furniture, and state-of-the-art gadgets. As they entered one of the rooms, he exclaimed, "What on earth's that?"

He pointed to what looked like a set of children's play blocks, only giant-sized. It was a unit made up of large plastic cells, emitting a soft hum. In that wood-paneled room, with its nineteenth-century furniture, they looked like cast-off pieces from an alien spacecraft.

"They're the backup batteries." Varatorta rested a hand on the unit. "This used to be the private dining room for the head lighthouse keeper's family, almost a century ago. Now we use it for this: There're over a hundred interconnected batteries, in case of an outage."

"And how are they charged?"

"With the solar panels on the back of the lighthouse," said Varatorta, pointing to the rainy window. "They work a bit better in the summer, obviously."

"Do you need to use them often?"

"Only sometimes, especially if lightning strikes near the lighthouse." Varatorta shrugged. "Sometimes it blows out the transformer."

"Must be a pretty hard life," Roberto said, shaking his head.

"Oh, hardly. We do just fine. You have to be cut from the right sort of cloth, but we also have lots of things to pass the time."

"Oh?"

"Of course! You can go fishing, go out walking, we've got a small vegetable garden . . ."

"And what about days like today?" Roberto said. "It must be like this a lot in the winter."

"Yes, well." Varatorta shrugged resignedly. "It's true; we sometimes get several weeks of this."

Roberto looked out at the rain, wind, and gloom, and shuddered. He could imagine little worse.

"Not my thing," he muttered.

"Hence our secret weapon." Varatorta winked. "Allow me to share it with you."

Roberto duly followed as Varatorta led the way into the next room. He was struck dumb by what he saw.

The room was lined from floor to ceiling with shelves, all completely filled with books. Like any booklover who gets access to someone else's library, Roberto stepped forward and eagerly began running his fingers over the nearest spines, hopping from one title to the next. There was a real mixture of genres and styles, from romance novels to military history, classics to modern bestsellers. Some were very old leather-bound editions, while others had the garish finishes of more recent cover designs.

"We've got more than three thousand books here," Varatorta declared. "It's a joint effort, the work of everyone who has lived and worked here, going back more than a century now. When we finish, we'll leave all these for whoever comes next, and they'll go on adding to it."

Roberto was so absorbed in what he was seeing that he only half listened. He wondered at the stories behind each book, at who might have read them and when.

"You're right, this lot would see you through plenty of storms."

"And that's not all." Varatorta pointed to the far side of the library.

There was a crackling woodburning stove, with a couple of armchairs and a comfortable-looking couch in front of it. Right next to it, a cabinet crammed with DVDs housed an old television.

"Where do I sign up?" said Roberto with a smile. The brief moment of intimacy had allowed him to forget all his pressing problems. "You guys know what you're about."

"This island can be very harsh in the winter—I won't deny it. But it also has a lot to offer, if you look in the right place."

"While we're on the subject," Roberto said with a grimace, "may I ask you a question?"

"Yes, of course." Varatorta gave him a quizzical look. "What's it about?"

"Have you been on the island long?"

"About three years. Why do you ask?"

"I'm sure it's silly but . . . Have you ever heard of someone called Tangaraño?"

Varatorta stared at him, a strange look on his face. He opened his mouth to speak but apparently thought better of it.

"I think whoever it is has some kind of problem with me," Roberto continued quietly. "I'd like to know who it is."

"Not who but what." Varatorta frowned. "Take a look at this."

The lighthouse keeper went over to one of the bookshelves and pulled out a slim, leather-bound book. On its cover, in faded gold lettering, it said *Myths and Legends of the Isle of Ons*.

"This book must be almost a hundred years old," said Varatorta, flipping the pages. "Where was it? Ah, yes!"

He held the book out to Roberto. On the page was an old engraving in black ink. It showed a stooped man, of uncertain age, dressed in a long overcoat and wearing a kind of hat made of braided greenery. Roberto shuddered to see three decapitated bodies at the man's feet.

But most disturbing was the expression on his face. His eyes were wide open but unfocused, shot through with madness and pain. The engraver had captured the moment perfectly, and the more Roberto looked, the more he felt himself drawn into the black pit of insanity that seemed to lie behind that gaze.

"The legend of the Tangaraño arose in the late nineteenth century," Varatorta said in a low voice. "Apparently, a sailor by that name came to believe that his wife and two small children were possessed by the devil. To free them, he drowned them and then chopped off their heads."

The cozy library had suddenly grown quite cold.

"This Tangaraño, either guilt stricken or fearing arrest, committed suicide by throwing himself into the Burato do Inferno, one of the shafts on the western side of the island. That part made the newspapers at the time, so it's taken to be true, and the myth begins from there."

"And what does the myth consist of?" Roberto asked hesitantly.

"Legend has it that Tangaraño's spirit is still trapped on the island because of his terrible deeds." Varatorta read from the book: "'On stormy nights, the spirit of the ill-fated sailor wanders the paths of the lush Isle of Ons, condemned to relive his family's gruesome fate. Any person or animal who has the misfortune to cross his path will meet the same fate as the two innocent children and his wife, all that time ago.'"

"What a horrible story."

"And that's not all." Varatorta turned the page. "'Legend has it that the Tangaraño lingers around people's homes, longing for the human warmth within, so that he can rid himself of his curse and place it on someone else's shoulders. That is what they call . . .'"

"The dead man's kiss," said Roberto, almost in a whisper.

"That's right." Varatorta looked up, surprised. "How did you know?"

Roberto swallowed. He didn't want to be taken for a madman, but he needed to tell someone. He began telling the lighthouse keeper everything that had happened since his arrival on the island, the discovery of the dead rabbit, the severed head on his front step, and his strange encounter with Elvira Couto. However, he said nothing about the money or Víctor Pampín's death.

"So? Think I'm making it all up?"

"Not at all." Varatorta shook his head. "Albert Camus said myths are more powerful than reality. If you want my opinion, someone's messing with you."

"That's what I think too," Roberto said, regaining his composure. "But who, and why?"

"Beats me." Varatorta shrugged, shutting the book. "But remember that curses only have power when the victim believes in them."

*Not a sentiment that Elvira Couto would agree with,* Roberto thought to himself.

"Is that also Camus?"

"No, no, that's Iker Jiménez." Varatorta laughed nonchalantly. "I wouldn't give it much importance. There's no such thing as ghosts, and the same goes for curses."

"True." He felt a little stupid. "Please don't tell anyone. These few days have been . . . quite challenging."

"Don't worry, it can be our little secret." He smiled warmly. "I'm sure that when the storm passes, you'll see everything differently. Nothing like a sunny day to chase away the fears."

"I hope it won't be too long."

"And don't believe a word that old witch Elvira Couto says," Varatorta scolded. "Still less when it comes to some crazy legend from over a hundred years ago. Someone who's seen as much of the world as you have ought to be above all that."

"You're right." Roberto shook his head. "With everything that's been going on, I've lost perspective."

"Absolutely!"

"Sometimes you have to take back control of your life," said Roberto, more to himself than to Varatorta, who he saw was looking at him strangely.

"Well, I see we understand each other."

"Of course we understand each other," Roberto replied, placing a hand on the lighthouse keeper's forearm and giving it a squeeze.

Varatorta looked down at the hand, and then at Roberto again with a peculiar expression. In a split second, it came to Roberto that the man had perhaps misunderstood his touch, and he instantly withdrew his hand, as if burned.

"What I meant to say was . . ."

Just at that moment, the overweight figure of Ibaibarriaga appeared in the doorway.

"What, what's happening?" he said. "Are we eating or what?"

"I was just telling Mr. Lobeira some stories of the island," explained Varatorta, winking at Roberto. "He's getting steeped in the true spirit of Ons."

"Well, enough talk." Ibaibarriaga gave Roberto a couple of fulsome slaps on the back. *"À table!"*

When Roberto sat down at the table, it once more struck him just how ravenous he was.

Just as they were uncorking a bottle of wine, the kitchen door opened, and in walked a figure wearing an oilskin. He pushed back the hood to reveal the face of a young man, no more than twenty-five, with frizzy hair and a haunted look. He gave Roberto a half smile.

"Were you going to start without me?"

"You're late, Pazos," said Ibaibarriaga. "Where have you been?"

"I was in back, securing the solar panels," Pazos replied as he struggled out of his raincoat. "With the wind tonight, they could easily fly off."

The head lighthouse keeper nodded with a grunt.

"Say hello to our guest, Mr. Roberto Lobeira. Roberto, this is Borja Pazos, our assistant."

The young man nodded in greeting, but his attention was more on what Varatorta was placing on the table. And that, Roberto had to admit, was perfectly understandable.

The first course was a tray of scallops that had been lightly browned on the griddle and gave off a delicious aroma of the sea. Next came some cuttlefish on a bed of sautéed vegetables, a platter of tuna loin with what Roberto guessed was homemade kimchi, and to finish, a plate of broad beans with shrimp in a sauce so thick that the spoon was almost standing upright.

They ate in silence, exchanging only a few comments, all food related. The three men were clearly used to one another's company—a gesture was all it took to communicate when they wanted something. Roberto supposed that if he lived cut off from the world in a lighthouse, he'd end up just as monosyllabic.

For his part, he savored every dish that was placed before him. When he didn't have room for another morsel, he leaned back in his chair, as satisfied as if he had eaten at the finest restaurant.

Pazos began to clear the table, and neither of the other two offered to lend a hand. When Roberto got up to help, Ibaibarriaga grabbed his arm.

"Let's go to the library for coffee," he said. "I've got so many questions I want to ask you."

It wasn't Roberto's first encounter with an enthusiastic reader who wanted to take advantage of some time with him. It was part of his job, and, if his host wanted to chat, he was hardly going to refuse, especially after such a feast.

They went back to the library, where the stove was still burning well. In addition to the books, there were all sorts of other items: a glass jar filled with tiny seashells, a bird skeleton, and the shell of an enormous spider crab. Roberto sank into the couch while Ibaibarriaga poured the coffee.

The lighthouse keeper came over with two cups, which looked tiny in his meaty hands. He sat down across from Roberto and fixed him with a hard stare. All his previous cordiality was gone.

"Okay, now that it's just the two of us, you're going to tell me everything that happened yesterday in the village. With no omissions. I want the unvarnished truth—otherwise there will be consequences."

# 17

## A Friendly Chat

For a moment, Roberto was speechless. It wasn't going to be the light-hearted book-related chat he'd expected. The lighthouse keeper, a hard look on his face, was watching him intently.

"I don't know what you're talking about," Roberto said.

"Oh, I think you do."

"I really don't. You'll have to explain a bit more . . ."

"Do I look like an idiot?" spat Ibaibarriaga.

"I beg your pardon?"

"I said, Do I look like an idiot?" Ibaibarriaga spoke slowly and deliberately. "Because I sure don't like being treated like one. I know something's gone down, and I want you to fill me in on all the details."

Roberto didn't like bullies, as Luis Docampo had discovered when the two had first met. And he also didn't like it when people tried to intimidate him.

"What if I don't feel like it?"

Ibaibarriaga shrugged, interlaced his fingers, and cracked his knuckles threateningly.

"This is a dangerous island in the winter," he said blithely, "especially on stormy days like today. Things happen to people, bad things, all the time. And you don't want bad things to happen to you, do you?"

"Are you threatening me?" Roberto got to his feet, his blood rising.

"Sit down, man. I was only joking," said the lighthouse keeper, with an ambiguous expression that was anything but reassuring, while pointing to the couch. "This is just a friendly chat."

"Doesn't seem very friendly to me."

"I'll tell you what I believe went down, and you can tell me if I'm right or not. How about that?"

Roberto stared at him for a moment but eventually sat down again. Although he didn't like the way the conversation was going, it seemed sensible to find out what the man wanted.

"The other day, soon after your arrival on the island, you went down to the village around ten in the morning. You sat on a terrace with Luis Docampo. The two of you talked for a while, and then you went to the beach, am I right?"

Roberto nodded, intrigued. The guy had been watching him through his telescope with all the patience of an entomologist who had just discovered a new species of insect. Still, there were gaps in the story. He'd said nothing about Roberto's encounter with Rosalía Freire and her daughter Helena. The telescope must have some blind spots.

"Somewhere along the way, you met up with the little Freire weirdo, that Diego." Ibaibarriaga paused to take a noisy sip from his coffee cup. "The two of you then walked to the end of the beach, and there was something floating just offshore, and you stripped off, dived in, and went and pulled it out."

Roberto felt the hairs on the back of his neck stand up. This was not sounding good at all.

"It looked like you and the kid didn't have the easiest time of it, but you managed to fish the bundle out in the end." He gave a wolfish smile. "A yellow one, about yea big. All coming back to you now?"

Roberto nodded mechanically. His coffee was getting cold, but he couldn't bring himself to drink it.

"After a while, Helena Freire and Tristán Docampo came to help get the bundle up to the village in a wheelbarrow." He paused briefly, looking pensive. "What was in that bundle, Lobeira? Tell me the truth."

"Just some fishing gear," he replied defensively. "Some lobster pots they wanted back."

Ibaibarriaga chuckled, a mocking look on his face that Roberto didn't like at all.

"This is where it starts to get interesting, because in a matter of minutes, at least a dozen Freires and Docampos came running into the village from all directions, and I'm wondering why. On account of some old pots?"

"You tell me," replied Roberto. "You seem like a pretty accomplished Peeping Tom."

"Well, unfortunately, from here you can't see the stretch of road in front of the church, which is where I assume the get-together happened. Or was it indoors?"

Roberto had to muster all his willpower to hide his feeling of relief. As chance would have it, the impromptu gathering and the opening of the bundle had happened right in one of the telescope's blind spots. That meant Ibaibarriaga wouldn't have seen Diego's attack on Pampín, or the body being carried to the adjacent store.

But the lighthouse keeper was interested in other things, of course.

"I'll tell you what I *think* went down." He gave another grim smile. "None of the day's events happened by chance. Someone tipped you off about whatever it was down in the water. I don't know if it was Docampo over that beer, or the Freire boy later on, and I don't care. You knew the bundle was going to be there, and that's why you went down to the beach. But that's not the most important thing."

"Oh no?"

"No." The man leaned closer and paused dramatically before going on in a knowing whisper. "The thing is . . . I already know what was in the bundle."

They sat staring at each other for a moment. The lighthouse keeper nodded significantly, leaned back again, and slurped a little more coffee. Roberto remained silent while the implications of this revelation flashed through his mind. It changed everything.

If Ibaibarriaga knew about the money, that meant he was in cahoots with its owners or, worse still, that he himself was the owner. Either way, it complicated things even more.

"Look, I didn't know—"

*"Cocaine,"* Ibaibarriaga said with the triumphant look of a poker player laying down a flush.

"What?"

"You heard me. I'm certain that bundle was full of cocaine. It's the only thing that could get all the Freires and Docampos to pounce like hyenas as soon as it came ashore." His grin grew wider. "It's fallen into their laps, and now those greedy bastards want to make some money out of it."

Roberto was dumbfounded and had to make a superhuman effort not to burst out laughing. Ibaibarriaga had been close but in the end clearly hadn't the faintest idea. For all his arrogance, he was miles off.

"Judging by the size of the bundle, I estimate about one hundred pounds, more or less." The man scratched his nose, making mental calculations. "At market price, that's about a million euros, maybe a little over."

"So what's your point?"

"That bunch of morons won't get a decent price for it, a quarter of a million max . . . and that's if they don't get caught red-handed," he said, spreading his palms. "They don't have any contacts, not unless . . ."

"Yes?"

"Unless you're the contact for the sale." He squinted at him. "Are you?"

Roberto laughed, despite himself. "No, no, I'm not their contact."

"Good news—I'm partly wrong, then—you didn't know what was going to be in the bundle." He frowned, clearly unsure on this point.

"Tell you what. I don't know what kind of agreement you and the families have come up with, and I don't care, because we're going to make a little modification. Tell them that one-third of the profit from the sale is mine."

"Wow," Roberto said. "That's quite a cut."

"I know people," Ibaibarriaga said. "I've got contacts on the mainland who can place that cocaine for a lot more than they'll manage to get. Possibly twice as much. It'll be win-win: I get my piece, and they get about the same as they were going to anyway. And you get yours, of course."

"And your colleagues, Varatorta and Pazos?" Roberto gestured to the kitchen. "Won't they want a piece?"

"Borja's like a son to me; he's a good kid; he'll do as I tell him." Ibaibarriaga shrugged. "As for Varatorta, don't worry about him. He has his ways, but I know how to handle him."

Roberto bit his lip. It wasn't great to be taken for a two-bit drug dealer, but that was nothing compared to the man's smugness as he presumed to give him orders.

However, it was hardly in Roberto's interest to disabuse him. As long as Ibaibarriaga thought it was all about a drug deal, with just a few hundred thousand euros up for grabs, it would keep him out of what was really going on. If he learned that tens of millions were in play, the situation could get seriously out of hand. Besides, Roberto was already implicated in a murder, and he didn't need anything new to contend with. So, though burning inside, he managed to compose himself and put on a heavyhearted, docile look.

"I'll talk to the others," he lied, before draining his coffee, now cold. "I don't think it'll be a problem, but I'll need a few days to bring them round. You know how pigheaded they are, and all the rivalry. It'll take some serious diplomacy."

"A couple of days is no problem. Have you seen the forecast?"

Roberto shook his head, and the lighthouse keeper stood up with a snort, going and taking a folder from a desk on which stood a radio transmitter. He pulled out a bundle of freshly printed papers. It was a weather forecast, showing several isobar maps and dozens of columns crammed with numbers.

"They're calling this one Storm Armand," he said. "It's a big one, and it's heading right this way across the Atlantic. It'll be on top of us in the next twenty-four hours. We're talking twenty-to-thirty-foot waves, and hurricane-force winds, seventy miles per hour. Do you know what that means?"

"Bad weather?"

Ibaibarriaga shook his head. "We're going to be completely cut off from the mainland for at least a few days. No boats, no choppers. Until Armand passes, nothing and no one is going to be coming or going on the island." He patted the radio transmitter. "The only comms will be via the cell tower or, if things get genuinely bad, with this."

Roberto stood up. "I'll go talk to them, but you'll need to bear with me."

"You've got until the storm passes," said Ibaibarriaga. "Not a day more. Or else I'll be calling the Guardia Civil. That'll be bad for the families but much worse for you, given how much you've got to lose. I'm sure your readers won't be very pleased to know the kind of trouble you're in. A serious mess."

*You don't know the half of it.*

"You'd better get going." Ibaibarriaga glanced out the window. "Looks like it's eased somewhat, but who knows for how long."

They left the library and started toward the front door. In the hallway, Varatorta and Pazos were busy stacking some heavy boxes.

"Off already, Mr. Lobeira?" Varatorta leaned on one of the boxes, mopped his brow, and held out his hand, clasping Roberto's for a second or two longer than seemed necessary. "It was a pleasure to meet you."

"Yes, I need to get off if I want to avoid getting drenched," said Roberto, attempting his best poker face. "Thanks for the meal."

"You're welcome. Come back soon—if it's all right with the boss, of course. And if you need something to read, feel free to use the library."

“Of course!” Ibaibarriaga said, shaking Roberto’s hand effusively. He was once again the friendly bookworm—all trace of the cold and calculating dealmaker had gone. Roberto almost admired his brazenness. “Thank you so much for honoring us with your presence! As Varatorta says, you’re welcome anytime.”

“The pleasure was all mine.” Roberto held his gaze defiantly.

“Don’t be a stranger!” Ibaibarriaga winked at him, as if sharing some particularly amusing joke. “It’ll be such a delight to see you again.”

Roberto didn’t deign to answer this. Bidding farewell to the other two, he stepped outside. The rain had stopped, but the sky was if anything more leaden. Under the roaring wind, a dull, deep rumbling persisted, the waves pounding on the cliffs—a foretaste of the savage blasts that were going to be unleashed in a few short hours.

He set off almost at a run. The need to talk to Antía Freire had become an absolute priority. There was too much going on—he couldn’t handle it all by himself.

He needed someone to help him with his plan, someone he could trust.

He didn’t know for sure if Antía was the right person, but he didn’t have much choice.

The clock was ticking.

# 18

## A Serious Problem

When Roberto woke the next day, it was immediately clear that all his plans would have to wait. Storm Armand had been unleashed in all its fury, and even the thought of going outside was madness. The windows rattled in the gale, and visibility was virtually nil. The house juddered and creaked as one gust after another assailed it.

He'd had time to think things over but had failed to come up with much. Until he managed to get hold of the hammer that had his fingerprints on it, the blackmailing Docampos would have him right where they wanted him. If Tristán kept his word and delivered it to him, then perhaps he could use the lighthouse keepers' ambitions against them. If he could get them in a fight with the islanders, he'd be left on the sidelines—at least until he managed to get off the accursed island and notify the authorities. But if not, he would have to find another way to evade their clutches.

And then there was the matter of the night marauder going around beheading animals. He found the tale of the vengeful Tangaraño hard to swallow. He didn't believe in ghosts. Or, at least, he didn't think he did. In any case, if it was a flesh-and-bone human, there was still the question of who it was and what they wanted from Roberto.

The alternative . . . ? He felt insane just thinking about it.

There was far too much on his mind, in any case, for him to get any writing done, as he saw to his dismay after struggling to make any headway on the second chapter. There was nothing he could do but let the hours pass until Armand let up. As soon as it slackened off a little, he wrapped up and left the house.

The footpath glistened with all the water that had come down over the preceding hours. The light had shifted, and a faint gloom pervaded everything, a harbinger of the absolute darkness that the stormy night would bring. He checked his watch: It was already past five o'clock, meaning nightfall wasn't far off.

He didn't know if Antía Freire would have accepted his proposal to meet, but there was only one way to find out: He had to go back to the lovers' hideaway to see if anyone had left him a note. If not, he would have to go to El Cucorno and make up some excuse, however implausible, to get a moment with her.

With that decision made, he quickened his pace.

Time was running out.

He'd been walking for some time when he realized something was wrong.

Out of the corner of his eye, he thought he glimpsed a human figure hiding in the thicket on the far side of the path. He stopped for a moment, pretending to tie his bootlaces, and took another discreet glance. Yes, there was definitely someone there.

Making a show of not having noticed, he continued along the path, before stopping just past the next bend. Removing his hood, he took a couple of silent steps in the direction of the ditch, pent-up anger roaring inside his chest. It was the same anger he'd felt when he arrived on the island and confronted Luis Docampo but this time multiplied by a thousand, bubbling up like lava.

He'd had enough. If someone was spying on him, there were going to be consequences—if he caught them off guard, all the better. Maybe it was one of the Docampos, making sure he didn't stray from the cottage and start making trouble. Or it might be one of the lighthouse keepers, monitoring their get-rich ticket. It could even be one of the Freires. Or, he realized irately, it could be the mysterious Tangaraño.

He didn't care. Whoever it was, he'd spotted them, and it was time to find out.

He retraced that stretch of the path, crouching to stay hidden behind the high vegetation. If his stalker broke cover, he'd have a perfect view of them, but if not, he'd soon be face-to-face with them. Either way, the spy would be revealed.

The person was still lurking. All he'd been able to see from the path had been a pair of maroon-colored pants, half hidden behind some dripping bracken. The rest of the figure was covered by the branches of the twisted oak tree beneath which it was sheltering.

Roberto crept through the bracken, trying not to make a noise as he approached the mysterious figure. Perhaps they'd fallen asleep, or been distracted somehow.

But all assumptions melted away as he dashed across the final few feet, squaring up to the figure with a growl . . . and in an instant, his anger evaporated.

Roberto braced against the tree and vomited up every last bit of his lunch.

*The Tangaraño, the Tangaraño, the Tangaraño . . .*

His mind spinning, he was unable to get the horrifying thought out of his head.

What he had taken for maroon-colored pants were actually light-colored jeans, completely soaked in blood. The man—it was a man, that much was clear—had been nailed to the trunk of the oak: two long, rough-looking nails had been driven through his bare chest. There was a vertical slit from below the navel to the sternum, and the guts were hanging out.

But the most terrifying thing was that whoever had committed this heinous crime had expertly decapitated the victim and taken the head away.

Roberto had witnessed many terrible scenes in his past as a war reporter, but this gratuitous display, this rejoicing in the mutilation of a human body, was something he was still unprepared for. It hadn't come about because of an explosion, a gun battle, or some uncontrollable surge of fury. It was the work of someone who, with incomprehensible levels of cruelty, had taken time over the torture.

It was one thing to decapitate a rabbit; quite another to take a human life in such ritual fashion.

*The dead man's kiss,* old Elvira Couto had called it. The curse of the vengeful spirit of a sailor who had been dead for more than a century, as Varatorta had explained.

Real or not, everything had just taken on a totally different dimension. Unconsciously, he gripped the charm the old witch had given him.

He couldn't just stay there. He had to find someone to tell.

Now, as if nature were toying with him, lightning flashed across the sky, followed by a prolonged thunderclap that he felt rumble in his chest. Briefly illuminated, the lifeless body seemed to be trying to move. Deeply shaken, Roberto turned and set off.

He rushed in the direction of the village. He ran headlong, barely breathing, with the mute expression of someone who has looked into the abyss and seen something unimaginable stirring in the darkness. He wanted to get away from that horror as fast as possible. When he reached the crossroads, he saw El Cucorno's brightly lit windows at the top of the hill. He took it as a sign and, gasping for air, started up the slope.

The old manor house, with a huge stone granary on one side, was one of the few buildings on the island that had two stories. All the shutters on the first floor were closed, and they creaked as the gale picked up. The huge double door was painted green, peeling somewhat and in need of varnish. Roberto pounded on it and felt he could barely wait for it to open.

After a few interminable seconds, he heard the slide and rattle of locks and bolts. A Freire man—one of the two whom Pampín had accused of trespassing on his patch—looked at him with bleary, somewhat confused eyes.

"What can I do for you?"

"I need to talk to Antía," he instantly blurted. "It's urgent."

"With Antía?" The man narrowed his eyes. "What about?"

"We don't have time for this," Roberto replied, and, ignoring the man's cry of protest, he barged past him and went in.

The entrance hall had high wooden ceilings, and at the back was an imposing twin staircase leading up to a gallery that overlooked the entire room. The floor was covered with a Persian carpet, beautiful and yet badly frayed and scuffed in places. The general impression was of decline and bygone prosperity.

"Antía!" he shouted from the middle of the hall. *"Antía!"*

A door on the upper floor opened, and there came the sound of footsteps approaching.

"Roberto! What are you doing here?"

Seeing Antía Freire's surprised face, he was overcome with a great wave of relief.

The sensation was short-lived, however, because the compact figure of Rosalía Freire appeared at her side, swathed in a padded robe and with her hair tied back.

"This is no way to enter a house, Mr. Lobeira," said the head of the Freire clan. "May I ask what it is that you want?"

"We have a problem," was his terse reply. He felt so tired, so utterly and completely spent. "A very serious problem."

# 19

## Outstanding Debts

Five minutes later, he was sitting in a small room with a mug of hot soup in his hands while Antía stoked the fire. Sitting by him, Rosalía Freire waited patiently for him to compose himself.

"So," she said, "what is it that's so urgent?"

Roberto placed the mug carefully on the table. "Someone's been murdered," he said.

"We already know that." Rosalía's face hardened, and her lips became a thin line. "But it was an accident. Diego didn't mean to hurt him."

"I'm not talking about Pampín," Roberto said, rubbing his eyes. *God, I'm so tired . . .* "There's another man dead," he went on. "I just came upon the body, not twenty minutes ago, on the path from the cottage."

Antía whimpered with surprise, and Rosalía Freire's expression softened for a moment, giving way to perplexity.

"What are you saying?"

Roberto began to explain how he'd happened upon the decapitated body.

"It's the Tangaraño," muttered the man who'd opened the door and who was now leaning against the mantelpiece. Shaking his head, he crossed himself.

"Don't talk nonsense," Antía spat. "Old wives' tales. There's no such thing."

But Roberto noticed that the slightest doubt had entered her face.

"Do you know who the dead man is? Someone from the island?"

"I don't know everyone on the island," he replied, exasperated. "And besides, his head's been cut off. That makes it kind of hard to tell."

"We have to go and see for ourselves, right now," said the woman. "Come and show us the way."

"Thank you," he muttered. "That's what I needed to hear."

Ten minutes later, a group of them—Roberto, Rosalía, Antía, and two men from the clan who looked so alike that they could only be brothers—were moving swiftly along the winding path back to the cottage. The rain was coming down hard, and they were all wearing oilskins, except for Roberto, whose elegant parka—bought in an exclusive Madrid store and more suited to strolling in fashionable neighborhoods on a Sunday than stepping out in a storm—was letting in water at all points. He was soaked from head to foot, and with every step came an uncomfortable squelch inside his equally unsuitable boots.

When they reached the curve in the path before the body, Roberto stopped and turned to the others.

"I just want to warn you," he said, raising his voice over the gale. "It's not a pretty sight."

"We're no strangers to seeing injuries," Rosalía said sharply. "Someone's always got some wound or another. The island's a pretty harsh place."

Roberto shrugged, feeling no desire to argue. "Don't say I didn't warn you."

When they finally came in sight of the body, Roberto had the small satisfaction of seeing all the blood drain from Rosalía Freire's face. One of the two men went over to one side and vomited, just as Roberto had done before. The other man crossed himself, made a sign with his fingers to ward off the evil eye, and seemed about to speak, but Rosalía silenced him with a hydra-like glare.

"This is . . ." stammered Antía, her eyes wide. "It's hideous. Who could have done such a thing?"

"Have you ever seen anything like it before?" asked Roberto.

Antía just shook her head.

"Are you sure?" he insisted. "No decapitated animals? Severed heads?"

"No, of course not!" she snapped, glaring back at him. "What are you getting at?"

He was silent for a moment, aware that what he said next could change everything completely.

"Your brother, Diego . . ." Roberto hesitated. "He says there's a monster on the island. And I think you know exactly what I mean."

Antía looked dumbfounded.

"Diego has the mental age of a ten-year-old!" she replied, wiping away the water dripping from her hood into her eyes. "He lives in a fantasy world! Half the stuff he comes up with isn't real!"

"Well"—Roberto gestured to the body—"this looks pretty real to me! And the night I arrived, someone left a rabbit's head on my doorstep, and I assure you that was real too. For a fantasy world, it's all disgustingly convincing!"

"It wasn't Diego!" she shouted. "He's been at home with me all day."

"I don't mean to imply that it was him." Roberto squeezed his temples, trying to ward off a growing headache. "But he must know something."

"Oh? What do you think he knows, exactly?"

He was silent for a couple of seconds. Finally, he let out a sigh. "The dead man's kiss," he said. "You know what I'm talking about."

"The dead man's kiss?" Antía shook her head. "That kids' story? It's just some absurd legend, a folktale!"

"Well, someone clearly doesn't think so," he said gloomily, pointing at the corpse. "The question is, who."

Everyone was momentarily lost in thought. The rain was coming down hard. At last, Rosalía Freire went over to the body and started carefully patting the pants. She extracted a battered wallet from one of the back pockets and opened it.

"Fuck!" The curse word took him by surprise. "It's Ricardo Docampo, one of Ramón's nephews."

"We have to tell the family," said Antía in a low voice.

"And although I know you won't like it," said Roberto, "we also have no choice but to notify the authorities. This is getting way out of control."

"That'll be their call," said Rosalía, steadying herself. "After all, he's one of theirs. But there's hardly any point. In this storm, it's going to be quite a few days before anyone can get to the island."

Roberto again looked at the body, and he had to admit that the woman was right. The torrential rain was doing its best to wash away any possible clues or prints that the murderer might have left behind. By the time the Guardia Civil showed up, nothing of any use would be left.

"Antía, Roberto, go tell Ramón Docampo. We'll wait here until you get back. And another thing . . ."

"Yes?"

Rosalía looked from the headless body to the two of them, worry etched in her face. "Be careful on the footpath. Whoever did this might still be out there."

The warning, though unnecessary, did little to raise their spirits. Antía produced a flashlight and shone it on the path. The swirling, relentless rain enveloped them, setting strange figures dancing in the beam.

They set off, walking in silence for a while until she stopped suddenly and gave him a grave look.

"Okay, I need you to explain something," she said. "Why me?"

"What do you mean?"

"You could have gone to the Docampos, or asked for my mother when you came to the house. That would have made sense. But you came in calling my name. Why me?"

Roberto hesitated for a moment. "You're the only person on this island I can trust. The only person who can help me figure out what's going on and solve the situation with the money."

"What makes you think that?"

"First, because you're clever, and I think you've got a good heart. I get the feeling that you actually care about people. Plus, you're not letting yourself get swept up in all the madness."

It all came out at once. The last part he'd let slip with no forethought.

Antía blinked pensively. Then her face relaxed, and she smiled.

"Well, that's the nicest thing anyone's said to me in quite some time," she said, looking down, "but the timing's pretty awful if you're trying to flirt with me."

Roberto felt his face flush. "You're totally right that it's all getting to be too much," he said, changing the subject. "All that money stashed in the church, Pampín's death . . . and now this."

Antía winced at the mention of the poacher's name, and tears sprang to her eyes. "Poor Diego," she sobbed. "He's just a kid! I don't know what we're going to—"

"Listen to me carefully," he said, taking her hands in his. "This is why I had to speak to you alone. There's something you need to know."

And Roberto began.

# 20

## Cards on the Table

Once he started speaking, it was as if a wall inside him had come tumbling down. As he recounted the chain of events since his arrival, he became aware of just how much had happened in the space of only six days. But when he got to the part about Luis Docampo murdering Víctor Pampín in cold blood, Antía's reaction reminded him that he wasn't the only one caught up in it all.

"Oh my God!" She covered her mouth. "But then, that means—"

"Diego didn't kill Pampín," he said, finishing her sentence. "Your brother isn't responsible."

Antía stood there, staring at Roberto wide eyed as she processed the information. She then launched herself into his arms, hugging him so tightly that he was forced to take a step back. He returned her embrace awkwardly as her perfume, mellow and sweet, invaded his senses. When they eventually separated, she looked up at him with glistening eyes.

"It's the best-possible news," she said, wiping away her tears. "You can't imagine the weight you've just taken from my shoulders."

"There's still a murderer in our midst," he said somberly. "Or two, most likely. I don't believe that Luis Docampo's killed one of his own, especially not like this."

"No, of course not." She grimaced. "Do you think this killing has anything to do with the money?"

"That's what I wanted to ask you." He held her gaze. "Could one of your family have had something to do with it, as a way of getting hold of the money?"

"Of course not!" she cried. "They're far from perfect, but none of them would do such a thing, especially without my mother's say-so."

"Then we really have a problem," Roberto mused. "Not only is there the money; someone else on the island is clearly willing to kill, and we currently have zero sense of the motive."

"That's not the worst of it." Antía's voice was bitter. "The money means everyone's on edge. This death, with the beheading . . . it could mean all-out war."

"You can't mean that."

"Just think about it," she said. "Our families have been at each other's throats for so long that no one really remembers how it all started. Every now and then, something comes up to stoke the hatred, but now with this money in the mix . . . it changes everything."

Roberto could see what she meant. There was a long-running feud, but both sides were trapped on the island. It couldn't ever go beyond contempt, harsh words, or unpleasant gestures, because the families shared the same space.

But now, if one of the parties was able to claim the money, it would put them in a position of definitive strength.

They were sitting on a powder keg, and the tiniest spark was all it would take. With the island cut off by the storm, and the atmosphere heightened by the appearance of the money, this cruel murder might be quite sufficient.

"And that's not all," he added.

He then proceeded to tell her about his encounter with the lighthouse keepers and the threat to report them if they didn't hand over a third of the loot.

"Another complication." Antía shook her head. "Please tell me there's nothing else I should know."

Roberto decided against sharing what he knew of the tryst between Helena Freire and Tristán Docampo. Not only had he promised the lovers he'd keep it a secret, but he also doubted very much that the revelation would be to anyone's advantage in that particular moment—just more wood for the fire.

"No, that's all," he said. "But we've got to be careful how we break this to the Docampos."

Coming to the village, the rain coming down hard, they turned onto the dirt path that led to the Docampos' house, their boots saturated.

The Docampo home was just as large as the Freires', but by contrast it was a relatively new construction, painted ochre yellow and with aluminum-framed windows. Antía, sheltering on the porch, knocked on the door and waited.

The door opened, and Amaia, Luis Docampo's wife, stood on the threshold. She eyed them suspiciously. If she was surprised to see the pair together, she didn't say as much.

"What do you want?" she spat.

"I need to talk to Ramón, Amaia," Antía replied calmly. "It's urgent."

The woman gave them another suspicious look but nodded, and, without asking them in, shut the door. A short while later, the door opened again, and the head of the Docampo clan stood before them.

"Antía," he grunted, and his gaze shifted to Roberto. "Lobeira. Well, what is it? Something happened with the money?"

"No, it's not about that," said Roberto. "It's better if she explains."

He had to admit, Ramón kept very cool as Antía quietly delivered the news. He paled slightly when she handed over the blood-soaked wallet, but managed to contain himself. Only the white of his knuckles betrayed the emotions presumably raging inside him.

"Wait here," was all he said before the door closed in their faces for a second time.

Roberto and Antía stood sheltering on the porch, not quite knowing what to do next. From inside the house came a muffled female scream, but nothing more. After a moment, the door opened again, and a large group of Docampos rushed out, led by Luis.

As he passed by, he looked resentfully at Antía. "If you had anything to do with this," Luis hissed, "my cousin's blood won't be the last that's spilled on the island tonight. That's a promise."

"It wasn't us," she said, trying to stay calm.

"Oh no?" Luis brought his livid face close to Antía's. "Who did it, then, huh?"

"Luis, that's enough," Ramón's steely voice cut in, giving Antía no chance to reply. "Go get our boy and bring him home."

"This isn't the last you'll hear of this," growled Luis, casting a final, hate-filled look at Antía before moving off.

Only then did Roberto notice that Luis had a hatchet hanging from his belt, and he wasn't the only one. A shiver ran through him. It wasn't the first time he'd seen something like this, and he knew from experience how it usually ended when things began to spiral and people took justice into their own hands.

"Antía, go back home," he whispered, squeezing her arm. "And call your mother. Tell everyone else to stay inside. If they run into the Docampos, it could get ugly."

"But what about you? What are you going to do?"

"I don't know. Take shelter somewhere, I guess."

"Why don't you come with me?" she suddenly suggested. "Better than being all alone in that cottage—"

"Lobeira, I need to talk to you," came a gruff voice from behind him. "Right now."

Roberto turned to find Ramón Docampo glaring at them. He had no way of knowing if he'd heard their exchange, but he couldn't snub the man without the risk of making things worse.

He exchanged a look of mute understanding with Antía before separating from her.

"Take care," she whispered, turning to leave.

"You too," he said, watching her slip away into the night. A feeling of dread came over him.

"Come on, then," snorted Ramón Docampo, pointing inside.

Roberto stepped uncertainly into the house.

# 21

## The Deep Roots of Hatred

Closing the door behind him, Roberto was surprised by the almost sepulchral silence that confronted them. Other people might have been at home, but the sensation at least was that Ramón Docampo and he were completely alone.

"Let's go up to my study." The man began climbing the stairs without looking back. "We've got a lot to discuss."

Roberto followed him to a room in one of the wings. It was a small, tastefully decorated study. Old lithographs of sailing ships hung on the walls, and there were burnished brass navigation instruments dotted around, their surfaces reflecting the dying embers in the fireplace. Heavy curtains covered the only window, and a cluttered desk was flanked by a pair of metal filing cabinets.

Ramón pointed him to the armchairs by the fire, between which stood a coffee table. Just as Roberto was about to sit down, the chandelier above them flickered and went out.

"The storm must have overloaded the generator," the old man muttered as darkness descended. "Just a moment."

Roberto heard the scrape of a drawer, followed by some rummaging. Ramón Docampo struck a match, and his face was momentarily lit in the darkness. Then, to the gentle hiss of a kerosene lamp, the whole room was bathed in amber light.

Ramón placed the lamp on the coffee table and went over to a bar cabinet in the corner. There was a chinking as he returned to the fireside with a couple of glasses and a bottle of Hankey Bannister.

"Okay," said Ramón, groaning softly as he sat down. "Now, I want you to tell me what happened. The detailed version."

"You already heard it from Antía," Roberto said cautiously. "There isn't much to add."

"Antía's a good girl," Ramón said as he poured two fingers of whiskey into each glass. "I've known her since she was a child, I've watched her grow up. I think she's the best in generations of Freires but . . . she's still a Freire. I'm sure you'll understand why I want a version of events from a more neutral party."

Roberto nodded and took a sip of his whiskey. It was lukewarm and could have done with a couple of ice cubes, but he guessed such luxury wasn't for now. He felt the liquor lining his throat and then hitting his stomach in a warm, comforting explosion.

For the second time that evening, he told how he had come upon the man's body and the state it was in. He also mentioned the macabre gift of the rabbit's head on the day of his arrival and Elvira Couto's story.

When Roberto finished, Ramón Docampo was on to his second glass and was watching him inscrutably.

"So, according to you, there's a monster loose on the island," Ramón said, speaking the words slowly. "Something out of legend, controlled by some curse, that's now gone and killed one of my family."

"I'm not saying that," Roberto protested. "I don't think anything supernatural's at work, but I do think that someone, taking advantage of the legend, has been going around killing animals, and for a long time. The rabbit the other day, your son's chickens, and lots of others besides. And now, for some reason, it's gone up a notch, and this person has started killing people."

"That's what *you* think." He leaned over the coffee table and tapped his nose a couple of times. "And you'll agree that it doesn't make much sense. Or that, if it is true, it's quite the coincidence that it's all started just now, when there are seventy-five million euros stuffed in a couple of bags behind the church altar. No?"

Roberto faltered. He had given only the outline of a theory, with all sorts of loose ends.

"I'm certain the Freires had nothing to do with it," he said. "I saw their faces when I took them to the body. They were as shocked as I was."

Ramón Docampo gave a grim chuckle, shaking his head, and took another sip. "That's because you don't know the Freires like I do," he replied. "You don't know how treacherous those people can be. The ambition that drives them. What they're capable of."

"Killing an innocent man with a hammer to the head, like your son did?" spat Roberto, unable to contain himself. "Like that?"

For a moment, Ramón said nothing, and the fear flashed through Roberto's mind that the old man hadn't known of Luis's crime. But then, a sad smile appeared on the patriarch's face.

"I know what my son did," he said simply. "Needs must."

"Needs must? Have you lost your mind?"

"If Pampín had survived, the authorities would have been called in. The money would have gone with them, and, what's worse, the rightful owners wouldn't have believed a word we said when they came calling for it later on." He struck another match and lit a cigar. "I know you won't understand, but Pampín's being dead is the best thing for us, for the Freires . . . and for you too."

Roberto tried to get his head around the man's twisted logic.

"Life on this island isn't easy." He exhaled a cloud of smoke. "Never has been. Let me tell you a story."

A clap of thunder rattled the windows, and the lamplight flickered. Roberto, feeling uneasy, took another sip from his glass.

"Ons hasn't always been inhabited," Ramón Docampo began, his tone teacherly. "Over the centuries, various people have lived here, and they all ended up leaving the island, for one reason or another. Sometimes it was an epidemic, sometimes on account of war or famine, sometimes pirates coming to plunder. It seems like a paradise to people now, but the location has always put it at the mercy of events in difficult times . . . and believe me, things have often been difficult here."

*You don't say*. Roberto thought of all he'd been through over the previous days, though he chose to keep it to himself.

"About two hundred years ago, the last attempt to colonize Ons happened," Docampo went on. "That was when the ancestors of both the Docampos and the Freires first arrived, as well as the forebears of everyone else currently resident here."

"Where's this heading?"

"Patience." He took another puff on his cigar. "Those settlers spent decades trying to make a life for themselves here. They cleared land, plowed fields, battled with the poor soil and all the storms—just like this one now—with pretty meager harvests their only reward."

Roberto remembered the weed-choked ruins he'd glimpsed on his walks over the previous few days.

"Nothing they did was enough, and the little they got from the land had to be supplemented by what they could get from the sea." He waved his hand vaguely. "They had to have detailed knowledge of the currents and the winds, and, even so, lives were often lost. But they managed to survive, although it was hardly what you could call the good life."

"*Some* didn't do so badly." Roberto gestured to the room around them.

"That's true, but you're jumping ahead." Ramón Docampo gave a half smile.

Roberto took a deep breath. The powder keg was going to blow at any moment, and the old man wanted to sit around telling stories.

"As I was saying, life on the island was hard, and the settlers had no choice but to work together." He interlaced the fingers of his two hands to illustrate the idea. "Unity is strength, and all that."

"Were the Freires and the Docampos at each other's throats back then?"

"Not at all. In the beginning, the ties were very close. I'm sure if we went through the old parish book, we'd find dozens of marriages between our two families over the years, just as between many other families." A sly smile appeared on his face. "Our blood's so mixed that it's only the surnames that differentiate us."

"So . . . what happened?"

Ramón Docampo shrugged. "Who knows? When you're barely managing to subsist, sometimes little things can lead to big disagreements. A farm boundary, a boat that needs repairing, a stray cow . . . only small things. But they build up and one day explode."

"In other words, you don't actually know how the conflict started."

"I wouldn't go that far," Ramón Docampo said. "Relations weren't fantastic, but then something happened that really kicked things up a notch."

"Okay, when was that?"

Ramón Docampo's cigar had gone out, and he paused to light it again. He puffed on it a few times, enveloping himself in a bluish smoke, until, satisfied, he resumed his story.

"May 15, 1945. Does that date mean anything to you?"

It rang a bell for Roberto, but much as he tried, he couldn't see a link and just shook his head.

"World War Two had ended one week before," Ramón Docampo explained. "The Russians were strolling around the ruins of the Reichstag, the Germans had surrendered unconditionally, and the Allied victory was being celebrated right across Europe."

"That was all a long time ago, and a long way from here. I don't see the connection."

"At that time, my father, Severino Docampo, was just one more man trying to eke a living from the island, like everyone else, including Orlando Freire, Rosalía's father." Ramón Docampo's mouth twisted contemptuously. "Orlando! As you can see, the Freires have a liking for pompous names. Well, that morning, my father and Orlando were fishing in the strait between the main island and Onza, the islet out there."

Roberto nodded, recalling the inaccessible-looking crag he'd seen to the south of the main island.

"According to my father, at about eleven o'clock in the morning, when they had just pulled in the nets, they saw bubbles coming to the surface between the two boats, which were a couple of hundred feet apart. At first, they thought it might be a whale surfacing, but then they found out."

"What was it?" Ramón's telling had turned more evocative, and the tale had Roberto in its grip now.

"A metal tower emerged from the water, followed by a long, dark metal tube. Imagine the shock of those two poor islanders when suddenly, right in front of them, a German U-boat appeared."

Roberto could not help but let out an exclamation. He suddenly pictured the iconic image of a German U-boat, one of those lone wolves responsible for sinking so many ships during the war. "Are you sure? What was a German submarine doing here?"

"During the war, or much of it at least, the port of Vigo was one of their reprovisioning bases," Ramón Docampo explained. "Throughout the war, they'd seen them pass by the island, often in the middle of the night, on their way to refuel and restock. But by the end of the war, that safe harbor no longer existed."

"So what happened?"

"According to my father, the sub was in bad shape. The tower was full of holes, and there was a big dent on one side, like it had been kicked by a giant. When they rowed over, they saw that it was leaking oil."

Roberto nodded pensively. In the closing stages of the war, the Allied pressure on the few remaining German-controlled ports had been ferocious. Ramón's description perfectly fit a submarine that had narrowly survived a depth charge. To have made it as far as the Rías Baixas was a feat in itself.

Ramón took another puff on his cigar. "One of the officers spoke a bit of Spanish, and he told my father and Orlando Freire that they were aiming for Argentina. While the three of them were talking, a group of men came out on deck for some air. They had different uniforms from all the rest. Apparently, they had skulls embroidered on their collars. Know what that means?"

Roberto swallowed hard. The so-called "ratlines" that had operated toward the end of the war were escape routes used by large numbers of senior Nazi officers to get to South America and thereby evade justice. There were dozens of known cases but not many firsthand accounts, and here was this man suddenly offering up a description of one such escape.

"They were short of everything." Ramón tapped the cigar in the ashtray. "Medicines, food, and especially fuel. There would be no crossing the Atlantic without that."

"And they requested it from your father and Orlando."

"They didn't request it." He shook his head. "They wanted to buy it. They gave them each a one-hundred-gram gold bar to ensure their silence, and promised them much more if they could get them what they needed."

"And did they?"

"Of course not!" laughed Ramón. "My father and Orlando Freire were poor as anything, and they lived on a remote island. Where were they going to get medicines, supplies, or thousands of gallons of fuel? This was Spain after the civil war we're talking about. Everything was thin on the ground."

"I see. And I guess they didn't notify the authorities either."

"The authorities would just have confiscated the gold and thrown them in jail."

"So they kept it a secret and didn't tell anyone."

"Well, they did a bit more than that." Ramón stubbed out the cigar now, crushing it in the bowl of the ashtray with three dabs of the wrist. "They came up with a plan to get their hands on the rest of the gold that was in that submarine."

"They what?"

"It was a perfect chance to escape a life of poverty." Ramón leaned back in his armchair. "They were tough men, accustomed to hardship, but they were also used to seizing chances when they came along. And this, without any doubt, was the best opportunity they'd ever had in their lives."

"Wait a moment," said Roberto. "Are you telling me that your father and Rosalía Freire's father stole gold from a bunch of fleeing Nazis?"

"Even better than that."

"Go on . . ."

"It's very simple," he said. "They took them all out."

# 22

## The Cell Tower

For a long time, the only thing to break the silence was the roaring of the storm outside and the rattling of the window as it was buffeted by the wind. Roberto looked at Ramón Docampo agog, simply unable to believe his ears.

"What do you mean, took them all out?" he eventually managed to say. "You're kidding, surely."

"It was the only way." Ramón shrugged. "As I said, those were hard times."

"How did they do it? It was two men against a whole crew, plus whoever else was on board. It wouldn't have been easy."

"On the contrary. Later that day, Orlando and my father crossed to the south of the islet, where the submarine was waiting for them. They took the largest cooking pot they'd been able to get their hands on, full of fish stew, freshly made."

"They brought them a meal . . ."

"Seasoned with a whole packet of strychnine, the stuff used in rat poison."

"They poisoned them!" Roberto was wide eyed. "But that's . . . awful!"

"Oh, hardly," Ramón said, quite blithely. "Think about it. Most of the passengers on that sub were war criminals; it isn't as if they didn't deserve it. They must have racked up goodness knows how many deaths among them. As for the crew, well . . . it was war; death was part and parcel. Just a few more for the grim reaper's tally."

"Even so, it's abhorrent," protested Roberto. "How could they just take the law into their own hands, and decide to keep the gold too?"

Ramón's low, monotone laugh made the hairs stand up on the back of Roberto's neck.

"You're still thinking like a mainlander," he said. "Authorities, processes, rules. I thought you'd have got it by now: Things work differently here."

Roberto finished his drink in one gulp. His head was buzzing, and the air in the study had become unbreathable.

"My father and Orlando Freire waited an hour and then boarded the sub," said Ramón, pouring himself another drink. "They stepped in through the hatch and found everybody dead. It smelled like shit, sweat, and engine oil in there. So now they had to find the gold, of course."

"And then?" Roberto felt as if his own voice were coming from some faraway place. For all his experience reporting on wars around the world, a dispassionate account of a cold-blooded mass murder still turned his stomach.

"That was when things went wrong." Ramón frowned. "My father and Orlando Freire had agreed to split the gold right down the middle. It was both families' ticket off the island, the chance to start a new life on the mainland, a future for both men's children."

"Let me guess: no gold."

"Oh, there was gold." Ramón nodded sadly. "But much less than they'd imagined, just a couple of pounds. There was a chest full of reichsmarks, too, but those were worth about as much as toilet paper by then. Basically, the bastards had been out to cheat them."

"And your father and Orlando Freire fought over what little there was, I suppose."

Ramón shook his head, clearly annoyed at such a suggestion. "My father was a good, trusting man," he said. "They agreed that Orlando would take the gold to the mainland for safekeeping while my father sank the sub. So they loaded the gold into Orlando's boat, and as he sailed away, my father set about looking for the flood faucets. Do you know what those are?"

Roberto shook his head.

"All different kinds of vessels have them—they're to let seawater in, in case of a fire on board. It took him a while, but eventually he found them. The submarine started to go down so fast that he almost got trapped inside. He at least had time to grab a souvenir . . ."

Ramón pointed to an object on the desk's polished top. Roberto had taken it for an old typewriter when he first came in, and only now did he realize what it was. He whistled. It was an Enigma machine, no less, the cipher device carried by all German submarines for encrypted communications. As far as he knew, there were hardly any left in the whole world, and here was one right in front of him now.

"Okay. And then what happened?"

"When he got back to the island, it was already dark." Ramón's voice was tinged with anger. "The next morning, Orlando Freire had disappeared. My father waited patiently for a week, until Orlando got back from the mainland. He was wearing an elegant suit, and his boat was loaded with food, clothes, and toys for the children."

"He'd taken the gold," said Roberto.

"He'd sold it and deposited the money he got for it in a bank," hissed Ramón. "And when my father asked for his share, he just laughed in his face."

"No honor among thieves," muttered Roberto.

"He hadn't just robbed him! He'd laughed at him, disrespected him!"

Here he sounded particularly bitter. Roberto now saw that the families' grudges had far deeper roots than he'd imagined—roots based on insults to honor, guilt, and the spirit of revenge.

"There's something I don't understand," he said. "Why didn't the Freires leave the island if they had all the money?"

"Because Orlando was a half-illiterate peasant and sold the gold for a fraction of its real value," Ramón muttered. "But it was still enough for them to build a house with, and over the following years, his family outshone all the others, ours included. And throughout all that time, until the devil took him to his grave, that bastard Orlando never stopped looking down his nose at us. My father died a bitter alcoholic, all because of him."

"I've been to the Freire house." Roberto recalled the air of the decay there, the old, moth-eaten furniture, the sense of imminent poverty lurking in every corner. "If they had money once, they certainly don't nowadays."

"No, nowadays they make a pittance renting out properties to vacationers." Ramón gave a spiteful laugh. "Houses that aren't even theirs but belong to islanders who have been gradually emigrating over time. At least we get that satisfaction."

"And the Docampos?" Roberto patted the elegant armchair he was sitting in. "Your family hasn't done so badly."

Ramón sighed. "An opportunity arose in the 1980s. Around the time of the tobacco-smuggling boom, post-Franco. We'd switched out the old sailing and rowboats for motorboats by then—the fast and furious kind. And nobody knew these reaches of the estuary like we did . . ."

"Did the Docampos get into smuggling?"

"Half the contraband tobacco that entered Galicia was carried on one of our boats." The old man puffed up with pride. "We didn't make that much, but a lot more than we did from fishing. That was when things started looking up for us. Then the smugglers worked out that you could make a hell of a lot more by moving drugs, and I saw that it was time to take a step back."

"You never smuggled drugs?"

"Never," said Ramón vehemently. "Too dirty, too dangerous. It was a good decision, even if not everyone understood it. But now it's been too long."

"Let me guess," said Roberto. "The money you built up then is also running out."

"Indeed. But there were years when we were the Freires' equals. What happened after isn't our fault."

Something in his tone made Roberto distinctly uneasy. "After?"

"When we pulled out of the smuggling business, Antía's father went to the drug smugglers and said the Freires would happily take our place." A baleful smile flashed across his face. "By then they were pretty broke and desperate."

"What happened?"

"One moonless night, trying to get away from the Guardia Civil, he crashed his speedboat into a boat moored out in the middle of the estuary," Docampo spat. "He died on the spot. The Freires blame us; they think we ratted him out."

Another piece of the complex puzzle of island relationships fell into place. The roots of mutual resentment spread like a weed that could clearly never, ever be pulled up.

"Just to be clear." He leaned over to Ramón. "Why are you telling me all this? Don't you realize you've just confessed quite a number of crimes to me?"

Docampo rubbed his chin, eyeing Roberto. "Everything I've told you is ancient history," he said. "It all happened a long, long time ago, and the only one still standing from the smuggling days is me. I don't mean to brag, if that's what you're imagining. No, what I want is something else."

"What?"

"That you understand what's about to go down," he said darkly. "And make the right call."

The ball of ice in Roberto's stomach grew a little heavier.

"I hope you don't mean what I think you mean." He shook his head. "That's crazy."

"The other day, when you pulled that bundle out of the water, I saw that all my prayers had been answered." A coldness had entered Ramón's tone. "Fortune had finally smiled on us, and the ticket off this island was being offered on a platter. And not only that, but also the chance for revenge on the Freire family."

"Revenge? For something that happened eighty years ago?"

"To right an injustice," he replied. "You're rich, so maybe you don't get it, but that money will change lives. Our lives."

"You want to keep all the money?" The words caught in his mouth. "Go back on your agreement with the Freires?"

"Live by the sword, die by the sword," Ramón replied. "Decades ago, the Freires reneged on an agreement. Now we've got a chance to collect the debt. If we don't act, they'll only do it again."

"What are you talking about?"

"Open your eyes!" Ramón smashed his fist down on the coffee table, causing the glasses to jump. "Right now, my boys are out there retrieving the mangled body of one of my kin! It was the Freires. They're trying to play us—again! But not this time! Do you hear me? Not this time!"

Roberto looked at him, feeling helpless and overwhelmed. He was sure that Ricardo Docampo's death had nothing to do with the Freires, nor with the money in the church, nor the deep-seated family feud. It was just too gory, too sadistic. It didn't fit.

There was another force at play on the island. But he could see there would be no way to bring Ramón around. The man's every word was freighted with paranoia, fueled by years of rancor and distrust. He was convinced that the Freire family intended to annihilate his own in order to keep the money for themselves, and there seemed nothing he wouldn't do to stop them.

He thought he was about to throw up. He saw the bloodbath that was coming and, like someone on a mad roller coaster, felt like a powerless observer, swept along by events.

"What you're saying is insanity," he said desperately. "When the storm passes, the authorities will get here, and the moment they find out what's happened, you'll be done for. The Docampos won't get the money, only jail, only more pain."

"Nothing of the sort." Ramón reached over and closed his hand tightly around Roberto's wrist. "Because you're going to stop that from happening."

"Me? How?"

"You're Roberto Lobeira, well-known journalist, bestselling author." Again, there was that icy smile that made Roberto's hair stand on end. "When the Guardia Civil show up, you're going to tell them that the Freires took the money, without our knowing anything about it. Later, the narcos whom it belongs to will come, and they'll take them out, every last one, to get back what's theirs. We'll save our skins by just keeping out of the way. They'll believe you. You don't have any ties to either family. You're the perfect witness."

"I'll do no such thing," said Roberto stubbornly.

"Oh, but you will," Ramón said simply. "Sometimes we have to do the right thing, even if we don't want to. And this is the right thing to do, especially for you."

"I don't see what's right about making myself an accessory to a crime!"

"You've already been through this with my son, if I'm not mistaken." Ramón's smile widened. "Something about a hammer covered in fingerprints, if I remember right."

Roberto held his gaze.

"Listen, Lobeira," he said, his tone more conciliatory. "I'm giving you the chance to be on the winning team. Accept my proposal, and I promise a couple million will go to you, as compensation for your trouble. Refuse, and I swear to God you'll be coming down with us."

There was a determination in his voice that seemed maniacal. Roberto saw in his eyes that he was absolutely resolved, and nothing Roberto could say was going to change his mind.

"You're crazy," he retorted. "Totally insane."

"Sanity is usually associated with making the right decisions." Ramón stood up, indicating that they were just about done. "Do the right thing, for your own sake."

Ramón held his hand out across the table for Roberto to shake. Roberto stared at it for a long time but refused the offer. The old man sighed and lowered his hand, ignoring the snub.

"Go back to your little cottage," he said. "Lock yourself in and don't come out, whatever you hear. Before the storm passes, this will all be done, one way or another."

Ramón went over to the desk and rang a bell. The door opened, and Amaia, Luis Docampo's wife, appeared—so quickly that Roberto suspected she had been eavesdropping on the whole conversation.

"Mr. Lobeira is leaving," he said gently. "See him out, please."

Roberto descended the stairs in a state of total confusion, ideas buzzing in his head like a swarm of angry bees. The enormity of what was about to unfold was more than he could even think about. Just when he'd thought he might take a measure of control, there was this new twist.

He caught sight of a spacious kitchen through an open doorway. Around the table, several of the Docampos were busy cleaning some old shotguns. Dozens of red cartridges, with their brass heads, were set out in rows alongside the gleaming guns. The stony-faced men and women, deeply absorbed in the task, did not so much as notice him passing.

Amaia Docampo saw him to the door, and he stepped out into torrential rain once more. The wind was so strong that it was a struggle just to stay on his feet. A bolt of lightning streaked across the sky, as if a ghostly photograph were being taken of the island, as if some bloodthirsty god wanted a memento of Ons just before the madness unfolded.

Roberto let out a groan that was a mixture of horror, despair, and impotence.

He couldn't have the deaths of any more innocent people weighing on his conscience. He just couldn't.

*You know it's the right thing to do. Do it.*

He took out his phone. He knew that once he made that call, his life would become a nightmare. Nothing would ever be the same. He would have to answer for Pampín's death, even if he wasn't the killer. His life, his career, it was all going to be totally and utterly ruined.

But he had no option. *Sometimes we have to do the right thing,* Ramón had said, *even if we don't want to.* Roberto smiled sadly at the irony of it. He was going to take the old man's advice but not as intended.

With trembling fingers, he called the emergency number for the Guardia Civil. It rang a couple of times; then there was a click at the other end of the line.

"Guardia Civil, Bueu Station," said a voice. "How can I help you?"

"Hi. Well, you see . . ."

Another, particularly intense, bluish flash of lightning streaked across the sky. And just before the thunderclap, Roberto was rocked by a huge explosion. He looked around in confusion, and a cry of helplessness caught in his throat.

"No!"

At the top of the hill, the cell tower had been struck by lightning. He watched as it collapsed before his eyes and was engulfed in flames.

# 23

## Erundina

Everything seemed to be happening in slow motion, or at least so it felt to Roberto as he stared at the collapsing cell tower. All he could do was gape at the flaming wreckage at the top of the hill as he tried to process what had just happened.

He realized he still had the phone clasped tightly in his hand. He shook his head like a wet dog, trying to clear his mind.

"Hello? Can you hear me?" he shouted into the device. "Is anyone there?"

But there was no answer, and although he walked about holding the phone up in the air, he couldn't get a single bar of signal.

The storm hadn't just made the island inaccessible by sea and air; all communications were now impossible too.

He put the phone away—it was little more than an expensive paperweight now—and rubbed his eyes.

*Think, Roberto. Think.*

The chances were pathetically slim. Outside assistance was out of the question. It was up to him and him alone to save the situation. Unless the Freires could be convinced to lend him a hand.

But to achieve that, he needed some kind of winning card to play. Something that would leave them no choice but to come in with him, whatever it was that he decided to do.

As he rubbed his aching neck, his fingers caught in the little chain on which the church key hung. At that moment, a realization struck him with blinding clarity. He broke into a run as a plan took shape in his head. There were a thousand things that could go wrong and a thousand things beyond his control. It wasn't much of a plan, but it was better than just doing nothing.

Coming to some buildings, he moved along, hugging the walls, advancing from one pool of darkness to the next in the gloom of the night. He dared not turn on his flashlight for fear of alerting someone to his presence. Instead, he moved forward, stumbling and cursing, praying not to catch his foot and fall.

At last, he found smooth cement underfoot, and the walking became easier. Now it was just a question of heading down to the village, which shouldn't be too hard. He only had to follow the slope down toward the shore.

Before he knew it, he was in the village, which in the summer would be so vibrant but now was as dark and silent as a tomb. Feeling his way along a wall, he mentally counted the steps and then ventured across the street, feeling absurdly exposed. He stumbled when his feet met the steps of the church.

He felt about on the door until he found the lock. He took the key from the chain around his neck and inserted it, entering the church and closing the door with some relief.

A dim light came from a few votive candles by the altar. A gentle stream of air coming in through a slightly open window shook the wicks, making everything quiver strangely, like in an old movie. As he'd expected, there wasn't a soul inside.

He went around the altar, passing by some wood carvings adorning the walls and a pile of religious banners folded neatly in a corner.

And there, at the foot of the altar, were the two sturdy duffel bags.

Roberto undid the zippers. By candlelight, the wads of euros, dollars, and Swiss francs lay silently, oblivious to the madness raging outside. Benjamin Franklin looked out at him from one of the bills, with that ambiguous expression reminiscent of the *Mona Lisa*'s, like a friend who's in on a joke.

With a couple of tugs, he closed the zippers and slung a bag over each shoulder. They were extremely heavy, and he grunted as the straps dug into his shoulders. Haltingly, he went back down the aisle, opened the door, and peered cautiously outside.

There was nobody around, or at least he could see no lights moving in the vicinity.

Taking a deep breath, he went out and locked the door behind him. The first part of the plan had gone perfectly. Everything was going well . . . for now.

Carrying the bags proved far more difficult than anticipated. He was soon panting under the extra weight, and every time one of his feet came to a treacherous puddle, he staggered and almost fell. He was also moving in complete darkness, and a couple of times, realizing he'd gone off course, he had to retrace his steps.

Only when he felt he'd gone a safe distance from the village did he turn on his cell phone flashlight.

He was able to move faster now that he could see a little, although he had to stop every now and then to catch his breath.

When he came to the sign for the old church, he breathed a sigh of relief. Making one final push, he negotiated the narrow, fern-choked path, until at last he was at the graveyard.

In other circumstances, he would have been genuinely scared at the thought of entering a lonely graveyard in the depths of night. But just then, it barely registered. He had more pressing problems.

Initially he had planned to hide the bags in one of the planters positioned along the top of the high graveyard walls, but he soon saw that wouldn't work. The actual greenery in the planters was minimal, given that it was winter, and so the bags would be easy to spot.

The ongoing rain had also turned the channels along the edges of the planters into small rivers. The bags were waterproof, but he didn't know if they would withstand prolonged immersion.

He dropped the bags to the ground, feeling his strength ebbing, and leaned against the wall. His eyes wandered across the graveyard, when suddenly he had an idea.

Setting off again, he moved forward between the tombs, looking for one with neither fresh flowers nor signs of having recently been tended. At the far end, by the back wall, he found just what he was looking for.

It was an old grave, moss covered and apparently untended. The lettering on the headstone, though faint, announced that one Erundina Quintáns lay there, having passed away at the age of ninety-five—something of a record in that graveyard. But the best part was the date: She had died in 1924.

It was perfect. He got down on his knees and dug his fingers into the earth, searching for the edge of the tombstone. It was not especially thick, chipped all over and missing one whole corner.

He stood up and looked around with the cell phone flashlight. He was delighted to find a broken branch, torn off in the wind, lying a short distance away. Ignoring splinters, he set about hastily yanking off leaves and twigs, until he was left with a fairly straight stake about six feet long. It was not the most sophisticated tool in the world, but it would have to do. With that improvised lever in his hands, he went back to Erundina's grave, jammed one end under the corner of the tombstone, and brought his whole weight down on the other end.

The branch creaked alarmingly, and for a moment he thought it would snap, but the wood, still green, flexed a little. He brought his weight down again, and this time, with a creak, the stone slab lifted up an inch or two.

Roberto felt his energy flooding back. Little by little, using the lever, he managed to get the tombstone off, until the deep hole below was revealed. He clambered down inside.

Time, the damp climate, and insects had combined to do away with the coffin, as well as the flesh of the woman buried there. A little over six feet down, all that remained were a few yellowish bones mixed together with scraps of half-rotted cloth, bits of wood that crumbled at his touch, and a few rusty nails. At the top, the skull of the grave's occupant stared up at him from empty sockets, with a laugh frozen for all eternity.

"I'm so sorry, Erundina," he whispered, feeling like some grave robber in Victorian London. "It's an emergency. I hope you understand."

Clambering out again, he dragged the duffel bags over and dropped them inside. With clenched jaw, he heaved the tombstone back into position. The old mortar had cracked, making it far more maneuverable.

Standing up, he cast a critical eye over his work. He pulled a couple of strips of moss from the wall and laid them along the edges of the grave, in the spots where he'd jammed the lever underneath. To finish, he scattered a few sticks over the top, until the grave looked just as untended as before.

Of course, it wouldn't pass a thorough inspection, but he doubted anyone was going to be checking the condition of the graves anytime soon.

His plan was coming along. Now he was the only one who knew where the money was. If the islanders wanted to get their hands on it, they would have to accept his conditions and help him avert the massacre that was about to be unleashed. That was the ace up his sleeve, his advantage over both families.

The only problem now was that he was utterly worn out. Every single muscle in his body ached. He had spent half the day running up and down the island, in a state of constant worry, and his body was warning him that he'd reached his limit. A gurgling in his stomach reminded him that it was almost ten o'clock at night, and nothing solid had passed his lips for hours. He had vomited up his lunch at the foot of the decapitated corpse.

Before anything else, he needed five minutes' rest. The whiskey he'd drunk with old Ramón Docampo felt prickly in the pit of his stomach, and his limbs were starting to go numb.

He spotted a small lean-to at the back of the church. It had a rickety wooden door with rusty hinges. Without a second thought, Roberto went over and, mustering the last of his strength, kicked open the door. The latch came off with a pop, revealing a dark, dusty interior.

It was full of garden tools and coils of moth-eaten rope. In one corner, covered with mouse droppings, a pile of old esparto grass sacks had been gathering dust for decades. Roberto dropped down on them with a groan of satisfaction. His eyes were heavy as lead, and he could no longer think clearly.

"Just five minutes," he promised himself. "Just five."

He rested his head on the sacks and, before he knew it, was fast asleep as the storm continued to rage outside.

# 24

## "Visitors First"

When he woke up, he struggled to remember where he was. He glanced at his watch and cursed: It was already past midday, although the light filtering in along the edges of the door was only very faint. He had slept far longer than he'd planned to and had lost precious time.

He still felt weak from hunger, but at least his mind was clear again. He couldn't say the same of his body, which resented the night spent on a hard floor. He got up from the sacks, aching all over. When he'd been in his twenties, he'd slept in far worse places—from a sniper's dugout to a rickety truck—but that was long ago.

*You're too old for this, Lobeira. When are you going to wise up?*

He took a few paces to stretch his muscles and stepped outside. The storm was still raging, but the heavy rain of the previous night had turned to drizzle. Black clouds scudded across the sky.

Checking Erundina's tomb by the light of day, he was pleased enough. It had turned out much better than he had imagined.

But he needed to hurry. He had no idea what the rest of Ons had been up to during the night, although he imagined that the Docampos would have been busy readying an attack while also keeping vigil over Ricardo's decapitated body.

He made a mental note of the urgent tasks ahead. He had reached the conclusion that the only way to prevent the massacre that threatened Ons was to create a stalemate. And the only way he could do that was by notifying the authorities.

The cell tower had been destroyed, and there was no way of making a call from the island, but there was another way of informing the mainland about what was happening. At the lighthouse, Ibaibarriaga had shown him a radio. The transmitter could be used to contact the authorities.

He didn't trust Ibaibarriaga as far as he could throw him, but he thought he could use the man's ambitions to get him to cooperate. Now that Roberto had sequestered the money, he could offer the keeper a juicy sum in exchange for use of the transmitter.

His plan would mean sharing the money between the families and the lighthouse keepers, but with the authorities notified, at least it would be an end to all the violence. And what was more, the perfect scapegoat for Pampín's death had materialized, so both he and Diego would be free of suspicion. The mysterious killer of Ricardo Docampo would take the rap for all the victims. Let the Guardia Civil go crazy combing the island for the damn psychopath, whether he was the Tangaraño or not; Roberto hoped he himself would be a long way away by then.

It was a risky plan, no doubt, and it all depended on Ibaibarriaga's cooperation, but he was sure the man's greed would win out. And if Roberto managed to prevent open warfare from breaking out, his newly acquired wealth was more likely to go unobserved.

Satisfied, he left the graveyard, carefully covering his footprints and checking that he hadn't left any trace of his presence. Ignoring the stabs of pain that accompanied his every step, he headed for the road that led to the lighthouse.

He felt weak, and his clothes were heavy with water, making the ascent slow and torturous. Luckily, he was now more familiar with the topography of Ons, and he had no difficulty in getting his bearings.

The paved track was an infallible guide to the colossus that dominated the island.

When he reached the gate, it was closed. A doorbell was fixed to one of the cement posts. Roberto pushed the button and waited patiently as he observed the lighthouse beacon.

The security camera buzzed and swiveled toward him. He imagined the lighthouse keeper at the other end, observing his unexpected visitor, barely forty-eight hours after their previous encounter. The gate clicked open, and he went through. Here at the highest point on the island, the wind was blowing so strongly that he had to hunch over to make progress.

Exhausted and at the limit of his energy, he was about to knock on the door, but it swung open before his hand reached the bronze handle. The lighthouse keeper had come to meet him, his eyes sparkling with curiosity.

"I didn't expect you back so soon," he said as he closed the door, and Roberto shook himself and stretched, grateful for the warmth inside the lighthouse. "So, have you got our little enterprise up and running?"

"We need to speak. There have been some developments."

"I don't like surprises," replied Ibaibarriaga, fixing him with a stare. "What's happened?"

"Could I have something to eat first? I'm famished."

The lighthouse keeper grumbled, but he gestured to Roberto to follow him to the kitchen.

A short while later, Roberto was sitting down to a juicy steak accompanied by two fried eggs with impossibly yellow yolks. He wolfed down the food with Ibaibarriaga, Varatorta, and Pazos all looking on.

"So, what's up?" the head lighthouse keeper finally asked. "Or did you just come for some free grub?"

Roberto gave him an inquisitive look and nodded at Varatorta and Pazos.

"You can speak freely," said Ibaibarriaga. "They already know about our little agreement. I told you it wouldn't be a problem."

The youngest of the three crossed his arms defiantly, in what he no doubt thought was the right pose for a merciless hard guy. Varatorta at least had the decency to bow his head in embarrassment.

"There are only so many times you can go into that library without feeling like you're a prisoner," Varatorta muttered by way of explanation. "The money's a way out for us."

Roberto cursed inwardly. Negotiating with the three of them would be more complicated, but Ibaibarriaga seemed to be the leader.

"The Freires and the Docampos are going to kill each other," he explained. "We have to stop them."

"Is it the cocaine?"

Roberto shook his head. "There's no cocaine," he said, weighing his words. "There never was."

"Like hell!" said Ibaibarriaga.

"It's money. Cash." Roberto put down his fork and looked straight at him. "Three million euros."

"Jesus fucking Christ!" exclaimed the lighthouse keeper. "Three million? I'm not surprised they want to kill each other."

"There's something else," Roberto added. "Yesterday evening, somebody murdered one of the Docampos, not far from here." He shuddered at the memory. "They decapitated him and nailed him to a tree."

The lighthouse keepers were silent as they absorbed the information.

Finally, Ibaibarriaga gave a low whistle. "Christ, you don't mess with the Freires," he said.

"It wasn't them." Roberto shook his head. "There's someone else."

"Someone else? What do you mean? It's not as if there are a lot of people on the island."

"I'm sorry, I can't explain everything right now," Roberto interrupted. "We have to stop this before it's too late. I need to use the radio."

"The radio? What for?"

"To notify the authorities. I don't know if you noticed, but the cell tower got taken out in the storm," Roberto said. "I saw it happen. It was struck by lightning, and fire completely destroyed it."

"So the radio's the only way to communicate with the mainland." Ibaibarriaga gave him his pensive half smile.

"And I have to do it as soon as possible, to stop something terrible from happening."

"And why would we let you?"

"Because if you do, I'll give you the money." He looked from one man to the other. "All three million of it. A million for each of you. And the Freires and the Docampos can explain the dead guy to the Guardia Civil."

He'd done it. He'd thrown the bait into the water, and now he had to see if the sharks would bite. The lighthouse keepers looked at each other in mute conversation. Finally, Ibaibarriaga shrugged and nodded. "Sounds good to me . . . but there's something I don't understand."

"What?"

"What's in it for you, Lobeira?"

"Don't you think that preventing a massacre is enough?" Roberto set his knife and fork noisily down on the table. "That's more than sufficient for me. And getting off this damn island as soon as possible, obviously."

"What about the islanders?" asked Pazos, scratching his head. "How are they going to feel about getting nothing?"

"They don't have much choice," he said. "I'm the only one who knows where the money is."

"Cunning." Pazos looked at him. "And where might that be?"

"Somewhere nice and safe," replied Roberto.

"And what are you going to tell the authorities when they show up?"

"Nothing about the money, obviously. That's between us. I'm just going to tell them about the guy who got his head chopped off. That'll give them more than enough to think about."

The three lighthouse keepers huddled together and whispered to each other. Finally, they seemed to have reached an agreement.

"Looks like you've got it all worked out." Ibaibarriaga nodded in approval. "You win. Let's make that radio call."

They exited the kitchen and walked down the high-ceilinged hallway. To Roberto's surprise, they continued past the door to the room in which he and Ibaibarriaga had spoken before.

"Isn't this it here?"

"That radio doesn't have a big enough range," the man explained. "We only use it to communicate with the patrol boats when they're close to the island. And in this weather, nobody will be out. We need the shortwave transmitter. It's in the other room."

They continued down the hallway and through a large room that was like a museum, full of old kerosene lamps, marker buoys, and a table strewn with whale bones that had been washed up by the tide. On the far side of the room was a door.

"Visitors first," Ibaibarriaga said.

As soon as he crossed the threshold, Roberto realized something was wrong. The room was completely empty, except for an old carpenter's bench in the middle. The floor was covered with paint and oil stains, but there was no sign of a radio.

"I don't get it." He turned. "There's no—"

He bent double as Ibaibarriaga punched him hard in the stomach. Panting, he tried to force air into his lungs and to avoid vomiting, all at the same time.

Pazos and Varatorta grabbed him by the shoulders and forced him to stand upright.

Ibaibarriaga brought his face right up close to Roberto's. "And now you're going to tell me where the money is," he said. "No lies."

"I don't . . . I don't . . ." Roberto panted. "I don't understand. We have to do something or they'll all kill each other."

"I don't give a shit about the Freires and the Docampos," the man replied. "If they're busy gouging each other's eyes out, it'll be easier for us to take the dough. And if you say there's three million, that means there's more, much more. Where is it?"

"I'm . . . not . . . telling . . . you." The last word came out mixed with a spray of saliva.

Another punch, this time to the ribs. Roberto began to see little sparks of color dancing before his eyes as he gasped like a fish out of water.

"I'm going to ask you one more time. Where's the money?"

Roberto shook his head and received another brutal blow. His legs buckled, and if the other two hadn't had a firm grasp of him, he would have fallen.

"You're going to force me to really hurt you." Ibaibarriaga rubbed his knuckles. "Pazos, search this idiot; see what he's carrying."

The younger man frisked Roberto, extracting his phone, his notebook, the key to the cottage, a flashlight, and the length of fishing line that Elvira Couto had given him. Ibaibarriaga looked the items over, becoming increasingly irate.

"What's this?" Pazos's fingers plucked at the chain around Roberto's neck, then pulled it clean off.

"Give me that." Ibaibarriaga took it from him. "Where's this key from?"

Roberto clenched his jaw and readied himself for the inevitable blow, but just then, Varatorta stepped forward and took the key in his chubby hands.

"I think I know," he said smoothly. "It's the key to the church."

"Are you sure?" asked Ibaibarriaga.

"Absolutely." Varatorta nodded so vehemently that his hair flapped over his bald patch. "It's a Fichet security key. The locksmith who came to install it last summer borrowed a drill bit from me. There isn't another one like it on the whole island."

A satisfied smile lit up Ibaibarriaga's face. "The church, eh?" He slapped Roberto on the cheek a couple of times. "If you'd told me that at the beginning, we could have saved ourselves all this unpleasantness. All right, lads. I think we should go and say a few prayers for the souls of the deceased, past and future. What do you say?"

They let go of Roberto, and he sank to the floor, dazed.

"You can wait here for us," said Ibaibarriaga from the doorway. "We'll decide what to do with you when we come back with the cash. In the meantime, make yourself at home."

He slammed the door shut, and Roberto heard the bolts slide on the other side. The men's footsteps faded away, and a few moments later he watched from the window as they disappeared down the path. He wasn't surprised to see that Ibaibarriaga had a shotgun over his shoulder.

Roberto hammered at the door with all his strength, but the effort was futile. The heavy teak door was bolted shut. He'd never be able to force it. And the window was sealed by iron bars. He could see the field behind the lighthouse, and the empty heliport, whipped by the wind and the rain. He shook the bars, but they had been set into the stone walls.

Desperate, he looked around the room, but the only thing inside it was the carpenter's bench, so heavy that he couldn't even move it.

Roberto buried his face in his hands.

His plan, hatched in a hurry, had been full of potential pitfalls. He'd known that and, even so, for want of alternatives, had forged ahead.

Well, things had turned out badly. And he had fallen right into the trap.

# 25

## "You Don't Fit but I Do"

The seconds turned into minutes and the minutes into hours. Roberto tried again to force the window bars, but he eventually gave up, his hands raw. He paced the room like a caged lion.

As the day wore on, the likelihood grew that the Docampos had already set out on their revenge mission. Antía would probably be wondering where he was, and might even have gone looking for him. The thought of her running into a party of bloodthirsty Docampos tormented him. But then again, she was nobody's fool. Surely, after giving the Docampos the news, she would have returned home, and the Freires would guess what was coming or, at least, would take some basic precautions.

That was what he wanted to believe, because the alternative was too awful to contemplate.

He checked his watch. Two hours had already passed since the lighthouse keepers had gone off in search of the money. By now, they would have reached the church and found no trace of the loot. He could imagine how angry they would be when they returned.

And what they would do to him.

He heard a faint noise somewhere in the lighthouse, and for a moment he feared it was them. He heard the noise again. It was the squeak of unoiled hinges, the sound of somebody opening a door.

"Hey!" He hammered at the teak panels. "Is there anybody there? Help!"

The sound stopped for a moment. Then he heard light footsteps approaching and, finally, a gentle knock on the door.

"My friend," whispered a familiar voice. "Are you there?"

Roberto almost fainted with relief.

"Yes, Diego, I'm here," he said, his voice shaking. "Please open this goddamn door!"

He heard the boy struggling with the bolts and, finally, the door opened wide. On the other side, Diego Freire—dripping wet, his clothes clinging to his body, and looking as if he were about to drop dead from exhaustion—observed him with his green eyes.

"I knew you were here!" shouted the boy. "I knew it!"

"Diego!" Roberto gave the boy a bear hug. "I've never been so happy to see someone in my life!"

"Why?"

"What do you mean, 'why'?" Roberto shook him by the shoulders. "You've saved my life, Diego."

"Really?" The boy's face lit up. "That's the second time, then! First on the beach, when you nearly drowned, and now here. I'm a superhero!"

"No doubt about it. But tell me, how did you know where to find me?"

Diego lowered his gaze, a guilty look in his eyes. "You can't tell Antía. Do you promise?"

"You have my word."

"Last night she told me that I didn't kill Pampín." The boy's voice was little more than a whisper. "That the bad man who took my toys did it. And that you found out."

"That's right, Diego." He gave the boy another reassuring hug.

"They said nobody was allowed to leave the house, that there were more bad men outside, that they wanted to hurt us." Roberto was surprised at the determined glint in the boy's eyes. "But I wanted to thank you. You saved me too. So I escaped when nobody was looking."

"Oh, Diego." Roberto ruffled the boy's hair. "They must be worried sick about you."

"I went to the cottage, but you weren't there," the boy said in a rush. "But the lighthouse keepers were. They'd broken down the door and were going through your things!"

Of course. When they'd found out that the money wasn't in the church, the next logical option was the cottage, and they'd gone there without realizing that the cash was safe and sound in Erundina's tomb.

"They seemed really angry, and they said they were going to do something nasty to you when they got back," Diego added. "So I guessed you'd be here, and I came running."

"Don't listen to what people say, Diego." Roberto gave him a kindly look. "You're a very clever lad. But right now, we have to get out of here, before they come back."

"That could be a problem." The boy furrowed his brow, as if trying to solve a complicated algebra problem. "You don't fit but I do."

Roberto was baffled by this, but his mind was already on other things. The cottage was about half an hour's walk away. The lighthouse keepers could appear at any moment, and he wanted to be long gone when they did, but first he had a radio call to make.

With Diego following close behind, he ran down the hallway toward the library. But there, another surprise awaited him.

"You've gotta be kidding me!" he said. "Is nothing going to go right?"

The transmitter was sitting there, its insides on display. Somebody had removed the cover, and all the electronic parts were arranged neatly around it. He picked up a circuit board and stared at it despondently.

He didn't have a clue how to put the device back together, and as if that weren't enough, they were running out of time.

"We have to get out of here, Diego."

They made their way to the front door, but it was locked tight.

"Diego," he said, turning to the boy, "how did you get in?"

The boy looked up and smiled at him. "Through one of the windows above."

"What do you mean, 'above'? This place only has one floor!"

"No." The boy shook his head. "Above. On the lighthouse."

Roberto stared at him in disbelief. He remembered the tiny windows that lit the spiral staircase leading up to the lamp. They must be at least fifty feet off the ground.

"Show me," he said.

Diego shrugged and set off. They crossed the hallway and climbed the stone stairs that led up into the lighthouse. Halfway up, one of the windows was wide open, and the rain had already left a puddle on the step. Roberto stuck his head out and cursed.

It was even higher than he had imagined. Built into the facade was a series of large, rusty iron rungs. No doubt they had once served to house a lightning rod that had disappeared long ago. Diego must have used them to climb up. The kid's agility was impressive, but Roberto couldn't say the same of his sense of danger. Climbing up the facade on a calm, sunny day would already have been quite a feat; to do so in the middle of a storm was verging on the suicidal. He looked at the boy with renewed respect.

"I already said you don't fit but I do," the boy said.

The window was little wider than an arrow slit. Diego had managed to squeeze himself through with some effort, but Roberto would be bound to get stuck. The very idea of the lighthouse keepers finding him in such a predicament made him shudder.

"Maybe you can climb down and open the front door from the outside," he said, though he knew it was unlikely.

"But I don't have the key."

"Okay . . . don't worry. We'll find some other way out."

His eyes stopped on the final flight of stairs that led to the metal structure at the top, and then he remembered the circular walkway near the top of the lighthouse that Ibaibarriaga had told him about.

He rushed up to the control room. There, next to the telescope, was the porthole-like metal door with the levers on either side. Roberto applied all his strength to one of the levers and just managed to make it budge, before doing the same with the other.

A violent gust of wind whipped through the open doorway.

Storm Armand was in full force. As far as the eye could see, the sky was packed with dark rain clouds, and the sea was a fury of seething white foam and roiling black water. The wind whipped the tower mercilessly, and Roberto gripped the handrail for dear life. Trying to make himself heard was out of the question. Peering down at the vertical sequence of iron rungs, he looked at Diego and shook his head. To even attempt the climb was madness in these conditions.

"We can do it!" yelled the boy. "It's easy! Look!"

Before Roberto could stop him, Diego swung his legs over the rail and grabbed the nearest rung. Then, instinctively compensating for the wind, the boy let himself drop down to the next rung, in a maneuver that took Roberto's breath away. Repeating the process, like some crazy circus acrobat, he kept going until he was no more than six feet from the ground. With one final drop he landed, rolled on the wet grass, and stood up. He brushed the grass from his clothes and, cupping his hands around his mouth, shouted something. Roberto couldn't hear a word, but it didn't matter. The message was clear enough: *Get on with it. If I did it, so can you.*

Roberto couldn't remember the last time he'd prayed, but he offered up a silent entreaty before he, too, swung his legs over the rail. Part of his brain screamed at him not to be an idiot and to get back to safety, but he forced himself to ignore it. He grasped the nearest rung and, imitating Diego, let his weight fall until he was hanging.

The wind whipped him pitilessly, and for a second, he was paralyzed, unable to move so much as an inch. He took a deep breath, and as soon as he sensed the wind slacken, he let go of the rung and dropped down onto the one below.

There was barely space for his feet, and for a moment, he was convinced he was going to slip, but he dug his fingers into the gaps between the stones and clung desperately to the facade. He had descended only a few feet, and he was already dancing with death.

Gradually, agonizingly, he repeated the maneuver. He was heavier than Diego and nowhere near as agile, but his greater height gave him an advantage because it meant that he was just about able to touch the next rung with the tips of his toes before he let go of the one above. As he climbed, he gained in confidence.

He was more than halfway down when disaster struck.

Roberto let go of the rung and placed all his weight on the one below. Then he heard a crack, and the rusty iron fixture split, releasing a shower of brown scales that were scattered by the wind.

For one terrifying moment, Roberto was in free fall. He thrust out a desperate hand and grabbed hold of the next rung. His fingers closed around it, halting his fall. Pain shot through his shoulder, but he didn't let go.

Panting, he closed his eyes and felt with his feet for the next rung. When he found it, he groaned with relief. He'd come close, too close.

"Be careful!" shouted Diego from below. "You're going to fall!"

*You don't say!*

Roberto took almost five minutes to cover the final section of the descent, moving with the speed of an arthritic old man. Whenever he was forced to swing from the rung above, it was as if someone were thrusting a red-hot poker into his shoulder. Finally, when he was only six feet from the ground, he dropped like Diego had. The landing on the rain-sodden ground was gentler than he had feared.

He stood up, legs trembling, and looked up at the lighthouse in astonishment. It was a miracle that they had made it.

His shoulder was throbbing, sending out waves of pain that forced him to clench his teeth.

"Let's go to your house," he said, leaning on the boy. "We need to talk to your sister."

"We can't go on the road," replied Diego. "The lighthouse keepers will come that way. But I know another route. A secret path. Follow me!"

He set off, and Roberto limped along after him, worried that time was running out.

Perhaps it already had.

# 26

## El Cucorno

If the descent down the outside of the lighthouse had been terrifying, Diego's "secret path" wasn't exactly relaxing. It was a narrow trail, less than a foot wide, and it went right along the edge of the cliff.

Roberto peered apprehensively over the precipice. Far below, the roar of the waves crashing on the rocks made any kind of conversation impossible.

Anyway, he was too busy concentrating on where to plant his feet. Every few steps, he felt the ground shift beneath his weight, and stones and clods of earth went tumbling over the edge.

"Diego!" He clapped the boy on the shoulder to get his attention and shouted at the top of his voice. "Are you sure this is the way?"

"Yes!" The boy nodded his head, quite sure of himself. "We're almost there. It gets easier soon."

Roberto had no choice but to trust in the boy, even though he couldn't help wondering what he meant by "easier." Fortunately, within a couple of minutes, the path widened out and swung inland, away from the edge. It was far from well trodden, and Roberto got a few scratches on his face from down-hanging branches, but he did feel safer. Eventually, they reached the main road, at a point far from the lighthouse, and raced along it to El Cucorno.

Arriving, they didn't need to knock on the door. The Freires must have posted a lookout, because Rosalía was already waiting for them.

"Thank God you're here!" she said as she flung her arms around Diego. "We were so worried! Particularly about you, you little rascal! Where did you get to?"

"That's a long story," said Roberto, feeling the reassurance of the heavy wooden door closing behind him. "But right now, what you need to know is that the Docampos are on a war footing."

"We already know that," Rosalía replied, grimacing angrily. "It was just a matter of time."

"They want to keep all the money, and settle some old scores into the bargain," he added. "They're not messing around, I promise you."

"How do you know all of this?"

"Ramón Docampo told me himself." Roberto dropped into a chair. Now that the adrenaline had begun to ebb, the pain in his arm had become close to unbearable. "I think he's out of his mind, but nobody can make him see reason. None of his family can, anyway."

"And nobody else either . . ." said Rosalía.

Roberto observed her carefully, and only then did he notice the grayish tone of her skin and the deep bags under her eyes, the product of a sleepless night. She was no longer the imposing matriarch he had first met, just a fragile, overwhelmed, exhausted woman. Even so, the flame of determination burned in her eyes.

"That arm of yours looks nasty."

"I think it's dislocated." Roberto clenched his teeth. "It hurts like hell."

"We're used to dealing with this kind of thing," Rosalía replied. "When you collect shellfish on the rocks, it happens all the time. Go upstairs to the first-aid station we've set up and ask Antía to take a look."

*A first-aid station? These people are preparing for war too.*

Roberto stood up with some difficulty and made his way up the stairs, gripping the banister with his good hand. When he passed the living room, he noticed that it had been cleared and a large mahogany table stood in the middle of it.

The scene was so similar to the one he had witnessed in the Docampo household that a bitter smile came to his lips. Around the table, three people were preparing a rudimentary arsenal of sickles, axes, and shotguns. He noticed that one of them, whom he recognized as one of the men Pampín had accused of trespassing on his patch, was holding an item that looked vaguely familiar. It was a moment before the penny dropped.

It was an old MP 40, a submachine gun with a folding stock similar to the weapons he had seen in the hands of German soldiers in countless war movies. The man was carefully loading bullets into the magazine. Roberto shook his head. The submachine gun had been carefully oiled and appeared to be in good condition, but it must have been more than eighty years old: It was almost certainly a souvenir taken by Orlando Freire from the German submarine.

He couldn't help wondering how many more relics like that were to be found on the island and, above all, what condition the bullets would be in, after sitting in a drawer for eight decades. Old munitions, as he knew by experience, tended to behave erratically and, sometimes, could be more dangerous for the marksman than his target.

Things weren't looking good. The Freires were planning to defend themselves using weapons that were old and unreliable, and the Docampos were both more numerous and had the initiative, but this lethal piece of gear tipped the scales.

He shuffled down the hallway until he reached the first-aid station, which was housed in a gallery that looked down onto an inner courtyard crammed with fish crates, lobster pots, and other junk. There were a couple of beds in the gallery, one of which was occupied. In it lay a young man with a long, deep cut on his right forearm, and Antía was tending to his wound, wrapping his arm in bandages that had been improvised by tearing a sheet into strips. On the floor was a bloody bandage that she had just removed.

"What happened to him?" he asked. "Was it the Docampos?"

Antía looked up.

"He doesn't know." She carried on changing the man's bandages. "Last night, he was coming back from checking the moorings when someone jumped him."

"I couldn't see him properly," her patient added, his voice trembling. "It was dark, and it all happened so quickly. He appeared out of nowhere and took a swipe at me. I raised my arm to defend myself, and then he tripped. I wasn't armed, so I ran straight home."

"All done," said Antía. "It's much better than yesterday, but try not to move your arm too much." She then turned to Roberto. "Your turn. You look dreadful."

"Thanks a lot!" Roberto said. "A brilliant diagnosis, I'm sure."

"What happened to you?" she asked, ignoring the sarcasm.

"I think I've dislocated my shoulder."

"Where? How?"

"Is there somewhere we can talk privately?" Roberto glanced at the bed where the young man was lying, his eyes closed.

Antía looked at him for a moment, hesitating. But Roberto's exhausted appearance seemed to make up her mind.

"Of course." She stood up and held out her hand. "Come with me."

She led him down a hallway, and as they entered the room at the end, Roberto realized it must be Antía's bedroom.

It was dominated by a large old-fashioned bed, covered with a brightly colored, handsewn bedspread. Against one wall was a mahogany closet, and on the opposite wall were a desk and a bookcase with half a dozen heavily laden shelves. The wallpaper, faded but elegant, gave the room a welcoming feel, in contrast with the worsening weather outside. There was the scent of candles, sandalwood, and perfume.

"Sit on the bed," Antía said, proceeding to examine him gently but firmly. "You've got a few minor cuts and bruises, but your shoulder's the real problem. We're going to have to do a reduction to get it back in place."

"That sounds painful."

"It is," she said as she wrapped a sheet around his torso and passed it under his shoulder. "I'll count to five and pop it back into place. Are you ready?"

"I don't know. How should I prepare for this?"

"Take a deep breath and close your eyes." Antía placed her hands on his shoulder and turned it toward her at an angle of forty-five degrees. "Ready? One, two . . ."

Before she had finished counting, she rotated Roberto's arm with a swift, surprising movement. The pain was so intense and unexpected that it made the room spin. For a moment he thought he was going to faint, and he let out a cry, half curse, half exclamation.

"All done," said Antía. "How does it feel?"

Roberto moved his arm gingerly. It still hurt like hell, but there was no longer a shooting pain as if someone were thrusting a knife into the joint. Whatever she had done, his shoulder was now back in place. Antía offered him a couple of painkillers, and he swallowed them in one go.

"Right, and now tell me what happened." Antía sat down on the bed, next to him.

Roberto took a deep breath and started to speak. He told her about everything that had happened since the last time they met, including the conversation with Ramón Docampo, and how he had been ambushed by the lighthouse keepers. Antía frowned at this part, but her expression turned to one of alarm when he described their escape down the facade of the lighthouse. "What on earth were you thinking?" she protested. "You could both have been killed!"

"True," he said, warily moving his arm in slow circles. "But the alternative was to wait until Ibaibarriaga and his chums got back."

"I never liked him," Antía muttered. "I never liked any of them, always keeping themselves aloof, so superior. But I didn't imagine they would do something like this."

"People always surprise you," replied Roberto, exhausted. The room had started to spin. "Look . . . Is it okay if I lie down for a bit?"

"Sorry!" She raised a hand to her mouth. "Of course you can. You must still be reeling from the pain."

Roberto lay down and sighed with relief. The bed was soft, and it smelled faintly of Antía's perfume. All of a sudden, it seemed like the most comfortable place in the world.

Roberto realized that it was the first time he had felt properly safe since he had set foot on the island.

# 27

## Antía

A comfortable silence fell between them as the rain drummed against the windowpanes. Antía was sitting next to him, close enough that, if he'd wanted to, he could have reached out and touched her.

"Tell me about yourself," he murmured sleepily. The painkillers were starting to take effect, and he wanted to hear somebody else's voice.

"What do you mean?"

"Tell me about your life. Who really is Antía Freire?"

"To be honest, there's not much to tell." She sounded faintly embarrassed. "I'm afraid my life will seem really boring compared to yours."

"Try me."

"Let's see." She sighed and unconsciously gathered her hair back in a graceful movement. "I was born in a hospital on the mainland, but I've lived on the island almost my whole life, except when I was at college."

"Really? And what did you study?"

"Marketing and business management," she replied, with a hint of pride.

"Really?" Roberto's eyes grew wide. "I wouldn't have guessed that."

"Why not?" Antía replied brusquely but with a half smile. "Thought I was some island hick who barely knew how to read?"

"That's not what I meant. I'm just surprised, that's all."

"I'm the first Freire to go to college. My family made a big effort to pay for it; I've always hoped to pay them back one day."

"How?"

Antía sighed again. "I wanted to set up a hotel on the island, maybe with a small fleet of boats that would serve as a ferry service, to bring guests from the mainland. More or less what I do now with the rental properties but in a place I could call my own, something I'd built up from scratch."

"Sounds like a great idea. Why didn't you do it?"

There was a brief pause.

"I was very young, and a bit of an idiot, and I was in love with a guy who turned out not to be who I'd thought he was. I married him."

"Oh dear." Roberto propped himself up on his good arm. "Are you still together?"

Another pause, this time shorter. Antía shrugged. "Not anymore. He was a sailor. Still is."

"That's a hard life."

"You don't know the half of it. Do you know what they call the wives of sailors—sailors who spend months at sea?"

"Not a clue."

"Grass widows." She pronounced the words as if they had a bitter taste. "Women who only see their partners for three or four months a year, if that. Lonely women, who often have to run the household and bring up the kids on their own, with an absent husband."

"Doesn't sound like a great arrangement."

"It wasn't," she replied. "And when he realized that Diego and I weren't going to accept that kind of life, he wasn't very happy . . . and I wasn't very happy with his reaction."

"Diego? What's this got to do with your brother?" asked Roberto, surprised.

By way of response, she sighed and stared straight back at him. Roberto suddenly understood.

"Diego isn't your brother!"

"No, he isn't," she replied, with the saddest smile he could imagine on a woman's face. "Diego's my son."

Immediately, everything made sense. Antía's protective attitude toward the boy. Her fierce, almost desperate reaction when she thought he'd killed Pampín. Their extraordinary physical resemblance.

"I don't understand." Roberto frowned. "Diego doesn't know either?"

She lowered her gaze and shook her head slowly.

"Why don't you tell him the truth?"

"It's a long story. We realized he was different from other children a few weeks after he was born. My ex rejected him and, I quote, said, 'A freak can't be my son,' before he disappeared."

"What an asshole!" Roberto said.

"My mother didn't want me to have to put up with people's gossip, so we behaved as if the child were hers. It might seem crazy, but you can't imagine how cruel people can be in a tiny place like this."

"Do the Docampos know?"

"I'm sure they have their suspicions, but they can't prove it. Diego and Helena were born on the mainland, a few days apart. Aunt and nephew became twins. I told you I married young."

"What happened to your husband?"

"Nothing I feel like telling." She shrugged. "Let's just say that things ran their course. We're divorced. It's all in the past."

"And what did you do after that?"

"I stayed on the island." She tucked a lock of blond hair behind her ear. "My father had died in the speedboat accident, my mother was on her own with a baby girl, and Diego needed me. You've met him. He wouldn't hurt a fly."

"And your plans?"

"I had to put them on the back burner. Then things on the island changed, what with the national park and all that." Her voice had grown quieter. "Now it's out of the question, but we have to find a way of carrying on. That's why I deal with the rental properties."

Roberto digested what he had just heard. The challenges of living on the island were once more brought home to him.

"Have you never thought about leaving? Going to live somewhere else? Starting a new life from scratch?"

"Not without Diego." She shook her head. "He needs me. And he needs a lot of extra support: specialist teachers, medical care, stuff that's too expensive and I couldn't afford on the mainland, even if I found a good job."

"That's why you hesitated when we opened the bundle and we counted the money," Roberto ventured. "Even though you knew we shouldn't keep it."

"Yes," she admitted. "For a second, I imagined that another life was possible. But you've seen what that damn money has led to."

"And now here we are."

"And now here we are," she repeated.

They fell silent, both soaking in the feeling of intimacy. Antía leaned back against the headboard, next to Roberto, who could sense the gentle heat of her body. If it hadn't been for the hell that was being unleashed all around them, it would have been the perfect moment. Suddenly, his gaze came to a halt on the bookcase, and he smiled.

"Looks like you already knew who I was." He pointed to a copy of *The Fleeting Glance*. "You never said."

Antía blushed. "I didn't want to come across like some crazy fan the first time we met. And now I'm dying of embarrassment."

They both laughed.

"There's nothing to be ashamed of," he said eventually. "And you could at least tell me if you liked it."

"I loved it." She stole a sideways glance at him. "You write really well."

"Now I'm the one who's blushing."

"You've had such an interesting life." Antía turned and looked straight at him. "You've traveled the world, been to exotic places, seen some terrible things, sure, but also had incredible experiences. After all that, I must seem really dull and boring."

"Not at all. It's just that . . ."

"What?"

"My life isn't so great. Being a reporter wasn't as interesting as you might think," he explained. "One dirty, ramshackle hotel after another—if I was lucky—never too long in the same place, almost always surrounded by poverty and suffering. I've seen enough death and destruction for several lifetimes, and I thought I'd left it behind . . . until I got here and everything went sideways."

"So that's why you gave up being a correspondent," Antía said. "That's why you decided to become a writer. To leave that life behind."

"More or less." His chest felt tight. His dark secret smiled at him, mockingly, inside his head. "There's something else."

"What?"

Roberto opened his mouth, but not a sound came out. There were things he had only ever told his therapist and Carmen Gavín. No one else. He couldn't.

But suddenly he realized that he wanted Antía to know. That this was the right time, the right place, and the right person. And if he couldn't say it now, right now, he might never be able to say it. He needed to share his story with her.

"I'm going to tell you something that almost nobody else knows," he began hesitantly.

"Don't worry, I'm good at keeping secrets."

There was a second of silence, a final moment of doubt that was overcome by a sigh.

"Do you know where the Gulf of Sidra is?" he finally asked, his voice tight.

"Somewhere in North Africa, off the coast of Libya, right?" she hazarded.

"Four years ago, I was there, covering the Libyan civil war," he began. "One of those long-running conflicts that the world has forgotten but where people are still dying on a daily basis. I was in a town called Ras Lanuf when I met a group of people who'd hired a boat to cross to southern Italy."

"Fleeing from the war?"

"Some of them. But most of them had reached Libya by traveling halfway across Africa on foot. They were desperate, exhausted, and hungry. God knows what they'd done to reach Ras Lanuf and get a passage on that boat. I decided to go with them."

"On a boat operated by people smugglers?" Antía's eyes opened wide.

"That's right. I thought it would be a great story, and if we came across an Italian patrol ship, my presence on board would make everything easier. I'd help them."

She listened, rapt.

"We set off on a cloudy, moonless night so we wouldn't be seen." Roberto's voice had fallen to a whisper as his secret emerged. "We were on this wooden boat that was falling to pieces, with a couple of wheezy outboard motors and a bunch of fuel drums to get us to Lampedusa. There was room for fifteen people, at most. The traffickers had squeezed fifty of us on board."

"Jesus Christ . . . !"

"More than half of them were young women who'd been through the most horrific experiences. All of them had been raped at least twice along the way. But out of everyone on the boat, I was the most scared . . . maybe because the other passengers didn't know how dangerous the crossing was."

"And what happened?"

"Three hours after we set off, one of the motors broke down." Roberto swallowed. "Two hours later, the other one failed, too, and so we were adrift, in a sea that was getting rougher by the minute. With power, we could have gotten out of there, but with our motors gone, the waves ended up capsizing the boat."

"Oh, Roberto . . ." Antía took his hand, but he didn't even notice. His mind was far away.

"Fifty people in the water, out in the Mediterranean, in the middle of the night." His voice faltered. "Can you imagine the noise that fifty people make when they're drowning in pitch darkness? The cries of panic, of terror? I won't forget it for the rest of my life. I have bad dreams almost every night."

Roberto shuddered. "I spent the next few hours clinging to an empty fuel drum, buffeted by the waves, floating in the darkness." His voice had fallen to a whisper. "And that wasn't the worst bit."

He paused, feeling for the words, not knowing quite how to express the last part. "I had to . . . I had to fight two migrants for possession of that drum. It was too small and it could only keep one person afloat. I hit them, kicked them . . . I don't know. I don't remember it properly." He stopped for a moment, his eyes full of tears. "The following morning, I was alive and they weren't. They drowned. It was my doing. I killed them."

"That's not true," Antía protested. "You didn't have any choice. Your life was at stake."

"Maybe." He gave a weary shrug. "But it's been with me ever since. I don't know how long I spent adrift. Dawn was breaking when I was picked up by a patrol boat that brought me ashore. Since then, I've been terrified of the sea. As soon as I got out of the hospital, I knew my days as a reporter were over. And that never again, for any reason whatsoever, would I hurt anyone."

"Shh, Roberto, it's okay." Antía leaned toward him and wrapped him in her arms as he began to sob.

His chest heaved as he let out a deep groan, the sound of a deadweight finally being released. His tears, a mixture of sorrow and relief, fell on Antía's shoulder. After a while, he dried his cheeks with the back of his hand, and looked into her eyes.

"Now you know who I am," he said in a shaky voice. "You know what I've done."

"You did what you had to do to survive," she answered, holding his face between her hands. "Like we do on the island. Like I did. You've got nothing to be ashamed of."

"I just want a quiet life, that's all," he mumbled. "I just want to be happy."

"To be happy," she echoed. "I'd settle for that."

They fell silent. Nothing else existed, not the island, not the quarrels or the money or the murder. The only thing that mattered was the moment, the bubble of their emotions. But just then, the bedroom door burst open.

"Antía!" Diego stood on the threshold, panting. "You're here! Thank God I found you!"

They both sat bolt upright on the bed, like a pair of teenagers caught in the act. Even so, the connection still flowed between them. Anyone else would have realized that something was going on, but Diego was too preoccupied . . . and, anyway, he was Diego.

"What's up?" Antía asked, blushing slightly as she composed herself. "What's so urgent?"

"It's Helena." Diego swallowed, and they realized that he was really worried. "She's disappeared. Nobody knows where she is."

# 28

## Helena

The boy's rambling explanation wasn't the easiest to follow, but in the end, they deduced that nobody had seen Helena for a number of hours.

"Mamma Rosalía's very worried," Diego concluded, frowning. "She's afraid the Docampos have kidnapped her."

"That's all we needed," said Antía. "Where the hell can that stupid girl have gotten to?"

"I think I have an idea," said Roberto, standing up. "I'll go and look for her."

"Don't be foolish." She turned toward him. "I've just done a reduction on your dislocated shoulder. You're not going anywhere. Anyway, how are you going to find her?"

Roberto bit his tongue. He had to tell Antía about the relationship between Helena and Tristán, but he didn't want to say anything in front of Diego. He wasn't sure the kid had much concept of keeping a secret.

"You have to trust me." He took her hands in his. "If I'm right, I'll bring her back soon."

"And if the Docampos have her? What are you going to do all on your own?" She went pale as another possibility occurred to her. "And if she's . . . ? Oh God . . ."

"Don't think about that. I'm sure she's fine, but I have to go right now. I'll explain later, I promise."

They left the room and, as they passed the living room where the improvised arsenal was being prepared, Antía stopped.

"Wait a moment," she said. She returned with something wrapped in a cloth. "Here, take this." She handed him the package.

Roberto unwrapped it to reveal an old Walther P38, a pistol that had no doubt once belonged to a German officer—another souvenir from Orlando Freire's little adventure eight decades earlier.

"I can't take it." He shook his head and handed it back. "I'm not using a gun."

"Are you crazy?" She looked at him, horrified. "You need to be able to defend yourself!"

"I already told you; I'm not going to hurt anybody. Ever again. And that includes the Docampos, however cruel they may be. I've got out of worse scrapes, believe me," Roberto replied, trying to convey a tranquility he didn't feel. "Give me an hour."

"Please be careful." Antía squeezed his hand. "I don't want anything to happen to you."

Roberto took his parka from the stand in the hallway and went back outside. It was no longer raining, and even the wind had died down a little. But the sky was still full of gloomy black clouds. The break in the weather wouldn't last long.

He was almost certain that Helena had gone to meet Tristán in their secret hideaway, not just because that was what he would have done if he'd been a lovestruck teenager in the middle of such chaos but also because of his request to meet Tristán there. The girl, surely unaware of how dangerous the island paths had become, had unwittingly put herself in peril.

It took him far longer than expected to reach the little huddle of houses. All his senses on alert, he trod carefully, trying to make as little noise as possible, checking behind every bush and tree, imagining potential ambushes every few yards. But he didn't meet a single soul.

Wherever the Docampos or the lighthouse keepers might be—assuming that the latter were searching for him—nobody was around in this part of the island.

When he reached the house, he tried the door but this time found it locked. He knocked impatiently, glancing nervously over his shoulder. He heard cautious footsteps inside.

"Who's there?" Tristán Docampo's voice sounded scared.

"It's me!" he growled, his nerves shot. "Roberto Lobeira! Open the goddamn door!"

The handle turned, and Roberto stepped inside.

"At least you're fully dressed this time," he snorted. "That's something. Can I ask what the hell you're doing here? Do you have any idea what's going on around you?"

"We needed to see each other," said Helena shyly. "I was going crazy. The phones don't work, and I was afraid something had happened to Tristán."

"Anyway, you're the one who asked to meet," Tristán added reasonably.

"I know, I know!" said Roberto. "But not when Ons was about to turn into Jonestown, for Christ's sake!"

"Jones what?" asked Helena in confusion, staring at him across the cultural abyss that separates the young from the old.

"It doesn't matter." He waved his hand dismissively. "We just have to get out of here. You both need to go home, and you have to promise to put the romance on hold until all this is over. Is that clear?"

The two young people looked at each other and nodded in a way that didn't exactly fill Roberto with confidence.

"Okay," he said. "Helena, I'm going to accompany you. Tristán, you head straight home but keep your head down, and if you see any of the Freires or the lighthouse keepers or a stranger, try to hide. All right?"

"The lighthouse keepers?" Tristán looked puzzled. "What have the lighthouse keepers got to do with all this? And what do you mean, a stranger? I know everyone on the island."

"I don't have time to explain just now. Please, just do as I say."

"Hang on!" the boy said. "Do you mean there might be someone else on the island, an outsider? And that they could have killed Ricardo?"

"I don't know." Roberto closed his eyes in exhaustion. "Yes, maybe."

*Personally, I'd kill for another painkiller.*

"That means it wasn't the Freires!" exclaimed Tristán.

"I told you," Helena reproached him. "Nobody in my family would have done something like this."

"Right now, your respective families are preparing for something far worse," interrupted Roberto as he opened the door. "The sooner we get out of here, the better our chances of preventing it. Come on, let's get going."

"Hang on! I almost forgot!" exclaimed Tristán, opening his canvas backpack. "Here. What you asked me to get."

Roberto was overcome by such a sense of relief that his knees almost buckled. The boy was holding a clear plastic bag, inside which was a hammer with remnants of blood and hair on the head.

"Thanks so much, Tristán," he said as he took it with shaky hands. "You've just saved my life."

"You can't imagine how hard it was to find," the boy explained. "It was in my grandfather's study, in a drawer in his desk. He almost caught me! I just about crapped myself."

"You did a great job." Roberto patted him on the shoulder. "Now let's get out of here."

He had to wait for what felt like an eternity as the two youngsters said goodbye to each other, with kisses, hugs, and whispered promises of undying love. Roberto impatiently shifted his weight from one foot to the other, worried that somebody would show up.

Despite the urgency, he felt a lot better. With the hammer finally in his possession, the Docampos had no way of implicating him in Pampín's death. Without that card to play, and with the money safely tucked away in the graveyard, the balance of power had unexpectedly tipped back in his favor. Of course, there was also the problem of the psychopath roaming the island, but if he managed to stop the Docampos and the Freires from annihilating each other, time would be on his side. As soon as the storm abated, communication with the mainland would be restored, the park rangers would return to the island and, with them, sanity.

When Tristán left them, Roberto turned to Helena.

"Right, let's get going—" He stopped mid-sentence and stared at the girl. "What the hell is that?"

"Nothing," she reassured him as she zipped her coat all the way up, looking shifty.

"What do you mean, 'nothing'? Let me see!"

Helena Freire unzipped her coat to reveal a huge hickey on her neck.

"Just what we needed! How are you going to explain that at home, young lady?" he grumbled. "How do you hope to keep your little secret if you turn up branded like a colt?"

"We didn't mean to," she said, blushing to the roots of her hair. "We got a bit carried away . . ."

"It looks like you've been bitten by Count Dracula, for Christ's sake," Roberto groaned. "Anyway, it doesn't matter. Try to make sure nobody sees it, and find yourself a nice scarf. The last thing we need now is for your mother to start asking questions."

They set off for El Cucorno in silence, Roberto annoyed by the teenagers' carelessness, Helena somewhat sheepish. When they finally reached the path that led to the Freire place, he let out a sigh of relief. They had made it without incident. Things were finally looking up. They stopped and looked at each other.

"We're here," whispered Roberto. "Now we need to decide what you're going to say when they ask you where you were."

"We can't tell them I was with Tristán!" the girl declared. "You promised that if we did what you asked, you wouldn't say anything!"

"And I plan to keep my promise," he replied, "but we still need a good excuse to explain your little excursion."

"I've already thought about that," she said, smiling triumphantly. "Look."

She opened her shoulder bag and showed him the contents. It was full of medicines, mainly painkillers and antibiotics, most of them in opened packets. Roberto was tempted to grab some for himself, but he resisted the urge. It was better to endure the pain in his shoulder and keep his head clear.

"Lots of tourists leave them behind when they go home at the end of the summer," explained Helena. "I'll tell them I checked a few of the houses for leftover medicines. That I thought we might need them, and, because I was sure they wouldn't let me leave, I snuck out. They'll be angry, but once they've had time to think about it, they'll come around. You'll see."

"You're one smart cookie." Roberto shook his head and smiled at the girl's cunning.

"Tristán and I owe you one," she replied.

"I try to do the right thing, that's all. And you don't owe me anything. The only thing I need is for you not to do anything foolish, at least not for a few days."

"We won't cause any trouble, I promise." The girl flashed him a dazzling smile. "Thanks so much!" She threw her arms around him and hugged him tight.

Roberto—taken completely by surprise—limited himself to patting her on the back.

It was an innocent gesture.

But fate had other ideas.

The Freire lookout had alerted people to their arrival. Just then, the door of El Cucorno opened, and the stout figure of Rosalía Freire came rushing out. When she saw Roberto and Helena hugging, she stopped sharp. They let go of each other, but it was already too late.

Rosalía Freire looked suspiciously from one to the other, and eventually her eyes came to rest on Helena's neck. An expression of surprise gave way to one of indignation.

"You son of a bitch." Her voice was ice-cold. "How dare you!"

"It isn't what it seems."

"I don't want your explanations," the woman replied. "I've got eyes in my head; I'm no fool. I know what I see."

"If you'd just let me explain—"

"What is there to explain?" she shouted. "That you've seduced a young girl? She's barely eighteen years old!"

Roberto felt as if the ground had opened up beneath his feet. It was just a stupid misunderstanding, but the woman was far too angry to listen to his explanations.

"Helena, please." He turned to the girl, who was as pale as death and in a state of shock. "Tell your mother that it's not what she's thinking. Please."

But Helena just stared at them, unable to utter a single word, caught on the horns of a dilemma to which there was no solution.

"Mom, I didn't . . ." she stuttered. "I didn't . . ."

"Don't say another word," Rosalía commanded. "Go inside. We'll talk later. You're a disgrace to the family."

"Mom . . ." Helena groaned as the tears welled up in her eyes. She looked from Roberto to her mother with the desperation of a caged animal.

"I said go inside!" roared her mother. "Now!"

With a sob, Helena ran inside, her shoulders slumped and her heart broken. Roberto remained rooted to the spot.

"I trusted you," Rosalía spat. "I let you into my home, offered you my hospitality, welcomed you into my family, and this is how you repay us."

"There's been a mistake," Roberto stammered. "You've got it wrong."

"I got it wrong when I offered you our friendship," she interrupted. "It won't happen again."

Roberto's mind was buzzing. If he told her the truth, she'd refuse to believe him, refuse to accept that her daughter was in love with the son of her worst enemies, the ones who were about to mount a murderous attack on them. And in the unlikely event that she did believe him, it would only make things worse because it would be obvious that he had covered up for them. It was a hellish situation.

"Don't ever darken the doors of El Cucorno again," she said. "Don't even think of trying to talk to any of my family—not Antía, not Diego, and certainly not Helena. For the Freires, you're a dead man. Is that clear?"

"Please let me explain," he begged.

"The time for explanations is over." She spat at his feet. "We're done here."

Rosalía turned and went back into the house. A key turned in the lock, and Roberto was left staring impotently at the front of the building, trying to understand what had just happened. Then he heard a sound, and he looked up. A ball of ice the size of a cannonball formed in his stomach.

From one of the windows above, Antía was looking down. Roberto had no idea how long she had been there, what she had seen or heard, but the expression on her face left little doubt.

Her eyes were full of confusion, anger, and disappointment—but above all, pain.

"Antía, wait!" he shouted but too late.

Antía slammed the window shut, and Roberto Lobeira—bestselling author, intrepid reporter, man of the world—was left standing all on his own in front of El Cucorno, feeling like the unluckiest man in the world.

It had started to rain again, and it felt like another downpour was on the way. Roberto stood like a half-wit for a couple of minutes, his brain short-circuited, trying to understand how everything could have gone to pot in such short order.

He'd lost Antía's trust in the stupidest way imaginable, and the thought of it broke his heart. But that wasn't the worst of it.

The last chance of preventing what was about to happen had vanished. The Freires had rejected him, their honor offended. He had become just one more of their enemies.

For their part, as soon as the Docampos discovered that the money was no longer in the church and that the hammer had disappeared, they would be after him.

And as if that weren't enough, Ibaibarriaga and the other lighthouse keepers were on his trail.

Finally, to complicate the situation even further, the mysterious murderer was still out there somewhere, searching for his next victim.

Roberto realized that he didn't have a single ally, and that he was alone on an island that was both completely cut off from the world and about to explode.

# 29

## Water on All Sides

By the time Roberto arrived back at the cottage, Storm Armand was raging with renewed strength. The rain was coming down in sheets, and visibility was almost zero. It was not until he stood in the front yard that he could see the full extent of the damage.

The lighthouse keepers had done a thorough job. The door had been battered open and hung loosely on its hinges, the lock had been smashed, and the doorframe was splintered. The windows were broken, and the shutters were banging against the wall.

He entered cautiously, a carpet of broken glass crunching beneath his feet. The interior had been completely destroyed.

The mattress had been slashed open, revealing the springs inside it; the same treatment had been meted out to the couch, a sea of yellow foam spilling from its wounds. His visitors had stripped the place from top to bottom; every inch of the cottage had been ransacked. Here and there, scattered over the floor, were his possessions, some stained with muddy boot prints. There were also holes in the wall, in places where they presumably thought he might have hidden the money.

He made a quick inventory of all his belongings. Although much had been badly damaged, the only thing missing was his laptop. He guessed that Ibaibarriaga and his mates had taken it, perhaps in the belief that it might contain some clue. Even if they managed to crack his password, all they would find was a brief outline of his next book, just a few thousand words.

*They're going to be disappointed.*

Both physical and mental exhaustion were catching up with him. He felt dulled, his senses confused and overwhelmed, every single muscle fiber screaming for rest.

He closed the door as best he could, jamming a chair against it. But there were still plenty of gaps through which the wind defiantly whistled.

The windows were beyond repair, but by closing the shutters, the space was at least more or less watertight, if gloomy. There was no electricity, of course. The propane lamp lay broken in a corner, and he had to make do with a few candles and the flashlight. His comfortable den had been reduced to a ruined hovel.

He turned the mattress over and collapsed onto the bed, defeated, a bottle of water in one hand, a piece of dry salami that had somehow escaped the rampage in the other.

It was a mixed bag. He had recovered the hammer that Luis Docampo had used to kill Víctor Pampín, freeing himself of that threat, and the money was safe and sound, but those were the only positive items on the balance sheet.

On the debit side, he had managed to earn himself the hatred of just about every single inhabitant of the island, and open warfare was about to break out. And to cap it all, he was as far as ever from identifying who the mysterious Tangaraño was and why he had gone from mutilating rabbits to decapitating human beings.

It was far from ideal. But all of this faded into the background when he remembered the expression of pain and disappointment on Antía Freire's face. He knew it was absurd, but that was what upset him the most. The woman had become the closest thing he had to a friend on this tiny patch of land. A friend with whom he had shared confidences. Someone to whom he had opened his heart and to whom he had entrusted a secret that had been eating away at his soul for years. And just when that promising friendship was starting to take shape, he had managed to ruin it with a stupid misunderstanding.

Roberto groaned with frustration as he turned over, and he felt the lumpy springs sticking into his back. He felt at the mercy of events, utterly unsure of his next move.

The smartest option, surely, was to lie low while the storm battered Ons. Go and look for a place where nobody would find him, let the islanders sort out their differences, just stay alive. And then, once contact with the mainland was restored, get the hell out of there and not look back.

He suspected it wouldn't be so simple, though, and every fiber of his journalistic soul rebelled against the idea of hiding in a hole while events unfolded outside.

First, in any case, he had to rest. The painkillers had almost completely worn off, his shoulder hurt like hell, and he felt incapable of taking a single step. At the same time, he suspected that, paradoxically, the ransacked cottage was the last place anybody would look for him. Or at least, that was what he wanted to believe, because the truth was, he didn't have anywhere else to go.

He felt sleep washing over him in an unstoppable wave. He didn't try to fight it.

When he woke up, the room was completely dark, a draft of wind presumably having blown out the candles. He felt around until his hands found the flashlight, but even though he pressed the button several times, it didn't give off so much as a glimmer of light. Cursing, he realized that he'd forgotten to turn it off before he fell asleep, and the batteries must be dead.

That meant that he must have been asleep for hours. He got up and groped his way toward the window. He bumped into what was left of the coffee table, grimacing as he knocked his shin against it.

When he opened the shutters, it was pitch black outside. He checked his watch: half past midnight. Then he remembered the lighter in his pocket. He used it to find the candles and lit them again, one by one.

He quickly took stock. He felt much better, more clearheaded, after resting. He searched among the clothes on the floor and picked out some clean garments to replace his torn, wet things from the day before. He had no way of replacing his parka, which was still soaking wet and would have appalled the sales staff of the elegant boutique where he'd bought it, but it would have to do.

*Right. And now what?*

His options were limited, although the first thing on his list, unquestionably, was to dispose of the hammer for once and for all. He approached the sink and opened the faucet, intending to wash it thoroughly and remove any hint of blood or fingerprints. But he suddenly stopped.

*Don't even think of it!*

He'd seen enough episodes of *CSI* to know that, even if he washed the hammer, traces of blood would be left in the drain. If things got complicated and the forensics department searched the cottage—something they would no doubt do, given all that had happened—they'd find those traces, and then he really would be incriminated.

He closed the faucet and leaned on the sink. The best option would be to throw the hammer into the sea, somewhere that nobody would ever be able to find it. But for that he'd have to wait until dawn. Going anywhere near the cliffs in the middle of the night with a storm raging was a surefire way to get himself killed.

But it would be foolhardy to keep it in his possession in the meantime. It would be hours before it was light, and if he'd learned anything, it was that things could change very quickly on this hellhole of an island. Every time he tried to get ahead of events, something unexpected happened.

With that in mind, he went outside and looked around. On one side, a low stone wall separated the cottage from the neighboring property, an abandoned lot completely overgrown with weeds. It was perfect.

He jumped the wall and pushed his way through the vegetation, trying to leave as little trace as possible. After he had gone a dozen yards, he bent down and started to excavate a hole with his bare hands, going deep enough to ensure that no curious passing animal would dig it up.

With the hammer in the ground, as he was clearing away any trace of his activities, it was then that he heard the first shots.

Three quick-fire reports were followed by a moment of silence and then another three shots. He looked up, alarmed, before retracing his steps back to the cottage.

He couldn't see a thing, and the noise of the rain and the wind drowned out any other sound, but he was absolutely certain. He'd heard too many gunshots in the course of his career to confuse them with anything else.

The war between the Freires and the Docampos had begun.

He felt a desperate urge to know what was happening, but he couldn't think of any safe way of obtaining information. Running down to the village under the cover of darkness was an easy way to earn himself a bullet to the head.

Even so, he went and climbed a nearby rise. From there, perhaps he would have some kind of sightline over the village. He scrambled up a tree and peered out into the darkness but in vain. Without any electricity, the lights that should have illuminated the main street had been extinguished, and only the automatic beacon on the breakwater, along with the intermittent moon, shed some faint light on the corner by the dock. That part of the island appeared completely deserted.

He remained where he was for a while, watching and waiting. There had been no more gunshots, but that meant nothing. As far as he knew, they might be knifing each other to death less than a mile from where he was. He was consumed by impotence and curiosity.

Just then, he saw flashlights, not far from his position, approaching along the track that ran down the middle of the island.

He cursed his recklessness. Concentrating on events in the village, he had forgotten to watch his own back, and now somebody had cut off his retreat. He descended from the tree and scrambled downhill, trying to make as little noise as possible. The lights had almost reached the cottage. They were looking for him; there was no doubt about it.

*Who is it? What are they after?*

He had no way to answer the first question unless he approached them, but the second was soon resolved when a member of the party opened fire on the windows of the cottage.

There came the harsh report of a double-barreled shotgun. Roberto clenched his teeth as the spray of shot hit the wall and shattered what few pieces of glass remained in the windows.

Instinctively, he crouched down. Someone issued an order that was lost in the noise of the storm, and the lights arced around the cottage, casting a net that nobody could cross without being caught.

It came to him that if he hadn't climbed the rise, he would have been cornered inside the cottage. For once, luck had been in his favor.

"That way!" shouted another voice, clearer this time.

They were moving closer to where he was.

He couldn't stay there. Taking a risk, he lifted his head and scanned his immediate vicinity.

The only path that would take him out of these newcomers' reach was one that led toward the isolated, virtually uninhabited northern tip of the island. There was nothing there other than a couple of wave-battered beaches . . . and Elvira Couto's hovel. Maybe, he thought, another visit to her wasn't such a bad idea.

*And you're hardly spoiled for options.*

Adrenaline coursing through his veins, he set off toward the dirt track. Every now and then, he sent pebbles flying beneath his feet, and he gritted his teeth, convinced that he could be heard for miles around. But the storm was his ally now. Its fury provided him with the perfect cover, and the only way he would be detected was if someone ran straight into him.

Having left his pursuers behind, he stopped in the middle of the track to regain his breath. He had walked this route before, but that had been in broad daylight and without anyone on his tail. He'd left his phone in the cottage, along with the flashlight, and had no means of lighting his way—not that he would have dared use them, for fear of revealing his position. His only option was to make his way in the dark, stumbling every few yards or getting caught in the vegetation, which made for miserably slow progress.

Fortunately, his eyes had adjusted. He could just about make out the track, a faint white thread through the darkness. Every now and then he looked up and cast a wistful glance toward the coastline of the mainland, a few miles away, beyond the roaring waves.

The yellow streetlamps and white light of the houses in Bueu were like a constellation of stars from another galaxy. He made out the headlights of an occasional car traveling along the coastal highway, and once he even spotted the flashing blue lights of a police patrol vehicle, oblivious to the drama that was playing out here, just across the water.

There was something atrocious about being cut off like this. An island was a piece of land with water on all sides. That was the dictionary definition. But what the dictionary didn't tell you was that an island could also be a death trap. People, civilization, safety . . . they were all so close, just an hour by boat. But at the same time, so far that they might as well have been on another planet. He could see the mainland, but it made no difference. He was on his own.

He walked in the rain for almost an hour, until the sound of the surf told him that Melide Beach was nearby. The strip of white sand was far narrower than the last time, and he was careful to steer clear of the huge waves that broke furiously on the shore. From here, it was not far to Elvira's hovel.

With a final push, he made his way up the steep slope to the old woman's home. There once more was the misspelled sign on its crooked, lichen-covered post.

The place was exactly as he remembered. The dream catchers and wind charms hanging from the eaves played a tinkling, discordant symphony. Roberto took a deep breath before knocking on the door.

"Elvira! Open up!" he shouted into the night. "It's me, Roberto Lobeira! Please, open up!"

He waited patiently in the rain but not a sound came from inside. He called a couple more times but to no avail.

*Maybe she's a deep sleeper. Or perhaps she's hard of hearing. She's very old, after all.*

He tried the handle, and it turned easily. The door swung open on its hinges to reveal an interior lit by weak yellow candlelight, and characterized by a peculiar smell. Roberto crossed the threshold, feeling like a thief.

"Elvira?" he called out. "Are you there? It's Roberto Lobeira. I'm coming in."

Once again, there was silence. Roberto stepped inside and repressed a gasp of horror.

Elvira Couto's diminutive body was suspended about a foot from the floor, as if she were levitating. One of her slippers had fallen off, revealing a small, dirty foot . . . Two huge copper nails had been hammered into her chest, pinning her to the wall like some giant butterfly. Her clothes were covered in blood, and her deformed, arthritic hands hung limply by her sides. But that wasn't all.

She had been decapitated.

And there was no trace of her head.

# 30

## You're Being Watched

The wave of nausea was overpowering. The musty smell of the room was mixed with the unmistakable stench of blood and feces that stained the woman's legs after she had lost control of her sphincters at the moment of death.

Nervously, Roberto checked the hovel, ready to flee at any moment. But the curtain that separated Elvira's sleeping quarters from the rest of the room had been drawn back, and he could see that the place was deserted.

He peered outside. Whoever was responsible for this could be hiding in the darkness, observing him, waiting to jump him when he emerged. The thought was enough to make him slam the door shut and wedge one of the stools against it, panting nervously.

Sweat poured down his back. He confirmed, much to his relief, that the blood on the floor was dark brown and coagulated. It was far from fresh, so there was no reason to believe that the killer was still on the scene.

Somewhat reassured but with his heart in his mouth, he walked around the room. In the guttering candlelight, things did not appear to have been disturbed.

He couldn't say if anything was missing in that jumble of possessions and pieces of junk, but it still appeared to be arranged according to a system that only the unfortunate Elvira had understood. Unable to bear the sight of her body any longer, Roberto removed the cover from the bed and draped it over her as an improvised shroud. Doing that made him feel slightly better.

This was the work of the same murderer who had killed Ricardo Docampo; there was no doubt about that. The same primeval violence, the same modus operandi, the same mixture of savagery and precision in the ritual arrangement of the victim and, above all, the absence of the head. The trophy. The proof of the killer's triumph.

He analyzed the scene meticulously. The door had not been forced, which meant either that the killer had a key or that Elvira had let them in. Either she already knew her murderer, or she didn't think they were a threat. Whatever the case, once inside, the killer couldn't have found it difficult to overcome the old woman.

*Inside. That's it!*

For the first time, Tangaraño had made a mistake. Unlike the previous murder scene, this location was under cover, and the rain hadn't washed away any prints. There might be some kind of a clue.

He began to systematically search the room but soon lost heart.

It was like looking for a needle in a haystack, particularly since he didn't know what he was looking for. The place was a perfect mixture of a chronic hoarder's sanctuary and the lair of a crazy old witch. It was impossible to say if anything was out of place.

"Come on, Elvira," he muttered, glancing at the body outlined under the bedspread. "There must be something. Where is it?"

Deflated, he dropped into the chair that was pulled up to the table, on which sat a cold dish of untouched, grilled mackerel and boiled potatoes, the woman's last supper, which she hadn't even had time to eat, interrupted by her lethal visitor. The fish stared at him with dead eyes, silent witness to whatever had happened there, as if it were laughing at him.

His feet encountered something beneath the table. Intrigued, he bent down and discovered the heavy wooden chest where the old woman kept the gifts she demanded of her visitors.

"This is it!" he exclaimed, unable to contain himself. "It has to be here!"

*Let's see what gift you brought to gain entry. I've got you, you bastard!*

He opened the chest and looked inside. It was like the treasure trove of a mad antique dealer. At the top was his old fountain pen, the one he had given her a few days before in exchange for the cleansing ritual she had performed.

His hopes faded. He had been sure there would be something more, some object that unequivocally gave away the murderer, but like all expectations based on illusions, the answer wasn't there.

Any gift that had followed his own visit should have been on top of the fountain pen, but everything else in the chest looked as if it had been there for a long time. Even so, he rummaged through the contents in the vain hope of coming across something.

His fingers closed around a hard, metallic object. To his surprise, he extracted an old Walther P38 from the chest, identical to the one Antía had offered him at El Cucorno but in much worse condition. Unlike the Freires' one, this had rust spots all over, was missing part of its handle, and had an air of neglect. It was impossible to know how long it had been in there, but it was clearly an offering either from a Freire or a Docampo.

He put it in his pocket. Did this gift mean that one of the two families was involved in the ritual deaths, or was there simply no connection? Things were becoming even more complicated.

Just then, he heard a distant noise over the storm. He wouldn't have picked it out if it hadn't been completely unlike all the other noises on the island. It was a sound he knew perfectly, but here it was completely out of place, and his blood froze.

It was the sound of an engine.

He rushed out of the house. No more than a quarter of a mile away, the headlights of an SUV bobbed along the track, making their way toward him through the pouring rain.

*What the hell?*

They'd found him. He had to get out of there right away.

He took one final, pitying glance at the woman's body. Ultimately, not even her spells and incantations had saved her from a far more powerful curse than any of the imaginary ones she had feared throughout her life.

If he was sure of one thing, it was that this was not the work of a ghost or some folk demon but of a person made of flesh and blood. Someone who was still out there, on the prowl, taking advantage of the chaos that had been unleashed on the island. Perhaps even the someone who was at the wheel of the SUV.

Without bothering to close the door, he ran off in search of somewhere safe to hide and to watch from.

Immediately, he realized it hadn't been the best idea. In the dark, he hadn't calculated the distance accurately, and the SUV was much closer than he had imagined. He raised his hand instinctively to protect his eyes from being dazzled by the headlights.

"There he is!" roared a man's voice. "It's him! In front of the house!"

The SUV accelerated toward him, its wheels churning up mud. He only just managed to throw himself to one side of the path to avoid being run over. His clothes were caught in brambles, and he struggled to stand up as the vehicle came to a halt a few yards away and executed a three-point turn.

"Don't let him get away!" the voice shouted again. "We've got him!"

"Luis!" shouted Roberto, as he staggered to his feet. "Luis Docampo! Have you all gone mad? What the hell are you doing here?"

The answer came in the form of a hail of shots that, fortunately for him, had been unleashed blindly. Roberto sensed the lead pellets whizzing past him and thunking harmlessly into the branches and leaves behind him.

"Turn the car around!" Luis shouted to the driver. "Point the lights at him!"

That was all Roberto needed to know. Not wasting another second, he rushed madly up the hill, pushing his way through the vegetation. The branches caught at his clothes and scratched his face, and he was soon bleeding from a thousand tiny cuts and scratches, but none of that mattered.

If he stayed there, he was a dead man.

The vehicle's headlights were finally pointing in his direction, and for a moment he could see clearly what lay ahead: a sea of low vegetation and a few twisted trees. His shadow stretched out ahead of him, shaky and blurred by the rain.

Another shot, this time closer, clipped the branches to his right. Panicking, he understood that—out here on the hill, in the glare of the headlights—he was like a sitting duck at a fairground shooting booth, and it was only a matter of time before his pursuers hit their target.

"Don't shoot!" he croaked. "I haven't done anything to you!"

*As if that were going to help. Run for your life, Lobeira. Run.*

His feet caught on something hidden among the undergrowth, and he fell flat just as a well-aimed bullet whizzed over his head.

Hunched over, he scrambled the last few yards to the summit of the hill, shielded by the scrub. His lungs were pumping like a blacksmith's bellows, and his vision was blurry. Suddenly, the earth beneath him gave way, and he rolled forward. He had reached the top of the hill, and the path now began to slope downward. Even more important, it put a protective screen between him and the shooters.

He scrambled to his feet and set off again, stumbling ahead at top speed. The terrifying possibility that he might be running headlong toward a precipice suddenly occurred to him, and he slowed down. The last thing he needed was to accidentally fall over a cliff in the middle of the night.

Just then, he felt some clear, level ground beneath his feet. He had hit another path. He looked in both directions, uncertain. From the other side of the hill came the muffled sound of the SUV engine revving. His pursuers hadn't given up the chase.

He had to get off the track as soon as he could. The going might be easier, but using it also meant staying somewhere the vehicle could reach him. His only chance was to seek refuge among the bushes and pray that they didn't find him.

One question echoed, unanswered, in his head: *Why?* Why were they after him? Ramón Docampo had sworn that nothing would happen to him, since he was their guarantee of getting off the hook. Perhaps they had discovered that the money was no longer in its hiding place, but who knew. These people were unpredictable.

That thought led to another, one far more worrying and more pressing.

*How did they find me?*

Nobody had known he was going to the old witch's hovel. Even he hadn't known until he'd taken the last-minute decision to flee.

And yet they had found him easily. There must be something he was missing . . . and that something could be the difference between life and death.

He had no way of knowing where he was. He tried to re-create a mental map of the island, but he was simply too tired. All he knew was that if he went west, he'd reach the cliffs that looked out onto the open sea. And if he followed the coast, he could work his way around the island until he came to the inhabited part. To El Cucorno.

Begging the Freires for protection was a long shot, but it was surely better than wandering around in the storm until somebody—a party of Docampos or the Tangaraño—got to him.

He had no compass, but he could use something else: the noise of the waves breaking against the cliffs.

The sound was a little louder to his right, and so he decided to head in that direction. That meant staying on the track for a little longer, but he felt it was worth the risk if it meant faster progress. The Docampos might have the advantage of speed, but he would be able to see them long before they saw him.

He broke into a run. The sky had cleared slightly, just enough for a few faint shafts of moonlight to illuminate his way. Just enough to see where he was placing his feet.

After a while, he slowed down—his lungs were about to burst. He squatted down, his hands on his knees, and rested for a moment, his heart pounding.

The island was a runner's nightmare, the constant ups and downs of the terrain aggravated by the treacherous surfaces of the tracks and paths.

A little farther ahead, the track divided, with one branch leading down to the coast. With some effort, he got going again until he came to the fork. A sign pointed toward the west, with the words Devil's Hole burned into the wood.

*Very fitting,* said a voice in his head.

The name was familiar. He remembered Rosalía Freire's mention of it: a huge shaft, more than forty yards deep, that connected to the sea. He had been warned of its dangers.

But here he was, walking toward it in the middle of the night as the sound of the waves grew ever more deafening. The irony of the situation would have made him smile in any other circumstances.

The path was narrower and traced a gentle curve down toward the cliff edge. He could smell the sea, the waves atomizing as they crashed against the rocks, sending tiny particles of salt water floating into the air. In the distance was the sinuous and constantly shifting line of the waves breaking at the base of the cliffs. He had reached the coast.

A faint click, almost inaudible, brought him to a halt, and his heart pounded. He peered into the darkness and then uttered a curse.

*Oh shit!*

This was bad.

He'd just discovered how they had managed to locate him so quickly at Elvira Couto's place.

And, worse still, he knew that his pursuers would be here any minute.

He was cornered.

# 31

## The Devil's Hole

Roberto crouched down next to the path, without taking his eyes off the black plastic device that was strapped to the trunk of a small, twisted pine tree. There was a motion detector at the front, and above that a black screen. Underneath were the words "Boly Guard," and on one side a sticker that read "Property of the Atlantic Islands National Land and Marine Park Service."

An infrared trail camera to detect animal movements.

"I should have damn well realized," he groaned. "We're in a national park!"

There must be dozens of the things all over the island to monitor the local fauna. The park rangers would use them to keep track of the island's wildlife.

The Docampos must have forced the door to the rangers' hut and availed themselves of the system. Every time he'd passed one of the cameras, a photo would have been taken, which would then have been transmitted almost instantaneously to the central control. He might just as well have been letting off flares as he went around the island.

He gave the camera the finger before ripping it off and tossing it into the bushes. He was furious with himself for having been so careless. But above all, he was scared.

The Docampos knew where he was, and there was only one way out. If he retraced his steps, he was sure to run into them, and all around there was nothing but low vegetation barely as high as his knees, and lichen-covered rocks. There was nowhere to hide.

As if fate had read his mind, just then he heard the SUV's engine and spotted the shifting beams of its headlights as the vehicle jolted down the track.

*You need to gain some time. Think, Roberto, think!*

His only hope was to reach the shore and pick his way carefully down the rocky cliff, trusting that they wouldn't follow him on such a reckless route. But if they caught him on the way down, he'd be as dead as if he'd thrown himself over the edge. Trapped between the roaring sea and their shotguns, he'd make perfect target practice for the Docampos.

The only question was how to win himself more time. There was nothing around that he could use.

Desperate, he searched his pockets, but the only thing there was the rusty Walther P38. Just then, his fingers came into contact with the little hank of fishing line that Elvira Couto had given him as an amulet. It had been lying there ever since, with no apparent use.

The idea appeared in his mind, from nowhere.

Absurd and unlikely, but it was all he had.

*Desperate times call for desperate measures.*

He unraveled the fishing line, praying that it wasn't broken. Quickly, he tied one end to a twisted root that emerged from among the rocks on one side of the path, and stretched it out across the track, some eight inches above the ground. He wrapped it around a large rock, which he balanced on top of another stone. Pulled tight across the path, it was invisible, but at most it would cause somebody to trip. He needed something more.

He took the pistol from his pocket and removed a cartridge from the magazine. The projectile, produced by some Nazi arms factory almost a hundred years earlier, had rust marks on one side and didn't look to be in the best condition. He buried it tip down, so that only the flat end was uncovered.

He was sweating profusely. He looked up and saw flashlights drawing near. The path was too narrow for the SUV, but its occupants were approaching, cautiously but relentlessly.

Time was slipping away. He took the badge from his coat and, very carefully, inserted it just a few fractions of an inch into the hole for the firing pin so that it sat upright. His hope was that, when someone came along the path and tripped on the fishing line, they would dislodge the rock, which would fall onto the badge pin, detonating the propellant.

There were a thousand things that could go wrong, obviously. He'd learned this trick from some Kurdish rebels in northern Syria years ago, but they had performed it with a Soviet anti-tank mine, not a miserable 9-mm bullet from almost a century ago.

Even so, it might give his enemies a fright and make them think twice about coming after him.

He checked the trap one last time, then set off toward the rocky cliff edge, just as he saw the flashlights shine directly on that section of the track.

It was no longer raining, but the booming sound of the sea crashing against the cliffs was deafening. This was accompanied by a searing, scraping sound, which he realized was the rocks being dragged back and forth like marbles across the foreshore.

He swallowed, awed by the force of nature. The idea of climbing down the cliffs seemed even less attractive.

But he had no choice. The flashlights had almost reached the spot where he had rigged up his trap.

*Please work. Please, I beg you . . .*

Nothing happened.

Either his pursuers had seen the trip wire, or the stone hadn't fallen on the cartridge. Or perhaps the ancient bullet simply hadn't worked. Just when he had convinced himself that his booby trap had failed, he heard a detonation, followed almost immediately by a shout of surprise.

A hail of shots was immediately unleashed. From his hiding place, Roberto could see the flash of guns as they unleashed their projectiles into the darkness.

"Hold your fire!" roared a voice in the distance. "Stop shooting! You're wasting ammo, you fools!"

"I've twisted an ankle!" came the voice of a woman who sounded as if she were in pain. "He's left trip wires across the path!"

"Can you walk?"

"I don't know," she groaned. "I don't think so. I'm sorry, Luis."

The wind, which was blowing in Roberto's direction, carried a sigh of frustration to his ears.

"Don't worry. Go back to the truck and wait for us there."

"On my own?" She sounded scared.

"Of course! What are you afraid of? We're the only ones here!" Luis Docampo sounded furious. "Go on, get moving!"

A long, heated discussion ensued, the details of which Roberto couldn't make out. But he'd given them something to think about, and he also had one pursuer less. The balance was still unequal, but he had tipped the scales. They'd be sure to advance more carefully now.

The path came out at a promontory at the cliff's edge. To one side, spattered with seagull shit, was an old information sign in various languages showing a cross-section of the Devil's Hole. But Roberto's attention was on the large opening surrounded by a precarious wooden guardrail that barely came up to his waist. He cautiously approached the edge of the shaft and looked down.

It was a black abyss, the bottom invisible. From below came a deep sound—half roar, half lament—every time the waves penetrated the narrow passage at sea level and crashed inside in a thunderous explosion. From the shaft came a series of deafening bangs followed by strange silences each time the sea retreated, before the cycle began again, as it had for thousands of years in the carving out of that extraordinary rock formation.

He took a step back. The place—which must have been awe-inspiring in daylight on a calm day—was terrifying in pitch darkness in the middle of a storm.

He saw now that his plan to climb down the cliff was doomed to failure. Picking his way blindly over slippery stones without knowing where he was going was a self-imposed death sentence. If one of those frenzied waves hit him, he'd be squashed like a bug on a windshield.

There was nowhere to go.

This was the end of the road.

His hands trembling, he took the Walther P38 from his pocket and turned toward the lights, which had almost reached the promontory.

There were four of them, he now saw, two men and two women, with Luis Docampo at the head. Three were carrying shotguns, and the fourth held a huge axe. They stopped a few paces away, and for a moment, nobody uttered a word.

"It's over, Lobeira." Luis Docampo's voice was full of tension. "You're trapped. Put down your gun."

"No way." He tried to control the tremor in his voice and pointed the P38 at them. "You put yours down and let me leave. Nobody needs to get hurt here, Luis."

Luis looked around, as if only just noticing where they were. "There are four of us and one of you," he replied. "Do you really think you can escape?"

"Your shotguns can each fire once, and I have a magazine with a dozen cartridges," replied Roberto. "I think that evens things up."

"Seriously?" Luis looked at him with wide eyes and clicked his tongue. "Do you think you'll kill all four of us before we fire? I doubt it."

"You don't want to find out." He gripped his pistol tight. "I'm serious."

"I don't think you are." Luis took a step toward him. "I don't think you've got the balls to pull that trigger."

Roberto swallowed with difficulty. His throat was tight.

Luis Docampo took a step closer, a sinister smile on his face.

Roberto raised the pistol and pointed at a spot slightly above his enemy's shoulder. Luis was right about one thing: Roberto would never fire at them in cold blood. He wasn't a murderer. But they didn't need to know that.

The old P38 trembled in his hand as he squeezed the trigger.

There was a dull click, and Roberto felt as if his heart had stopped.

Decades of salt and rust. A complete lack of maintenance. Old, damp ammunition. There were a thousand possible explanations. He couldn't know the cause, but the pistol had jammed, just as he had feared it might. He registered a fleeting look of terror in Luis's eyes before the man realized that the weapon hadn't fired.

Roberto squeezed the trigger again, desperately, but the mechanism was locked solid. Luis's expression went from fear to surprise and, finally, to comprehension and triumph. He approached Roberto, who was staring at the pistol with the funereal expression of someone who has just received a terrible piece of news. Almost delicately, the islander removed the gun from his hand while the rest of the party kept their shotguns trained on him. Luis inspected it for a moment, then tossed it into the Devil's Hole.

"Turns out you did have the balls," mused Docampo. "I definitely didn't see that coming."

Before Roberto had a chance to ready himself, Luis punched him hard in the stomach. Roberto gasped and took a step back, and felt the ground sloping away behind him, marking the edge of the shaft. Being punched by these people was becoming a tiresome routine, but he suspected that worse things were about to happen to him.

"I've never liked you." Luis Docampo grabbed him to stop him falling and, in a delicate, almost intimate gesture, pulled him close. "You have no idea how much I'm going to enjoy killing you."

Roberto struggled to his feet and, after getting his breath back, gave him a faint smile. "That's . . . never . . . going to happen," he panted. "Ever."

"Really? And can I ask why not?"

"Because if you kill me, you'll never find the money." Roberto gave him a defiant stare, having just thrown his winning card onto the table. "I've hidden it well. You can turn the island upside down and you'll never find it, not a single cent. You need me alive."

Luis Docampo stared at him for a moment. Then, to Roberto's surprise, he laughed. But it was mirthless laughter, full of pain. "Do you really think I give a damn about the fucking money?" he asked quietly. "After everything you've done?"

"I don't understand," Roberto replied, with a horrible sense of foreboding. "I don't know what you're talking about."

"I'm talking about my cousin Ricardo, the one whose head you cut off," whispered Luis furiously. "About old Elvira Couto, who you murdered in cold blood. Don't worry, we had time to see what you did at her place. You're a sick, twisted son of a bitch, Lobeira."

Roberto's whole body went numb. Luis thought that he was the murderer roaming around the island. That he was responsible for the two deaths. The injustice of the situation made him want to scream.

"The moment you showed up, things started going wrong. You just happened to find my cousin's body." Luis was seething with rage. "And we just happened to see you coming out of the home of a woman who'd been murdered in exactly the same way. You come to Ons, and people start dropping like flies and, guess what, you always just happen to be close to the scene of the crime. Don't insult my fucking intelligence!"

"It isn't what it seems. I . . . *oof!*"

Another punch, this time to the face, made Roberto lose his footing. He tasted blood inside his mouth.

"Don't lie to me! I know you did it, you bastard! Tell me where my son is! Where have you hidden him? What have you done to Tristán?"

Roberto froze. The last time he'd seen Tristán, the kid had been heading home just after saying goodbye to him and Helena Freire. For some reason, he'd never reached the Docampo house, and the boy's family thought Roberto had something to do with his disappearance.

"I don't know where Tristán is." He shook his head. "The last time I saw him, he was heading home. That's the truth."

"I don't believe you."

"That's all I know. I'm sorry." Roberto stood up, defiant. He'd seen enough situations like this to know that his death sentence had already been signed, no matter what he did. If he was going to die, then at least he would do it standing upright, with dignity.

"Tell me where my son is."

"I swear I don't know."

Luis Docampo looked at him, his eyes blazing with pain and rage. "If you aren't going to tell me anything," he said, spitting out the words without taking his eyes off Roberto, "you can tell the devil."

He shoved Roberto, a hard, direct jolt to the sternum, winding him. Trapped in a sensation of absolute panic, Roberto staggered back, as if in slow motion, and toppled over the low barrier.

Finally, with a scream of terror, Roberto Lobeira plunged into the shaft of the Devil's Hole.

# 32

## Something Exceptional

Fifteen minutes earlier, four miles out to sea and far from the sight of anybody, a set of conditions, each of which on its own would have been insignificant, combined to give rise to something truly unique.

The power of Storm Armand shook the surface of the sea, raising waves the size of four-story houses, fully thirty and forty feet high, which began running toward the shore in what appeared to be an infinite succession. Just then, a blast of warm air, driven by a sudden temperature change, collided with one of these waves, pushing it in the opposite direction from the current that was driving it toward the coast of Ons.

The blast, which could easily have torn the roof off a house, made almost no impact on the thousands of tons of water that constituted the wave, other than to slow it down momentarily, enough to ensure that the next wave hit it, at a precise angle of 120 degrees, not a single degree more nor less, and with a speed differential of less than five knots. If it had hit in any other way, the two waves would have collapsed, like thousands of other waves that collided chaotically in the fury of the storm, but in this case it was different.

The two waves merged to form a single, much larger one, loaded with their combined inertia. Advancing more rapidly, it swallowed up the waves ahead of it, in a complex process known as nonlinear compression, and gradually transformed into something else: a behemoth the height of a ten-story building headed for land with all the force of a freight train.

A killer wave, any sailor's nightmare.

The wall of water, two hundred yards long, its weight incalculable, took twelve minutes and thirty-five seconds to reach land, and struck the cliffs of Ons just as Roberto Lobeira hurtled into the Devil's Hole, destined for a certain death.

And that was the coincidence that saved Roberto's life.

He was plummeting into the shaft. The mouth of the hole receded as gravity claimed him. From his throat came a cry of pure, primal terror.

And just then, that whole section of the coast shook as if a bomb had exploded. The walls of the hole reverberated, and fragments of rock, blasted loose by the impact, rained down. The water entered via the channel at the foot of the cliff, which was too narrow to accommodate such a great volume all at once. The bottom of the hole turned into a bubbling, foaming, rising pool.

As the water rose, the distance between its surface and Roberto's free-falling body became shorter. What should have been a deadly, 150-foot drop was reduced to a fall of barely a quarter that distance. When he hit the water, Roberto was swallowed in a crazed pandemonium of turbulent foam. He managed to surface, and he gulped down some air before he was sucked down into what had now effectively become a huge drain.

He wheeled about helplessly in the water. Surrounded by impenetrable darkness, he had lost all sense of up and down. At breakneck speed, the stream of water carried him out through the channel, and he caught one of his knees on the side wall of the rock formation as he passed. The pain shot up his leg and set his brain on fire.

The sea spat him out on the surface just as he was running out of oxygen. He drew a frantic breath as the battery by water continued. The coast, a line of huge boulders covered with razor-sharp barnacles and mussels, loomed threateningly not a dozen yards away.

Just then, the next wave lifted him fifteen feet up in its final dash to the cliffs. Roberto screamed as he was hurled against the dark reefs that emerged like the decayed teeth of a monster of the deep. There was a brutal impact; he recoiled in pain . . .

And then, nothing.

# 33

## Waking Up

As if churned up by the waves, his mind feverishly mixed memories of the night spent adrift in the Mediterranean with his fall into the hole. Huge waves picked up the lifeless bodies of the migrants and dashed them against black walls made up of ravening mouths that then ground them to pieces. In the midst of it all, he was a powerless spectator, his trauma finally unleashed, freed of all controls and restraints.

It was the pain—a stabbing sensation in his chest every time he breathed—that made him regain consciousness.

He opened his eyes and, as he tried to focus, groaned in agony. At the same time, a feeling of relief exploded inside him.

*I'm alive. I'm alive, I'm . . .*

The sensation of joy drained away, however, as he realized that above him was not the cloudy sky of Ons but a damp and irregular stone ceiling, its far corners lost in darkness.

*Where the fuck am I?*

He carefully turned his head and realized that he couldn't move a single muscle from his neck down. He was struck by the terrifying possibility that he had been paralyzed, but the shooting pain in his knee brought him back to reality.

As he succeeded in wiggling his toes inside his sodden boots, never had he felt so happy at something so trivial. He then tried to do the same with his fingers but, hard as he tried, found he couldn't move them at all. That was when he realized he had been tied up.

He was lying on an old wooden table, which swayed a little when he moved. His hands had zip ties around them, and a thick rope had been lashed around his chest, securing him to the table.

He tried to process it all. His last memory, before suddenly waking up in a cave, trussed up like a turkey, was of being thrown against the rocky shore. That was enough to disorient the most levelheaded person.

He breathed deeply and instantly regretted it as he felt a sharp pain in his side. He must have a couple of broken ribs at the very least. The shock kept the pain at bay for the moment, but it was just a question of time before he truly began to suffer.

He closed his eyes and counted slowly to ten as he tried to calm the crazed beating of his heart. Then he opened his eyes again and looked around, a little calmer now.

He was inside a long, high cave, the stone floor covered with dry sand and the pulverized remains of seashells. In the openings in the walls, here and there, somebody had placed small kerosene lamps, which hissed softly as they bathed everything in their yellowish glow, although most of the light came from an old beacon connected to a gasoline drum by an antiquated rubber pump that looked at least a hundred years old.

Music played through a loudspeaker. The powerful voice of Rocío Jurado sang passionately of how she had found love, against a background of clicks and crackles as an old audiotape wound around the bobbins. That incongruous detail, more than anything else, made his hair stand on end.

He gradually took in more details, or at least as many as he could observe from the position in which he found himself. There were a few old pieces of furniture, including a bed that consisted of an old straw mattress on some fishing crates. Fixed to the walls were hooks from which hung oilskins, nets, and various implements.

Just then, Roberto sensed the presence of two faces in the shadows. He painfully turned his head to try to find out who those two people were, observing him, motionless, silent, and unblinking.

Almost immediately, he wished he hadn't.

The two people neither moved nor spoke because they were dead.

From a shelf, in two enormous glass jars full of alcohol, the head of Elvira Couto and a man who he assumed was Ricardo Docampo observed him through lifeless eyes. An inarticulate cry of terror caught in his throat.

"Help!" he finally managed to scream with all the power in his lungs. "Help! Is there anybody there? Help!"

He shouted himself hoarse, but nobody appeared. He struggled against the zip ties and the rope, but these only dug into his flesh, biting deeper the more he moved. His hands tingled, and he was soaked with sweat.

Just when he was beginning to think he would be trapped there forever, he heard footsteps approaching from the far end of the cave.

"Hello! Who's there?" he shouted. "Help me! Please!"

The steps came to a halt a few feet away, but try as he might to turn his head, he couldn't see his visitor. Then he heard the sound of a chair scraping as it was dragged across the floor, and a shadow came between him and the light.

Roberto focused his gaze, struggling to identify the person, and when he did so, he gasped.

In front of him, with a satisfied air, was Varatorta, who observed him with a friendly smile.

"Hello, Roberto," he said in a smooth, polite voice, as if they had just bumped into each other while strolling through the park. "Welcome to my secret lair. You have no idea how much I've been looking forward to seeing you again."

# 34

## There Is a Monster Among Us

Roberto remained silent, too confused to say anything. His mind, already befuddled by the fall into the sea, refused to process the mass of information that was now assaulting his brain.

"It's you," he finally managed to say. "You're the Tangaraño. You're the murderer."

"Come now," Varatorta said with a smile. "'Murderer' is a very ugly word. I think of myself as an artist. Or someone who investigates human nature, if you prefer."

"Where are we?"

"I already told you: in my secret lair. My refuge. My laboratory, you might call it."

"No." Roberto shook his head. His throat was in agony. "I mean . . . what is this place?"

"Ah, this!" Varatorta smiled, satisfied, and swept his hair back over his bald spot. "It's an old sea shaft, similar to the Devil's Hole that you fell into last night. Thousands of years ago, in this very place, the water came crashing in and ate away at the cliff above us. At some point, a rockfall blocked the entrance. Now, there's only one way in. Incredible, right?"

"How . . . how did I get here?"

"Oh, I thought that was obvious!" The lighthouse keeper opened his eyes wide in surprise. "I brought you."

"How is that even possible?" Roberto closed his eyes. "I don't remember . . . I don't know . . ."

"My dear friend, when you arrived at that woman's house," Varatorta said, pointing his plump thumb over his shoulder, in the direction of Elvira Couto's head, "I was outside, waiting in the bushes."

"You were waiting for me?" A shiver ran down his spine.

"I didn't know it was you." He shrugged. "I saw someone walking along Melide Beach and guessed they must be on their way to Elvira's place, so I decided to wait. I was curious to know who was out on a night like that."

Roberto struggled on the table and was rewarded with a shooting pain in his side.

"I was about to come and introduce myself to you there," the lighthouse keeper continued, "when all those people showed up, and I decided it was better to wait."

Roberto recalled how he had felt as if he were being watched when he arrived at Elvira Couto's hovel. Perhaps the Docampo party had unwittingly saved his life . . . before trying to kill him themselves.

"I was very intrigued, if I'm honest." Varatorta stroked his goatee. "I didn't know what was happening or what scores the Docampos might have wanted to settle with you, so I followed them."

"How come nobody saw you?"

"Everyone was concentrating on you," the lighthouse keeper explained. "It was a piece of cake. By the way, I was very impressed by your little trick with the fishing line. You should have seen the surprise on their faces when the bullet went off!"

"I need some water," croaked Roberto, becoming increasingly uncomfortable. "Please."

"I'm so sorry. I'm forgetting my manners! I'll bring you some right away."

Varatorta went over to the shelf where his victims' heads sat in jars, and came back with a flask. As he gently poured liquid into Roberto's mouth, Roberto savored the taste of fresh water.

"You must have swallowed a lot of seawater," Varatorta said. "Your throat will be raw."

"Tell me how you got me out of the sea." Roberto shuddered as he remembered the moment when the waves had dashed him against the cliffs. "I don't understand."

"Well, that was a stroke of luck." Varatorta sat down again, placing the flask at his feet. "When the wave washed you up against the rocks, I lost sight of you for a while. But then I saw you floating, unconscious, with your head above water. Your parka saved your life."

"My parka?"

"Yes." Varatorta pointed to Roberto's disheveled coat, hanging on a hook and dripping slowly onto the floor. "When you fell into the sea, it got wrapped around your neck, and because there was lots of air trapped in the filling, the parka acted like a life jacket. If it hadn't been for that, you'd have been pulled down, and I'd never have found you."

Roberto licked his cracked lips. He'd been cursing his leaky parka ever since he arrived on the island, but in the end, it was only thanks to it that he was still alive. He was sure that was something the coat's designers couldn't have even begun to imagine.

"The current washed you to a slightly calmer spot," Varatorta explained. "As soon as the Docampos left, I pulled you out of the water and, well"—he opened his arms wide—"here we are."

"I suppose I should thank you."

"That would be polite"—Varatorta nodded—"but such formalities are hardly necessary between friends. It doesn't matter, seriously."

"Why am I tied up?" He struggled on the table. "Let me go."

"No, no, no." The lighthouse keeper shook his head vehemently. "You've been through a lot. You have several fractured ribs, you have a cut on your head, and one of your knees is in a bad way. I think it's better if you stay there, for now. And it will make everything much easier."

"Easier? What are you talking about?"

"Slow down. There's no hurry. We've finally got time to chat. You'll find out soon enough." Varatorta tapped his nose with a conspiratorial gesture. "I'm hungry. Do you mind if I have a little snack?"

Without awaiting a reply, the lighthouse keeper got up and disappeared from Roberto's field of vision. A moment later, Roberto heard him clattering around at the other end of the cave. He took the opportunity to try to loosen his restraints. The plastic cables around his wrists were tight, but there was some slack in the rope that tied him to the table. Carefully, he puffed out his chest to make some space, and the pain in his broken ribs brought tears to his eyes. But even if it was just a few fractions of an inch, he could feel that the rope was now looser.

That small triumph revived his spirits. He rocked a little, and the table creaked under his weight, squeaking ominously. Roberto stopped, fearing that the lighthouse keeper had heard him, but the noise of the dishes continued uninterrupted. He repeated the movement, and the rope loosened again. Bit by bit, he was making space.

After a few minutes, he heard his captor approaching, and he stayed still. Varatorta dragged an old school desk over and put it next to the chair. Ceremoniously, he covered it with a cloth, on top of which he placed a plate of scrambled eggs with bacon, and a glass of red wine.

"Breakfast is the most important meal of the day," he said as he sat down. "That's what my mother always said. I'm sure yours told you something similar, Roberto."

"I don't understand," Roberto said, sounding slightly dazed.

Varatorta looked at him, his fork halfway to his mouth, a look of mild surprise on his face. "You don't understand why my mother said that?"

"No." Roberto nodded toward the glass jars sitting on the shelf. "I meant those."

Varatorta followed his gaze and contemplated the jars in silence. Then he turned back and gave him one of his strange smiles. He delicately rested the silverware next to the plate and took his time before speaking.

"I'll answer your question, but before I do, I'd like to know what you think about it."

"I think it's the work of a madman. A psychopath."

There was a tiny spark of annoyance in Varatorta's eyes, but it was replaced almost instantly by an expression of pity.

"You disappoint me, my friend," he sighed. "That wasn't the reply I'd expected from you. It's so . . . unimaginative. I'd hoped for much more from a writer of your reputation, to be honest. Please, have another try."

"What do you want me to say?" Roberto asked, measuring his words carefully. He couldn't help noticing how sharp the knife resting just a few inches from his head was. "Give me a clue, at least."

"I was sure you'd recognize the intrinsic beauty of my work." Varatorta was suddenly very serious. "From one artist to another, onc creator to another, an objective valuation of the delicate balance and subtlety of a work of art."

*Jesus, he's out of his fucking mind.*

"I'm not sure we're the same kind of . . . artist," Roberto replied cautiously.

"Think about it!" The lighthouse keeper waved his hands in the air, enraptured. "We're like soulmates! We both take the human essence and mold it until we've transformed it into something else, something that transcends the vulgarity of daily life."

"I'm just a writer."

"You're far more than that! You're a dream weaver—you allow people to escape from their boring lives and have exciting adventures. And I . . ." Varatorta looked at him with a faraway expression. "I take their tired, fragile, failing bodies and transform them into works of art that exceed the imagination. How can you not see that?"

"I don't know if Elvira Couto and Ricardo Docampo would agree," he replied dryly. "Perhaps they were happy with their bodies as they were."

*Mind your tongue. Don't provoke him.*

Varatorta banged the table, and the silverware clattered. "No!" he roared with an anger that didn't fit his peaceful appearance. "That's not true!"

Roberto swallowed again. He wasn't in a position to argue with the man. He decided to try another tack. "Tell me, then. I want to understand. From one artist to another."

Varatorta gave him a hurt look but with a flash of hope. "Really?"

"Absolutely. I want to know everything about your work."

"What a delight to meet someone who understands me!" Varatorta clapped. "You don't know what it's like to spend years here with nobody to talk to about all this. It's such a relief."

Roberto took advantage of the moment to puff his chest out again. The ropes loosened a tiny bit more.

*Keep him talking. Say anything, just keep him talking.*

"Well, I have to admit it took me a long time to reach this level of virtuosity," the man boasted, unaware of the bacon fat that was trickling down his beard. "I had to master the technique that enabled me to take the conversion of bodies to these heights."

"And how did you do that?" Roberto inflated his lungs once again, enduring the pain of his broken ribs.

*Just a bit more. Keep going.*

"It's a very long story." Suddenly, Varatorta seemed embarrassed, almost ashamed. "I don't know if you'll want to hear the whole thing."

"I wasn't planning on going anywhere. In case you hadn't realized. Please, continue."

"Well, my friend, from a young age, I was a solitary and somewhat dreamy child." Varatorta sipped his wine and settled into his chair. "I didn't have many friends. I mean, to be honest, I didn't have any.

Nobody understood me, and Mother always said I was too good to mix with people who didn't appreciate me."

"A lonely childhood, I imagine."

"Worse than that." Varatorta's expression changed, as if the wine and the memories had a bitter taste. "The other kids always mocked me. Tubby Tony, Freaky Tony, Wacko Tony . . . It was like they came up with new nicknames daily."

"I'm so sorry. Nobody should go through that." Another breath, another fraction of an inch.

"It doesn't matter." He shrugged. "It's ancient history now. When I turned sixteen, they stopped teasing me."

"What happened?"

"There was a boy in my class. His name was Guille Juncal. I looked up to him. He was tall, handsome, a good athlete, witty . . . The girls were all crazy about him. He was everything I wanted to be."

"Let me guess. He was the one who made up the nicknames?"

"Not at all. He never said an unkind word to me!"

"And?"

"I wanted to know how he did it. What he did that made everyone like him, how he always managed to be in such a good mood. I needed to know what I had to do to be like him."

"And what did he think of the idea?"

Varatorta stared into the depths of the cave, far away, as he remembered.

"I went to his house one Sunday in the summer, one of those days when it's so hot that nobody wants to go outside." He ran his hands through his hair, a gentle smile on his lips. "His parents were away, and he invited me in. I told you he was very kind. He gave me a glass of water, we talked for a bit, and as soon as I had the opportunity, I did it."

"I don't understand . . ."

"I whacked him on the head." He gave another of his weird smiles. "I killed him in the living room of his own house, and then opened him up to see what he was like inside. To find answers. To discover what made him tick. That was where it all began. That was when I discovered my gift."

Roberto held his breath, shocked. The man was confessing to murder as if he were talking about the weather. There was no remorse in his voice, no sense of guilt. Nothing. A complete absence of empathy.

"Your . . . your gift," he stuttered.

"That's right—my gift!" Varatorta's voice went up an octave. "That day, I realized I could see things beneath the skin that others didn't see. Things that make us unique and special but are hidden from our comprehension. You need the hand of a true artist, of someone like me, to bring them to light. I'd found my path. After that day, everything changed. I felt stronger. More confident. More . . . myself. Guille saved me. He showed me the path."

"I can't imagine his parents were too pleased that you'd killed their son."

"Oh, they never found out." Varatorta shrugged. "Mother took care of everything after I told her what I'd done. As far as I know, Guille is still buried in the same spot in our vegetable garden."

"Your own mother . . ."

"She wasn't at all happy." He frowned. "She didn't understand my art, but she loved me too much to let anything happen to me. She made me promise not to do it again. And I was a good boy; I did as she asked." He shrugged again. "But then, when Mother died, well, I thought I could start again."

"And nobody's ever suspected?"

"Never." Varatorta smiled triumphantly. "I've always been very careful."

"It can't have been easy."

*Keep him talking. Play for time.*

"In that sense, this place is perfect for me. I realized as soon as I got here, three years ago. Isolated but close to the mainland, and quiet enough in the winter that nobody interferes in your business."

"What about the summer?" The rope let out a groan, but the lighthouse keeper didn't appear to have noticed.

"Oh, this place fills up with tourists, people wandering around, sticking their noses everywhere. I spend the summer on the mainland." Varatorta's smile widened. "I travel. I enjoy my freedom."

Roberto's gaze jumped to the glass jars. He suspected that this "freedom" concealed a whole world of horror.

"You know what most people have in common?" Varatorta leaned toward him with a conspiratorial air. "They only see what they want to. They allow their prejudices and their beliefs to come between them and reality. They prefer what they know to what they don't know when they're trying to explain what surrounds them."

"Like myths," Roberto guessed, feeling as if he were swallowing broken glass. "Like the Tangaraño."

"She was the one who put me onto that little disguise." Varatorta nodded in the direction of Elvira Couto's lifeless head. "The rest was in the lighthouse library, as you well know. All I did was connect the dots, and suddenly I realized I'd discovered the perfect alter ego for the long winter months. The perfect way to cover my trail, in case I slipped up."

"But you never ki—" Roberto corrected himself. "You never practiced on an islander until now."

"That's true." Varatorta's expression turned cunning. "Never mix business and pleasure. I couldn't call attention to my hiding place. Practicing with animals helps to calm my nerves, and I improve my technique as part of the bargain. But it isn't the same; I'm sure you understand . . ."

Roberto nodded, humoring him. He was dealing with a textbook psychopath, someone with no moral or ethical boundary whatsoever, and for whom his victims were mere fodder, not human beings. And who was also clever enough to have led this life for years without being caught.

"I only really give myself over to my art when the occasion arises." Varatorta stood up and stretched. "When there's a sign to say the moment is right. What I didn't expect was that it would happen here, on the island, and so explicitly."

"And what was the sign?"

"I wasn't expecting *you* to ask that." The man looked at him in surprise. "I thought it was obvious."

"Sorry, I'm being a bit slow."

"Isn't it clear?" Varatorta seemed genuinely surprised. "You gave me the sign."

Roberto gulped when he heard that. "I gave you the sign? How? When?"

"In the lighthouse, in the library." Varatorta recited his words back at him. "'Sometimes you have to take back control of your life.' Those were your words, don't you remember?"

"But I didn't mean . . ."

"You told me we understood each other; you even squeezed my arm," the lighthouse keeper insisted. "There was no room for misunderstanding! First you asked me about the Tangaraño in the library, and then that. It was crystal clear that you'd seen what nobody else had. That you understood me."

Roberto didn't even blink; he was paralyzed by horror.

"When I saw you getting off the boat, I realized that another sensitive soul had finally arrived, another artist like me, someone who could really appreciate my work, someone with whom I could share a moment like this." Varatorta's voice vibrated, swollen with passion. "I generally keep a souvenir of all my works, but that day, I decided to make an exception . . ."

"The rabbit's head on my step," Roberto guessed.

"That's right!" he said, nodding with the enthusiasm of someone revealing a particularly good magic trick. "I assumed that as soon as you found it, you'd realize there was someone else like you on the island, someone with the sensitivity to create magic out of nothing."

"So when I went to visit you at the lighthouse . . ."

"I knew you'd understood my message as soon as we exchanged our first glance." In Varatorta's mind, the pieces fit perfectly in his twisted template. "And when you said you understood me, that you'd guessed who I really was . . . I almost told you on the spot! I hope my work hasn't disappointed you. I hope I've lived up to your expectations."

A bitter aftertaste filled Roberto's mouth as he realized that he had unwittingly provoked this orgy of blood and gore on the island. First by chancing upon the money, and now this. His arrival on the island had detonated a thousand accumulated tensions all at once. He and he alone was to blame. The weight of responsibility, however random and unfair, crushed him like a slab of stone.

"Now I've finally been set free." Varatorta took his hand. His touch was soft and slightly damp, like a fish. "That's why I want to thank you. For setting me free, for making me understand that I shouldn't worry about the consequences. Now, finally, I can finish my work on this island."

"Your work?"

"Yes, my work!" he shouted, excited. "A collection of different people, all distinct from one another, a variety of interiors exposed to the light, shining in their constellation of delicate differences. I've already got Elvira, an old woman who—without realizing it—gave me the thread of this magnum opus with her Tangaraño and her dead man's kiss."

Just then, Roberto remembered the plate of grilled fish, already cold, that he had seen on the woman's table, in her hovel. Searching for clues to the murder in the chest full of offerings, he had not realized he had one right in front of his eyes. Varatorta, the lighthouse keeper. Varatorta, the friendly cook. Who knew how many plates of food he had taken to the old woman while she recounted her old tales. He had forged his macabre plan while the woman ate in front of him.

"I've already got one of the Docampos," the man continued. "It was exciting, but I wasn't very pleased with the results. It . . . lacks sparkle. I'm sure you understand."

Roberto didn't answer. He was concentrating on loosening the ropes a little more.

"Now I have an urge to work with my companions at the lighthouse," he said, raising an eyebrow. "I know they seem brutish and unrefined, but I'm convinced I can get excellent results, particularly with Ibaibarriaga. It would be quite a challenge to open up that great big body of his; I'm sure of that."

"They don't know who you really are . . ."

"They've never asked." He shrugged. "But if they were observant, they'd have realized, as you did so perceptively in the library. I always do the cooking. I'm the one who repairs anything if it breaks. Always an artist's hands, obviously. Always me. Me, me, me."

"You dismantled the lighthouse radio transmitter." He remembered the way the pieces had been laid out, almost obsessively, on the table. "You cut off our communications."

"Of course it was me," the man laughed. "I'll put it back together later; that won't be a problem. As soon as I've dealt with Ibaibarriaga and Pazos, obviously."

"You won't be able to. They're stronger than you, and now they've been alerted—and they're looking for the money."

"Trust me." Varatorta smiled. "I'm one of them. But before that, I have to do something else, something very special."

Roberto looked at him, holding his breath. He didn't want to know what he meant, but he had already guessed.

"I need a Freire for my work of art. One of the Freire women, rather. I think Antía Freire's head would make the perfect contrast with the Docampo in that jar." He pointed at the shelf. "Feminine delicacy and masculine strength. Intelligence and its absence. Isn't it marvelous?"

"Stay away from her!" grunted Roberto, writhing on the table.

"Come now, let's not get sentimental." Varatorta waved his hand dismissively. "I'm fond of her, but you can't make an omelet without breaking eggs. It's just what has to happen."

"If you lay a finger on her, I'll kill you myself." The threat sounded hollow, even to his own ears. "I promise you."

"You see? That's exactly why you have to wait for me here, in my lair, enjoying my hospitality, while I take care of things. Anyway, you're forgetting something very important."

"What?"

"I need you to complete my work." He leaned over, until his lips were brushing Roberto's left ear, in an almost erotic gesture. "Because when I finish with them, it will be your turn, my friend. The culmination of my picture. The interior of an artist, of a creator, by moonlight. It will be a marvelous moment."

Roberto turned pale. He struggled furiously on the table, which rocked with his movements as he unleashed a string of curses and insults.

"See you in a few hours, my friend." Varatorta donned his oilskin. "I'll be back in a while. In the meantime, make yourself at home!"

With a smile, the lighthouse keeper turned and disappeared into the far end of the cave. Roberto was all alone, his brain vibrating like a tuning fork, his spirits at rock bottom.

There was a monster loose on the island, on the hunt.

And the only person who knew the truth and could stop him was held prisoner in this cave.

# 35

## So Near, and Yet So Far

He lay on the table, trying to put his thoughts in order. He had the final piece of the puzzle, yet there was nothing he could do to prevent what was imminent.

Nobody had the slightest inkling as to what was about to hit them. Everyone trusted Varatorta, taken in by his peaceable bearing and polite manners. With Storm Armand as cover, the lighthouse keeper felt at liberty to carry out whatever insane plans had been germinating inside his head, without worrying about the consequences. He had entered a spiral from which there was no exit. And he didn't care. His only concern was to complete his grisly artwork.

Roberto had to escape, come what may. On the cassette player, Rocío Jurado had given way to Juan Gabriel, whose silky voice and mellifluous Mexican accent urged the listener to hug him tight, tighter than ever. Bound like a parcel, Roberto couldn't help noting the bitter irony.

He counted to three and puffed up his chest once again to loosen the ropes. The stabbing pain in his lungs was so intense that he cried out in agony. Dejected, he realized that his efforts had made almost no difference. At this rate, he'd never manage it. He'd have to find another way to free himself of his bonds.

As he writhed in frustration, the table let out another alarming creak . . . and an idea popped into his head.

He began to rock from side to side, gradually building up momentum. With each movement, the table creaked and groaned, louder and more ominous all the time, as it threatened to fall to pieces under the weight of the assault.

Suddenly, the table let out a rasping squeak that echoed off the walls of the cave, and, almost simultaneously, one of its legs gave way. Roberto fell to the ground in the middle of a sea of broken, half-rotten boards. The sudden, jarring impact on the stone brought forth another cry of pain. This was no way to treat a set of broken ribs.

He lay on the floor for a few seconds, his face buried in what was left of the table, while he struggled to get his breath back. The rope had come undone, but the zip ties continued to dig into his wrists. His situation had improved but not by much.

*Think! How the hell did he do it? You know the answer. Just try to remember!*

His mind traveled far back in time, to a bomb-torn hotel in Kandahar, Afghanistan. A guy from Blackwater, the US mercenary company, a red-faced, suntanned kid who was a mountain of muscles and tattoos, drunk as hell, had bet Roberto and some other war correspondents that he could easily free himself from an ensemble of zip ties exactly like these. They had been unconvinced, of course, but in the end, the mercenary had won his free round of beers.

He shut his eyes tight and remembered the scene, striving to recall every last detail. Then, still lying on the ground, he tried to reproduce each of the mercenary's movements.

Varatorta, so that he could lay him face up on the table, had made the mistake of tying his prisoner's hands in front of him, and now Roberto could make use of that fact. He started by untying the laces of his boots, although it wasn't easy as his fingers were stiff from lack of circulation. When he finally managed to undo the knots, he passed one of the laces through the central zip tie that joined the zip ties around his wrists, and then tied it to his other bootlace with the most secure knot he could manage.

He cast a critical eye over his handiwork. His bootlaces were strong, and now he had a cord passing through the center of the zip ties. Roberto lay on his back, straightened his legs as far as the laces allowed, until they were tense, and then began to move his legs as if he were pedaling a bicycle, faster and faster.

The laces made a rough hissing sound as they rubbed at the zip ties. Each time he straightened his injured knee, an explosion of agonizing pain flooded his body, launching waves that reverberated through every fiber of his being. His forehead was beaded with sweat as he struggled to ignore the pain and keep the zip tie as taut as possible.

*Clack.*

That was it. The zip tie had snapped from the accumulated tension and friction.

His hands were finally free.

He rubbed his aching wrists. Then he got to his feet, only to realize what a mistake that was. His knee made a stomach-churning crack, and he very nearly fainted from the pain. He fell back to the floor in agony, and it was a whole minute before he was ready to try again.

This time, he stood up very carefully. The zip ties were still wrapped around each of his wrists, cutting off his circulation. He looked around, and his eyes alighted on a stone shelf on which an array of tools and instruments was laid out.

He struggled over to it. Each time he placed weight on his wounded leg, his knee screamed, but he gritted his teeth and continued to inch his way forward. By the time he finally reached the shelf, he was bathed in sweat and his head was spinning.

He inspected the items on the shelf: various screwdrivers, some electrical components, a few other bits and pieces, and among them all, some pliers. He picked them up, but they immediately slipped out of his sweaty hands.

"Steady now," he whispered to himself. Sweat had dripped into his eye, making it sting, but he ignored it. "Nearly . . . there. Nearly . . . there."

With one final effort, he got hold of the pliers again and managed to snip the zip ties. He was free.

He had to lean on the shelf as he recovered his strength. From where he stood, he could see the full extent of the cave. It was much smaller than he had imagined, no more than thirty feet deep, and lower at the back as the rocky roof tapered to meet the floor. There at the back, he spotted a kitchen with a work surface, on which stood a 1980s cassette player. He limped over and switched it off. The silence came as a relief.

Dragging his bad leg behind him, he inspected the rest of the cave, looking for something that might be of use to him. Unconsciously, he moved in a wide circle, trying to stay as far as he could from the shelf bearing the heads of Elvira Couto and Ricardo Docampo, which observed him unseeingly, a rictus frozen on their faces for eternity.

Almost all the furniture looked like castoffs, just one step away from becoming firewood. When he opened one of the drawers, he let out a sigh of relief. This had to be Varatorta's first-aid kit. He rummaged around in its contents until he found some Valium. Then, right at the back, he spotted a plastic canister.

*Amphetamines. I wonder why that doesn't surprise me.*

Roberto hesitated for a moment before slipping a dextroamphetamine pill into his mouth. His body was almost at its limit, and he needed one last burst of energy, even if that pushed the needle into the danger zone.

The rest of his search was fruitless. There were no weapons apart from the silverware the lighthouse keeper had used to eat with. Wherever it was that Varatorta kept the knives and saws he used to carry out his crimes, it wasn't here.

*He's got them with him. He needs them to finish his work.*

There was no time to lose. Every minute counted.

He struggled into his wet parka, which he now viewed with grateful eyes, and limped toward the end of the cave. A pile of huge boulders, evidence of the rockfall that had closed the shaft many centuries ago, barred his way, but he saw that, off to one side, a small path led upward. A gentle draft of air, redolent of salt and moisture, caressed his face from above.

*That's where the exit is.*

He was about to head for it when a sudden thought stopped him. He couldn't just leave the place as it was.

He limped over to the gasoline drum that powered the beacon, and disconnected it. The light went out, and the cave was plunged into gloom, illuminated only by the two propane lamps hanging on the wall. Roberto shook the drum and heard liquid sloshing about inside it. It was still half full, and it must still contain at least thirty gallons of fuel.

He tipped it over, and his sinuses were inundated with the smell of the gasoline that came gurgling out. The fuel spread across the stone floor, trickling under the furniture and the shelves, soaking every last corner.

He grabbed one of the propane lamps and hurled it to the ground. The glass shattered, and the fuel caught. The heat drove him back as the ball of fire spread throughout the cave, burning everything inside it. Taking one last look before he made his exit, he saw the flames engulf the glass jars that contained the heads of Varatorta's victims.

He left the hellish scene behind, relieved by his act of atonement. The monster was still on the loose, but his work had been reduced to smoke and ashes.

The opening was little more than a narrow crack that he could only enter on his stomach, but he crawled along the passage until he reached a homemade wooden ladder that ascended up into the darkness above. Gingerly, he placed his foot on the first rung.

It seemed solid.

He began to climb laboriously up, using only his uninjured leg. In the meantime, the smoke from the flames below was searching for an exit and enveloped him like a shroud. Soon, he was coughing and his eyes were watering. If he lost his footing and fell, he'd end up being devoured by the fire that he himself had started.

Burning Varatorta's lair had seemed like a great idea just a few minutes ago, an act of divine justice. Now he wasn't so sure. Luckily, as he ascended, with the current of fresh air blowing downward, the sound of the waves breaking against the shore grew stronger. He was very close.

Finally, his head emerged into the cold night air that ruffled his hair. Roberto gasped, seeking oxygen, as his fingers grasped the edge of the shaft. He breathed deeply, once, twice, three times. He'd never have imagined that a mouthful of air could both hurt so much and taste so sweet. He wiped his eyes on his sleeves, and blinked a couple of times. And then he frowned.

He sensed something was wrong. He turned his head, trying to orient himself.

Then he let out an impotent groan.

Storm Armand was still blowing, but the rain had stopped and the wind had dropped slightly. The clouds had disappeared, and above his head, the sky was full of stars, twinkling icily. The full moon shed its white light on the whole scene, and Roberto could see almost as well as if it had been day. Just across the water, a few hundred yards away, rose a huge black bulk, at the base of which he could make out a foamy line of waves beating against the shoreline.

There was nothing that size anywhere near Ons . . . apart from the island itself.

Roberto realized there was only one place from which such a view was possible: Onza, the islet just off the main island, a chunk of wild and deserted rock that was completely uninhabitable . . . and of course, cut off.

Varatorta had established his refuge on the only place where he could be sure he would never have unexpected visitors.

And Roberto had no way of escaping.

# 36

## Roberto Lobeira's Big Problem

The low hum of an outboard motor carried to Roberto on the wind. It could only mean one thing.

Varatorta was crossing to Ons, heading for one of the beaches at the south end of the island. The storm had abated somewhat, but the sea remained wild. You had to be either very stupid or very skillful to sail in such conditions.

Varatorta, Roberto suspected, had both qualities in spades.

Lifting himself out of the shaft with a final push, Roberto lay flat on his back, trying to catch his breath. Among the patches of cloud above, he caught the twinkling of an airplane at low altitude. He watched it traversing the sky, hypnotized, still unable to believe his good fortune.

He was alive, unbelievably enough. In the span of a few hours, he had been chased, shot at, had fallen from a very high cliff, and had survived an encounter with a serial killer. If he were a cat, that would be almost half his lives gone.

As far as he was concerned, his guardian angel would be well within its rights to ask for a raise. Or a promotion to archangel, for that matter. The only thing he couldn't give it was a vacation, because this was all far from over.

Roberto, with a salty taste in his mouth, saw that this dance with death had at least one more song to go. He had to gamble his life blindly, and just cross his fingers for his color to come up again on the roulette wheel.

*Get moving. You have to keep moving.*

The pain shooting up from his knee mingled with that of his broken ribs, his dislocated right shoulder, and the dozens of cuts and bruises all over his body. He should be in the ER, being tended to by doctors, and not lying on some desolate rocky crag.

But you play the hand you're dealt.

If he stayed lying down too long, he knew he'd never be able to get up. He forced himself to his feet, wincing, gritting his teeth, and started moving down to the shore.

What would normally have taken him five minutes took several times that, every excruciating step bringing tears to his eyes. At last, he felt sand underfoot—the unreal white sand of Onza's only beach, a narrow strip no more than thirty feet long. He could see Varatorta's footprints and the track left by the boat when it was dragged down to the water, but apart from that, there were only seaweed, the odd bit of plastic, and driftwood.

His spirits sank. There was no boat in sight. He was trapped on the islet. There was no way out.

To try to swim across, in his current state, was out of the question. In such treacherous waters, in the dark, he'd be sure to drown.

Unless . . .

Maybe there was a way. Something that was staring him in the face, and yet was at the same time too terrifying to consider. He shuddered.

He had caught sight of something at the back corner of the beach, half-hidden in some scrub: an empty, half-rusted oil drum like the one he'd knocked over in the cave. God only knew how long it had been there. Though rusty, it looked otherwise in decent enough shape—not full of holes.

Looking out across the channel, Roberto spotted a cove on the far side, into which the wind and tide appeared to be driving the waters. With the oil drum as a makeshift raft, he would surely get there—it was only a few hundred yards away.

In theory, it was simple.

But he couldn't do it. The voice inside Roberto Lobeira's head mocked him.

*Forget it. You know it's impossible,* it whispered.

Roberto gulped. It was one thing to get in the water in daylight, as he had done to retrieve the bundle a few days earlier. This was entirely another matter. To be out in dark waters, clinging to some ad hoc flotation device, would mean reliving the very trauma that kept him awake so many nights. It would mean turning his recurring nightmare into a reality.

And he was seriously thinking of submitting to that torture.

*No. No way . . .*

Instinctively, he took a step backward, but then the image of Varatorta entering Antía's room, a lazy smile on his face, jolted him.

*Sometimes you have to take back control of your life,* he'd told Varatorta. Which Varatorta had, in his idiosyncratic way, taken quite literally.

Now he had to follow his own advice. There was no other choice.

Roberto let out a roar, a mixture of fear, despair, and defiance.

*Don't think about it. Do it. Do it.*

He rolled the drum down to the water's edge. It was instantly snatched by the undertow, and he flung his arms around it. Before he knew it, he was out of his depth and being swept out across the channel.

There was no turning back.

Roberto gritted his teeth and concentrated on not letting go. Without the drum to keep him afloat, he knew he'd be a dead man. A wave crashed over his back, and he let out a shriek. He screwed his eyes shut, trying to control his breathing.

When he opened them again, it seemed that things were working in his favor for once, as the current was indeed taking him directly toward the main island. He just let himself be carried along, bobbing up and down at the mercy of the waves, while the landmass ahead loomed progressively larger.

But then, one of his hands slipped. As he regained a hold, he took a gash from one of the drum's edges. Inside his head, he heard drowning people all around him, flailing, battling with the waves. Reality had turned blurry—his heart was pounding even harder on account of the amphetamines, while panic, that ravenous monster, was dragging him toward the seabed . . .

At that very moment, as he was doing battle with every single one of his inner demons, he saw something he hadn't accounted for.

A few hundred feet away, a powerful spotlight and a pair of lights, one green and one red, were dancing across the waves. A speedboat was approaching Ons, in spite of the conditions.

There was no doubt about it. Someone was about to land on the island.

And in the midst of his nightmare, a spark of reality exploded in his head.

Because Roberto knew perfectly well who it was.

And what was about to happen.

# 37

## The Speedboat

Osvaldo Salazar was no coward. This was beyond all doubt.

He had demonstrated as much when, at the age of just twelve, in his native Cali, Colombia, he had joined the Norte del Valle Cartel and killed his first man. That rite of passage, which had turned him from just another street kid into a gunman, a full-fledged cartel *sicario*, had been the start of a brilliant career that had culminated in his current lofty position, to which he had ascended at the age of just forty. Tall and sinewy with crew-cut gray hair, he looked out at the world with ice-blue eyes that never failed to send shivers down the spines of his enemies.

At forty, the majority of people consider themselves to be just hitting middle age, but for a cartel member to survive that long was a major accomplishment. Violent deaths or long jail sentences had invariably claimed Osvaldo's kind by then.

The fact that he had reached that milestone without serious injury or arrest said much about his skills, or his good luck. Along the way, his original cartel had ceased to exist, and he was now working for another organization, and divided his time between Mexico and Colombia. But it was all still part of the same game.

No, he could never be called a coward. But even he was struggling with the sheer terror of the stormy sea-crossing he was currently contending with. And there was no way he could let on about it with his men.

He hadn't liked the assignment from the start. He had long since graduated from petty courier jobs, so being sent to Spain in search of a mislaid package had felt like an insult to his pride. But he hadn't refused, not when the boss himself had selected him for the task. And when the details of the operation were explained, he saw why the boss had thought of him.

It turned out that a Spanish group operating in the Rías Baixas, the Ferreiros clan, owed his boss a considerable amount of money. Money that was supposed to have been left anchored at an agreed-upon pickup point but that, when their local contacts had arrived to get it, hadn't been there. The Galicians swore blind they'd done as instructed.

Of course, the boss hadn't believed a word of it. That wasn't how things worked in his world.

And that was why Osvaldo was here.

He and his men had been in Spain a week. They had caught a scheduled flight to Madrid, and after a brief meeting with a fixer who'd provided them with the necessary equipment in exchange for a considerable sum of money, they had rented a car and made their way to Galicia.

The interview with the members of the Ferreiros clan, in an abandoned warehouse in an industrial park in Cambados, was brief, intense, and ultimately very satisfactory—at least for Osvaldo Salazar. The two men he'd tortured to death, who were now lying dead in a ditch, probably weren't of the same mind.

He'd managed to establish that the Galicians weren't lying. Storm Armand had been preceded by a less violent storm, and during that, the bundle must have slipped its moorings and since then had been drifting loose in the estuary.

If those men had bothered to undertake a proper search rather than making excuses about the storm and the difficulties of sailing in such conditions, they'd still be alive. They'd overestimated the boss's patience, but, worse than that, they'd been sloppy.

And if there was one thing Osvaldo could not stand, it was sloppiness.

However, he now knew where the bundle was.

It should have taken only a few hours to resolve the matter, but Storm Armand's untimely arrival had complicated matters. He and his men had been forced to hole up in a hotel in Bueu for several days, waiting for the weather to settle.

Going out for air had been unthinkable, and not only because of the foul weather—four burly Colombians strolling along the quay would have been sure to attract unwanted attention in a tiny fishing port. And that was something that Osvaldo, in all his meticulousness, could not allow.

Finally, the conditions had started to improve. After several hours spent waiting in a bar in the port of Beluso, a short distance from Bueu, drinking cup after cup of the foul stuff the Spanish had the temerity to call coffee, Osvaldo and his men had been given the all clear to set sail.

All of which was why the four gunmen now found themselves being flung from side to side and up and down in a fiberglass speedboat, negotiating the most terrifying waves Osvaldo had ever seen, with four huge Yamaha engines booming out behind them.

No, he wasn't a coward. But he was still looking forward to having dry land underfoot again, even if it was on the gloomy, forbidding island now coming into view up ahead through the freezing foam and spray.

The man at the helm was something of a character. His face was so weather-beaten that he could have been eighty years old rather than his true fifty. Short and squat, he had hardly a decent tooth left in his mouth, and the odd gold replacement glittering here and there gave his smile an ominous aspect. His name was Francisco "Chuco" Barreiros, and according to numerous sources among the local drug runners, he was one of the best speedboat skippers in the area. Half an hour into the crossing, Osvaldo could attest to that.

Chuco expertly steered a course between the waves, accelerating in bursts at just the right moment when he had to bring the vessel over the crest of one. They would reach the top and seem to hover momentarily, before hurtling down the other side. A deft flick of the rudder, and Chuco swerved around the next oncoming breaker.

His steering was a spectacle in itself, as was the sight of Osvaldo's men, three of the toughest guys imaginable, leaning overboard to empty every last drop of their stomach contents.

"Nearly there!" Chuco bellowed.

"Can we dock in this?" Osvaldo held on tight as the speedboat bucked wildly.

"Dock?" Chuco laughed derisively. "If we go anywhere near the dock, we'll be smashed to pieces!"

"So what are we going to do?"

Chuco Barreiros lifted one hand from the wheel to point to a whitish line that was rapidly growing closer. "Straight onto the fucking beach!"

"Sure that'll work?"

"Death and taxes, man!" shouted Chuco, gunning the engines. "Those are the only things you can be sure of in this life!"

He seemed half crazed or drunk, or both, but there was no doubt he knew how to handle a speedboat. Once they were in the lee of the island, the swell diminished, and the boat stopped bucking like a wild stallion. Chuco then leaned over and switched on the landing lights, along with a powerful spotlight on the prow.

"What the fuck?" Osvaldo shouted. "We'll be spotted!"

"I have to be able to see!" the skipper called back as he also turned on the Fathometer to gauge the depth of the water. "You don't want me to fucking ground us. Now, let me do my goddamn job!"

Glancing between the sea up ahead and the Fathometer screen before him in the instrument panel, Chuco slalomed his way through the reef on the approach to Ons. With the occasional sudden sharp flick of the rudder, he managed to steer clear of the treacherous rocks lurking just below the surface.

If he hadn't been so focused on those things, he might have seen, a few hundred feet to the left, a person clinging to an oil drum. But the idea of anyone being desperate enough to get in the water in such conditions didn't so much as enter his thoughts.

With a final, almost suicidal burst of throttle, after which he cut and expertly tilted all four engines inside by jamming down a lever, Chuco Barreiros launched the speedboat straight at the beach. The nose hit the sandy bottom with a rasping hiss and carried the vessel—about two-thirds of the hull—firmly ashore.

"Made it!" cried the skipper.

With the din of the engines gone, the sudden quiet onshore—there were only the wind whistling in the bare trees and the waves lapping against the shore—was almost eerie.

Osvaldo stood up, which felt strange after having just about acquired his sea legs on such a bumpy crossing. He gave himself only a few seconds. They had to move.

"All right, men, lock and load! First, we secure the beach. Carlito, Joel, you take the right side. Python, you take the left. I'm covering. Move out!"

The Colombians jumped out of the boat with practiced movements. If any of them still felt discomfort from the bumpy ride, it didn't show. Osvaldo watched them with satisfaction. He had handpicked these three for their extensive military experience. They were ruthless and remorseless, the best in the field.

They fanned out across the beach, handguns at forty-five-degree angles to the ground, fingers hovering on the triggers. After a short while, Osvaldo heard a series of confirmatory whistles. All clear.

"See you back here," grunted Chuco, taking a cigarette between his ruinous teeth. "Don't take too long—the tide's going out, and it'll be a job getting the boat down over bare sand."

"We'll be quick," Osvaldo said, patting him on the shoulder. "I'm not here on vacation."

Osvaldo knew Chuco would wait for them, however long it took. The man knew whom he was dealing with.

Osvaldo caught up with his men, and the four of them, with the deserted vacation homes the only witnesses, moved soundlessly along the track to the village.

When they reached the road, they were amazed at what they found.

"What the . . ."

The street, which in the summer would be crowded with tourists just off the ferry, was desolate—it looked like a hurricane had been through the place. Shotguns seemed to have been fired at the pitted front of the Docampo supermarket, and someone appeared to have smashed the door down with an axe. The ice cream sign, full of holes, creaked dully in the breeze.

There was evidence of fighting everywhere they looked. Broken glass covered the ground, and a barricade, formed of yellow garbage containers, old tires, and fish crates, had been set up in the middle of the road. Whatever had happened there had taken place some hours earlier, and none of the combatants were anywhere to be seen.

Python moved a little way to the side. He was short and barrel-like, with arms like pistons, and his half-unbuttoned shirt revealed the sizable snake tattoo from which he got his name. He crouched over something glistening on the ground, touched his fingers to it, and brought them to his nose.

"Blood." He nodded. "Still fresh. Shoot-out happened less than two hours ago."

"I can see that." Osvaldo frowned.

He didn't like it. He thought he was showing up on a cute little island inhabited by the type of people he could simply scare into handing over the money. And here was the aftermath of what appeared to have been a full-scale gunfight, outcome uncertain. Maybe the victors were hiding in the shadows, with him and his men in their sights at this very moment.

"Change of plan," he hissed. "Shoot first, ask questions later. We move together, and we stick to the cover."

They crept forward along the street, observing the damage. There didn't appear to have been many casualties, apart from whoever had left the patch of blood. The bullet holes seemed scattered rather than concentrated, and to Osvaldo's clinical eye, it looked more like an act of vandalism than a bona fide assault.

The work of amateurs, he concluded. Civilians, most likely, out to cause a ruckus and give whoever it was a fright.

Nonetheless, he would have felt better with an assault rifle in his hands just now. He and his men each had a Beretta 92S—provided by the fixer in Madrid for what was supposed to have been a simple in-and-out job—but these had only fifteen-round magazines. But he might as well have asked for the moon to be made of cheese.

You play the hand you're dealt.

One of his men, his olive-skinned face leathery and sporting a pencil mustache, tapped him on the shoulder.

"What, Carlito?"

"Over there," whispered the gunman, pointing across the street. "The church."

Ons's church was in a pitiful state. Part of the door had been hacked down, and the remaining portion swung pitifully in the wind.

"Let's go," he muttered.

It was even worse inside. What little furniture there was had also been hacked to pieces, and bits were scattered everywhere. The altar had been toppled and lay broken at the foot of the steps leading up to the small tabernacle. Flagstones had been pried up, exposing the bare earth below. Here and there, someone had drilled holes in the walls that looked like the entrances to giant burrows. They had no idea that they were contemplating the results of Ibaibarriaga's and his men's meticulous yet ultimately fruitless search for the money.

"Mother of God." Carlito crossed himself. "What's been going on here, chief?"

"Someone's been looking for something!" Osvaldo said. "And it seems they were pretty determined. Question is, did they find what they were looking for?"

"Our package?"

"Beats me. Python, why don't we find out? Get the tracker."

Python swung his backpack onto his front, unzipped it, and took out a rectangular device about the size of an iPad. He pressed a button on the side, and the screen came to life as the GPS device inside started sending out a signal. After a minute, a pulsing green dot appeared on the display.

"It's really near, chief," Python said, proffering the device. "Like a few hundred yards."

"Well, let's go find it," Osvaldo growled, "and then get the hell off this island."

They left the church, guided by the green dot on the device, which Osvaldo carried, while the others moved stealthily ahead, guns at the ready.

It wasn't long before they came to a halt, at a point where several footpaths met.

"Joel," Osvaldo said, pointing. "Open that up for me and let's see what's inside."

It was a yellow garbage container on wheels, intended, along with a dozen or so others distributed around the island, for the use of tourists. Although barely used in recent months, it still gave off a very pungent smell indeed. Shining a flashlight inside, they found it empty except for a bright orange buoy—the same one Roberto had spotted floating offshore. Python leaned in and pulled it out. Still attached were some shreds of yellow plastic. Python took out a jackknife and plunged the blade into the buoy, opening up a slit about eight inches long, and then pulled out the small locator device and the attached battery.

Osvaldo grimaced. Someone had gotten to the bundle first. He couldn't help but think of the Ferreiros and their negligence. If those sloppy bastards had done their job, he wouldn't be on this shithole of an island, and he wouldn't have this mystery to solve. Disconnected from the tracking device, the money could be absolutely anywhere.

"What now, chief?" asked Carlito.

"Let me think." Osvaldo rubbed his eyes. "First up—"

But before he could finish, from somewhere in the distance there came a salvo of what sounded like rifle reports. Instinctively, the gunmen all dropped to one knee, aiming their guns in the direction the sound had come from.

"Let's go pay our respects," Osvaldo said with a half smile.

"We're light on tools," Python said, waving his gun. "Sounded like rifles, right? They'll shit all over us."

"We've got the element of surprise. Plus," Osvaldo chuckled, "you're an ugly bunch. One look at you and I reckon they'll throw down their weapons in an instant."

"Seriously," said Python, "there's four of us. Shouldn't we go get some backup?"

"By then, the storm will be over, and the money will be long gone."

They set off in the direction of the gunfire, which started up again with a few furious bursts, followed by silence, and then a further exchange. As they were getting closer, Joel, at the head, raised a clenched fist and dropped to one knee.

Osvaldo crept forward until he was next to him.

"Enemy spotted, twelve o'clock," Joel said under his breath. "In that ditch."

"You sure?"

"Boss, I spent two whole years hunting guerrillas in the jungle. I'm sure."

"Okay, how many?"

"One. Don't think he's seen us yet."

"All right, you and Carlito circle round and come down on him from the bank. I'll hold here with Python in case he decides to move. And save your bullets. Let's take him alive."

Joel and Carlito left the track and slipped into the undergrowth. Osvaldo waited patiently. After a few minutes he heard a scuffle, followed by muffled shouts and a thump. Shortly, the two gunmen reappeared, dragging a crumpled figure between them.

"Any more?" said Osvaldo as his men flung the individual at his feet.

"Just one," Joel said. "Like I said."

"Armed?"

"Just this." Joel held out a penknife as the prisoner eyed Osvaldo in terror.

"Who the fuck are you?" Osvaldo asked.

"Tris . . . Tristán Docampo, sir," he stammered. "Wh-what's happening? Are you friends of Roberto?"

"I'll ask the goddamn questions." Osvaldo glared. "And if I don't like the answers, motherfucker, you're going to die in the most horrible way imaginable."

# 38

## The Siege

Over the years, men far more hardened than Tristán Docampo had buckled under pressure from Osvaldo Salazar. A terrified young man of twenty was no match for him. The Colombian had little difficulty in getting him to talk, and he was shortly describing everything that had happened on the island over the previous days.

"Let me see if I understand," said Osvaldo when the boy had finished filling them in. "Right now, your family is laying siege to the house of your sworn enemies, the Freires?"

"That's right, sir," Tristán said, gulping. "Please don't hurt me . . ."

"So why aren't you there with them?"

"I already said! Helena's inside the Freire house! I refuse to take part in this madness, but I also don't know how to stop them."

"Oh right, your girlfriend." Osvaldo again squeezed his temples. "What a sad tale. And would you like your sweet Helena to go on living?"

"Of course!" Tristán straightened up, summoning a shred of courage from somewhere. "I'd do anything for her!"

"Then be smart and tell me where the money is. That's all I want to know."

"The money was in the church, sir, like I said. That's all I know."

"We've been here already." Osvaldo puffed out his cheeks. "Try harder, kiddo, or things will get very ugly, very quickly."

"I've told you everything I know!" Tristán protested. "Maybe Roberto knows."

"Ah, the journalist. And where's he just now?"

"Beats me." He shook his head. "I last saw him the day before yesterday, when he was taking Helena home."

"So he might still be there?"

"I don't know." Tristán was trembling. "I've already told you everything I know, sir. Please let me go."

"Not just yet. We're going to hold on to you just a little bit longer."

With Tristán between them, Osvaldo and his men set off once more. They soon arrived at the flat area of ground in front of El Cucorno, the Freire family home. Crouching in some bushes, they contemplated the scene.

The Docampos had created a barricade out front, with piled-up garbage containers, pieces of timber, and overturned boats. From there, a group of them were keeping the house under constant fire.

The facade of the old farmhouse was riddled with shot and bullets, and several windows had been smashed. From time to time, the muzzle of a rifle would appear at one of them, shooting blindly in the direction of the Docampos, who would instantly and wildly return fire.

The assault on El Cucorno, if it could be counted as such, had not succeeded. A kind of stalemate seemed to have set in, and neither side appeared to know how to end the game.

*Very good,* thought Osvaldo. They were total amateurs, just as he'd imagined.

"Joel, you stay here with the kid. Carlito, Python, with me. Nice and quiet, you two."

Treading lightly, the three Colombians broke cover. Speed was of the essence because, although the Docampos' backs were to them, the defenders inside the house might spot them, and there was no telling how they might react.

Osvaldo, with his two men alongside, felt the adrenaline coursing through his veins. In situations where he might have his head blown off, he felt strangely serene, almost happy.

Although he'd never stopped to think about it, Osvaldo Salazar was the kind of person who, in situations where people usually lost their cool, became singularly lucid. Everything shone with a special light, every detail stood out sharply as time slowed down. It was a magical sensation. You could almost say he enjoyed the challenge.

Creeping up behind Ramón Docampo, he thrust the barrel of his Beretta into the back of the old man's head. Ramón stiffened in surprise. Meanwhile, Carlito and Python had done the same with Luis Docampo and another of the men behind the barricade. The surprise was total. The rest of the Docampos looked on, dumbfounded, with no idea who these new arrivals were or where they'd sprung from.

"Tell them to drop their weapons," Osvaldo commanded. "Or the next thing they'll see is your brains all over the floor."

Ramón tried to turn his head, but Osvaldo thrust his gun harder against the old man's neck. Osvaldo glanced across at his men, a strange electricity in his body. This was the key moment. If the Docampos realized that there were only three of them and reacted, a bloodbath would ensue.

"Tell them to drop them," he insisted. "Now."

"Fuck you," growled the old man. "I'm not going to . . ."

"We've got your grandson, Tristán, back there, with a gun just like this one to his head." Osvaldo pressed a little harder. "If you want his blood on your hands, that's no problem . . ."

Ramón turned pale, seeming to visibly deflate. Then, in a broken voice, he said, "Drop them!"

"But, Father!" Luis exploded.

"They've got your boy, you idiot!" he retorted. "Do as I say!"

Osvaldo, keeping his eyes on the old man, heard rifles and hatchets clatter to the ground. The satisfaction was mixed with a touch of disappointment. It was a little too easy for his liking.

Carlito went along the barricade, grabbing the weapons and then making a pile of them at Osvaldo's feet. Osvaldo finally allowed the old man to turn and face him.

"Who are you?" said Ramón, eyes blazing. "Where are you from? Do you work for the Freire family?"

Osvaldo shook his head.

"I've come to get something that belongs to me, Don Ramón." He stroked his temples slowly, gun still raised. "You know what I'm talking about."

He was pleased to see the old man turn ashen. Always an intriguing moment. Sometimes when it dawned on people whom they were dealing with, they actually pissed themselves.

"We . . . We don't know where the money is, I swear."

"But you knew it was ours, didn't you?" Osvaldo clicked his tongue. "Your grandson told us everything. You should have been smarter and not gotten mixed up in this. You know how the business works."

"They've got it!" Ramón pointed at the house, fury breaking through his fear. "Those traitorous sons of bitches—you should kill the lot of them!"

"I'm sure you'd love that, but I'm the only one deciding who lives or dies today."

"It's like a castle, that house. You won't get them out of there unless you've brought a cannon."

"Oh, I won't need one." Osvaldo looked up at the house. "I've got a much better idea. Joel! Bring me the boy!"

Joel appeared from up the bank with Tristán by the collar, manhandling him as they moved down to the barricade.

"Are you crazy? They're going to kill us!"

"Maybe." The sweet sensation of risk, that drug more potent and delicious than anything the cartel ever sold on the streets, flooded Osvaldo's chest. "But something tells me they won't."

The Colombian led his hostage out in front of the barricade. He forced Tristán to kneel. Noisily cocking his gun, he pointed it at his head, while Luis cursed loudly from the barricade.

"Helena!" cried Osvaldo. "Helena Freire! There's someone here who wants to talk to you!"

He was met with a resounding silence.

"I'm going to put a bullet in this guy's head"—he looked at his wristwatch—"in exactly one minute if you don't come out here. Clock's ticking, Helena."

There came the sound of startled, angry voices from inside, followed by a muffled female scream.

Osvaldo felt his pulse quicken. If she didn't come out, Ramón Docampo was right: He had no way of forcibly removing the Freires from the house, other than by setting fire to it. But if he did that, he risked the money burning too.

Just as he was preparing to pull the trigger, there was the sound of bolts sliding open and locks turning. Osvaldo watched with satisfaction as the girl ran out, despite someone's apparent efforts to restrain her.

She dashed over to them, breathless and disheveled. Osvaldo noticed that one of the sleeves of her dress was torn, presumably from her struggle to get out of the house. Helena dropped to her knees beside Tristán, and the two of them embraced tearfully.

Osvaldo let out the breath he had been holding in and allowed himself another of his rare smiles. Once again, the coin had landed just as he'd called it.

Osvaldo let the lovers enjoy their reunion, wanting to be sure that all present saw and understood what was going on between them.

"Nothing sweeter than two young people in love," he said at the top of his voice, to no one in particular. "Right?"

He looked around, radiating calm, completely in control.

"Two young lovers, their whole future ahead of them, a house on the hill, maybe even the pitter-patter of tiny feet . . ." He stroked

Helena's hair absently and clicked his tongue again. "It'd be a shame if that were all cut short. A real shame."

Helena and Tristán looked up at him, roused from their embrace by the threatening edge to his voice.

"Everyone in the house, you've got thirty seconds to lay down your weapons and come out!" He hauled Helena to her feet, and she let out a screech as she felt the cold metal of his gun thrust against her chin. "My name is Osvaldo Salazar, and I've come for what's mine!"

Five interminable seconds of silence ensued.

"If you do anything to my daughter, you're a dead man!" Rosalía Freire's voice rang out from one of the windows. "You've got four guns on you right now!"

"Maybe," Osvaldo said, feeling another burst of adrenaline, every last pore of his skin electrified. "Everybody dies, sooner or later. But if I go down, I promise you, my men'll leave this little bitch so full of holes, you'll be able to use her as a sieve. Twenty seconds!"

His heart was pounding, and he felt more alive than ever.

He could almost feel the sights of the rifles on him. He lifted Helena's chin with the barrel of his gun until she cried out in pain.

"Ten seconds!"

"Don't shoot!" Another voice, this time Antía Freire's, came from one of the windows. "We'll come."

Just as the count was about to reach zero, a dozen Freires emerged, unarmed and dejected. Python went over and frisked them one by one, before herding them together with the Docampos. The rival family members, all prisoners now, looked at each other in dismay.

"See?" Osvaldo said, letting go of Helena, who took refuge in Tristán's arms. "If everyone's reasonable, no one has to get hurt. But hold on, where's the journalist, that Roberto?"

"We don't know," said Antía firmly. She seemed the calmest of everyone. "He was here, but he left hours ago. I'm certain he's already notified the police and they're on their way. Get out of here and leave us alone, while you still can."

"Ooh." Osvaldo whistled. "You're a wild one. Don't you worry, we'll be long gone before anyone gets here. So, once again: Where's our money?"

"We don't have it," Antía replied. "Search the house if you want."

Just at that moment, Python was coming out of the house, with the old MP 40 slung over his shoulder as booty.

"No one else in there, chief," he said. "I didn't see the money, but it could be anywhere."

Osvaldo took a deep breath and massaged his temples pensively. Time was not on his side. The sun would soon be up, and the storm was almost over. He turned to Helena and Tristán, who were once again in each other's arms.

"Come on, enough fooling around," he said, placing himself between them. "Okay, someone is going to tell me exactly where our money is, right now, or these lovebirds are going to get it. And the rest of you will be next. We'll take you out one by one until there's nothing but a pile of corpses left on this mangy island. Do I make myself clear?"

"We don't know where the money is!" wailed Rosalía Freire.

"And neither do we!" cried Ramón Docampo. "I swear!"

"Why is it that I just don't believe you?" Osvaldo shook his head. "Don't you see how easy this all could be? Right, who's first?"

Swinging the Beretta slowly back and forth between Helena and Tristán, he sang softly, "Eeny, meeny, miny, moe . . ."

The gun ended on Helena, and she gasped in terror. Osvaldo shrugged and pulled the trigger.

# 39

## The Confession

There was a collective, horrified scream, and Helena cowered—but only a loud click came from the gun. The girl opened her eyes wide, as if she were unsure whether she was still alive.

The Colombian opened his left hand to reveal a gleaming 9-mm bullet in his palm.

"Empty chamber that time, just for fun!" Then, sliding back the rack on top of the Beretta, he pointed it at her again while gently stroking her hair. "Shh, don't cry." And then, to the families, "This time I'm not playing. Come on."

"No!" came a voice. "Stop!"

Osvaldo turned and saw a skinny boy in the center of the group who had tears rolling down his cheeks.

"I know where the money is," he said. "I'll tell you, but please stop."

"No!" shouted Antía, yanking on the boy's arm, but he pulled away.

"That money made me hurt someone. I don't want it to happen again." He looked at Antía tearily. "That money is bad. Bad, bad, bad! Let this man take it away, and everything can be okay again."

"Oh, little one." Antía's voice quavered. "I wish it were that simple . . ."

"At least this guy's got some sense," Osvaldo said. "What's your name, kid?"

"Diego," came the answer, between hiccups. "Diego Freire. Don't hurt them. Please."

"You have my word." Osvaldo opened his palms innocently. "Tell me, Diego, how come you know where the money is?"

"Roberto hid it." The boy's nose was running, and the snot mingled with his tears. "He thought he was on his own, but I followed him. I like following him. I'm always saving him. He says I'm a superhero."

Osvaldo arched an eyebrow. "Well? Where is it, then?"

"In the old graveyard. Quite near."

"All right, Diego Freire." Osvaldo tucked the pistol into his belt. "Lead the way; we'll follow. Everyone."

"Everyone, chief?" asked Python.

"Yes, everyone," he hissed, leaning over to whisper in his subordinate's ear. "We can't leave them behind—we'd have to set a guard. There aren't enough of us to divide forces."

Python nodded, then gestured to Carlito and Joel, who took up position on either flank of the intermingled Freires and Docampos, while he took up the rear. Osvaldo set off in front with Diego at his side.

A little light was entering the sky as the group moved slowly along the road toward the old church. Seen from afar, the singular procession had the look of some kind of popular pilgrimage, but that was rather undercut by the participation of the grim, gun-toting Colombians and the islanders' distraught expressions.

Osvaldo smiled to himself. He held all the aces, and he knew it. Once again, he was getting to show his expertise. He would soon have one very happy boss.

When they reached the old church, the gunmen herded the group into a corner of the graveyard, up against a wall, forcing them to sit on the ground with their hands clasping their necks. The tension had built up even more on the short walk, and the Colombians were increasingly brusque. Dawn's arrival left them under no illusions as to the need for haste, and the accumulated fatigue and nerves were beginning to tell.

Carlito and Joel guarded the hostages while Osvaldo and Python followed Diego over to Erundina's grave. Osvaldo eyed the ramshackle monument suspiciously.

"It's this one." Diego nodded vehemently.

"Okay, kid, get back to your family." He patted him on the back. "We'll take it from here."

Python picked up a branch—the very same one Roberto had used—and did likewise in making a lever of it. Leaning his considerable weight on it, he succeeded in lifting the tombstone, which he and Osvaldo, now able to get their hands around it, heaved aside.

Osvaldo peered into the grave. Inside were the two duffel bags. He pulled them out and immediately unzipped one. He sighed with relief at the sight of the jumbled wads of euros, dollars, and Swiss francs. He quickly checked the other bag too. He didn't have time to count the money, but it looked like it was all there.

He got up and dusted off his pants.

"We good?" Python said.

"We sure are."

He glanced around. In the growing light, the graveyard looked bucolic, like a picture postcard. The old church, the gravestones, the flower beds—just perfect for what he had in mind next.

"Carlito, separate the two families," he said. "And bring one of the groups over to the church."

Carlito hurriedly did as he was told. There were murmurs of concern and a few shouts of protest, but the guns pointed at their heads quelled any possible revolt. The families were separated, and the Freires were herded over to the front of the church.

"No, not like that." Osvaldo moved around the graveyard, observing the group with great concentration, like a director of photography. "Not so tight, give them some space. That's right, that's good. Now, the other group on the other side. A little farther away. That's it."

Osvaldo turned around, taking one final look. The islanders were positioned across the graveyard in two almost symmetrical lines, some twenty feet between the two. Some of them were trembling, fearing the worst.

Osvaldo approached Python, gun in hand. "You know what to do, don't you?" he whispered.

The man nodded, glowering. "Leave no witnesses."

"Leave no witnesses," Osvaldo repeated. "You and I will take care of the ones on the right. Joel and Carlito can do the ones on the left. Nice and quick, nice and clean, okay?"

"They'll start running," Python said. "There're too many of them."

"No, even better." Osvaldo stroked his temples. "Then it'll look like they did each other. The more scattered about the corpses, the better. We wipe the guns and leave them in their hands." His blue eyes sparkled. "Let the Spanish cops lose their minds trying to figure out what went down."

Python transmitted the orders to the other two, who silently went and stood between the two lines. A few cries and pleas began to be heard.

"What's going on?" Diego was holding Antía tight. "Are the bad men leaving? Why are they separating us?"

"Oh, Diego." Antía wrapped her arms around him. "It'll all be over soon."

"You sons of bitches," cried Ramón Docampo. "You swore you'd let us go!"

"Well, Don Ramón, you know better than anyone the consequences of stealing in this business." Osvaldo gave him one of his reptilian looks, but the old man glared defiantly back. "I am sorry. It's nothing personal."

The Colombians raised their guns, readying to shoot. A chorus of cries rose up from the cowering islanders as they awaited the imminent hail of bullets.

The sound of gunshots was deafening, so loud that it must have been heard on the other side of the island.

# 40

## The Ambush

But it wasn't the hail of bullets that Osvaldo had been envisaging.

The first one hit Carlito in the shoulder—with such force that he spun right round and dropped to the floor. Bullets raked the ground just in front of Osvaldo's feet, raising small tufts in the earth, like tiny volcanoes.

For the first time since arriving on the island, Osvaldo felt afraid. He cast around, trying to establish where the shots were coming from as his men ducked down behind the nearest gravestones. And then he saw them.

Two men were peering over the wall at the far end of the graveyard, hunting rifles leveled at him. In a split second, as he dived for cover, he took a mental photograph: One of them was burly, with a sweaty bald pate and a ferocious look in his eyes, and the other was a younger man with a messy shock of hair, his tongue sticking out the corner of his mouth as he took aim.

*Who are these motherfuckers?*

"That money's mine!" yelled Ibaibarriaga as he fired another shot. There was an impact, and the marble gravestone by Osvaldo's head showered him with fragments. "Hands off, you bastard!"

That was the signal for chaos to break out. Suddenly, all the islanders were running hither and thither, fleeing from the exchange of gunfire. The gunmen, too busy returning fire, could do nothing to prevent them from scattering.

"Boss!" Python shouted, dropping down beside him. "It's an ambush!"

"I can see that!" Osvaldo hissed.

"We can't stay here! The cover is for shit, and they've got the high position, plus more firepower! We have to retreat!"

"The money's over there!" Osvaldo pointed to the duffel bags, which had been left in what was now no-man's-land. "We aren't leaving without it!"

"But, boss, we're almost out of ammo! Carlito's hit, and for all we know, they could be about to flank us!"

Osvaldo swore. His lieutenant was right; they'd been caught completely off guard. He didn't have a clue who the attackers were, or if they were part of a larger force. For all he knew, this could be part of a pincer movement. If they were also coming up from behind, he and his men were done for.

Osvaldo Salazar was clever, but he wasn't all-seeing.

Had he known that it was only two of the lighthouse keepers, he might have made a different decision. Had he known that his adversaries had barely a dozen bullets left each, he would no doubt have proceeded differently. Had he known that they were far more terrified by the situation than his own men were, he would have made a stand.

Then things would have had a different ending.

A far bloodier one.

But Osvaldo had no way of knowing any of this, and he instead ordered the retreat.

The calm nerves that had kept him alive all those years won out over the rage. But this thing wasn't over.

*No way.*

This was just a deferral.

"Head back to the beach," he shouted to Python. "You help Carlito. Me and Joel will cover you."

The four of them began moving back to the gate, Carlito wincing at every step, while Osvaldo and Python loosed off some shots at the lighthouse keepers. Ibaibarriaga and Pazos ducked as the bullets crunched into the stone wall.

The islanders were all racing to escape from that hornet's nest. For a moment, Antía was right next to Osvaldo, but the gunman didn't even notice.

The chaos was total.

Osvaldo's whole plan, which had gone so smoothly until now, was unraveling.

# 41

## "It's All Your Fault"

"Come on, Diego!" Antía urged the boy, who was staring open mouthed at the chaos around him. "We have to go!"

"What's going on? Who's shooting?"

*It's the lighthouse keepers—but right now, that doesn't matter. If we don't get out of here, we're dead.*

There was no time for explanation.

"Come on!" She tugged on the boy's arm, panting. "This way!"

A bullet hit the gravestone next to them, taking a smoking chunk out of one corner. Antía instinctively ducked and gripped Diego's hand even tighter.

They rushed out of the graveyard. In the general disorder, the Docampos and the Freires moved as one, all simply bent on getting out of there alive. Antía caught sight of Amaia Docampo tripping and hitting the ground, to be trampled in the terrified onrush as everyone fought to get through the gate at once. Panic had seized them all. They hurtled along like a blind mob.

Antía went down a narrow, overgrown track. With one hand she swiped aside the branches in her way, and with the other kept hold of Diego behind her.

All she could think of was to run, to get as far away as possible from the bullets flying in the graveyard.

Just then she found a bulky figure barring the way.

"You!" growled Luis Docampo, as startled as she was. His eyes darted over to Diego, who was cowering behind Antía. "All this is because of this little imbecile, him and the writer!"

"What are you talking about? We have to get out of here! Those people are going to—"

"If they hadn't pulled that damn money out of the water, none of this would have happened! They've fucked us all!"

*You weren't saying that when we were all counting the cash. When you thought you'd struck gold.*

But she didn't have time to voice her thoughts, and Luis wasn't listening in any case.

In a blind rage, needing someone to blame for the nightmare that was unfolding, and at the same time seeing a chance to settle old debts, he leaped at her, knocking her to the ground.

"Luis, no, wait!" Antía cried, but it was already too late.

He was at least twice her weight and strong as an ox. She cried out, feeling his hands close around her throat. She heard a muffled shriek from Diego. She gasped, her feet scrabbling in the sodden earth.

Then, just as she was about to lose consciousness, she saw a shadowy figure behind her assailant, carrying some sort of club, which was then lifted high and instantly came down on Luis's head.

There was a thud, and Luis was knocked sideways to the ground, unconscious, like an ox in the slaughterhouse. With his hands released from her neck, Antía spluttered and then gulped down air.

"Roberto!" she croaked, coughing and spluttering. "It's you!"

"It's me, yes." Roberto helped her to sit up. "Are you all right? Are either of you injured?"

"Diego! Are you okay?" Antía staggered over to her son, who was trembling with fear. She engulfed him in a protective embrace before turning to her savior again.

Roberto looked terrible. His clothes were little more than a collection of wet rags, and his face was a constellation of cuts and bruises. One arm hung limp at his side, and he had a makeshift crutch. He looked as if he had just stepped out of a washing machine filled with sharp rocks.

Which in a sense wasn't all that far from the truth.

Time stood still. Antía was unable to speak, trapped in Roberto's feverish gaze. For an instant, the shooting, the violence, the money, all the chaos that had been unleashed on the island, simply stopped.

"Antía, I . . . I need to tell you something. There's nothing between Helena and me. It's a misunderstanding. In fact . . ."

"Shut up . . ." She got up and moved closer to him. "I know. Helena told me everything after you left."

"Really? I didn't want you to think that . . . I mean . . ."

"I know," she repeated before hugging him tight. Roberto yelped with pain, and Antía instantly let him go. "I'm sorry."

"It's nothing. I think I've cracked a rib, that's all."

"I don't mean that." She looked in his eyes. "I'm sorry I doubted you. I was an idiot."

"Antía." He looked at her hard. "I . . . you . . . I mean . . ."

She squeezed his hand. That was enough. Their trusting connection had returned. It pulsed between them once more, as if it had never gone away. They were fighting on the same side again.

"Are you boyfriend and girlfriend?" Diego's voice interrupted the moment of intimacy with all the delicacy of a chain saw.

"No!" they chorused, blushing. A little too quickly to sound convincing, perhaps.

"I was worried about you," Diego said. "I didn't know where you'd gone."

"It's a long story." Roberto gave him an affectionate wink. "Seems you knew about Erundina's grave, though. Can't hide anything from you."

"I'm a superhero," Diego said proudly. "I look out for you."

"Of course. If it weren't for you, who knows where we'd be."

"What happened to you?" Antía was checking Roberto's injuries. "Who did this to you?"

"Now isn't the time." Roberto's eyes were strangely bulging. The amphetamines were keeping him on his feet like a doped-up racehorse, but his dilated pupils gave him a manic look. "We should get out of here, before we bump into anyone else."

"I thought you said you would never hurt anyone," Antía said, gesturing to the body of Luis. "I see you've had a change of heart."

Roberto used his foot to turn Luis over, eliciting a low whimper. "It's just a scratch. He'll get over it. Plus"—he grinned—"I thought I could make an exception for Luis. He killed poor old Pampín, after all. Besides, he gave me a push."

"A push?"

"Really, it's a long story." He glanced around. The sound of gunfire had died down, and there was no one left in the vicinity of the graveyard. "I'll fill you in, I promise. When there's time."

"These gunmen who showed up, the money's theirs! In the graveyard, they were about to . . ." She shuddered at the memory.

"I saw," Roberto said. "I followed you from El Cucorno . . ."

What he didn't say was that he had come across guys like the Colombians before, too many times in his life. Ruthless professionals, the kind who didn't tend to leave loose ends.

"So Ibaibarriaga is trying to get in on it. That changes things slightly, but still . . ."

"Don't you get it?" Antía wrung her hands. "It's going to be a bloodbath! My family, the Docampos . . ."

"Not necessarily," replied Roberto, smiling slyly. "It might all end without another shot being fired."

"How can that be possible?"

Maybe it was the mixture of adrenaline and amphetamines coursing through his body, or maybe it was because he was absolutely convinced of his plan. Whatever the reason, he had never been so sure of anything. And that feeling, after so many days of uncertainty, was comforting.

"It's very simple." Roberto's smile grew a little wider. "Because I have a plan. And this one's going to work."

# 42

## Roberto's Plan

The sun hung low in the January sky when Roberto, Antía, and Diego reached the village. For the first time in almost a week, a patch of blue could be seen, a sign that Storm Armand was finally moving away toward the interior of the Spanish mainland.

In the thin early light, the main street presented a bleak picture. The damaged facades looked as if they were covered in some terrible rash, and not a single window had gone unharmed. They moved down the deserted road, broken glass crunching underfoot, looking around with a mixture of astonishment and concern. It was like being in a ghost town. Finally, they stopped outside the tattered church so that Roberto could have a brief rest.

"Are you okay?" Antía said. "We can wait a little longer, until you feel stronger."

Roberto slumped down on the stone steps. Surrounded by the boards that had been ripped from the door, he was assailed by the memory of all that had happened since the day when, right in that spot, with the excited Freires and Docampos around him, he had opened a mysterious bundle that the tides had carried to Ons.

Somehow it all seemed like someone else's memories.

"I'm okay," he said, leaning on her to bring himself to standing once more. "We don't have time to rest. There's still a lot we need to do."

*And every minute counts.*

As they'd been walking, Roberto had given Antía a whistle-stop account of everything that had happened since he had left Helena at the door of El Cucorno. This included a description of Varatorta's blood-curdling hideout, and he tried to ensure that Diego didn't hear all the horrifying details.

At the part where the lighthouse keeper had told Roberto about his designs, Antía had clapped her hands over her cheeks in horror.

"I could have never imagined such things from Varatorta," she said bitterly. "All the years he's been living here . . . We should have noticed something, seen the signs."

"But Diego did, remember? He told us there was a monster loose on the island. He just didn't know how to explain it."

"Poor Diego," she said, looking over at the boy, who at that moment was deep in concentration, making a pile of pieces of glass on a stone. "We all just thought it was his imagination. Another one of his fantasies."

"Everyone looks down on him because of his condition, but that's exactly why he sees and hears more than anyone else, because people just act as though he isn't there . . ."

"So where's Varatorta now?"

"He could be anywhere. I don't suppose you saw if he was with Ibaibarriaga at the graveyard?"

"I didn't. It all happened so fast. I *think* it was just Álvaro and that young assistant of his, Pazos, but I'm honestly not sure . . ."

"That's a problem." Roberto frowned. "It's hard to predict Varatorta's next move. I get the feeling that all his mental dams have burst, and he doesn't care about consequences anymore. But, on the other hand, we have dealt with the most important thing."

"What's that?"

"The war between your family and the Docampos—it's over, or it's on pause, at least."

"You're right there. They'll all be holed up somewhere or other, licking their wounds."

"With the fright they've had today, I imagine they won't be quite so eager to see any bloodshed for a while . . . But you know them better than I do."

"Yes," Antía said. "It's the money. Everything's gotten out of hand since the money showed up. At least those Colombians have gone off with it, so we might have a bit of calm again."

"I'm afraid it's not going to be that easy. They don't have the money, Antía."

"Don't they? I thought they ran off with the bags?"

Roberto grimaced.

"No, I got a good view of that part. They left the bags, and one of them had taken a bullet, but the others managed to grab Helena and Tristán as they were escaping. I saw them heading down to the beach, and they had guns to Helena's and Tristán's heads."

"They took my sister?" Antía shuddered. "Why? Where have they taken them?"

"No idea." Roberto bit his tongue. "But what I do know is that they won't give up easily. They've been sent here to recover that money, and in their line of work, failures aren't tolerated. The guy who's leading them, the one with the blue eyes who never blinks, he's a pro. As soon as they've regrouped, they'll be back."

"Back? Where, though?"

"To wherever the money is, of course." They set off down the ravaged street again, Roberto dragging his injured leg.

"The money? Do you know where it is? What are you up to?"

"Like I said, I have a plan. I had time to think it over when I was crossing from Onza."

"What can we do? We don't have any guns, and there are only the two of us—three if we count Diego—and you look like you could pass out just about any second!"

"You'll see . . ." Roberto said. "First, we need to contact the mainland."

"The phones aren't working, remember?" she said. "The cell tower? And the only radios we have are short range, for communicating on the island . . ."

"Right," Roberto said grimly, still hobbling on. "But if we can't make ourselves heard, we'll have to make sure we're seen."

"What are you talking about?"

"We're going to light a fire," he said. "The biggest fire Ons has ever seen, something they can't help but see from the mainland."

"What do you have in mind?"

"Very simple." He stopped and grinned at her. "We're going to set fire to this damn village."

# 43

## The Fire

"Burn the village? Our village? Have you lost your mind?"

"Far from it," Roberto said, setting off once more. "The moment people on the mainland see the smoke plume, all kinds of alarms will be activated. We're in a national park here—there are protocols for such cases. When they try to contact the island and get no response, they'll have no choice but to send someone over."

"The estuary's still bad. After a storm, the swell is incredibly strong for days . . ."

"Sure." Roberto glanced down toward the dock. "But the wind's almost completely died. There's nothing to stop them from sending a helicopter."

"The heliport next to the lighthouse!" She opened her eyes wide. "Of course!"

"Now," he said, smiling wryly, "if you happened to be an arsonist, where do you think you'd choose to start a fire?"

Antía thought for a moment. She scanned the buildings, and her eyes came to rest on one in particular.

"There." She pointed to one adjacent to the dock. "The Docampo restaurant. It's got propane bottles for the kitchen and its own generator connected to a fuel tank. It's also full of wooden chairs and tables . . ."

"Okay, a Docampo property! And there I was thinking the war between the two clans might be over . . ."

"Once a Freire, always a Freire . . ." Antía shrugged. "And it would make one hell of a blaze."

Roberto leaned against a wall and watched as Antía and Diego went down and climbed into the restaurant through a broken window. He heard them rooting around and furniture being moved, and after a short while saw them clambering back out at top speed. At their backs, an orange glow indicated that the fire was gathering strength. A smell of burning reached their nostrils at the same instant as the first wisps of gray smoke began appearing through the gaps in the restaurant's front.

"We'd better get out of here," said Antía, an excited gleam in her eye. "When the fire reaches the gas bottles, it'll blow sky high."

"Boom!" added Diego, skipping around in excitement.

For him, it had all become a thrilling adventure again. Roberto envied the boy's ability to simply put traumatic moments out of his mind. With Diego, nothing existed but the present moment.

"Well, there's your smoke signal." Antía gestured to the restaurant. "Now what?"

"We go get the money, of course," said Roberto matter-of-factly.

"What do you want that damn money for?" She frowned. "It's been nothing but trouble."

"I need it for the next part of my plan." At that moment, a pair of windows on the top floor of the restaurant burst, sending a shower of glass flying. "And I think I know who has it. Let's get going."

They had gone a few hundred yards when there was a colossal explosion. They turned around in time to see an immense fireball going up from what had been Luis Docampo's business. A shower of debris, shattered tiles, and bricks flew in all directions, falling mostly into the sea and fortunately well short of their position.

"Whoa!" Antía said. "They must have heard that across the estuary!"

"I hope so. But we've also given the whole island a pretty clear sign that the clock is ticking." Roberto looked at his watch and frowned. "This is busted. Do you have the time?"

"Almost half past nine," she said.

"Okay. I reckon the cavalry will be here in an hour or two. Come on."

"Want to tell me where we're going?"

"We're almost there." Just then, he stopped in the middle of the road, suddenly on the alert. "Quickly, behind those bushes!"

There was no doubt about it. There was the clear sound of footsteps approaching.

# 44

## "Let's Make a Deal"

They dashed over to a cluster of low bushes. The trio crouched down in silence, hardly daring to breathe.

"Are you sure somebody's coming?" Antía whispered. "I can't hear anything . . ."

"Shh," Roberto said, "here they come!"

Just then, two familiar figures appeared on the road. Álvaro Ibaibarriaga was leading the way, with his hunting rifle slung over one shoulder and with the two heavy duffel bags in his hands. Borja Pazos came stumbling along beside him. The younger man was gripping his stomach, and with each stride he gave a pained groan. He was very pale and, from his blood-soaked clothes, appeared to have taken a bullet.

"Come on, Borja, we're almost there!" Ibaibarriaga urged. "Hang in there, damn it!"

"I can't make it," moaned the younger man. "Think I'm about to . . . pass out. Need to . . . rest."

"We can't stop now," Ibaibarriaga urged him on. "Those gunmen could be back at any moment. As soon as we're safe in the lighthouse, you can lie down. No one can get us in there!"

"What about Varatorta, where's he?"

"That's exactly what I'd like to know. The bastard bolted just when we needed him. As soon as I see him, I'll give him both barrels."

But Pazos had stopped in the middle of the road and was staring up ahead. Ibaibarriaga followed his gaze and, seeing what his assistant was seeing, smiled.

A little way ahead, the rangers' battered SUV—the same one the Docampos had used to chase Roberto—was parked on the roadside, and it was empty.

"Finally," Ibaibarriaga cried. "A bit of luck! We don't have to walk all the way to the lighthouse. We'll be there in no time."

The two lighthouse keepers walked over to the SUV. From the hiding place, Roberto saw that Pazos was leaving a trail of blood in his wake and was extremely pale. Undoubtedly, the wound was more serious than he had imagined.

"What now?" hissed Antía as the pair went over to the SUV, and Ibaibarriaga opened the trunk and flung the duffel bags in. "There goes the money! We can't keep up with them in the SUV! By the time we get to the lighthouse, there'll be no getting them out, and it'll be too late for your plan . . ."

"Don't worry," Roberto said, taking a bundle of keys out of his pocket. "I came across the SUV before they did, on my way to the graveyard. They won't be going far."

Meanwhile, Pazos had collapsed against one of the rear wheels of the SUV. He was shaking slightly all over, and on the verge of going into hypovolemic shock. Ibaibarriaga, who was coming around that side of the vehicle, saw him and frowned.

"Come on, kid," he said, a note of concern in his voice, "not long to go now. Let me help you, come on."

Ibaibarriaga lifted him and gently eased him into the passenger seat. As Ibaibarriaga leaned over to fasten Pazos's seat belt, Pazos let out a gasp of pain and promptly passed out.

"Listen to me, Diego." Roberto turned to the boy, who was looking on in fascination. "I need you to do something for me—something very important. You have to be very, very brave. Can I count on you?"

"Is it a superhero job?" He beamed.

"Of course it is." Roberto squeezed his shoulder, and then proceeded to whisper conspiratorially in his ear. "Got it?"

"Yeah, of course!"

"Okay, well, off you go now, and make sure no one sees you."

But Diego was already on the move. Grinning excitedly, he slipped off through the undergrowth. A couple of seconds later, the only trace of the boy was the swaying of the tall grasses as he went away.

"What are you doing?" Antía said, scandalized. "He's just a kid!"

"There's nobody better at moving around this island unseen. He'll be fine. Now for our part . . ." He stepped out from behind the bushes.

"Get down," Antía said. "They'll see you!"

"Exactly."

He moved serenely along the road, like a visitor taking the morning air. Ibaibarriaga, who was furiously rummaging around for the keys, looked up, his eyes widening in surprise.

"You!" he exclaimed. "What the hell are you doing here?"

"Looking for these, Álvaro?" Roberto brandished the keys.

Ibaibarriaga's look of confusion shifted to one of cold determination. He got out of the vehicle and pointed his shotgun at Roberto.

"Yes, as it happens," he said. "And you'd better hand them over, or you're dead meat."

"Not so fast!" Roberto took a step to the side and kneeled down. There at the roadside was a manhole, with the cover off—Roberto's doing, on his way up from the beach. He dangled the keys just above the opening. "Not unless you want to spend the next few hours swimming around in shit."

Ibaibarriaga's eyes sparkled with fury.

"Just hear me out," Roberto said.

"What is it?" Ibaibarriaga grunted.

"First, stop pointing that thing at me," Roberto said.

"Fuck you."

"Your decision." Roberto moved the keys a little closer to the manhole.

"Okay, okay, wait!" Ibaibarriaga snorted, lowering the rifle.

"Antía, come over here, please," Roberto said, watching Ibaibarriaga all the while.

Antía emerged from behind the bushes and stood beside him. The lighthouse keeper's gaze flicked back and forth between them.

"What's she doing here?"

"She's coming with me. With us."

"Us? What are you talking about?"

"It's very simple," Roberto said calmly. "There are some pretty pissed Colombians on the island, and they're looking for the money you've just loaded in that SUV. They'll stop at nothing to get it back."

"Tell me something I don't know."

"The authorities will be here soon." He pointed at the black plume in the sky. "I don't think they'll be long, but in the meantime, we need a safe haven to avoid unexpected encounters. And I can think of no better place than the lighthouse. So let's make a deal."

Ibaibarriaga narrowed his eyes. "Okay. You're offering me the keys in exchange for letting you into the lighthouse. Why would I agree to that?"

"Because if you don't, they'll get you first." Roberto shrugged. "You won't even make it as far as the lighthouse. You've got the money to carry, and your partner doesn't look in great shape. You're no match for a team of professional hit men."

Ibaibarriaga squirmed, clearly furious. Roberto, a knot in his stomach, did his best not to give away what he was really keeping an eye on.

*For the love of God, don't turn around. Keep on looking at me, please . . .*

Out of the corner of his eye, he watched as Diego emerged behind the SUV, tiptoeing closer to it.

All their hopes rested on him.

Though with Diego you could never be sure, he seemed to have understood the instructions perfectly. Furtively, without making the slightest noise, he appeared to be doing precisely as Roberto had asked.

*He needs more time. Keep this bastard talking.*

"You lied to me at the lighthouse," Roberto piped up. "You locked me in that room."

"You weren't exactly truthful with me," Ibaibarriaga said. "There's far more than three million in those bags."

"I guess we're even."

"As long as you aren't expecting an apology . . ."

"No, not at all. A lot's happened since then."

"Right." Ibaibarriaga looked Roberto up and down, one eyebrow raised quizzically. "You look like shit. What happened to you?"

"I fell off a cliff."

"Sure! You'd be fish food by now."

"They may not like the taste of me." Roberto watched as Diego completed his task and slipped away again. "So . . . what do you say?"

"The money's mine," said Ibaibarriaga finally. "And I don't intend to share it."

"We don't want one cent of that money, don't worry," Roberto said. "All I care about is getting to safety."

"Fine," Ibaibarriaga said after a few moments' reflection. "But let's bury the hatchet, okay? I know you and I haven't exactly gotten along."

"Consider it buried." Roberto nodded. "I just want to get us out of here before the Colombians show up."

"Well then, let's go." Ibaibarriaga nodded to the SUV. "You drive, and I'll go in back with the lady and the money. I don't want any funny business."

"He's coming too." Roberto pointed to Diego, who had just appeared behind him, with a shy expression, as if he had been hiding behind the bushes all along.

"Another one?" Ibaibarriaga snorted.

"Yes, just the three of us. Shall we?"

The lighthouse keeper nodded and turned back toward the van. Roberto got up, doing his best to control his shaking legs.

Three minutes later, at the wheel of the SUV, Roberto was driving at full speed along the road to the lighthouse, with Borja Pazos unconscious beside him and Ibaibarriaga in back, watching Diego and Antía like a hawk.

He allowed himself a smile. It was all going according to plan.

But the hardest part was still to come.

And if it went wrong, the consequences would be enormous.

# 45

## Always Another Way Out

When they reached the esplanade in front of the lighthouse, the column of smoke behind them was already hundreds of feet high, a thick dark line bisecting the clear morning sky. The sun bounced blindingly off the mirror at the top of the lighthouse, and there was an absolute stillness to the air, broken when the SUV came to a screeching halt outside the building.

"Get him inside!" Ibaibarriaga jumped out almost before Roberto had stopped. "I'll go open the door!" He dashed ahead with the duffel bags. He hadn't let them out of his sight for a moment and didn't appear to intend to do so even now.

"Pretty clear where his priorities lie," Antía said as she and Roberto struggled with the inert Pazos.

"The money's gotten hold of him," Roberto said, lifting Pazos by the shoulder. "Like everyone else on this island. But that's a good thing."

"Why?"

"Because it makes people lose perspective. They don't see the whole picture. We need to keep it that way."

"You and your plan," Antía sighed as they started toward the lighthouse, carrying Pazos between them.

Roberto bit his cheek, trying to bear the pain. Carrying an unconscious, fully grown adult was like carrying a block of cement. Doing it with a shattered knee and several broken ribs was out-and-out torture.

When they finally got to the tiled entrance hall, Ibaibarriaga was there to lead them through to a small room with posters of bands on the walls and a record player in one corner, as well as an ancient-looking computer.

"Put him on his bed," he said. "He doesn't look good."

"I'll see what I can do," said Antía. "Do you have a first-aid kit?"

"There's one in the living room. But I've decided to keep one of you in my sight at all times. Diego, you can come with me."

With them gone, it meant Antía and Roberto were finally alone. They were walking a tightrope.

"You're crazy, you know that?" she said, shaking her head. "Jumping out and just walking up to Ibaibarriaga like that!"

"Well, in the last forty-eight hours, I've been beaten up, I almost fell off a lighthouse, I've been shot at, thrown off a cliff, a psychopath has tied me to a table," he said casually. "I've had to more or less swim from Onza in the darkness, in the middle of a storm . . ."

"Okay, okay, I take your point. Another normal day in Ons!"

"More or less!" Roberto laughed, but that brought an excruciating stab in his ribs. "You could have warned me when I showed up here. I would have appreciated that."

"I said don't go wandering by the cliffs at night. It isn't my fault if you chose not to listen."

*"Touché,"* Roberto said, tilting his head.

They fell silent, basking in a rare moment of peace. They were both aware of the strange sense of calm that sprang up between them.

"So what's next?" Antía said eventually.

"The Colombians will show up before too long," Roberto said, again wincing, "and we'll have to play our final hand."

"How do you know they'll come here?"

"They saw Ibaibarriaga go off with the money. By now they'll have worked out from Tristán and your sister that he's the lighthouse keeper. The only logical thing is for them to come straight here."

"You seem very calm," she said with a tired smile. "I hope you know what you're doing."

"Ever since I came to this place, I've been behind the curve," Roberto said. "It's just nice to be ahead of it for once."

"And Varatorta, where's he?"

"That's a good question," he admitted. "It's the one loose end right now."

"He can't be far. Let's have a look around."

They went down the hallway to Varatorta's bedroom. Unlike those of Pazos and Ibaibarriaga, it was sterile and Spartan, almost completely devoid of decoration. There were a table and chair, a bed with a faded gray cover, and a wardrobe with nothing but clothes inside it—nothing at all to suggest its occupant's desires or the way he kept himself entertained.

"Gives me the creeps," Antía muttered. "There's a weird . . . *nothingness* about it."

"His real game room is elsewhere." Roberto clenched his fists as he remembered waking up tied to the table in the spine-tingling cave. "This is merely what he wants others to see."

Just then, Diego appeared with the first-aid kit. It was in a sturdy, leather-bound case bearing the insignia of the Spanish Ports of the State.

"Thank you, Diego," Antía said, taking it from him.

"He's got a bullet in his stomach," Roberto said uneasily. "What can you do?"

"There's no doctor on the island. I've done a few first-aid courses but . . ." She trailed off.

It was clear to them both that if he didn't get to the mainland soon, he'd be dead.

"Where's Ibaibarriaga?" Roberto asked Diego.

"He's boarding up the ground-floor windows," the boy replied, flapping his arms around. "The planks are gigantic! I don't know how he can lift them."

"Stay with Antía. I'm going to give him a hand."

Roberto limped down the hallway to the kitchen. There he found Ibaibarriaga lifting up a plank and slotting it into brackets on either side of one of the windows.

Diego was right to be amazed. Each of the planks was indeed enormously wide and thick, but the lighthouse keeper, brawny forearms bulging, picked them up with seeming ease.

"All done," he said, wiping the sweat from his bald head. "We put these up for hurricanes. No chance of anyone getting through them!"

"Have you done all the windows?"

"Every last one. The front door's sturdy as anything too. Even God couldn't break that down."

"Aren't you worried about us getting stuck inside? What if we need to get out for some reason?"

"Jesus, all that trouble to get me to let you come in, and now you're thinking about how to get out?" Ibaibarriaga then added, "Besides, nothing to worry about on that count. There's always another way out."

"What about Varatorta? Where do you think he's gotten to?" He tried not to let his anxiety show.

"No idea," Ibaibarriaga grunted. "He comes and goes like a house cat. Why?"

"We could use all the hands we can get."

"He'll show up. He can't have any idea what he's in for."

*If only you knew . . .*

"Someone should go up top and keep watch," Roberto said. He was feeling distinctly woozy, but the Colombians could be there at any moment.

"Good idea, let's go this way."

"Can't you go? I'm not sure I can manage the stairs."

"No way," Ibaibarriaga said menacingly. "Like I said, I want to keep an eye on one of you guys at all times."

Roberto grumbled but pushed himself on nonetheless.

*Just keep going a little longer. Nearly there.*

Climbing the narrow spiral staircase was agony. Each step was a summit to be conquered, his shattered knee a continuous fireworks display of pain. Ibaibarriaga finally took pity on him and slipped an arm around his waist to help him up the last stretch.

By the time they reached the landing for the light, Roberto was drenched in sweat. Above their heads, they could hear the low swishing of the light as it spun on bearings that floated in mercury. Ibaibarriaga threw open the door. Unlike the last time they had been there, there was only a gentle if drizzly breeze.

Roberto went over and put an eye to the telescope.

"Anything?" Ibaibarriaga said.

"Not yet," answered Roberto, still scanning around. "Wait a second . . . There they are!"

Some way down the cement road, the Colombians were approaching on foot. The one at the back, wounded in the shoulder, was limping badly, while Helena and Tristán came with them at gunpoint. Roberto could also see that the gunman who was particularly short and thickset was carrying the MP 40 he had last seen at the Freire house.

That was bad news.

They hurried back downstairs, where they found Antía and Diego in the kitchen. Diego had curled up on one of the benches and was snoring like an exhausted puppy, while Antía had found some tins of food. She handed Roberto some sardines in oil, and realizing just how long it had been since he last ate, he proceeded to wolf them down.

"Help yourselves!" Ibaibarriaga huffed.

Roberto was about to come up with a retort, when they heard a thump followed by a scraping sound. To their astonishment, one of the kitchen sideboards, complete with platters, bowls, and plates, began to move, and then, as if by magic, it slid to one side, revealing a secret passageway.

There, looking disheveled and wearing a backpack, stood Varatorta. He gave an indecipherable smile.

# 46

## A Difficult Truth

Varatorta's gaze shifted from Ibaibarriaga to Antía, from her to Diego, and finally from Diego to Roberto. Finding the writer sitting there at the kitchen table, he showed a flicker of bewilderment, but this was quickly replaced with a beaming, satisfied smile—a look of pent-up excitement.

"Christ, Varatorta," Ibaibarriaga exploded. "What took you so long?"

Varatorta didn't respond immediately but stared steadily at Roberto. For some reason, he seemed delighted by the writer's presence, rather than seeming to have any thought about Roberto giving him away. Grinning, Varatorta gave Roberto a slow, complicit wink.

"I went down to the beach, like you told me to," he said at last, his voice soft.

"Where does that passageway come out?" Antía said.

"At the old woodshed," Ibaibarriaga said.

"And what were you doing at the beach?" Roberto interrupted, trying to control the tremor in his voice.

"It was his job to check on the Colombians' rearguard and the place they docked," Ibaibarriaga said. "But I don't get what took so long. Did you run into anyone?"

"There was nobody there, Álvaro." Varatorta took off his oilskin and sat down at the table, completely serene. "Just an unmanned speedboat pulled up on the sand, that was all."

"So why didn't you come and help out at the graveyard?" Ibaibarriaga growled. "Borja's been hit! If you'd been there, things might've gone differently."

"I was still on the beach when I heard it all kicking off." Varatorta shrugged. "And then I had to make a detour. I couldn't just walk up the road with those gunmen heading right this way!"

"Well," Ibaibarriaga snorted, "we need to get ready. They'll be here any minute."

"I love it when we have visitors." Varatorta stretched his delicate hands across the table, right in front of Roberto. "Especially the unexpected kind."

"I swear to God," Ibaibarriaga said, "I don't get you sometimes. Okay, I'm going back up to see where they've gotten to. Don't let this lot out of your sight. I'll be right back."

Ibaibarriaga went off again. For a moment there were only the crackling of the fire in the corner and the ticking of an ornate grandfather clock. It was like the room was holding its breath.

"Well, this is a surprise," said Varatorta, leaning back in his chair. "I thought you'd still be . . . in the place we last saw one another."

"Your secret cave, you mean." He was pleased to see a glimmer of apprehension enter Varatorta's face. "It's all right. She knows everything."

"As in . . . everything?"

"Not every single detail. I didn't want to spoil the surprise."

Varatorta gave an excited whimper, as if he'd just opened a long-awaited Christmas present. "Really?"

"Really."

Antía was observing Varatorta quizzically. He gave her one of his contorted smiles.

"It's so nice that you brought her," Varatorta said, and then nodded at the sleeping Diego. "And him too. I knew you'd get it in the end."

"What's all this?" Antía gave Roberto's hand a fearful squeeze. "What are you talking about?"

Roberto said nothing, all his focus on the man across from him as he weighed up his next move.

*Careful,* he thought. *Be very careful now.*

"From one artist to another?" he finally said.

"From one artist to another," Varatorta said, all smiles. "Oh, I knew it! I knew I should have talked to you sooner, when there was more time! All the incredible work we could have done together! But now—"

"Now the curtain's about to drop." Roberto sighed. "The authorities will surely be here soon, probably no more than half an hour."

"I know." Varatorta, with a sad smile, reached into his pocket, pulled out a handful of bloodstained gold teeth, and dropped them on the table.

Roberto picked one up, with a mixture of disgust and horror.

"I was actually held up because I met someone down at the beach, by the speedboat," Varatorta said conspiratorially. "He had a mouthful of these things. I didn't like the way they looked on him, so when I cut off his head, I thought it'd be nicer to take them out."

Roberto suppressed a shudder, forcing a smile. "Lovely—really nice."

He squeezed the tooth in the palm of his hand so hard that it hurt, while Varatorta calmly gathered the rest of the gold teeth and put them back in his pocket. In the midst of his madness, he exuded serenity, like a kamikaze pilot about to embark on his final flight.

"I have something else," Varatorta added, as if this were all the most regular thing. "A little something for you, Mr. Lobeira. A token of admiration and friendship." He reached for his backpack and offered it to Roberto.

"What's this?"

"Go on, open it!" Varatorta said, eyes sparkling. He looked jubilant, gleefully expectant, like he was the one now presenting a long-hoped-for present.

Roberto took a deep breath, wincing at his broken ribs, while at the same time trying to avoid letting on just how much pain he was in. The pain, more than anything else, served to clear his mind.

He didn't know what was in the backpack, but he could be pretty certain it wasn't going to be something pleasant. Precisely as he'd anticipated, it was very much a Varatorta kind of gift. As he unzipped the backpack, it was all Roberto could do to keep himself from vomiting, while Antía, looking over his shoulder, let out a horrified scream.

There inside the backpack was Luis Docampo's severed head, staring up at him with lifeless eyes, the mouth half open and the swollen, bluish tongue poking out between nicotine-stained teeth.

"If I'm really honest," Varatorta enthused, tittering, "I wasn't planning on using him for one of my pieces. Such a *brutish* man. No sparkle, if you know what I mean. But then I bumped into him on the road, and he was stumbling along—"

*Because I'd just hit him over the head with a big piece of wood . . .*

"And I remembered that he was the one who pushed you down that shaft . . ." Varatorta shook his head, looking like a displeased schoolteacher. "And he shouldn't have done that. So I just thought—"

"That I'd like you to take care of him," Roberto said, finishing the sentence. "Another gift for me, like the rabbit's head."

"That's right!" Varatorta drummed his hands on the table in delight. "See? See how you and I really understand each other? I realized I maybe went over the top when I tied you up, and probably that would have been unpleasant for you, so . . ."

Roberto closed the backpack, his mind whirring. From Varatorta's perspective, this was the greatest peace offering possible. What Varatorta didn't know was that, in his twisted attempt to ingratiate himself with Roberto, he had inadvertently done away with the only other person on the island with blood on their hands. He had avenged Víctor Pampín's murder. But for it to have been done in such a manner . . .

"What about the body?" Roberto said. "Is that also . . . ?"

"Oh"—Varatorta waved his hand dismissively—"fish food, like the guy at the beach. Trash, second-rate material, nothing like what's coming in now."

"Now?"

"Of course! I'm just going to say hello to my old colleague Borja." He stood up and winked again, before giving Antía a hair-raising, head-to-toe look. He appeared to be evaluating her. "Later on, we can discuss how to use what time we have left."

"Sure," Roberto said, managing, despite everything, to maintain a faint hint of a smile.

"Oh, and by the way, the passageway." He jerked a thumb at the sideboard behind him. "At the far end, there's a steel door, three inches thick. I've got the only key. Just mentioning it in case our lady friend here felt like making an early exit."

To make completely sure, Varatorta now produced the key, shoved the tip into a crack in the countertop, and brought the palm of his hand suddenly and violently down on the bow of the key, succeeding in snapping it.

"Nobody's going through this door," he said, looking at them both. "Whatever happens, this thing ends here."

With that, he left the kitchen, making for Pazos's bedroom. As soon as he was out of earshot, Roberto groaned and collapsed forward on the table, trembling.

"What the hell was that all about?" Antía said, a horrified expression on her face. "Was that part of your plan too?"

"No." He shook his head. "Not at all. Just trying to buy some time."

"So you just go along with that psychopath? He's killed two more people, and he's talking about killing me, like it was the most normal thing in the world!"

"We don't have much choice," replied Roberto. "We're locked in. This place is like a fortress. There's a two-hundred-and-fifty-pound lighthouse keeper who's obsessed with getting rich, and a serial killer who seems convinced that time's against him in trying to complete his work . . ."

"So what on earth are we going to do?" Roberto's reply made her blood run cold.

"Honestly, I don't have a clue. Varatorta's being here changes everything. Unless . . ."

"Unless what?"

But Roberto didn't answer. He was staring at the wall, thoughts seething. Just then, Ibaibarriaga's heavy footsteps were heard approaching along the hall. The lighthouse keeper burst into the kitchen.

"They're nearly here," he said, and then frowned. "Where's Varatorta?"

"He's gone to see Borja," said Roberto, recovering his composure. "Álvaro, we need to talk. It's Varatorta. He's been lying to us."

# 47

## "It's Not What It Looks Like"

"What the hell are you talking about?"

"Exactly what I said," Roberto said patiently. "Varatorta's got a secret."

"We've all got secrets," Ibaibarriaga snapped. "What's so important about this one right now?"

"It could decide whether we live or die."

"Go on."

"He lied about why he took so long to come back. I realized as soon as he said there was no one else on the beach."

"Bullshit!" Ibaibarriaga said, but a few worried creases appeared on his forehead. "Varatorta's like family. He'd never lie to me."

"Think about it," Roberto insisted. "Do you really think those Colombians could have made it to the island in a speedboat on their own, in the middle of that storm? Ons is hardly easy to get to, especially in those conditions. They'd have needed a local skipper, someone who knows these waters."

Ibaibarriaga's brow grew even more furrowed. "That's true," he muttered, more to himself than to Roberto. "But . . . why would he lie to me?"

"Isn't it obvious? He's planning something. If you ask me, I think he's done a deal with the Colombians. They're his chance to get his hands on the money. Your money. As soon as they get here, he'll go and throw open the door to them, and we'll all be screwed. They'll kill us all. Those people don't leave witnesses."

"Surely not . . ." Ibaibarriaga shook his head in disbelief. "He's one of our own. I've been living with him under this roof for three years. I know him . . ."

"How well do you really know him? Do you know anything about him, apart from day-to-day stuff at the lighthouse? The things he likes doing, his past? His ambitions in life? You don't know what goes on inside his head. Really, you know next to nothing about Varatorta, apart from what he wants to show you . . ."

The shadow of doubt, a horrible, gripping doubt, was spreading in Ibaibarriaga's heart. His expression went from one of doubt to one of confusion and from there, in quick succession, to one of anger.

"For all I know," Roberto said in a low voice, "he could be at the front door right now, about to let them in. Given the deal I suspect he's done with them . . . Why do you think it took him so long to come back? Varatorta isn't what he seems. You have to act, Álvaro, or your money's going to be gone."

A dense silence descended, accentuated, if anything, by the crackling of a log in the fireplace. Then Ibaibarriaga slammed a fist down on the table, making the crockery jump.

"There's only one way to get to the bottom of this," he growled. "And if it turns out to be another one of your games, I'll sling the two of you straight out the door, and you can fill in the Colombians."

In a fury, he jumped up and ran out of the kitchen to find Varatorta.

"Hurry!" Roberto urged Antía. "Let's go after him!"

Ibaibarriaga hurtled down the hall, moving surprisingly quickly for a man of his size. Reaching Pazos's room, he stopped dead in the doorway, confounded by the scene that presented itself.

Sitting at the foot of the bed, next to the unconscious body of Borja Pazos, Varatorta had opened out a cloth roll containing an array of scalpels, a small saw, and a number of long copper nails. He looked up at the intruder in surprise, which quickly turned to annoyance. Ibaibarriaga looked from Varatorta's sinister set of instruments to his face.

"What the hell's going on?" Ibaibarriaga cried. "What's all that?"

Varatorta's only answer was another of his freakish smiles. Then, at lightning speed, he grabbed one of the scalpels and leaped at Ibaibarriaga.

But Ibaibarriaga was not an easy man to knock down. When Varatorta crashed into him, the big man wrapped his huge arms around him, and the pair whirled like an enjoined spinning top in the small space of the room. They fell into the table in the corner, sending the record player and computer flying. With grunts and flailing fists, the two men were locked in what would clearly be a fight to the death.

Varatorta brought his elbow down on the nose of Ibaibarriaga, who let out a howl as blood cascaded from it. With a roar, he returned the favor with a brutal headbutt to his opponent's forehead. A watery crack sounded, and as Varatorta staggered back, sight swimming, Ibaibarriaga took full advantage, going after Varatorta, getting him by the throat and, arms locked, beginning to throttle him. The pair fell to the ground, kicking and struggling, but Ibaibarriaga kept up the stranglehold, progressively squeezing tighter and tighter.

Varatorta's thrashing soon grew weaker as he ran out of oxygen. His wild eyes spun, and for a second, they focused on Roberto and Antía watching in the doorway. He stretched out one of his hands to them, in a final, pleading gesture.

Antía tried to go in, but Roberto held her back.

"No," he said. "He deserves it."

"But . . ."

"Leave him."

As Varatorta's gaze clouded over, a final glimmer of understanding and rage shone through, before disappearing altogether as Ibaibarriaga gave a last, brutal squeeze, bringing a dull crack. Varatorta's legs kicked for a couple of seconds, and, finally, he was still.

For a moment there was absolute silence in the room, a second frozen in time.

"Goddamn . . . goddamn bastard." Ibaibarriaga, panting, lifted himself to standing. "He . . . he tried to kill me. You saw! Oh, fuck!"

The big man doubled over in pain. His gaze came to rest on the handle of Varatorta's scalpel, which was protruding from his groin. A bright red bloodstain was rapidly growing around it.

"Shit," he muttered, his voice gummy. "Now I'm really screwed."

And just at that moment, two gunshots echoed from the esplanade outside the lighthouse.

Osvaldo Salazar and his men had arrived.

# 48

## Just in Time

Some people lose their temper when they are angry.

These people allow their anger to simply take over, and it begins making decisions on their behalf. That means they can be dangerous, even violent, but at the same time predictable and easy to manipulate.

Osvaldo Salazar was not that kind of person.

When he became angry, which happened only rarely, an icy calm would settle in his chest as on the surface of a frozen lake, giving him an extraordinary clarity of mind. This, of course, made him an even more dangerous adversary than usual.

And at that moment, Osvaldo Salazar was very angry.

Everything had seemed under control. The money had been in their hands, and they'd been well set to get away from the island—only for everything to flip in an instant. He'd been forced to leave the money behind and scuttle back to the beach with his tail between his legs, one of his men wounded, and his pride crushed. Only to learn that, although the sensible move, it had actually been totally unnecessary.

The two trembling teenagers now trailing along behind him had revealed the truth. It had been two men, three at most, who had put them to flight. A couple of nickel-and-dime lighthouse keepers armed with hunting rifles had made Osvaldo Salazar, the Scorpion of Cali himself, flee. If anyone ever found out about it, the stain on his honor would be irreparable. Fury and shame came flooding in, but he managed to keep them locked under the ice sheet.

To make things worse, Chuco, the skipper, had vanished along with the speedboat's keys. All they'd found was a pile of trampled cigarette butts and a half-empty beer bottle. The ground of the island had seemingly opened up and swallowed him whole.

The gunmen behind Osvaldo maintained a wary silence. They knew not to bother him at such moments.

Osvaldo raised his pistol and fired two shots into the air, the sudden burst of noise echoing off the facade of the lighthouse before ebbing away.

"You in there!" he cried. "Show yourselves!"

There was no response. Nor was he surprised. But at least they knew he was there.

"Python." Osvaldo turned to his lieutenant. "Is the package ready?"

"Nearly, chief." Python took off his bulky backpack. "Nearly there."

One of the principal reasons Osvaldo had survived so long in his chosen field was his ability to adapt to changing circumstances. As they'd been making their way up to the lighthouse, he'd spotted a small, corrugated shed in a roadside field, inside which someone had left a couple of sacks of ammonium nitrate—fertilizer, for when the land came to be plowed.

The interesting thing about ammonium nitrate is that, when combined with a few other ingredients, it can easily be converted into a powerful explosive known as ANFO—ammonium nitrate and fuel oil. It had long been a go-to bomb component for terrorists all around the world. Osvaldo himself had made car bombs with the stuff in Colombia during the widespread violence there during the late 1990s.

So, as he watched Python carefully dousing the fertilizer with some gasoline from a can they'd taken from the speedboat, he allowed himself a momentary sense of satisfaction. He might yet come out on top.

Python finished mixing and carefully inserted one end of the improvised detonator—a long copper wire—into the top of the backpack. He connected the other end to a battery—only one of the terminals, though. The second that circuit was closed, the devastating bomb would blow.

"All done, chief."

"Now it just needs placing," Osvaldo said, nodding to the front door of the lighthouse. "Go on, off you go."

"Me?"

"That shit must weigh like a hundred pounds! You're the strongest. Come on, man up, off you go!"

Python sighed but made no further protest. It meant crossing a considerable stretch of open ground with a hundred pounds of high explosives on his back, but ultimately, that was his job. He might not be a man of many scruples, but his bravery was beyond question. Without giving it too much thought, he slung the backpack over one shoulder and set off at a run.

To his relief, he made it to the door unscathed. He propped the backpack against the door and, having paid out the electric cable, dashed back to the ditch in which the others were now bunkered.

"Good work." Osvaldo patted Python on the shoulder as he handed over the battery. "Let's give them a final warning before we ring the doorbell."

Osvaldo got up and walked to the center of the open ground in front of the lighthouse. He was totally exposed but at the same time felt strangely calm and alert.

"Listen up! We've just laid enough explosives to blow the door all the way to Pontevedra! You've got two minutes to come out with the money."

Once again, absolute silence was the only response.

"We can still do this the easy way," he said. "Give me the money, and I'll let you live. If you make us come in there, we won't be going easy on you."

His words sounded muffled through the wooden planks boarding up the windows. In Pazos's room, Roberto and Antía exchanged an apprehensive look.

"What do we do?" she said.

"Hand over the money." Roberto shook his head. "We have no choice."

"Fuck that," gasped Ibaibarriaga, growing paler by the minute. "We're safe in here. They can't get in."

"Didn't you hear?" Roberto turned to him. "They're about to blow the door. Then, if the blast doesn't kill us, they'll finish us off in no time. We have to give them the money!"

"Besides," Antía added, nodding to Ibaibarriaga's wound, "that blood isn't slowing down. You're in need of urgent medical attention, or you're done for."

"You can patch me up." Ibaibarriaga was bathed in sweat, but there was still a gleam in his eye. "Like you did Pazos."

"He's dead," Antía said quietly. "He went just now."

"Dead?"

"I'm not a doctor, and I don't have the right things!" she exploded. "If you don't want to end up like Pazos, we have to settle this thing."

Ibaibarriaga cast an incredulous glance at Pazos's lifeless body. A guttural wail of grief rose from deep in his throat.

"Where's the money?" Roberto said.

"In my room, under the bed," Ibaibarriaga whimpered. His eyes were growing dim.

"I'm going to get it."

"Roberto, wait!" Antía grabbed his arm, but before she could say any more, a shrill beeping struck up. They both looked over at Ibaibarriaga, who was struggling to unzip his jacket.

"What's that?"

"It's the security cameras at the front gate. They've picked up some movement. Someone's coming." He held out a device reminiscent of a large cell phone. A black-and-white image showed a large group of people surging through the front gates at that very moment.

"Thank goodness," sighed Roberto. "Just in time."

Antía looked over his shoulder and gasped in surprise. "No way!"

"There you have it." Roberto gave a relieved smile. "The Docampos and Freires side by side. The Colombians didn't see this coming."

"Helena and Tristán," Antía said. "They're here for them."

"The families might not be the best of friends," Roberto said, "but there's one thing they hate even more: an outsider who's dumb enough to make a common enemy of himself. They're actually very closely knit. And right now, they seem pretty pissed."

"You knew this was going to happen!" Antía marveled. "This was part of your plan!"

"It wasn't so hard to foresee." Roberto shrugged. "I've seen it plenty of times in rural societies: They have their differences, but when the chips are down, they pull together. Ons isn't so different from the rest of the world, after all."

"So what next?"

"You stay with Ibaibarriaga," he said, hobbling toward the front door. "And when I give you the word, tell Diego to bring the money out to me."

"What are you going to do?"

Roberto smiled at her, as it struck him this might be the last time he ever set eyes on her. But he kept that to himself.

"I'm going to talk movies with Osvaldo," he said. "I hope he's into cinema."

And without another word, he turned and went down the hallway.

# 49

## What Things Are Worth

Osvaldo was pleased to hear a key turning in the lighthouse door. His call was being answered. At the same time, gripping the battery in his hand, he felt a touch of regret. A part of him would also have loved to blow the door . . . Maybe he'd do so anyway, he said to himself, when he'd dealt with this part.

Just then, however, there came a cry from an agitated Python.

"Chief! Look! It's all those farmers—they're back, and they've got their guns."

Osvaldo turned to look, eyes blazing. Pouring through the main gates at the entrance to the lighthouse grounds was a group of the islanders. Grim-faced, Freires and Docampos advanced side by side.

"Hold them off!" he shouted. "And don't let Carlito take his gun off the lovebirds for one second! If anyone makes a false move, tell him to take them out!"

"Sure thing." Python patted the MP 40. "I can stop them by myself with this baby!"

Nonetheless, they were trapped between the lighthouse and the angry islanders, with no apparent way out.

Osvaldo rubbed his temples. The islanders had quickly found cover. Two of them, Ramón Docampo and Rosalía Freire, holding out white handkerchiefs, moved forward cautiously, looking to parlay.

"That's far enough!" Osvaldo shouted when they were some twenty feet away. "What do you want?"

"Our children!" Ramón thundered. "Helena and Tristán!"

"Sure, once I get my money." Osvaldo motioned to the lighthouse. "Not a second earlier."

"We've heard that one before," Rosalía said bitterly. "We don't trust you, Osvaldo Salazar. Do what we say or you're dead."

Osvaldo grinned, but the look in his eyes remained frosty. "You seem to have forgotten something," he said as Carlito appeared over the ditch, shoving Helena and Tristán ahead of him at gunpoint. "If I go down, so do those two."

There was a moment of absolute tension, with no one willing to yield. Sweaty hands gripped guns as both sides braced themselves. One false move, one ill-judged response, was all it would take for the carnage to begin.

And at that moment, Roberto stepped through the door.

He squinted in the sun, shielding his eyes. And then, dragging his injured leg along, he started moving toward the group in the middle of the open space.

Never in his entire life, not even in terrifying war situations, had he felt so exposed. He imagined every single shooter, on both sides, watching him, fingers on their triggers, asking themselves the same question: "Whose side is he on?"

And yet in spite of that, he somehow mustered a winning smile.

# 50

## *The Good, the Bad and the Ugly*

"All together at last," Roberto said in the cheery tone of someone sitting down to evening drinks with friends. "We haven't been introduced. You must be Osvaldo Salazar. My name's Roberto Lobeira."

"I've heard about you," the Colombian hissed. "Got my money?"

"Don't worry, there's plenty of time. Tell me, are you a movie lover by any chance?"

"What the—"

"Movies, cinema, you know."

"I don't have time for this—"

*"The Good, the Bad and the Ugly,"* Roberto went on. "Clint Eastwood, Lee Van Cleef, Eli Wallach? It's a classic, from 1966, you must know it."

Osvaldo gave a dubious grunt but allowed him to continue. Rosalía and Ramón looked on in bewilderment.

"I love the ending of that movie. The three main characters are in this graveyard; each of them wants the money for himself, but nobody dares shoot—they can only hit one opponent at a time, and if they do, the other one will take advantage and shoot the survivor."

"Mexican standoff," Osvaldo said, comprehension dawning.

"Mexican standoff, exactly. I always wondered where the phrase came from. Well, I'm afraid our situation is much like the one in the movie. You and your men here, the islanders over there, and over in the lighthouse behind me, Ibaibarriaga with his rifle, sitting on a mound of explosives. A perfect triangle."

Roberto was silent for a moment, letting the idea sink in with all present. He had said it loud enough to be heard by everyone else, too, and he was pleased to hear some concerned murmurs strike up on both sides.

"No one can win here," he continued. "Whoever shoots first will be open to attack from the third one in the triangle. That's what makes it awkward. But beautiful, too, if I may say so."

Osvaldo gave a half smile and looked at him with renewed respect. "You did this," he muttered. "You planned it to happen like this."

"Let's just say I've had quite a lot of time to think it through," Roberto said, modestly tilting his head. "And I believe I've come up with a solution that suits everyone, and that means this can end without violence."

"I'm all ears."

"Okay. Salazar, you release Helena and Tristán and let them go back to their families. In exchange, the islanders guarantee you safe passage to the speedboat so you can get away from here."

"No way," Osvaldo said. "I'm not going anywhere without my money."

"I'll give you the bags with the money—and the keys to your speedboat—in exchange for that detonator you have in your hands." He pointed to it. "You can leave with your money, and we can all part on good terms."

"Let me get this straight," Osvaldo said. "I get the money, and they get their kids, right?"

"Right."

"What about the lighthouse keeper?" He pointed to the lighthouse. "What does he get?"

"Ibaibarriaga gets to live, which isn't bad in the circumstances," Roberto said. "Everyone in the triangle comes away with what's most precious to them right now. I think it's a good deal."

Osvaldo was silent for a few moments, weighing the offer. Roberto kept up his smile, though a tiny bead of sweat trickled down his forehead. It all rested on the gunman's response now.

"There's just one thing I don't get," Osvaldo said at last. "Everyone gets something . . . apart from you. What does Roberto Lobeira get out of this?"

"I get a wonderful story to tell," he said nonchalantly. "Don't forget I'm a writer."

Osvaldo gave him a long, calculating look. Eventually, the rarest of occurrences: He let out a hearty, resounding laugh.

"All right! Deal. But no real names in that book of yours."

"You have my word," replied Roberto gravely, holding out a hand to shake.

"How do we do this?" Ramón said. "We don't trust this guy as far as we can throw him."

"You'll just have to trust me," Roberto said. "First, the detonator."

Osvaldo searched his face, still trying to ascertain the trap, but finally, very slowly, held out the battery to Roberto, who immediately disconnected the wires.

"Now it's my turn." Roberto turned to the lighthouse and shouted, "Antía, the money!"

Antía and Diego appeared through the door, each carrying one of the duffel bags. When they brought them over, Roberto undid the zippers, showing the wads of money inside.

"I'm sure you'd like to count it, but I don't think you have time. It's all there."

"I believe you." Osvaldo pulled out a wad of bills and in the bright morning light ran his thumb over the edges, satisfied. He tossed it back into the bag and gestured to Python, who came over and grabbed the bags.

"Let the lovebirds go," he ordered.

Helena and Tristán went running over to the islanders, to be enveloped in hugs and cries of relief.

"Tell me, Lobeira." Osvaldo scrutinized him again with those cold eyes. "What is there to stop me from just killing all of you anyway?"

"The fact that you don't know if you'd manage it—you'd still be trapped between two armed opponents. Besides, you're a practical man. You got what you came for, and the authorities will be here any minute. Everyone's capable of appreciating what things are worth, right?"

The Colombian looked pensive for a moment and at last gave another of his rare smiles. "You're a clever man, Lobeira. I hope we meet again."

"Don't take this the wrong way, but I hope we don't." He handed him the speedboat and SUV keys. "Have a good trip."

"What about Barreiros, the skipper? Was he in on this?"

"I don't know who you're talking about. The keys were in the ignition; I just thought it prudent to have something up my sleeve."

Osvaldo stared at him and finally blinked. "Okay, we're out!" He whistled and pointed to the SUV. "Move, men!"

The men trotted over to the vehicle and climbed in, gunning the engine as they raced away. Osvaldo caught Roberto's eye as they passed, and then the SUV was disappearing around the corner.

Roberto let out a massive sigh and doubled over. He felt dizzy. "I can't believe it," he gasped. "It worked."

"You did it!" Antía cried. "It's all over!"

"It'll only be over once they're off the island," Roberto said, and then looked over at Rosalía and Ramón. "And when these two finally decide to call it quits."

Rosalía and Ramón looked at each other in embarrassment. In the light of day, under the sharp winter sun, everything seemed quite different.

Doubtless they were being assailed by all the bad calls they'd made—all they had done, all they had been on the verge of doing.

Without the nefarious presence of money, it was as if a black cloud had dissipated and things as they really were had been revealed.

Docampo looked around, no doubt searching for Luis. Antía and Roberto exchanged a sad look. Even if he had been a murderer, Luis Docampo had also been somebody's son, and a husband and father. There was still a lot of pain to get through.

But now wasn't the time for them to say anything. That would come later.

"I think . . ." Ramón cleared his throat. "I think I owe you an apology, Rosalía. On behalf of all of us, for everything."

"Us too, Ramón." The woman puffed out her cheeks. "I can't believe we let it get to this point."

Tentatively, she held out her hand, which the man hastened to shake. If they had been in a movie, everyone would have burst into cheers of joy at that moment, but there was only a disbelieving silence.

It was over. Finally.

"Your daughter and my Tristán." Ramón shook his head. "Who would have thought?"

"Oh, come on, Ramón." The woman patted him on the back. "We Freires and you Docampos have been hooking up for more generations than anyone can count. They're hardly the first."

"If only they'd told us . . ."

"They're young and stupid," the woman concluded. "Time will heal both those things! As it will our differences, Ramón."

Ramón gave a half smile.

"Sure, sure." He nodded. "Although . . . this doesn't mean we're even."

"You're right about that!"

The two became embroiled in a heated argument. Roberto gave Antía an incredulous look.

"Some things will never change, right?" he whispered, instinctively putting his hand in hers. Antía squeezed his hand in return, as if worried that he might be about to disappear.

"If they didn't have something to argue over, they'd both die. They need each other like that."

"As long as it's just words, everything will be fine." Roberto straightened up with a wince. Then he remembered something. "What about Ibaibarriaga?"

Antía shook her head disconsolately. "He's gone. He lost too much blood."

"Poor guy," Roberto muttered. "I don't think he was actually bad. The money just clouded his judgment."

"I think he felt guilty about Pazos's death," she added. "He was devastated. His final moments weren't pretty."

"I hope he rests in peace. It's too high a price."

"Same with Pampín, and Ricardo and Luis Docampo, Elvira Couto too. They've all paid dearly."

Roberto walked over to the lighthouse and slumped against the wall. He was exhausted. The amphetamines were wearing off, and his eyelids felt like lead, but he still couldn't relax completely. Not yet.

He patted his pockets, looking for his cigarettes, before remembering they were doubtless somewhere at the bottom of the Devil's Hole. He sighed and simply leaned his head back, enjoying the warm caress of the sun's rays, the feeling of being alive.

Antía went and sat down beside him, and a few minutes later, they heard Diego shouting with excitement.

"Look, look!" He was jumping up and down. "Over there, by the headland!"

Everyone looked out to sea. The Colombians were racing away in the speedboat, although the efforts of whoever was at the helm would have horrified the late Chuco Barreiros. The sea was still choppy, and rather than negotiating the waves, they were trying to shoot directly through them like an arrow. Huge walls of water broke constantly over the vessel.

"They shouldn't be going that way," Antía muttered. "They're heading away from the channel. There are sandbanks there; it isn't safe . . ."

At that moment, with a burst of throttle, the speedboat tackled a particularly tall wave. As it reached the crest, the inexperienced skipper failed to cut the speed, letting it go hurtling down the far side, so that the nose was caught under the next oncoming wave.

Even from up on the hill they could guess what was going to happen next.

The rear of the boat flew up and over, and the vessel proceeded to turn a near-somersault. The crew were thrown violently overboard—dim human silhouettes could be glimpsed arcing through the air. The next wave slammed down, swallowing bodies and boat in a foaming whirl of gray surf. The capsized hull glistened briefly like a wounded sperm whale before disappearing into the depths.

In less than fifteen seconds there was nothing but floating scraps of plastic and fiberglass, and an oil stain in the water. It was as if the speedboat had never existed.

*That's an end to Osvaldo's career. Probably for the best . . .*

Roberto looked up. In the distance, he could already hear the syncopated beating of rotor blades, and after a few moments, a helicopter came into view, in the white-and-green livery of the Guardia Civil, approaching at full speed.

He looked at it with satisfaction. And relief.

It was all over. They had weathered the storm.

And with that, he collapsed.

# 51

## Stormy Night

***One year later. Madrid.***

The line stretched out the bookstore and into the mall in Plaza de Callao. On either side of the door stood six-foot posters of the book cover, announcing that Roberto Lobeira would be signing copies of his latest novel.

Inside the store, behind a book-covered table, Roberto sat smiling and writing dedications. The success of *Stormy Night* had put that of *The Fleeting Glance* in the shade, and Roberto's life had been a nonstop whirl since publication day. The articles and interviews had been coming thick and fast, all feeding the insatiable monster of public interest.

Roberto suspected that the phrase printed on the cover, *Based on a True Story*, had a good deal to answer for.

After passing the latest signed copy across the table, and then having his photo taken with a female reader, he took a moment to sit back and rub his sore wrist. He had been signing flyleaves and penning dedications continuously for the last two hours, and he still had a lot more to do. The line, rather than diminishing, only kept growing longer.

Resting against the side of the table was the ivory-handled walking stick that had become his constant companion over the past year.

Although he had undergone several surgeries, his injured knee had not returned to full functionality, and the doctors doubted that it ever would. His limp looked set to be a permanent reminder of the night he had fallen down the Devil's Hole, the price he'd paid to make it off the island alive.

Every time he looked at the walking stick, Roberto said a quiet prayer of thanks. The toll could have been far higher.

"Are you all right?" Antía leaned over and rested a hand on his back. "Do you need a break?"

"I'm fine," he said. "The doctors say I should be sitting down, and I am! I'm doing as I'm told."

"That would be a first," she teased, looking into his eyes.

They smiled at each other, in a secret conversation with neither beginning nor end—the best kind.

Neither of them could put a name to whatever it was that existed between them. It was a timid, fragile thing, and it had been doing its best to grow in two souls that were still healing. They both wanted to love, but the fear of being hurt meant they proceeded warily, with all the caution of a caged animal that suddenly finds itself released into the wild.

They still didn't believe they could be so happy.

"Are there a lot of people outside?" he asked as the next book was placed in front of him.

"Quite a few, I'm afraid. I got Diego to hand out tickets, but you know what he's like. I think he got excited and gave out at least twice as many as he should have."

"Damn kid." Roberto smiled. "Always making trouble for me."

Roberto had never been so happy in his life. First, just that they were alive. His plan, which had been born out of desperation and had seemed almost certain to fail, had somehow come off. He was still amazed to think of it.

Within hours of the Guardia Civil arriving, the tragedy of Ons had hit the news. Broadcasters had shown up, the incident was all over the TV, and it filled column after column in the papers for weeks.

Fortunately, the inhabitants of Ons knew how to keep a secret. Everyone stuck to the story: During Storm Armand, a boat of Colombian gunmen had appeared on the island, looking for a lost consignment of cocaine, which turned out to be in the possession of the lighthouse keepers. When they had refused to hand over the drugs, a gunfight had ensued. With the terrified islanders safe behind locked doors, after a night of shots and explosions all across the island, the Colombians had won out. Only to crash their speedboat in the stormy waters and drown.

As a story it had its fair share of holes, but there was physical evidence to back it up. The only dead bodies the police found were those of the three lighthouse keepers: A group of Freires and Docampos had collected those of Elvira Couto, Ricardo Docampo, and Víctor Pampín, and stashed them together in Erundina's grave.

As far as Roberto knew, they were still there, resting in peace.

A few days later, the bodies of the Colombians had also washed up . . . except for Osvaldo Salazar's. Nobody knew where it was. That was a mystery that had caused Roberto more than a few sleepless nights.

While recovering in the hospital, and over the following, feverish months, Roberto had hammered away at his laptop, creating a fictionalized version of everything that had occurred on the Isle of Ons. The book had found an instant readership among a public enthralled by an episode of violence and chaos right on the doorstep of civilized Spain, and yet hidden to all.

Of course, the book omitted the feud between the Freires and Docampos, as well as any mention of Varatorta's exploits. That was for another manuscript—for his eyes only. Some things were better left in the shadows.

Between signatures, Roberto looked up and saw Diego come into the store, an empty book of tickets in hand. The changes he had undergone since moving to the mainland were incredible. With the help of specialist teachers and, above all, surrounded by so many new stimuli, his adaptable mind had soaked up all sorts of new information. He would always be different, of course, but he was becoming more and more independent, and most important, he was happier than ever.

Roberto looked at him tenderly, unaware that in the boy's heart he was already occupying the space of the father he had never known.

Diego had always known that Antía was his mother, even though everyone assumed he would never find out. They should have guessed, really, that his intensely curious nature would lead him to discover the truth. But Diego had quietly assimilated that secret, as he had so many other things.

And with Diego and his mother, Roberto shared another, even bigger secret.

They alone knew the whole truth of that stormy night . . .

When Roberto, clinging to the oil drum, had drifted ashore, he had spotted the speedboat, and, taking care not to be seen by the skipper, he had gone to the Docampos' wrecked store and grabbed two duffel bags identical to the ones containing the money, from the same pile from which the first two bags had come. He had then gone to the visitor booth and stuffed them full of hundreds of tourist brochures and maps of the island.

The most onerous part had been carrying the heavy bags. He had taken them and hidden them in the ditch by the SUV. The rest had been down to Diego.

While Roberto kept Ibaibarriaga busy, Diego had done something incredibly brave. He had slipped through the undergrowth, picked up the duffel bags containing the brochures and maps, crept over to the SUV and switched them out for the ones containing the money—first of all placing several handfuls of bills as a false top layer in both bags.

Osvaldo Salazar had sunk to his watery grave with a load of old brochures and maps, and a tiny percentage of the overall millions.

And that secret was known only to Antía, Diego, and Roberto himself.

Two days after Roberto was evacuated from the island with a leg splint and a neck brace, Antía and Diego had quietly boarded a boat moored at the jetty. Among their belongings were two duffel bags containing more than seventy million euros in various currencies.

That accursed money was now securely hidden away in a safe-deposit box.

It was all theirs.

Or almost all.

Using anonymous donations, they had invested some of it to help the islanders rebuild their homes. Antía had even insisted on paying for the reconstruction of Luis Docampo's restaurant to help his widow, Amaia, who would continue with the business. The bank accounts of the Freire and Docampo families were well stocked for generations to come, which, with any luck, would make for less conflict in the future.

The Ibaibarriaga and Pazos families had also each received a tidy sum through an old friend of Roberto's, who had acted as an intermediary. To his disappointment, much as he had tried, Roberto had been unable to locate any relatives of Víctor Pampín or Elvira Couto.

Helena and Tristán had gotten a house together in Bueu. They were a young couple, full of hopes and dreams, and like all such couples, they were forever arguing. Antía was sure they would be very happy. Roberto thought they wouldn't last six months.

And then there were the three of them. Scarred, both inside and out, beaten, scratched, and exhausted, but alive. And happy.

The next reader in line stepped forward, and Roberto looked up.

Only for his heart to stop. Because the person before him, smiling and clutching a copy of *Stormy Night* in his hands, was someone he knew all too well. Someone he would have preferred never to have seen again in his life.

Standing there in an expensive suit, Osvaldo Salazar looked back with his cold, reptilian eyes.

"Good afternoon." The soft Colombian accent took on a threatening tone. "Nice to see you again, Mr. Lobeira."

# 52

## Happy Endings Are Only in the Movies

They looked at each other without saying a word, like two chess players about to embark on the endgame.

"I thought you were dead," Roberto eventually managed to say.

"You aren't the first to make that mistake." The cold smile on Osvaldo's face grew a little wider. "A costly one."

*Antía. Diego. I have to get them out of here.*

"Uh-uh." Osvaldo shook his head, guessing Roberto's thoughts. "If you're wondering about that woman of yours and the kid, they're outside. Someone's asked them to go pick up a present for you. A little surprise."

"Let me guess. No present."

"But it is a surprise, right?" Osvaldo raised an eyebrow. "Anyway, they're in good company, don't worry."

"What do you want?"

Osvaldo looked at him with mock astonishment. "What do you think I want?" He held out a copy of *Stormy Night*. "Your signature. And a little chat, of course."

As he took the book, Roberto felt he had fallen into some kind of nightmare. No one in the line had noticed anything—they all continued to wait their turn, chatting away like normal. Carmen Gavín, who was accompanying Roberto for the signing, was over in a corner, engaged in a seemingly lengthy phone conversation. He looked around in desperation, but not a single employee of the bookstore was nearby. It was a Saturday afternoon, and they were all run off their feet.

He spotted three guys who looked very out of place. Tall, muscle-bound, pretending to be browsing the shelves but each clearly with one eye on Roberto and Osvaldo.

"Don't do anything dumb," Osvaldo said, "or this thing turns ugly."

"I can cry out. Call for help."

"And what are you going to say? That I threatened you? That I'm one of the characters in your book?" Osvaldo rubbed his temples. "Nobody knows me, I don't have a record in your country, and neither do any of my men. Besides . . ."

"Besides what?" Roberto's mouth was dry.

"I'm sure you'd love to see that girl of yours again, and the kid. Am I wrong? Like I say, they're outside, and they're being well looked after."

Roberto bowed his head, defeated. "What do you want me to do?"

"First, sign the book." Osvaldo glanced over his shoulder. "People are beginning to stare."

Mechanically, Roberto opened the book and wrote his signature inside.

"Great book, I really enjoyed it, but it's full of lies."

"I changed the names, like we said."

"I don't mean that," Osvaldo said sharply. "I'm talking about the money."

"I don't know what you're talking about."

"Oh, yes you do." Another icy smile. "Before the boat capsized, I had time to look. There was some actual money in the bags but mainly just a crapload of flyers and maps. You can imagine how upset I was."

Roberto shrugged. There was no use denying the obvious.

"You tricked me, Lobeira. And I don't like being tricked."

Just then, the next person in line blew out their cheeks loudly and said, "Man, this guy's taking his time. We've been waiting an hour now . . ."

Osvaldo turned and gave the man a death stare. The man flushed and dropped his gaze.

"Now, you're gonna tell me where the money is," Osvaldo said, turning back to Roberto with a wolfish smile. "Every last bill."

Roberto squeezed the marker pen in his hand and briefly entertained just stabbing Osvaldo in the eye with it. But he knew there was nothing he could do as long as they had Antía and Diego.

"Let's just look at this quickly," said Osvaldo.

Osvaldo took out a cell phone, moved around the table so that he was beside Roberto, and placed the phone in front of them both. Draping an arm over Roberto's shoulder, he smiled. Anyone would think they were taking a selfie.

"You said you liked movies," he whispered. "Here's one I want to show you . . ."

He tapped the screen, and the video began to roll: In the middle of an empty, white-walled room, a man sat naked and tied to a chair, his body covered in welts and bruises, his head inside a burlap sack. Suddenly, his head having been drooping forward, he seemed to be alerted by a sound—Osvaldo had the video on mute—and started manically casting around for the source.

His whole body began to tremble as a shadow passed behind him, and then there was Osvaldo beside him. He wore a white plastic apron and was holding a pair of pliers.

Roberto was almost grateful that the video was on mute for what happened next. Osvaldo, with an icy smile, grabbed one of the man's hands and proceeded to cut off his fingers, as the man writhed and struggled madly with his bindings.

"This is nothing compared to what your woman and the kid will get—if I don't get the money in the next twenty-four hours." Osvaldo pocketed the phone and walked back around to the other side of the table. "Surely you know that happy endings are only in the movies. Now, you're gonna make your apologies and come with me to—"

"No."

"I beg your pardon?"

"I said, no."

"I don't think you understand the situation here, Lobeira."

"Oh no, I understand perfectly." He smiled and nodded reassuringly at Carmen Gavín, who, still on the phone, was now looking over, no doubt wondering why he was taking so long with this particular fan. "I think you don't understand."

The Colombian blinked very slowly a couple of times. The fluttering of a deadly butterfly. "All it takes is a signal from me," he said, "and they're gone."

"As you've already said. But there's also a movie I want to show you." Roberto took his own phone out. "You know how much I love movies."

Osvaldo gave him a severe look, but there was just the smallest hint of worry in his eyes too.

Roberto tapped the screen, and a video started to play. It was in black and white, shot from an elevated position, and there was a time code in the bottom left-hand corner.

"Look familiar? It's from the security camera at the lighthouse," he said. "Amazingly clear, right?"

Out in the center of the lighthouse yard stood the two of them, talking, with the members of the Freire and Docampo families looking on.

"I don't know what you're trying to—"

"Just a moment . . . Now!"

Antía and Diego entered from the right, carrying the duffel bags. They placed them down in front of Osvaldo, who took out a handful of bills and thumbed it before, looking satisfied, putting it back in the bag and turning away. The video ended there.

"So what?" Osvaldo shrugged. "I know what happened. I was there."

"Precisely. Now, I suppose you know I was a journalist before I became a writer, right?"

Osvaldo just gave a noncommittal grunt.

"I still have lots of contacts, especially in Mexico." He looked the Colombian squarely in the eye. "People who know people. People who know things, like who your boss is. And how to reach him by email."

There was a sharp intake of breath from Osvaldo.

"Your boss is not a person known for his patience, or his compassionate nature. Some say he's even slightly paranoid after so many years of playing cat and mouse with the authorities. I'm sure you can imagine how he might view this video, showing you receiving the money."

"It changes nothing. I'll tell him what happened. He trusts me. I'll just tell him—"

"Hold on, hold on," said Roberto, cutting in. "Now comes the best part. The money happens to be sitting in an account in the Cayman Islands, and I want you to guess whose name it's in."

Osvaldo's expression went from bewilderment to understanding in a split second. And from that, to one of panic.

"My name," he finally said, his voice tiny.

"Yours, exactly! Seventy-five million euros in the name of Osvaldo Salazar, the Scorpion of Cali himself. I've also had time to do a little research on you . . ." He smiled. "Sadly, you don't have the access code to the account."

Osvaldo gulped, a hot flush running through him. But that was nothing compared to the whirlwind tearing through his mind.

A whirlwind of possibilities.

A whirlwind of ramifications.

All of which, at best, concluded with him ending up just like the man in his video.

"Just so we're really clear," Roberto continued mercilessly, "I have no interest in keeping that dirty money for myself, but it is my life insurance."

Osvaldo tried to say something, but his eyes were glassy as if he'd just been dealt a knockout blow.

"If I see you again, even from afar, I'll send the video and the bank account information to your boss. If anything happens to me or to anyone close to me, the email will be sent automatically. If you should so much as breathe within a hundred yards of me again, the email will be sent. If you chew in a way I don't like, the email will be sent. Anything, any attempt to fuck with me, the email will be sent. Have I made myself clear?"

"Very clear." Osvaldo sounded like he was being strangled. He said nothing more. He didn't need to. They both remained silent for a few seconds, staring at each other. The game was up; there were no pieces left to move.

"It's time you left," Roberto sighed, and pointed to the door. "There are lots of people waiting. And tell Antía and Diego to come back in, if you'd be so kind."

Roberto gestured to the next man in line, who stepped forward, paying the stunned Osvaldo no mind.

Osvaldo Salazar was not a coward, but he wasn't stupid either. No one reached his age in his line of work otherwise. He knew when he had lost.

With slumped shoulders, he turned and signaled to his men that they were leaving.

"Osvaldo!" Roberto called out, and the man swiveled back around. "You're forgetting this." Roberto held up the signed book. "So you have something to read on your way home."

Osvaldo gave him a withering look but grasped hold of the book without a word. There was nothing to say.

Roberto held his breath until the gunmen had gone out, away into the crowds of Plaza de Callao. When Antía and Diego entered again, both looking confused, he finally exhaled. He smiled to signal that it was all over, and the relief on their faces was obvious. He would explain everything later.

They had survived the storm.

More important, they had survived its consequences.

And for now, the sun was shining.

# About the Author

*Photo © Nines Minguez*

Manel Loureiro is the international bestselling author of the Apocalypse Z series, *Only She Sees*, *The Last Passenger*, *Twenty*, *The Door*, *The Bone Thief*, and *When the Storm Passes*, winner of the 2024 Fernando Lara Novel Prize, one of Spain's most prestigious awards for commercial fiction. Born in Pontevedra, Spain, Manel is published in more than thirty countries and has been translated into more than twenty languages.

# About the Translator

*Photo © Thomas Bunstead*

Thomas Bunstead has translated numerous Spanish-language writers, including Manel Loureiro, Agustín Fernández Mallo, María Gainza, and Enrique Vila-Matas. He is the recipient of two PEN Translates awards, an O. Henry Prize, and the McGinnis-Ritchie Award, and was short-listed for the Art Seidenbaum Award and National Translation Awards. His writing has appeared in such publications as *The Paris Review* and *Brixton Review of Books*.